OF BLOOD AND ONYX

AN AKRANI GODS NOVEL

Cover Design | Editing | Book Design and Typesetting
Enchanted Ink Publishing
Map: Alyssa Green, using Wonderdraft software.

ISBN: 978-1-963126-00-6 (E-book)
ISBN: 978-1-963126-01-3 (Paperback)
ISBN: 978-1-963126-02-0 (Hardcover)

WWW.AUTHORALYSSAGREEN.COM

For my readers

Author's Note

Although the characters in this series are fictional, some of the obstacles they face are real-world situations. This book contains sexual assault by the villain, gore, explicit sex scenes, and mental manipulation/abuse by a parent. Read at your own discretion.

None of the politics, worldviews, or cultures represent any country in present society.

ALYSSA GREEN

OF BLOOD AND ONYX

AN AKRANI GODS NOVEL

N
W
E
S
BEHEMOTH T
MELIWE FOREST
CALUN
AZUREDEN MOUNTAINS
THESSALY
ATTLEMIS OCEAN
GRELAN FORES
HAVEN
LE
AADER FOOTHILLS

RRENMIS MOUNTAINS
BALAM
N FOREST
WYNDOVER WOODLANDS
AKE
ONYX MOUNTAINS
BLACKROCK HARBOR
LATORA
LAOSIAN SEA
CRENITHA

THE ANSWERS
ARE
IN THE FLAMES

PROLOGUE

HE NEWLY CROWNED QUEEN SANK INTO the dark waters of the sanctum's pool. The room was in utter chaos, and no one seemed to notice their queen disappearing into the depths. He chuckled to himself, knowing it would go unheard in the rumble of scattering footsteps. It was all going exactly as he'd anticipated.

He watched while the Alchyra rushed after the escaping Mathias.

A young maiden escaping with the crowd caught his eye. She screamed, "The queen!"

He gave her a curt nod and darted down to the pool's edge. He dragged Blaise's limp body from the sanctum pool. The large room was nearly empty by the time he carried her to the closest bedchamber.

Gods, she's heavy. Damn sentinels and their godsforsaken training. He heaved Blaise onto the huge mattress. Her shallow breathing was the final piece that would allow him everything he wanted.

"And so it begins." He retrieved a crystal from his pocket.

Next to Blaise's unconscious body lay a corpse.

A grin crept onto his pale features as he placed the crystal to Blaise's forehead. It changed from translucent white to yellow in a matter of seconds.

He walked around to the corpse, which he'd alchemized for this mission. He slid the crystal into the gold-prong setting that hung from the chain around the dead body's neck. The corpse's skin became smooth, and its facial features mutated. Blaise lay beside herself in front of him.

The new Blaise opened her eyes to meet his cold gaze. He touched the symbol on his sternum, and it tingled. "It's done. You know what to do."

She nodded and sat up, swinging her legs over the side of the bed.

He caught a glance of the glowing symbol at the edge of her low neckline. "That is *never* to be seen," he hissed.

Without a word, she adjusted her bodice in the mirror next to the door, then walked out of the room.

He stared at the real Blaise. He could practically taste his immortality.

I have done what you've asked. Break free from your bonds and come forth. Reclaim what is yours.

1
KAIDEN

IT HAD BEEN THREE WEEKS SINCE HE'D LEFT her. Even though he was back with his family, he wasn't the same without her. He would never be the same without her. Kaiden Atherton didn't stand as tall as he used to. His shoulders slumped forward, and he often stared at his boots while walking.

He was a celebrated hero upon his return to Elatora. He'd secured his inevitable promotion to commander of the Sentinel Order. It should've made him happy, should've had him jumping for joy. In the past, he would've been thrilled, but the thought left him over-whelmed and empty.

Now that he knew the truth about everything, it was difficult to go back to the routine he'd left, difficult to go back to the way things had been before he'd met Blaise. She was the lost heir of Balam and a half god, and Kaiden was half-ellorian. Since he'd left Balam, something inside him had become hollow. And he didn't know what that feeling meant.

Blaise's vibrations haunted him at night despite their distance and how they'd parted. Kaiden still wanted Blaise, *longed* for her. The familiar humming itched at his back. He could feel her breath in his chest and her pulse in his neck. He'd convinced himself the feeling would pass but was beginning to realize leaving her had been the biggest mistake of his existence.

Blaise's coronation ceremony had been three weeks ago. Mathias had stayed in Balam after their suicidal mission, and he should've been back. It was unlike him. If he'd run into trouble, Mathias would've sent word, but none had arrived.

That last mission had left the unit broken, forcing Kaiden to take some time for recovery. It was thanks to that mission he'd learned his mother, Beatrice, was an ellorian—a peacekeeper of the realm created with pure akrani by the lower god of peace, Colvyr. During his break, he'd spoken to his father, Commander Stephen, and had asked about his bloodline.

The commander had avoided saying anything more than general details about Beatrice. Kaiden knew it was painful for his dad to reminisce about his mom, so even though he had more questions, he'd refrained from pushing too hard.

Hopefully King Vaughn will be more willing to talk about her.

King Vaughn had been busy traveling to and from the nearby port. This was the soonest he could meet, and Kaiden was itching to ask questions—to discover the truth about his mother.

The musky scent of rain filled Kaiden's nostrils, and a crisp breeze caressed his dirt-covered cheeks. He strode through the large oak doors of Cloveshire Castle, the dull stone clacking with each of his booted steps. He slowed his pace, passing a row of arched floor-to-ceiling windows on his right. The sun hid behind dark clouds. Raindrops hit the windows at an angle and trickled down the glass panes. This type of weather wasn't uncommon for the time of year, yet Kaiden couldn't help but wonder if he'd ever see the sun shine again.

"Captain Kaiden," a familiar deep voice bellowed from behind him.

Kaiden turned and grinned. "George."

The burly man pulled him in for a hug. "It's good to see you."

Kaiden noticed his dark green tunic and black trousers. "What's this? No armor?"

George shook his head with a smile, combing his fingers through his long auburn beard. "After being chased by the kynarah, I decided it was time to retire. The kids are growin' fast. They need their father. And my wife needs her husband."

Kaiden admired George for putting his family first. He chuckled, clapping him on his shoulder. "It's about gods damned time. What brings you to the castle?"

"Pickin' up a few things I left in the armory. What about you, Captain? How you farin'?" George asked.

Kaiden didn't know how to answer that. He had everything he'd ever wanted in life. Well . . . everything he'd *thought* he wanted. His lips curved up, and he lied, "Fine. I've been put in charge of the squires' training. They're to graduate soon."

"That's great, Captain. Do you know how Blaise is doing?"

Kaiden's eyebrows rose, and he inhaled. "I'm not entirely sure."

"Oh." A concerned look crept onto George's rugged features. "Captain, if you need to talk, I'm here."

Kaiden appreciated his offer, but he wasn't one to open up to others. "Thank you, George. Now, if you'll excuse me, I have a meeting with the king." He started toward the throne room.

"Of course. I'll be seein' you."

"Give my best to the family," Kaiden replied, then turned the corner into another wide corridor.

Kaiden stopped in front of two oak doors embossed with the Bere family crest, inhaled a deep breath, and glanced at each sentinel standing guard.

"Captain Kaiden, how are you today?" the woman sentinel asked.

"I'm well, Sergeant Bianca," he replied.

"The king seems to be in good spirits today." Her lips curved up, and she winked.

Kaiden was glad to hear it. Maybe it would be easier to coax some answers from King Vaughn.

"Good," he said.

The other guard rolled his eyes and pushed through the door to announce the captain. Kaiden followed the sentinel into the throne room. The clouds had cleared, allowing beams of sunlight to stream in, casting a warm glow over the gray stone floor.

King Vaughn sat on his throne, the oak tree mural behind him making it appear as though it were part of the trunk. Despite his loose dark trousers and tunic, he hadn't foregone the simple gold crown adorned with oak leaves. He shook a strand of chestnut hair from his eyes as his gaze snapped to Kaiden from the parchment he'd been reading. "Ah, Captain, I apologize for the late meeting."

After the guard left the two men to their privacy, Kaiden bowed, hinging at the waist. The leather of his armor creaked, and as he straightened, his steel pauldrons lightly clinked, and a few flecks of dirt fell to the floor. "No apology necessary, Your Majesty. I know you're eager to get Blackrock Harbor up and running again. And the sun celebration is happening soon."

This tradition had been going on for over five hundred years, and Kaiden loved it, mostly because he would get to indulge in his favorite treats: custard tarts and Sun Cake, which was customary to eat during the eclipse to keep negative energy at bay. It was an annual event that brought all the peoples of the realms together.

The king nodded and massaged the bridge of his nose with his thumb and forefinger. "Don't remind me. I'd cancel it if I could." He stood, setting the parchment roll on his seat. He walked down the steps and came within a foot of Kaiden, scanning his muddy boots and dirty armor. He flicked a piece of crud off Kaiden's chest plate with his index finger, amusement shining in his dark eyes.

Kaiden didn't falter at the king's proximity. "I apologize for my appearance. I was running the final trials with the squires this morning."

He smiled. "How are you, Captain?"

Kaiden rolled the tension from his shoulders and rested his forearm on the hilt of his sword, which hung off his right hip. "I'm fine, Your Majesty."

"Well rested?"

How should I go about this?

Kaiden replied, "Yes, Your Majesty."

"You look like you have questions." King Vaughn took a step back. "Ask them." He clasped his hands behind his back.

Kaiden had left Blaise in order to ask the question that had been burning holes in his mind and keeping him up most nights. "Can you tell me about my mother and her lineage?"

King Vaughn averted his gaze. "Have you asked your father about this?"

Kaiden pushed back the strands of dark hair covering his forehead. "Tried and failed."

What if his mom turned out to be a villain or had been involved in some terrible things? What if she wasn't the hero he believed her to be? He had always looked up to her, even in her death, and didn't want to think she could be anything other than perfect. If she wasn't the person Kaiden thought she was, the remnants of his heart would shatter.

"Where to start?" King Vaughn walked back up the steps to the throne, picked up the parchment roll, and sat.

Kaiden braced himself for the truth.

"Your mother was one of many ellorians who lived in Crenitha. She served alongside the sentinels for years. Beatrice's satori allowed us to counter Rowena's revenants. It was because of her that Haven and Elatora survived as long as we did."

Kaiden's shoulders relaxed, and he loosed a breath. "Why did Rowena betray her own kind? Did anyone know she was an ellorian?"

King Vaughn shook his head. "No one knew Rowena's true lineage until your most recent mission. I'm not sure your mother knew either until it was too late."

Kaiden cleared his throat. "Do you know the details of my mother's death?"

"Your mother was tired of seeing units of sentinels and Haven soldiers slaughtered. You showed great promise as a young boy, and she was fearful for your future. Your father and I believed you could carry some of your mother's abilities—her physical strength or her satori." The king stared off into the distance, and sorrow came over his face. "She was confident in her satori and decided she should face Rowena alone."

Mom never wanted me to become a sentinel. Kaiden's eyebrows came together. "If I had her satori, wouldn't it have manifested by now?"

King Vaughn grinned. "Akrani isn't always so absolute. It can be subtle. Something I learned from your mother."

Could it be possible that his akrani had been developing gradually? That he could use satori to read minds like his mother? Was that what the vibrations were? He still had so many questions about his ellorian bloodline and his alleged satori. Unfortunately, he'd not paid attention in squire lectures when they'd discussed the many complexities of akrani, the second life source.

The king cut him a sidelong glance. "Is there something else you wish to ask, Captain?"

Kaiden released another breath. "I have some concerns for Sergeant Mathias. He hasn't returned, and I've received no word from him."

"I see." King Vaughn's face softened. He stood, descended his throne and walked a few feet, stopping in front of a painting that depicted Colvyr with short dark hair. His eyes were entirely white. The god of peace's arms were outstretched, a warm smile gracing his serene features.

Beatrice had been a servant to Colvyr. An ellorian.
What does that mean?
Would Kaiden have to serve the god of peace as well even though he was only a half blood?

"It seems we share similar concerns, Captain. I invited Queen Blaise to attend the squires' graduation ceremony as my guest of honor. I have received a response from her, but she declined due to an assassination attempt."

Kaiden's eyes widened, and his heart sped up. "What happened?"

"There was no other information given in the letter."

Kaiden's chest tightened. "What would you have me do, Your Majesty?"

The king faced Kaiden. "Return to Balam with an official peace treaty for the queen to sign. You'll go as my emissary, Captain. And while you're there, figure out what Mathias is doing. Bring him back in one piece, or I'll have to send the hounds after him. If they find him, I'll have to send him to the dungeon."

Mathias would not want that. Kaiden held back a wince. With the way things had ended, how could he go back and confront Blaise? Then again, he couldn't say no to the king. The last sentinel to fuck up had been assigned a horrible position on the Teaos wall guarding from midnight to noon. Kaiden did *not* want to see the king's bad side.

"Consider it done, Your Majesty," Kaiden said with a slight bow.

"Good. There's no time to waste. I'll assign another sentinel to take over the squire unit. You'll need to gather a small team to accompany you on this mission." The king rubbed the scruff on his jaw. "I recommend Sergeant Elric Maddock; he's strong and has a good head on his shoulders. Corporal Simone Pythias has been consistently inquiring about a mission with you, though I'm not entirely sure why," King Vaughn said. "Regardless, she's well trained."

The first name the king had mentioned sounded familiar. Kaiden remained in silent thought. Where had he heard that name? It dawned on him.

"Are you talking about Mad Dog Maddock? Wasn't he thrown into the dungeon for losing control over his akrani?"

The king waved his hand. "That's just a detail. Besides, it was an accident. He has been doing well since then," he said. "Don't you trust my judgment, Captain?"

After the lack of honesty King Vaughn had shown regarding Blaise, no, Kaiden didn't trust him, but he couldn't tell the king that. "Yes, of course, Your Majesty."

It was getting late, and King Vaughn was right. Kaiden needed to assemble his team of sentinels, gather provisions, and set out for Balam.

"Thank you for indulging me, Your Majesty. I'll take my leave."

"Of course, Captain. May the gods be with you on your journey."

The gods. Kaiden hadn't believed in them before, but after meeting Blaise, he'd been forced to at least acknowledge their existence. She was a half god, a deime.

Kaiden bowed and returned the sentiment, then walked out of the throne room.

Once he made it into the hallway, his mind burst with thoughts of Blaise and the potential danger she could be in. Surely Mathias wouldn't let anything happen to her. What if they were both compromised? Or what if they had formed a bond? It wouldn't have been the first time a woman chose Mathias over him.

Kaiden hurried down the wide corridor, and a wave of dizziness hit him, stopping him in his tracks. He leaned against the closest wall and closed his eyes. White blurred his vision. Blaise appeared before him, chained between two pillars on her knees. His teeth began to chatter from the icy chill of what appeared to be a windowless room.

He called out her name, reached for her, but he received no response. The slump of her body caused his heart to sink. Why was there so much blood? What had happened to her? Where in gehheina was she?

With another flash of light, he opened his eyes to the hallway of Cloveshire.

A young squire approached him. "Captain, are you all right, sir?"

Inhaling, Kaiden straightened and cleared his throat. "I'm fine." He recognized the boy. "Aren't you on weapons maintenance?"

With a nod and fear in his eyes, the squire hurried away in the armory's direction.

Maybe once Kaiden arrived back in Balam, he could speak with Zade about what he'd experienced. Maybe he'd find what he was looking for there since he clearly wasn't finding it in Elatora like he had hoped.

KAIDEN MADE IT A PRIORITY to stop by the apothecary after his visit with the king to pick up Helena's elixirs. He'd been paying frequent visits to Blaise's grandmother and brother, helping with household chores along with any maintenance that needed to be done to the estate. He liked the hard work Helena assigned him, but she often chose chores that resulted in him being shirtless from the heat. Working on the property allowed Kaiden to forget about his responsibilities as a sentinel. It also made him feel closer to Blaise.

Forty-five minutes later, he stood on the Carringtons' doorstep, a small pouch in hand. He knocked on the dark wooden door and waited.

It opened, and Helena greeted him, a smile on her pale pinkish face. "Captain Kaiden, it's so good to see you again." She wrinkled her nose at his full body armor.

He grinned and held up the burlap bag. "Hello, Lady Helena. I wanted to get these to you before you ran out." It hadn't been that long ago that Kaiden had promised Blaise he'd buy her gram's elixirs for the rest of his life. That promise had been made on the condition that Blaise would win their duel to join his unit. She'd lost to Kaiden but had won in other ways.

Helena took the elixirs, held the door open, and gestured for him to come inside. "What did I say about calling me that? I'm Grams to you."

Kaiden smiled, then stomped his boots at the entrance and walked into the foyer. "Very well, Grams. I'm afraid I can't stay as long as I usually do."

Grams tapped her forefinger to her chin. "That's a shame. I just finished baking a batch of custard tarts."

Damn. She knew how to get to him.

"Come along, Captain. Don't leave me to finish them on my own." She led him into the kitchen.

"If I'm to call you Grams, then it's only fair you call me Kaiden." He drew up to the dark oak cabinets, his fingers drifting over the smooth worn countertop where Blaise had likely prepared her meals. He sat at the small wooden table, and his heart fractured as he pictured her sitting next to him, having her buttered toast and hot tea.

Grams limped over with two plates of custard tarts and silverware in hand. She placed one in front of him. "Something bothering you, Kaiden?" she asked, taking the seat across from him.

Kaiden smirked, his mouth watering. He took a bite and chewed, and the crust crumbled and melted. He savored the sweetness of the creamy custard. "This is delicious."

"Don't avoid the question." She shot him a severe look.

He knew she'd hear about his mission from Daniel eventually. If that man spent half his time practicing sword techniques rather than gossiping, he'd be an expert. "The king has assigned me to act as an emissary."

A worried expression dawned on her face. "Why?"

"He invited Blaise to attend Daniel's graduation ceremony, but she declined due to an attempt on her life." Kaiden took the last bite. "And I've received no word from Mathias."

Grams dropped her fork onto her plate and sat for a moment, shifting her gaze to the tall windows a few feet away. "I see . . ."

"I'll take care of this, Grams. I'm sure she's fine," Kaiden said, placing his hand over hers.

She inhaled and breathed out a heavy sigh. She put her other hand on her heart. "I carry her everywhere I go."

He placed his hand on his chest. "A hollow feeling?"

Grams tilted her head. "Go on."

"Since I met Blaise, I can feel her. Each breath, each beat of her heart. It's almost as if she's a part of me. But since I left Balam—left *her*—there's been a void right here. It's almost unbearable." Kaiden didn't know how to say it without sounding crazy.

Gram's pale blue eyes met his hazel ones, and she tucked a strand of her long white hair behind one ear, studying him in the silence.

"You can tell me I'm losing my mind, Grams." He brushed his fingers through his hair.

A breathy laugh escaped her. "I don't think that at all. But I do think you two share a special bond." She rubbed the bridge of her nose, eyes closed. "There's a word for it in the old language. I'm afraid old age has taken its toll on me."

"You've seen this before?"

"Yes. Between your mother and father." Grams finished her custard tart, then brought their empty plates to the sink.

Kaiden was unaware Grams knew his mother. After all the conversations they'd had the past three weeks, Beatrice had never come up. "You knew my mother?"

Grams glanced at him, scrubbing one of the plates, and nodded. "I did. I thought I told you I met her in Balam when she was an ambassador for Elatora."

Had King Vaughn left that detail out on purpose? Kaiden's family had been connected to Blaise's long before they met.

"What do you remember about her?" he asked.

Grams placed the dishes on the drying rack next to the sink. "Well, she was quite the diplomat, but caring at the same time. That's rare amongst political types."

He smiled as warmth grew in his chest. "I'm glad she left that kind of impression on you."

"Not just me, Captain. Everyone around her too." She shuffled over and took her seat across from him once more.

He wished he'd known his mother the way Helena knew her. She seemed to have been a light in everyone's life. Maybe that was why his mom's death had taken such a toll on his father.

Grams spoke of the visits Beatrice had made to Balam as an ambassador. Hearing the stories about his mom sent waves of comfort through Kaiden.

"I do appreciate what you've done for me these past weeks." Grams's lips curved up.

"Before I forget." He untied a small coin pouch from his utility belt. "This should cover your elixirs for a few months and anything else you might need."

With a frown, Grams held up her palm in protest. "You don't have to—"

"I want to," he insisted. "Coming here has given me something to look forward to after a long day. Please take the gald."

She reached for the pouch, her eyes brimming with tears. "Thank you, Kaiden," she whispered.

"I should go. Thank you for the delicious tart." He stood, and she followed him through the foyer to the front door.

"Please . . . take care of my Pooka," she said.

He couldn't hold himself back and enveloped her slight frame in his arms. "You have my word, Grams."

She returned the hug. "Good. Now go on. I know you have much to do."

Kaiden straightened, stole one last glance at her, and then turned on his heel. He made his way through the open pathway to the stable. Cedric stood in one of the stalls, munching on hay. Kaiden led Cedric by the reins into the open. He climbed into the saddle and headed home.

Kaiden longed to know his mother. In all honesty, he truly longed for purpose again. Before he'd met Blaise, his purpose had been to eventually be promoted to commander of the Sentinel Order and follow in his father's footsteps.

I thought after learning the truth about Mom, my purpose would be clearer.

KAIDEN WALKED INTO THE ATHERTON house, unbuckling his sword and placing it on the table in the foyer. He gazed at the steps of the open staircase of his home, his mind a million miles away, thoughts of Blaise and Mathias haunting him. He hoped they were safe.

His father, Commander Stephen, burst through the front door and stared at Kaiden, a chastising look on his rugged face. "We need to talk."

Kaiden assumed his dad wanted to know about the meeting with the king. He followed the commander into the study with a sigh.

In past years, a much younger Kaiden had explored the dark oak shelves lining the walls. He'd learned about the history of the kingdoms of Crenitha. Some books were full of past Athertons' adventures, and some had information about the gods. A framed picture of the family Kaiden had drawn when he was younger hung on the wall next to the small fireplace.

I can't believe Dad kept that.

His father took a seat at the oak desk sitting in the middle of the room and clasped his leather-gloved hands on the smooth surface. "The king told me you asked about Beatrice."

Kaiden stood in the threshold of the doorway and leaned against the frame, attempting to keep his posture relaxed. "You should be glad. You won't have to avoid my questions anymore." He hadn't meant for it to come out so harsh.

Stephen let out a slow breath. "Your mother wanted certain things to be kept hidden. Aren't you the least bit worried about the consequences should you uncover them?"

"What're you talking about? Don't you think I deserve to know who I am? Who she was?" Kaiden bit out, frustrated with this whole situation.

His father stood, walked around the desk, and placed his hands on Kaiden's shoulders. "You are a captain in the Sentinel Order, and you are my son. Is that not enough?"

Kaiden wanted to tell him it was, but that would've been a lie. It was never enough. His throat constricted as he gazed into his father's dark eyes. "It used to be."

Stephen stepped back, arms dropping to his sides, an unreadable look on his face.

Kaiden crossed his arms over his plated chest and pushed away the rising sorrow. He couldn't afford to let his emotions get the best of him—not now, not while he had a mission to complete. So he took a deep breath and forced himself to focus on the task at hand. He would deal with this later, when he had time.

"Where's Elizabeth?" Kaiden asked.

"She went with Sergeant Isaac to the training grounds at Cloveshire." Stephen made his way back to the desk.

"Isaac?" Kaiden cocked a brow.

The commander nodded. "Yes. I thought she would've told you. He started courting her a few days after returning from Balam."

Since Kaiden's return, a rift had developed in his relationship with his sister. She'd distanced herself from him, and he wasn't sure if it was intentional. "If you have nothing else for me, I need to prepare for my assignment to Balam as emissary."

Stephen glanced at Kaiden, and for a split second, it looked like he wanted to say something more. His eyes softened. "Your assignment," he muttered, then cleared his throat. "May the gods guide your path."

Kaiden wished things with his father weren't so strained. So difficult. So frustrating.

The commander was so caught up in the kingdom's safety and preservation that he'd forgotten about his family. Even more so when Beatrice had died.

Kaiden only hoped he wouldn't end up like his father.

2
MATHIAS

Casimir Octo homed in on a hare in the clearing, tiptoeing closer. The trees of Grelan Forest provided cover for the most wanted person in Crenitha: the man who'd tried to assassinate the new queen of Balam.

He wasn't *that* man. Before Nira had saved him for the second time, she had run into an akrani-produced double of the man they had just taken to the dungeon, a prestae. No one would ever call him Sergeant Mathias Gage again. He would no longer be on King Vaughn's shit list. He would no longer protect the kingdom of Elatora—his homeland.

Mathias and Nira had managed to lose the Alchyra in the foothills on a stolen horse. He didn't want to admit it, but he owed her. He was thankful she had helped him dye his hair and the stubble on his face with coal. He hated having to hunt outside of the kingdom wall, even with the slim chance of being recognized.

He released a steady breath, set his iron sights on his target, and pulled the trigger on his crossbow. The arrow pierced dinner through its eye. After he field dressed it, he headed toward the cottage in Haven, where he tolerated Nira.

It was almost time for his shift at the tavern. He still couldn't believe he'd let Nira talk him into taking the job as a barkeep. But until he found who'd set him up, that job would have to do. And it wasn't all that bad. The free ale was worth it.

Mathias passed the Haven soldiers guarding the entrance of the vast kingdom. The guards shot him a quick glance, and he sucked in a breath and held it, his palms growing sweaty. He released the breath once he'd made it through the gate, thankful he hadn't been recognized.

Mathias walked through the front door of the cottage and passed the sitting-sleeping area. He wished they could afford a bigger home, but this was the best they could do. In a few long strides, he was in the small kitchen.

He retrieved the heavy cutting board from a cabinet below him and placed it on the square counter next to the sink. He began preparations for a stew.

Has Elatora received word of the accusations against me? Will Kaiden know better than to believe such a lie?

They'd grown up and trained as squires together. Commander Stephen had treated him like an Atherton from the moment his parents died. Elizabeth and Mathias had easily fallen into the roles of competitive siblings. Although, she had surpassed him and Kaiden in academics. She probably had the whole Cloveshire archive memorized.

Nira strode through the front door a few moments later, pulling him from his thoughts. She worked the day shift at the same tavern as Mathias. She had gone by Veda since they'd reached Haven, but Mathias had another name for her.

He washed the meat in the kitchen sink, giving her a sidelong glance. "You're looking rough, sweetness."

She pulled the string that tied her hair up, letting dark thick waves fall over her shoulders. The hem of her navy dress hovered just above the dirt floor with each step she took across the room. "And you don't look like a charming husband."

Mathias couldn't keep his arousing thoughts at bay. He imagined gripping her long dark hair in one hand, holding her close as he thrust into her.

He cleared his throat, pushing the thought far away. "Hunting's a dirty job, sweetness." He tore his gaze away, knowing that nickname would rile her up.

"Stop calling me that." Nira rolled her eyes, hands placed firmly on her hips.

Mathias shrugged. "I think it's ironic, don't you?"

Her brow furrowed. "What in gehheina is that supposed to mean?"

He stepped toward her, their bodies mere inches from each other. "I'm talking about the fact that you're *anything but sweet*."

Her cobalt eyes narrowed and captured him, enamored him. It had to be some kind of akrani. Every time he got too close to her, he felt—no. He shoved that thought away too.

"Only because you are so difficult," she bit out.

His eyes wandered to her dusky pink lips. He cursed himself for wanting to taste them. "I have work soon." Tearing himself away, he returned to cooking.

He was grateful to her for saving his life, but she'd been an absolute nightmare to live with. She always had to have things a certain way, from the cleaning of the dishes to how they were put away. She had an opinion about everything. So the less they saw each other, the better. It was good they worked opposite shifts. Mathias had never thought he'd end up loathing Nira. At least, that was what he told himself.

"About that, the boss said to take the night off."

Goddess of chaos, not an evening alone with Nira.

"Do you have any more leads?" Nira asked.

He added vegetables to the pot. "Maybe."

"Were you planning on telling me?" she asked, putting more wood into the stove.

He loosed a breath, his patience already wearing thin. "I heard there's a man who contracts mercenaries here. He owns the Scarlet Crown. Maybe you've heard of him, Tarren Mandelbaum."

Nira nodded. "I've heard of him. There are rumors he also runs an underground fight club. And he's supposedly good friends with King Theod." She added water to the pot. "So, what's the plan?"

How does she know so much?

"Well, tonight would be a good night to observe the Scarlet Crown." The liquid had begun to boil.

Her eyebrows came together, her gaze meeting his. "What do you mean by 'observe?'"

"Precisely that."

She huffed, and an annoyed expression crept onto her face. "Could you be more vague?"

"Probably." He grinned.

She dipped the ladle into the soup, brought it inches from her lips, and puckered, blowing on the hot liquid.

He gritted his teeth, refusing to stare at the velvety show of her luscious lips.

"When are we leaving?" She carefully sucked in the cool broth.

He swiped his tongue over his bottom lip. "We?"

She faced him once more. "Yes, *we*. My ass is on the line too, you know."

He leaned closer, their faces inches from each other.

This is dangerous territory.

It had been over a month without sex at this point. For him, that was a long time.

He whispered, "You're not going."

"Yes, I am." She didn't falter.

Stepping away, he inhaled, trying to calm himself. "I can't risk you fucking anything up."

Her nostrils flared. "Me? You're the one who got me into this mess in the first place."

Damn, she had a point. Maybe bringing her along would prove helpful.

He conceded with a loud groan. "Fine. We leave at dusk. If you're not ready by then, I'm going without you."

Her blue eyes narrowed. "I'll be ready." She handed him the ladle and walked outside onto the small wooden porch.

Gods, that woman is infuriating. Why does she always make it a point to push my limits at every opportunity?

Mathias couldn't deny his attraction toward Nira despite her being seven years his senior. And it didn't help that she wasn't willing to satiate his more primal needs. His body didn't care about her age. He still wanted her. He couldn't exactly go to the pleasure house as a "married man." That wouldn't be good for Casimir's reputation.

AFTER DINNER, MATHIAS PUT ON a tunic, jacket, and scarf. He walked out of the small cottage so Nira could get ready. The sun drifted toward the horizon, painting the sky in hues of orange, yellow, and red. He let the crisp evening breeze fill his lungs, and the day's tension left his body on his exhale. A flicker of hope coursed through him. Maybe tonight would be the night he'd finally uncover the truth. Mathias was going to make whoever was responsible for this situation suffer.

About half an hour passed, and Nira finally walked out. Mathias's lips parted while he took in her appearance. She wore knee-high black boots, fitted trousers, and a burgundy button-down jacket that revealed the soft curves of her waist and stomach. Her hair was styled in waves that cascaded over her shoulders, and she'd wrapped a black scarf loosely around her neck. Her makeup consisted of heavy black eyeliner and a dark red lip color. His eyes drifted back down to the gold hoop piercing in her belly button. It was at that moment he realized the gods must hate him. This had to be punishment for the hearts he'd shattered in the past.

"Stop staring. Are we going or not?" She shot him a narrow-eyed glare, then walked past him off the porch.

This is going to be a long night. Mathias adjusted his hardening length in his pants and followed her lead.

Once they made it out of the wooded area onto the busy main road of Haven, they caught a carriage the rest of the way. It didn't take long to arrive in front of the three-storied building bustling with patrons.

The Scarlet Crown had been established within the last five years. The business was known for its gambling tables and satiating the desires of Haven's people. Lights illuminated the front of the pleasure house, and several windows on the second and third floors were lit with silhouettes of positions he longed to enjoy. *Lucky bastards.*

Mathias helped Nira out of the carriage. "It should be pretty easy to get what we need with this crowd."

Nira tucked a strand of dark hair behind her ear. She nodded, shifting her gaze to the busy crowd. She fiddled with the same strand, pulling it back down to the side of her face.

"What's wrong?" he asked as the coachman pulled away.

"What if we get caught?" Her eyes met his.

A glint of apprehension shone in her stare. He reached for her hand and gave it a reassuring squeeze, then intertwined her arm with his. "We won't have to worry about that if we're a convincing couple." He glanced at her one last time and led her in. "Shall we, sweetness?"

She winced, let out a breath, and smiled. "Yes."

It had been a while since Mathias had stepped into an establishment like this. They passed through the double doors. Perfume, tobacco mixed with cinnamon apple ale, and malt liquor filled Mathias's nostrils. He took in their surroundings, marking the exits. Most of the gambling tables were spread out on the main floor. There were two bars and an elevated loft area he assumed was for the privileged patrons. Scantily clad attendants escorted their clients up and down the wide grand staircase.

He noted two men standing at the base of those stairs. *Is that the only way to the second floor?*

"Why don't you play a few rounds?" Mathias suggested, gesturing to a card game at one of the half-circular tables.

"You're leaving me alone? What're you going to do?" She shot him a look of concern, tucking a strand of hair behind her ear. She hugged herself and shifted in discomfort.

"I'm going to get a drink. Don't worry, I'll have my eyes on you." Mathias walked away to one of the two bars, tallying the armed guards. He counted about fifteen of Tarren's men. There had to be a few undercover, but Mathias wasn't too concerned about that.

Now to find Tarren.

The barmaid was a pretty blond with chestnut eyes who filled out her uniform quite nicely. Despite Mathias's admiration for her, she didn't compare to Nira. There was something about Nira that this woman didn't have. He just hadn't figured it out yet.

"I'd like to buy two drinks. One for me and one for Tarren Mandelbaum. Keep it anonymous though, beautiful." Mathias tipped her an extra gald piece from his coin purse. She nodded and carried out the order.

Mathias watched the barmaid carry the drink on a gold platter through the gambling floor, up the loft steps, and straight up to a man who appeared rather young to own such a prestigious establishment. The first thing that stood out was the thick gold ring on his index finger. His shoulder-length blond hair was pulled back in a sleek ponytail, and he wore a plum-colored velvet jacket. Tarren was sitting amongst some mixed company, laughing and enjoying himself.

After Mathias finished his drink, he searched the gambling tables for Nira. He recognized her long dark hair and started toward her. Nira came up behind him, brushing her fingers over his forearm.

His attention snapped to her. "Oh, hey. I thought you were over there." He gestured toward one of the tables.

"Nope." She smiled. "I'm right here."

He leaned in. "Have you been drinking?"

"I might've had a glass or two."

He refocused on the task at hand. "Well, I found Tarren. We should be clear for a bit to investigate upstairs."

"What precisely are we looking for?" she asked as they sauntered toward the staircase.

"Anything. But I'm not sure how to get past those two." Mathias gestured to the guards who had just stopped a couple from going up the stairs.

Nira pushed up on her toes, her lips grazing his ear. "Follow my lead."

A corner of his mouth rose. He'd never seen her like this before. "What're you going to do?"

"No more questions." She undid the top buttons of her jacket, revealing a hefty amount of cleavage, then hooked her arm in his. "Shall we?"

Nira swayed on his arm, leaning all her weight on him and pulling him off-balance.

Mathias held back his surprise, steadying himself and her. *Goddess of chaos, this woman.*

He glanced at Tarren, who sat contentedly in a section of the loft, flirting with the barmaid—that same blond who had served Mathias earlier.

Shit, they seem familiar with each other.

One of the men guarding the staircase stopped Mathias and Nira at the landing.

"I haven't seen you here before," the guard said to Nira. "I would've remembered you." His gaze roamed her body with shameless desire, and a tinge of jealousy coursed through Mathias's veins.

Nira staggered over to the guard and slurred, "This is my first time." She smiled, sweet and seductive.

The other guard had a smirk on his scruffy face, arms crossed.

Mathias grabbed Nira's forearm, pulling her off the guard. He draped her arm around his neck and leaned toward the guard. "She's a bit overstimulated. Do you think I could buy a room for maybe thirty minutes?" He reached for his coin purse and took out a few pieces of gald.

The guards exchanged glances, then looked back at Mathias with raised eyebrows.

With a huff, Mathias retrieved two more gald pieces and passed them to the first guard.

"Welcome," the guard said with a sweeping hand gesture. "You sure you can handle her by yourself? Why don't you come find me? I'll be off in about an hour."

"She's my wife; I can handle her just fine without you," Mathias growled, walking past him.

Once on the second floor, Mathias stared at Nira. His lips formed a straight line, arms crossed. What in gehheina had gotten into her? She was like a woman possessed. They'd only lived together a few short weeks, but he'd never thought she could have that kind of . . . sex appeal.

Her brow furrowed. "What?"

"You surprise me, that's all," he replied, starting down the hallway.

"This way." Nira took the lead. "His study is at the very end."

The hallway was lined with dark wooden doors on both sides.

"How do you know that?" Mathias followed her. Moans of pleasure filled his ears as they passed several closed doors.

She glanced over her shoulder at him. "I might've subtly asked around."

"What does that mean?"

They stopped at the last door at the end of the long hallway. "It means we don't have much time." She dropped to her knees, retrieved two small pins from her hair, and picked the lock.

Mathias ensured the coast was clear for her to continue. Voices echoed from the staircase. A couple was walking up. "Hurry up," he prodded.

"I can let you do this alone," she snapped at him.

Finally, there was a click, and she tugged him into the room. The couple climbing the stairs had reached the second floor, and their heavy footsteps resounded against the carpeted floor.

Mathias released the tension from his body with a sigh. "Fuck, that was close." He leaned against the dark oak.

Nira immediately went to the wooden desk and started rummaging through the drawers.

Mathias kept an ear out for anyone nearing the study while he searched through the cabinet in the corner of the office. "He sure does like a lot of red."

"The place is called the Scarlet Crown," Nira pointed out, reading through a small stack of parchments. "I'm not finding anything," she said, putting papers back in the drawer. "I think we've hit a dead end here."

Mathias stopped his search and walked over to the desk. He examined the inside of the top drawer. "This looks like the desk my father used to have in his study. If it is, there should be a trigger—" Something clicked inside the compartment, and the top of the oak desk popped open. Everything on the surface fell to the burgundy carpet. "That's something."

Pinned beneath the top of the desk was a map of Crenitha with coordinates. Mathias realized they led to the Onyx Mountains. The papers in the bottom compartment of the desk were letters. Nira read one.

"What is it?" Mathias leaned close, inhaling a scent of charcoal. Where was the jasmine he'd grown so accustomed to? Then he remembered she had stoked the fire when they'd been cooking.

"This letter is written in the old language. But whoever sent this is searching for the Onyx Crystal," she replied.

He glanced over her shoulder and frowned. "I didn't know you knew other languages."

She shot him a sweet smile. "You never asked."

That's fair. He continued to ask, "What is the Onyx Crystal?"

"It looks like King Theod is searching for it to trade for more resources for the expansion of Haven," she said.

"So, it's valuable." The symbol at the bottom of the parchment had two overlapping circles and a pentacle in the middle. "Who's the letter from?"

Nira stared at the symbol for a moment, and then her dark blue eyes met his. "I don't know. But Blaise is to marry King Theod to unite the kingdoms. He's included coordinates to the galydrian mines." She picked up another parchment. "This appears to have been ripped from a tome. Look."

He studied the frayed edge.

"The stamp in the corner tells me it's from the Balam archives." She pointed to the top right corner. "We need to take this to Blaise. Make sure she finds the Onyx Crystal before they do."

Mathias wanted to question Nira about how she knew all this, but there was no time.

Heavy footsteps were approaching.

"We need to go." He grabbed the parchments from her, folded them, and stuffed them into his coat pocket. They glanced at each other for a heartbeat, then rushed through the other door in the study, which led to a bedroom.

The boom of deep voices echoed from the office as Mathias and Nira tiptoed to the door leading into the hallway. He couldn't tell how many men had entered the office.

Two? Maybe three?

They crept into the hall and quietly sprinted down the length of it. Mathias peeked over his shoulder to make sure no one was following them.

About halfway, Nira stopped, opened a door, yanked him inside, and closed it behind her.

Mathias scanned the bedroom. It was empty, thank the gods.

"What are you doing?" He could hear heavy footsteps approaching.

She stripped off her scarf and jacket, then peeled off her undershirt, revealing the white strip of cloth covering her breasts. "Quick, take off your shirt."

"What?" He cocked a brow.

"Just take off your shirt and get under the covers," she said through gritted teeth.

Doors were opening and closing. It sounded like the men were going through all the rooms lining the long hall.

"They're still here somewhere," one man bellowed.

"Did you get a look at them?" asked the man with a deeper voice.

"The boss won't be happy about this."

Mathias finally obliged and got under the covers. Nira straddled him and began writhing her hips against his. She leaned forward and captured his lips with hers.

Gods, she's so soft. His hands roamed the silky skin of her back.

She placed her hands on either side of his head, hips still rocking against his hardened length. There was no hiding the fact she turned him on.

He asked in between kisses, "Why didn't we do this sooner?"

"Be a good boy and stop talking." Her lips curved up against his mouth as the bed creaked beneath them. She massaged his tongue with hers, moaning and quickening her pace. If she kept that up, he was surely going to explode in his pants.

One of Tarren's henchmen burst into the room and stared at them for a moment.

"Do you mind? I only paid for half an hour," Mathias said, a smirk on his face. With the way the blanket was wrapped around them, it looked like they were naked.

The muscular man scanned the room. "Pardon me." Then he walked out, closing the door behind him.

Nira smiled. "Thank the moon goddess."

She started to climb off, but his grip tightened around her hips, holding her in place. "We could finish what we started," he said, only half joking.

With an eye roll, she said, "There are men after us, and you want to play?"

He shrugged. "I promise it'll be fast."

She actually giggled for the first time ever. The sound sent strange tingles through his body.

"Maybe later, honey."

She'd never called him that before. Mathias let her go, and she climbed off.

He sat up and began to dress as well. "Did you just call me honey?"

Nira threw her scarf around her neck and studied him for a few seconds. "Aren't you supposed to be my husband?" She winked.

He cocked a brow but didn't prod the issue further. Maybe later he'd talk to her about everything.

He made his way over to the door leading into the hallway and opened it slightly. "It's clear. Let's go."

Mathias descended the steps onto the main floor. Tarren's men were searching the patrons, making them empty their pockets onto the gaming tables. The exit was only twenty feet away. Could they make it without being noticed?

Nira waved her hand. "Go, get out of here." She covered her face with a crimson veil.

Where did that come from? He frowned. "What're you going to do?"

She gestured to the wooden stage near one of the bars. "Cause a diversion." She walked up to the musicians, talked to them for a few seconds, and then traipsed onto the stage. That alone caught the attention of the crowd.

The melody started. Nira slowly moved her hips in small circles, keeping with the rhythm of the music, and the strange tingle reminded him of their little moment upstairs.

He shook his head, remembering what he was supposed to be doing. Glancing at the exit, he patted his coat pocket, ensuring the parchments were still there, and then made his way to the door.

With every couple steps, he would turn and steal a glance at Nira. She was hypnotizing the crowd through her dance, and he couldn't help but fall under her spell too.

Stop ogling her. You're supposed to be leaving, idiot. He held his breath and passed one henchman, who appeared occupied by Nira's performance. Placing his hand on the door, he pushed it open and stepped out of the Scarlet Crown.

He hurried into a dark alleyway across the street and waited for Nira in the shadows. The odd sensation had dissipated. He was sure a few of the men would stop her after her intoxicating performance. The thought set his insides on fire.

Mathias waited another thirty minutes for Nira to walk out of the establishment, but she never did, and he couldn't risk going back in there. He headed home. Maybe she'd taken another exit he didn't know about. This whole situation caused a wave of unease to roll through him. He'd never seen that side of Nira before.

Strolling a few streets down, he hailed a coach and hopped inside. Gods, he hoped Nira was okay.

Mathias spent the ride thinking about the night's events and what to make of them. He reached into his pocket and grasped the two parchments he'd taken from Tarren's office. He hoped Kaiden or someone was onto this treachery. The only problem was, how would they know? Nira was right. They needed to warn Blaise.

The driver parked on the side of the road. There was no way the carriage could make it through the thicket. Mathias climbed out and made the short trek to the cottage, the full moon lighting his path.

He walked through the front door, and his eyebrows rose at the sight of Nira sound asleep in her bed. *How in gehheina did she get home so fast?* Plopping onto his makeshift bed in the sitting area, he contemplated waking her and decided it wasn't worth suffering her wrath.

He pulled the folded parchments from his coat and placed them beneath his pillow. With a yawn, he lay down and turned onto his side.

We're that much closer to clearing our names. Mathias couldn't wait for his life to return to normal.

He lay in bed a few feet from Nira. Despite everything that had happened, he couldn't get the taste of her lips out of his mind or forget how her soft, warm body had felt against him. The way she'd stared with those piercing blue eyes of hers, like he was all she'd wanted at that moment. He had to be mistaken. She'd acted like she loathed him these past three weeks. What in gehheina was happening to him?

Why do I even care?

3

BLAISE

LAISE COULDN'T BREATHE. THE SURFACE OF the water seemed so far away, so out of reach. Her blood mixed with the dark water of the pool, caus-ing her sight to blur crimson. A current pulled her deeper, where the light couldn't reach her. Her lungs longed for oxy-gen, and her eyes drifted closed.

Help me . . . The deep, masculine voice came through, muffled in her mind.

She opened her eyes, but only darkness filled her vision.

Release me . . .

With a lurch, Blaise regained consciousness. A pierc-ing cold enveloped her body. Spikes of pain erupted in her wrists, like a thousand tiny needles jabbing into her skin. She tried to cry out, but her throat was bone-dry.

Her hands instinctively clenched into fists. The pain was so intense, she felt like her wrists were on fire. She tried to pull her hands free, but the cuffs were too tight.

She was trapped. Chained between two gray stone pillars.

What happened? How in gehheina did I get here? Her lips trembled. She didn't know if it was the arctic chill or the fear coursing through her.

Blaise yanked on the iron chains, the shackles digging into her wrists. Dizziness caused her to stumble back, and a churning in her stomach ensued.

She lifted her head and scanned the room. Darkness cloaked most of the windowless vestry. A sense of emptiness filled her. She glanced up at the snowflakes falling through a large moonlit hole in the ceiling, coating her skin in a thin layer. In seconds, the snow melted despite the icy wind entering the chamber.

Memories flooded her: a sharp unwelcome pain; Mathias's sky-blue eyes, void of emotion. He'd shot her with a bolt, and it had sent her crashing into the sanctum pool. Blaise peered down at herself, wincing with the movement. The bolt stuck out from her stomach. She pursed her lips, breaths shaky from the agony of the memory.

It didn't make sense. Her mind flashed back to the moment in Calun when they'd been captured by the Balam refugees.

I made a promise to Kaiden that I'd protect you, and I couldn't imagine telling him I'd failed. Mathias had seemed so sincere. On the verge of tears. She could tell he'd meant it.

Her fingertips buzzed, and she didn't know if it was the cold or the akrani coursing through her, begging for release. She called upon her katai and tried to use lightning like she had done in the past, attempting to free herself from the iron cuffs. Nothing happened. An intense vibration roiled through her to the point of agony, like it was trying to escape.

A block was preventing the use of her akrani. For every try, she only failed. The pain was too intense, too exhausting.

She sank down in a jerking motion, the chains pulling her arms farther apart. An audible pop came from her right shoulder, and an ear-piercing scream escaped her lips. Tears fell from her eyes onto the cold stone floor.

Blaise's heart plummeted at the memory of Kaiden leaving before her coronation ceremony. He'd said he needed to find answers about his lineage back in Elatora. But he'd never asked her to wait for him, never said he'd be back for her. He'd never said he wanted her. Not only was her body broken, but her heart was as well. She wanted him, but she wasn't sure if they could work out their issues.

I will be free soon, and you shall no longer carry this burden . . .

It was that deep disconnected voice again.

Who in gehheina is speaking to me?

And how were they speaking to her? Could it be her satori, or could she be losing her mind? It wouldn't have surprised her.

"Ah, you're awake." A familiar voice sounded from the darkness surrounding her. "Your existence has caused quite the disturbance in the higher realms, deime." He stepped just beyond the light encircling her, his hands clasped behind his back. His thick black coat, along with his trousers, were covered in snow. His boots were caked with mud, which told her he'd traveled quite the distance.

She choked while the pain continued throbbing through her shoulder. "Why are you doing this? Let me go."

He bowed, staying in the shadows. "Apologies, Queen, but you must remain in these restraints. Everything fell into place perfectly. Your blood opened the portal, allowing your father's bonds to weaken. Once he escapes gehheina, he'll come for you. And I'll finally be immortal again."

Her fingertips in her right hand went numb. Remnants of sharp pain shot through her arm. Though her mind was cloudy, her eyes widened, and realization crashed into her like a violent wave.

"Who are you?"

He rolled his shoulders back. "A scavenger created by the god of death, Teival. More importantly, someone on the road to redemption. I failed once. I won't do it again." He reached into his jacket pocket and removed a yellow crystal.

"Does that mean Teival is my father?" she bit out through the agony pulsing in her body.

His voice echoed through the darkness. "Don't worry, he'll find you."

A chill trickled down her spine. She glared daggers at him. "There will be an uproar amongst the people once they discover what you've done."

A throaty laugh escaped him, and he stepped around her, avoiding the circle of light. He placed the rough stone to her forehead. "They won't even know you're gone."

She couldn't respond. Tendrils of akrani were being forced out of her inner well of power. When he pulled the meta crystal away, the life source sealed itself inside with a brief burst of yellow light. All the air left her lungs like someone had punched her in the gut. It took a few moments for the searing within her body to dissipate.

Fuck, that hurt . . .

She panted. The surge of akrani was gone. "What . . . did you do?"

His voice became distant. "A favor."

"Wait, you can't leave me here."

The sound of his bootsteps faded.

"Come back here!"

He drained my akrani! For what purpose?

Had someone close to Blaise betrayed her? Was that person truly Mathias Gage?

The icy wind howled through the cracks in the walls and ceiling as though confirming her suspicion. She shivered, praying for warmth to save her from this all-consuming cold, praying to the gods to relieve her of this pain, praying for *something* to fill the frigid void in her heart.

$$4$$

KAIDEN

THE FIRST STOP KAIDEN MADE WAS THE Cloveshire training grounds. He wanted Isaac on his team, mostly so he could keep an eye on him. The thought of Isaac courting Elizabeth made his stomach churn.

When did she grow up? She was no longer that little girl who asked for nightly bedtime stories.

Kaiden strode through the armory, his boots echoing on the gray stone floor. He passed rows of weapons, all neatly arranged and ready for use. He pushed open the door and stepped out into the breezeway that led to the large green training field. The crisp air hit his cheeks, and the sun shone through the white clouds.

In the distance, he made out Elizabeth's long dark blond hair. She sat cross-legged, reading. The book was most likely from the Cloveshire archives, which she maintained.

Isaac held a sword, practicing his technique. He swung the sword in a wide arc, then brought it down in a swift strike. He repeated the motion over and over, his movements becoming more fluid with each repetition. Once he noticed Kaiden, he stumbled over his feet and somehow managed to land on his back.

Kaiden held back a laugh as Elizabeth rushed to Isaac's side.

"Your form looks good. Except for that last move there," Kaiden teased while Elizabeth helped Isaac up. "Might need to work on that one."

Isaac dusted himself off. "Captain, this is unexpected."

"First of all, why didn't you tell me about this?" Kaiden gestured between the two of them.

Elizabeth and Isaac exchanged a glance. She replied, "You've been so moody since you arrived home. When was I supposed to tell you?"

Kaiden crossed his arms. "That's no excuse, Liz."

She scoffed. "Oh, now you want to take an interest in my life?"

"What's that supposed to mean?"

She rolled her eyes. "Face it, you're not the same as when you left. And frankly, I don't know if that's a good thing."

Kaiden's nostrils flared, and he turned his attention to Isaac. "I want you on my team."

Isaac opened his mouth to speak, but Elizabeth intruded. "You what? Where are you going this time?"

"If you must know, the king requested I go to Balam as an emissary," Kaiden replied, trying to act unbothered by her attitude. It was difficult though. He had always been able to sense her emotions easily—a bond he loved but sometimes cursed.

"Did something happen?" Isaac asked, a look of concern on his face.

"The queen rejected the king's invitation to attend her brother's graduation ceremony."

"I see," Isaac said. "Count me in."

Elizabeth looked back and forth between Kaiden and Isaac, brow furrowed. She let out a breath. "I suppose I can't get in the way of your sentinel duties."

"You have nothing to worry about, Lizzie. I'm sure everything's fine," Isaac told her. "She's probably just busy."

Elizabeth nodded, seeming to understand. She turned to Kaiden. "You better take care of him. And come home safe. Both of you."

Kaiden pulled her petite body into a hug and embraced her tightly. "Didn't I come home last time?"

She gasped. "Kai, can't breathe."

"Sorry." He released her.

Isaac leaned in and kissed Elizabeth on the cheek. "Don't worry, I'll carry you in my heart."

Kaiden huffed, rolling his eyes. "Let's go. We have much to do."

He didn't like the idea of her and Isaac, though they were well suited for each other. Isaac did enjoy books just as much as—if not more than—Elizabeth. Kaiden may have to accept that Isaac could be the one for her.

Isaac matched Kaiden's pace while they made their way off the training grounds. "Where are we going?"

"We have two more sentinels to gather for the mission," Kaiden said.

"Do I know them? What're their names?"

Kaiden released a breath. He'd almost forgotten how talkative Isaac could be. "Sergeant Elric Maddock and Corporal Simone Pythias."

Isaac stopped in his tracks.

Kaiden looked over his shoulder. "What's wrong?"

Isaac caught up. "I heard Sergeant Elric is a wild card. There was an accident during a field exercise due to his lack of control over his akrani."

"Yeah? Well, he came highly recommended by the king. Anyway, I didn't think you were the type to gossip. Have you been hanging around Daniel again?" A corner of Kaiden's mouth rose.

Isaac released a breath and moved on from the topic. "Corporal Simone should be at the tavern by this hour."

Kaiden's eyes narrowed. "How do you know that?"

Isaac shrugged. "It's common knowledge."

"Right." Kaiden shot him an incredulous look.

They retrieved their horses from the Cloveshire stable, saddled up, and rode off in the direction of the Bootless Sentinel. A wagon of handmade furniture passed them, followed by a black carriage. Kaiden's stomach rumbled from the aroma of fresh midday bread.

Kaiden and Isaac arrived at the tavern twenty minutes later. They tied their horses to a wooden rail just a few feet from the establishment and walked inside.

Isaac strode up to the bar and ordered two pints while Kaiden's eyes roamed the area.

Kaiden asked, "Do you have any idea what she looks like?"

The barmaid slid Isaac two foaming pints of ale, the frothy head threatening to spill over the sides of the glasses. He picked them up and ambled up to Kaiden, offering him one.

The scent of the alcoholic beverage was intoxicating, and Kaiden's stomach rumbled in anticipation. "No. We're on orders."

"Come on, you know nobody follows that rule." Isaac shot him a coy grin.

Kaiden's lips formed a straight line. "Oh really?" He canted his head.

With a defeated sigh, Isaac gave the pints to two patrons nearby.

"You cheating bitch!" A man stood from the table in the corner, unsheathing a dagger from his hip.

Kaiden reached for the handle of his sword, ready to intervene. A tiny white-haired woman straightened from the other side of the table.

The armed man lunged at her. She swooped beneath the table and between his legs, ending up behind him. Kicking the weak point behind his knee, she forced him to the floor, then slammed his face into the wooden table. Her technique was familiar.

The man shrieked and dropped his blade, reaching for his bloody nose.

She searched his trouser pockets and pulled out two cards, throwing them onto the table with the rest of the pile. "Who's the cheater now?"

Isaac had a grin on his face. "That's who we're looking for."

Where have I seen her?

Kaiden's lips parted with a sigh. "Great." He was beginning to wonder if the king was setting him up for failure. Walking up to the woman, Kaiden greeted her. "Corporal Simone Pythias?" He hoped Isaac was mistaken, but to his misfortune, she responded, facing him.

"Captain Kaiden. Sergeant Isaac." Her gaze stayed on Kaiden, who stood several inches over her. She adjusted her black tunic and swiped the gald coins off the table. "What can I do for you this fine afternoon?"

The man with the bloody nose walked out of the tavern, and the few patrons went about their business—except the barkeep, who kept giving the three sidelong glares.

"You were recommended by the king himself," Kaiden said. "He said you're eager to go on assignment."

Simone sat down and tossed her booted feet onto the table, leaning back in the chair. "He's not wrong," she said. "Are you the lead?"

Kaiden's brow rose. Okay, he was beginning to understand why King Vaughn had recommended her. "The king appointed me as emissary to go to Balam and establish a peace treaty with the queen." He left out a few details but figured she didn't need to know them at the moment.

"Whatever the mission is, I'm in." She sat upright in her seat. "Just tell me when we leave, and I'll be there."

Kaiden studied her. "Why are you so eager to join my team?"

She cocked a sculpted eyebrow. "I haven't been outside these walls since the revenants were wiped from the land."

Isaac muttered, "It's overrated."

Simone curved her fingers, examining her nail beds, seemingly bored. Kaiden accepted her answer with a nod and told her the time and place to meet the next day.

As he and Isaac walked away, Simone called out, "Just like old times, right, Isaac?"

Kaiden disregarded her comment and continued out the door of the tavern, but he wondered about their history. He didn't have time to concern himself with such things.

With one more person to recruit, he climbed onto Cedric and rode toward Sergeant Elric's estate. He hoped the sergeant would be as compliant as Simone.

They rode down a less busy street of Elatora. The trees lining the road swayed gently in the crisp breeze.

"Remember trying to get Blaise into our unit? That was like pulling teeth," Isaac said.

"How could I forget?" Kaiden replied, staying slightly ahead of Isaac. "It took a duel to finally get her to agree." The thought caused the corner of his mouth to rise.

"You miss her, I can tell."

Isaac was a blunt little shit. It seemed his promotion to sergeant had given him an ego boost.

However, Kaiden couldn't deny it. He remained quiet, listening to Cedric's hooves clop against the dirt road.

"Captain, I overheard someone talking about an arranged marriage amongst the royals. Do you think it could be Blaise?" Isaac asked. "Maybe that's why she declined."

Kaiden's grip tightened on the reins. His heart sank at the thought, but Isaac was the last person he wanted to talk to about this. "Drop it, Isaac," he said through his teeth.

Isaac fell back a few feet and said nothing more about it.

Warmth rose in Kaiden's stomach. He didn't want to think about the possibility that Blaise would agree to something like that. Could he really blame her if she had? He was the one who had walked away, after all.

Kaiden and Isaac rode through the iron gates of a grand estate. Acres of land surrounded the stone-pillared house ahead. Trees and wildflowers were spread around the property. His eyes flicked to a beautiful fenced-in garden of various vegetables.

This guy must have a lot of free time on his hands.

Isaac scrutinized the place with admiration in his eyes. "From the looks of it, Sergeant Elric has been out of his cell for a while now."

Kaiden and Isaac secured their steeds, then climbed the stone steps of the patio. Kaiden banged on the dark oak door.

"Do you think he's home?" Isaac asked, standing slightly behind Kaiden.

An unfamiliar vibration washed through Kaiden. A medley of sweetness, bitterness, and sourness lingered on his tongue like licorice. With a frown, he scowled, shivering from the flavor.

What is that?

The new vibration grew stronger in one direction. He followed without hesitation, heading around the porch.

"Where are you going, Captain?" Isaac asked, trailing him.

Kaiden shushed him.

They came to a terrace that overlooked more foliage and a hedge maze. On the far side sat a dark-haired man clad in a black tunic, trousers, and boots, with chess pieces set in front of him. As Kaiden neared, he noticed the stone table itself was the board, and the pieces were crafted of the same marble. Had he made those himself?

"Sergeant Elric?" Kaiden walked into his periphery.

"Captain," the man said, moving the rook three squares forward. He looked like he could be around Kaiden's age. "To what do I owe this surprise?" He really didn't appear surprised at all.

Kaiden gestured to the wooden seat across from him. "May I?"

Elric glanced at him with his blue-gray eyes and nodded. "What's this about?" He kept moving the pieces on the board, concentration apparent on his face.

"I'll just remain standing. Don't worry about me." Isaac walked to the balustrade behind Kaiden and leaned back on it, arms crossed.

Elric seemed unbothered with Isaac's remark while he waited for Kaiden to continue.

"You came recommended by the king for a very specific mission."

Nothing but the rustling of the foliage could be heard. A chill ran down Kaiden's spine. Was it from the dropping temperature or merely being in the presence of this man? Kaiden assumed it was the latter.

Elric made one last move, rendering checkmate to the alabaster king on the board. "You say His Majesty recommended me. Did he tell you anything else?"

Kaiden shook his head.

Elric leaned forward, placed his elbows on the table, folded his hands, and stared at Kaiden.

Gods, why couldn't Kaiden get a read on this guy? That vibration rolled through Kaiden once more, causing gooseflesh to rise on his nape.

"The assignment is to establish a peace treaty with the new queen of Balam."

Elric interlaced his hands in his lap and leaned back in his chair. "If the king recommended me, I'd hate to say no and suffer his wrath."

Sergeant Elric didn't appear enthused about this mission, but he didn't come off as the type of person to show it either.

Kaiden said, "We'll meet at dawn in front of the Teaos gate."

"I'll be there," Elric replied, cleaning up the pieces.

Kaiden stood, the chair legs scraping against the stone. "We'll take our leave now." He made his way back around the house and down the steps of the porch.

Isaac caught up and asked, "Did I sense a bit of fear from you back there?"

Kaiden untied Cedric's reins from the tree in the courtyard. Isaac wasn't wrong. Kaiden had felt uneasy the whole time he'd been in Elric's presence. He just didn't know what to make of it.

"Don't be ridiculous."

"It's completely understandable, Captain. I was creeped out by him as well." Isaac had a smirk on his face.

They rode through the gates of Elric's estate, and the vibrations settled in Kaiden's chest. "Do me a favor."

"Sure." Isaac perked up in his saddle and almost fell off at the sudden movement.

Kaiden shot him a tight-lipped glare. "Shut up."

5

KAIDEN

KAIDEN ROLLED OUT OF BED AFTER ONLY A few hours of sleep plagued by the emptiness in his soul. Barefoot, he padded over to the window and gazed at the stars lightly dusting the dark sky.

This assignment was a godsend. Kaiden could finally speak to Blaise about everything. That was if she granted him an audience. It had been over three weeks since he'd last seen her.

Surely she isn't still angry.

An image of Blaise using her lightning on him coursed through his mind. His eyes narrowed.

She wouldn't.

After filling his satchel with necessities for the journey ahead, he woke Cedric. The horse didn't seem too happy, huffing and shaking his head.

"Sorry, Ced. I'm tired too." Kaiden petted the horse's neck. He wrestled Cedric into his bridle and saddle, then headed toward the Teaos wall.

The revenants no longer infested Crenitha, so King Vaughn kept the Elatora gates open, though visitors were screened by guards. Kaiden respected and admired the king for wanting to protect his people, but the world wasn't full of ill intent anymore.

Sergeant Elric's black armor gleamed in the orange hues of the rising sun. He rode up to Kaiden, who was waiting near the drawbridge. Kaiden didn't know what to think about this mysterious sentinel, but instinct told him Elric was trustworthy. Until proven, Kaiden would keep an eye on him.

Isaac and Simone joined them seconds later, coming from the same direction. Kaiden briefed his small team on the travel route. He signaled to one of the sentinels guarding the gate. *Alpha unit en route.*

The guard signaled back. *Copy.* Then he saluted.

Kaiden waved his hand, and the unit followed him into Grelan Forest.

A FEW HOURS LATER, THE unit stopped to rest the horses and have their noon meal. Kaiden scarfed a portion of bread and cheese, then went to fill his canteen with water from the small stream nearby.

A refreshing breeze rustled the leaves of the trees.

Kaiden inhaled, securing the lid on his full canteen and admiring the beams of sunlight streaming through the canopy of leaves above him. He wished he could share this miniscule moment of serenity with Blaise.

Kaiden and his unit traveled through the Onyx Mountains pass, the scent of soot and smoke filling the air. The sporadic rumbling of the ground intensified the vibrations in his chest, putting his senses on high alert. The volcano had become active after their return to Elatora weeks ago.

Isaac rode beside Kaiden. "A gald for your thoughts."

Kaiden glanced at Isaac, then scanned the mountains. "Do you know anything about this volcano?"

"Well . . ." Isaac inhaled as though preparing to give a long lecture on the topic. "From what I've read about these mountains, the volcano is dormant for one hundred years at a time. But it's a little early. Hopefully the creatures are still in hibernation."

Kaiden kept his gaze on the path ahead. "What creatures?"

Just as Isaac opened his mouth, Simone guided her steed up to the other side of Kaiden. Her black armor glimmered in the setting sun. A shortsword hung on her left hip. "I've heard talk that you and the new queen of Balam have history, Captain."

I'm going to kill Daniel. Kaiden let out a breath, tilting his head to the sky.

Isaac seemed to welcome the interruption. "They were lovers."

Kaiden couldn't believe he'd said that. He shot Isaac a wide-eyed scowl, then turned back to Simone. "Things are . . ."

"Complicated," Isaac interjected.

"I don't care if you're courting my sister. I'll still hurt you." Kaiden sped Cedric up, taking the front of their formation.

"Oh, come on, Captain, we're practically brothers now," Isaac teased.

Simone caught up to Kaiden, a grin on her lovely face. A sense of familiarity flowed through him while he stared at her features. It mixed with the vibrations in his chest and unsettled his insides, leaving a sour taste in his mouth. He didn't know why she had that effect on him.

Kaiden was finished with that particular conversation. He heaved a sigh, stealing a glance at her. "Tell me, Corporal, what made you volunteer for this assignment?"

She didn't seem fazed by the sudden shift. "I didn't want to miss the opportunity to go on a mission with *the* Captain Kaiden."

"Brownnoser." Isaac coughed, and she glared at him.

Kaiden grinned. He peeked over his shoulder at Elric, who appeared oblivious to their conversation.

A strong tremor struck Kaiden, causing him to stop Cedric in his tracks. He held up a hand, bringing his team to a halt. He examined the steep grade of the surrounding mountains. Peering over at Isaac, he said, "We're being watched."

"How can you tell?" Isaac asked, his head on the swivel.

"Incoming." Simone pointed her crossbow at the mountain closest to them.

At a quickening pace, four razor-toothed beasts flanked their unit. The creatures circled them, mouths dripping with strings of saliva. They closed in, the jagged spikes on their backs bristling. Their long claws crunched against the dark soil. The thick brown fur covering their bodies was matted.

"Saroga!" Isaac pulled out his crossbow. "They must've come out of hibernation when the volcano became active."

Elric unsheathed his sword and dismounted, ready for their attack. "How do we kill them?"

"Yes, kill them," Isaac replied, two saroga chasing him toward the mountains.

"Not helpful." Simone followed Isaac, shooting at the creatures.

Despite their size, they were still fast, and they dodged her bolts, their hungry growls echoing through the pass.

A saroga charged Kaiden while he dismounted and brandished his sword. He swiped at the creature, slicing deep into its throat. The beast gurgled but didn't seem disturbed by his strike. Kaiden dodged its razor claws a second too late. One claw grazed his backplate, knocking him off-balance. He regained his footing. The creature was already upon him. It lunged forward, its claws outstretched. Kaiden ducked out of the way, but the creature's tail whipped around and caught him across the face. He staggered, dazed.

With blood trickling down its throat, the creature snarled and charged again. Kaiden drew his sword, attempting to parry the attack. He swung once more. The creature stealthily dodged the blow. It swiped at Kaiden with its tail, and he jumped back, narrowly avoiding it. There was no way he could fight like this much longer. The creature was too strong and too fast. He needed to find a way to defeat it.

Kaiden steadied himself and tightened his grip on his sword. He glanced at his unit, who were battling the other three. With a loud war cry, he slid on his knees toward the saroga, dodging its claws. With one long, deep cut, the creature's warm intestines splattered all over the volcanic soil. The beast collapsed in one big heap.

Four more emerged from the mountains while Kaiden moved to assist Elric.

"Fuck," Elric cursed, then took down a saroga with his blade. It slowed the creature, giving Elric the chance to unsheathe a dagger from his utility belt. He plunged it into the beast's eye, finishing it off.

Another saroga approached, roaring and swiping at him with its claws, but Elric was too quick and precise. He elegantly ducked under the blow and slashed at the creature's leg. The beast whimpered and lashed out with its leathery tail. Elric was already gone, dancing around the beast, striking at it from all sides.

What a show-off.

The animal was powerful, but with Elric's agility, he dodged its attacks and kept striking. Ultimately, the beast fell dead to the ground. Elric stood over the creature, his sword and dagger dripping with blood.

"They're probably hungry," Kaiden said, loading a cartridge into his crossbow.

"Good observation, Captain." Elric flung his dagger into the forehead of a saroga coming up behind them. It swiped and growled, then crumpled to the ground.

Kaiden aimed his crossbow at the beast. Taking in a deep breath, he focused on his target. Shooting something that was sprinting toward him was no easy feat. Kaiden placed his finger on the trigger, and at the bottom of his breath, he squeezed it. The bolt whizzed through the air and pierced straight through the eye of the saroga. It fell to the ground in a heap of dirt. He let out a sigh of relief.

Kaiden was about to pull the trigger again when a huge winged beast flew over one of the peaks. It snatched the last saroga up in its jaws, blood spurting everywhere. Burgundy scales covered its whole body, and it had horns and teeth that could grind bones.

"What in gehheina is that?" Simone gaped at the vicious creature tearing apart the saroga.

Isaac sat behind her, wide-eyed. "I think that's a vissera." He'd apparently lost his steed.

Elric sprinted to his horse, mounted, and kicked it into a gallop, heading away from the winged beast.

Kaiden knew—even with the four of them—they couldn't take on this creature. "He has the right idea. Let's get out of here. Head toward those trees." He whistled loudly for Cedric, and the horse came running. Kaiden climbed on and nudged him with the heels of his boots.

The small group raced toward the patch of dead trees ahead. The winged beast roared, giving chase. Kaiden didn't think any amount of bolts would take that creature down.

Kaiden was pushing Cedric to his limits. All the horses would need a long rest if they survived this.

Just a few feet more . . .

They made it into the thicket of the dead forest. The vissera circled above them for a few moments. It roared and returned to the mountains, giving up on its pursuit.

BEFORE SUNSET, THE UNIT SOUGHT shelter at a small inn a few miles outside of the Onyx Mountains pass. The angular stone structure stood with a thatched roof and had bars on the doors and windows. They tended to their horses, making sure the animals were unharmed, and then settled them into the stalls.

Kaiden walked into the inn, taking in the stone-and-timber interior. Warmth emanated from the large slate fireplace in the common room. Tapestries and paintings of the gods and their servants decorated the walls.

A woman with graying hair greeted them and offered a hearty dinner. They graciously accepted the meal, eating it in the small tavern. With full stomachs, they headed up to their rooms.

Tired of Isaac's mouth, Kaiden decided to bunk with Elric. The fight against the saroga had left him depleted. Kaiden sighed in relief at the sight of two beds across from each other. His mind flashed back to the Lerwick Inn, where he'd shared a bed with Blaise. He'd told her about his mother and how she died. A corner of his mouth lifted at the memory.

With a groan, Kaiden plopped face-first onto the bed closest to the open barred window. The mattress springs were anything but quiet. They squeaked while he turned onto his back, struggling to find a comfortable position.

Elric had walked in by then and settled onto the bed. It made as much noise as Kaiden's did. Elric's feet nearly hung off the end of the bed.

"Are you afraid of me, Captain?" he asked, staring at the wood-paneled ceiling.

Kaiden didn't want Elric to think he was weak, so he lied, brow creased. "No. Why?"

"Just curious. Most people are."

Kaiden cleared his throat and brushed off that remark. He stole a glance at Elric. "Why *are* people afraid of you?"

Elric's eyes were closed. "A story for another day."

The room was enveloped in silence. Elric was most likely a private person and didn't like to be in the midst of any drama. Kaiden respected that. In fact, he shared the sentiment.

Kaiden wanted to ask about Elric's past but didn't want to pry too much, plus his eyelids were becoming heavy. The cool breeze drifted through the small space while beams of moonlight streamed through the window. It didn't take long for sleep to find him.

KAIDEN ALLOWED THE UNIT AN extra hour of sleep. After yesterday's attack by the saroga and that other beast, they all needed the rest. They still had about a day and a half's ride until they arrived at the Balam fortress, and he didn't know what he would be walking into when they arrived.

Elric and Kaiden woke up almost simultaneously. They armored up, and Elric volunteered to make sure Isaac and Simone were ready. Meanwhile, Kaiden thanked the innkeeper for her hospitality and left the woman a few extra gald pieces.

With the Daagan Forest on his left and Wyndover Woodlands on the right, Kaiden and his team traversed the flatlands to the north, toward Balam. From this distance, the massive snowcapped peaks of the Terrenmis Mountains appeared to only be the size of Kaiden's thumb.

The day of travel passed with no more attacks by the creatures of Crenitha. With the sun set over the horizon, Elric managed to kill a small deer for dinner. They stopped to make camp and had a nice, quiet evening—aside from Isaac complaining about not having a horse. Kaiden was thankful. He would not take these moments for granted.

6

KAIDEN

THE SUN SHONE HIGH IN THE CLOUDY SKY, contrasting with the gray stone towers of the Balam fortress. Riding through the outskirts of the fortress, Kaiden and the unit passed many stalls of traders selling wares, vegetables, and baked goods. They passed an outdoor tavern. Kaiden nodded at the patrons and gave the barmaid a polite smile. She gave him a flirtatious grin, and he snapped his gaze to the path ahead.

Kaiden rode through the fortress gates, his unit trailing behind. He hadn't expected to be met by two stable hands. The men gathered the sentinels' horses, guiding them toward the stables of the massive structure.

Kaiden made his way up the steps, staring at the intricate detailed patterns on the heavy wooden doors. He raised his knuckles to the mahogany and attempted to knock, but a servant opened the door and greeted the group, confusion apparent on her tan face.

"I'm Captain Kaiden Atherton, emissary of King Vaughn. I'm here to establish a peace treaty with Queen Blaise." Kaiden introduced his unit, and the servant invited them into the large foyer of the fortress. A cold draft ghosted across his cheeks, dreariness overwhelming him.

"Please wait here while I fetch the queen's advisor, Sir Andreas." The servant walked away.

Isaac stepped next to Kaiden. "So . . . how's it going?"

In all honesty, Kaiden's heart had started pounding against his rib cage the moment they entered Balam. How he'd managed to keep a calm demeanor was beyond him.

"I'm fine, Isaac," he said, unable to keep the irritation out of his voice.

"You sure? It's just, you haven't seen her since before the coronation, and—"

"I swear, Isaac, I will put you on the Teaos wall for the rest of your sentinel career if you don't stop talking," Kaiden said.

"No need to be hostile, Captain." Isaac half grinned.

Gods, how does Liz put up with him? Kaiden rubbed the space between his eyes with his index finger and thumb.

Anxious vibrations roiled through him, dragging him into a dark place. It caused his stomach to churn, and a wave of nausea hit him.

Simone was busy looking at the paintings decorating the foyer, and Elric actually appeared quite bored.

"I . . . *like* what they've done with the place," Isaac murmured. "Do you think Blaise is going to be happy to see you again since you left?"

Kaiden gave him a sidelong glare. "I'm not sure."

His mind was preoccupied with the nausea and anxiousness washing through him. He didn't want to alarm the others by telling them that something didn't feel right about any of this.

A moment later, the blond-haired Andreas came traipsing down the wide corridor. He stepped in front of Kaiden and bowed. Kaiden returned the gesture, his unit following suit.

"Captain, it's so nice to see you again." Andreas's hands were clasped in front of him. "We weren't expecting a visit from you. I assume you want a meeting with Her Majesty?"

Kaiden nodded. "Yes, that would be greatly appreciated. I do apologize for the unannounced visit. It's nice to see you as well."

"No apology necessary." Andreas looked to Isaac. "I remember you, young Isaac, but I don't recall the other two."

"Corporal Simone Pythias, Sir Andreas." She curtsied.

"Sergeant Elric Maddock." He gave a tight-lipped nod of his head.

Andreas nodded to them both. "I have the servants readying your chambers. The queen is otherwise occupied at the moment. We would be honored if you'd join us for dinner tomorrow."

Kaiden agreed. He assumed Blaise was still angry at him for leaving. It wouldn't be an easy feat to earn her trust back.

"Good, then it's settled," Andreas said.

Kaiden had questions he needed answers to. "Sergeant Isaac was just commenting on how he liked the decor." He shot Isaac a coy smirk and could've sworn his face turned pale.

Andreas exchanged a look with Isaac, then turned back to Kaiden. "Would you like a tour of the grounds, Sergeant Isaac?"

"A tour would be great," Kaiden replied. It would give him the opportunity to ask about Mathias.

"I'd be delighted. Keep up." Andreas strode down the wide hallway.

The alabaster quartz walls of the corridors were a drastic contrast with the obsidian stone floor. Black iron chandeliers loomed overhead. Matching sconces caged the light beside every door. Unease washed over Kaiden. It was clean. Spotless. Yet there was no warmth.

Kaiden kept pace beside Andreas while the other three trailed close behind. Upon walking into the courtyard, he breathed in the sweet aroma of lavender and honeysuckle. The scent triggered memories of Blaise.

The feeling of her plump dusty-pink lips. Her laugh—sweet like his favorite pastry. And the heat of her infuriatingly fiery attitude.

Gods, I miss the tranquility and completeness I feel around her.

The midday sun warmed Kaiden's face, a pleasant contrast from the bitter chill of the fortress. Green shrubbery lined either side of the walking path, and beyond those, colorful flowers were arranged in a chaotic motif. Young oaks were planted aesthetically throughout the garden. In the center was an obsidian stone fountain.

"I assume you've come to investigate the assassination attempt," Andreas said.

Kaiden inhaled, letting Andreas's words sink in. "The response from the queen was vague, and there was some confusion since she declined to attend her brother's ceremony." He tried to keep his voice calm. "Could you elaborate on what happened?"

"It's quite simple. Sergeant Mathias attempted to assassinate the queen at her coronation." A firm expression appeared on Andreas's pale aged face.

Kaiden's brows came together. "Is the queen okay? Are you sure it was him?"

"Yes, she's fully healed. I was able to procure an akrani gitros for her wound," Andreas assured him. "We're quite positive it was Sergeant Mathias, Captain. We have witnesses, one of them being General Zade of the Alchyra. We're not sure what the sergeant's motives were, and we attempted to capture him, but he had an accomplice. It seems Lady Nira assisted in his escape. We lost them in the Balam foothills. I have two trackers still searching for them."

Bile rose in Kaiden's churning stomach. Kaiden had been there for Mathias through the deaths of his parents, his many breakups, and fights they'd had over women. In truth, Mathias had become part of the Atherton family the moment he'd stepped onto the estate. Kaiden didn't want to believe that his best friend would do such a thing.

If there were witnesses, what choice would he have? Rolling his shoulders back, he tamped down the disappointment and anger. "I must speak to General Zade."

"He and half of the army are somewhere between the

Terrenmis Mountains and Meliwe Forest for training." Andreas stopped.

Kaiden's brow furrowed. Blaise knew better than to send half her army away. Her kingdom wasn't exactly at its strongest.

Why would she do that? He glanced at his team behind him.

"Is something wrong, Captain?" Andreas pushed a loose strand of hair behind his ear.

"No." Kaiden stared at the sparkling water spraying from the spout in the fountain. "Is it possible for me to speak with the queen in private?"

"Oh . . . I'm afraid not, Captain. The queen has a very busy schedule. Besides, anything you say to her will eventually make its way back to me." A grin crept onto Andreas's rugged face. "But I could deliver a *private* message to her if you'd like."

Kaiden fought the urge to shake Andreas by the shoulders and demand an audience with Blaise.

How could she so readily trust this man?

One of the servants caught up to them and told them their chambers were ready. Kaiden and his unit followed the woman up a couple flights of stairs to the guest wing.

Despite the fire burning in the hearth, Kaiden's bedchamber had that same glacial ambience as the rest of the fortress. He brushed his fingers along the purple velvet curtains of the canopy bed and then wandered out to the balcony and breathed in the crisp breeze.

There had to be more to this whole situation than Andreas had let on. Was the queen being evasive, or was Andreas keeping them apart? Why in gehheina had Mathias tried to kill her?

BLAISE

BEADS OF SWEAT TRICKLED DOWN BLAISE'S temples. She tried to spark her well of akrani while an excruciating pressure imploded in her chest. She threw her head back, screaming. The infection must've be worsening. Her vision blurred, and when the darkness drifted in and out, a husky masculine voice echoed.

Come to the portal.

"Where? Who are you?" she bellowed into the shadows.

With no concept of how much time had passed, Blaise knelt on the cold stone floor, the skin around her wrists rubbed raw from the iron restraints. Her body trembled from the pain and bone-chilling conditions, yet she was so hot that she couldn't even shed tears. The last drops of water she'd consumed had been at the bottom of the sanctum pool.

Her lips quirked up. Gods, she would do anything to have a bowl of Grams's beef stew in front of her, to hear the latest gossip from Daniel. The gravity of her current situation interrupted her moment of bliss.

I'm dying.

Yes, looks to be that way, Little Flame, an unfamiliar female voice said from the shadows.

Blaise scanned the open space, her eyes landing on a frozen pool. The light of the moon loomed through the rough opening in the ceiling. Her brow creased.

"Who's there?" Ripples of akrani overwhelmed her already overflowing senses.

Your light in the darkness.

She winced and let her head fall forward. "Do me a favor and stop talking in riddles."

Whoever was speaking stayed in the darkness. *Come now, is that any way to speak to the goddess of chaos?*

Goddess? Blaise's eyes widened. "I thought the gods had abandoned us."

A cackle echoed through the room, leaving Blaise's ears ringing.

Oh, trust me, Little Flame, we've all been watching. But I could not stand by and allow you to make the wrong choices. Her voice was like silk.

"Where were you when all of this happened?" Blaise's brows came together. Blood rushed from her face to her pounding heart. She swallowed. "Have you come to kill me?"

A feminine figure stepped into the circle of light. Her tight dark red curls were tied in a high ponytail, and she wore polished silver armor, a sword sheathed on her right hip. From what Blaise could make out in the dim lighting, Jynx had a subtle red glow in her eyes.

No. I haven't come to kill you, said the goddess, a firm but exasperated expression on her sharp features.

"Then are you here to rescue me?" Blaise asked, hope rising in her nearly burning chest.

Jynx let out a huff like she was annoyed by Blaise's questions. *I have not come to you in physical form, Little Flame.* Just as she said it, her body flickered like a dying candle. *The portal is opening, and the highest of the gods is regaining strength. He will search out the one who has his power. Once he escapes, he will wreak havoc upon the realm.*

Blaise opened her mouth to speak, but Jynx went on. *We're running out of time. Your time here is coming to an end. The one who will balance you is coming.* Her image flickered once more, becoming translucent. She was fading. *When you're free, you must find Chaos Island.*

"Wait, how do I get there?" Blaise called after her. "What about my akrani? Why is this happening to me?"

The goddess's body flickered, and she said, *Because you're dying. Don't worry, they'll be here soon.* Jynx disappeared.

Damn goddess and her riddles. Blaise struggled against her restraints, against the excruciating pain of her dislocated shoulder. The heat of her akrani filled her to the brink, and the fever raged in every cell, through every pore. *How long will I have until the god of death comes to collect my soul?*

8

KAIDEN

NO MATTER HOW HARD KAIDEN TRIED to push them away, the memories taunted him. He'd asked for her forgiveness, and she'd given it to him. Even though he hadn't deserved it. Even though he'd left her before she took her crown.

He could still see her in that beautiful violet gown, walking down the sanctum aisle at her coronation. Knowing he could never have her fractured his heart. His commitments to the Sentinel Order and to himself had solidified his purpose for leaving. But the moment he'd walked out of the fortress, he'd felt the emptiness settle into his chest.

I should've stayed.

The moon shone high in the starlit sky. A gentle breeze flowed through the open balcony doors. He wouldn't spend the rest of the night wrestling with memories and the void. Giving up on sleep, he swung his legs over the edge of the bed and decided to take a stroll.

Kaiden threw on his trousers, tunic, and boots, then walked out of his bedchamber into the moonlit corridor. He was mindful of his steps, keeping quiet as he padded to the end of the hallway. Blaise was in everything. She was in the cold obsidian floors, in the alabaster walls, in the iron chandeliers. No matter where he went, she was there. Torturing his soul. Leaving it to rot in the expanse of his hopelessness.

He turned the corner and made his way down another wide hallway, where a sliver of light shone onto the black stone floor. It came from an open door. Curiosity snaked through him. He crept closer, and muffled voices spilled out of the room. One of them was Blaise's.

Sweat trickled down Kaiden's forehead while his pulsing heart plummeted into his stomach. The last conversation with Blaise slipped into his mind.

He'd stared at her soft lips and remembered how she tasted before looking into her chestnut eyes.

I'll stay for your coronation ceremony, he'd said.

She'd gazed at him for a long moment, letting out a slow breath. *I don't want you to feel obligated to stay. You have a long journey ahead of you, after all.*

Is that how you truly feel about it?

All she had to do was ask him to stay.

Instead, she said one word that broke him completely.

Yes.

Blaise's voice snapped Kaiden back to the present. "Will the captain's visit hinder our plan?"

"No, Your Majesty. We'll continue with the wedding plans, and you will marry King Theod." It sounded like Andreas's nasally voice.

"You don't think he'll suspect anything?"

"No. Everything will be fine," Andreas drawled. "Anyway, the king will arrive in a few days to help with the plans."

Kaiden's chest flared with heat and constricted like a vise was tightening around him. *It can't be.* He turned on his heel, making his way back to his bedchamber. Had she forgotten about him? All that had happened between them? He couldn't. Every kiss haunted him, every touch still lingered upon his skin, and her scent . . .

Kaiden burst through the doors of his room, then slammed the only barrier between him and the loss of the love he'd never had. He leaned his back against the heavy wood, shutting his eyes. He inhaled, and the tiniest hint of lavender teased his senses. Opening his eyes, he skimmed the moonlit chamber, inhaling once more. *Her* true scent was gone. He wrapped his arms tightly around his hollow, aching chest and slid down the smooth oak to the cold stone floor. Maybe it wasn't her. Maybe it was the remnants of his shattered hope.

KAIDEN'S BOOTS CLACKED AGAINST THE dark stone fortress floor. Stopping in front of a window in the corridor, he took in the view. The sun hid behind gray clouds, and the Terrenmis Mountains were barely visible in the haze.

He focused on his reflection. He'd not slept the night before, and his pale complexion and the dark circles around his eyes matched well with the gloomy decor.

The shadows of this place seemed to grow inside him, transporting him to regretful pasts. The memories of everything he'd done wrong hung in the air around him. A pounding in his chest caused him to lurch forward. Grasping at his heart, he steadied himself against the glass pane.

What in gehheina? As he continued through the hallway, another hammering pang reverberated through him, but he was able to keep his balance. The farther he went, the stronger it became. Panting, he braced himself against an open door. Droplets of sweat slid down his face. He wiped his forehead and realized where he'd ended up.

The sanctum.

Kaiden stepped through the wide doorway. Dizziness swept through him, and a blinding light filled his vision. He closed his eyes. His eyelids instantly snapped open when screams echoed in his ears. Disoriented, he took in the scene unfolding all around him. The scattering crowd pushed and shoved one another as they ran through him and vanished at the threshold of the sanctum.

A female voice bellowed across the room, "The queen!"

His attention snapped to Blaise, who stood on the wooden stage holding the bolt that protruded from her stomach, blood covering her hands and soaking her dress. Her eyes focused across the room, face contorted in pain and confusion. She stumbled, falling into the pool behind her.

He followed her line of sight to the other side of the sanctum, where Mathias stood holding his crossbow.

The stoic expression on his friend's face seemed almost inhuman.

What would make him do this? Mathias sprinted from the room, knocking people over in his haste.

Andreas clasped his hands and strode calmly toward Blaise's submerging body. He stared at her for a heartbeat, then hauled her from the dark pool.

Light overwhelmed Kaiden's senses once more. He fell to his knees. Somehow he'd ended up at the dark pool's edge. He peered into the water, where a hint of crimson swirled in circles.

Blood. He squeezed his eyes shut, willing the sight to go away. *I should've stayed.*

Breathless, Kaiden climbed to his feet and strode through the sanctum doors, nearly bumping into Elric.

"Captain." Elric walked closer and examined his appearance. "You look like shit."

"I'm fine, Sergeant. Did you need something?" Kaiden managed to push the disturbing images away for the moment.

"Now that we know the queen is alive and well, shouldn't we head back to Elatora?" Elric asked.

"We don't know that for sure. I'll feel more at ease once I see her with my own eyes. And besides, I haven't established the peace treaty yet," Kaiden replied, starting down the hallway.

Elric nodded, but it looked like he wanted to say more.

"Why don't you tell me what's on your mind, Sergeant?" Kaiden stopped near the staircase.

"I can sense it, Captain."

Kaiden cocked a brow. "Sense what?"

"Your akrani."

Shit.

Blood rushed to Kaiden's face. "I don't know what you're talking about."

Elric's stare didn't falter. He crossed his arms.

Kaiden decided there was no hiding it from this man. He leaned closer. "Take a walk with me."

The courtyard was flooded with the golden radiance of the midmorning sun. Kaiden sat on a stone bench in front of the water fountain, tilting his head skyward. *No more clouds.*

Elric combed his fingers through his black hair and remained standing.

Kaiden inhaled. "This is a recent development." Deep down, he knew it wasn't, but he was steadfast in his denial. "Is it that obvious?"

It was difficult for him to get a read on Elric. That neutral expression seemed to be permanently etched onto his face.

"No. I wasn't sure at first. But I know now. Satori, right?" Elric's eyes scanned the area.

Kaiden appreciated his attentiveness to their surroundings. "Yes, my mother had it. She was an ellorian."

Elric nodded. "That explains it. I've heard of your mother, Captain Beatrice. There's not much on record about her in the archives," he said. "Take care. Your satori could have dire consequences."

Kaiden remembered what Zade had once said about satori when they were crossing Thessalynne Lake. *Every time I use it, I lose some of my own memories. Sometimes it's temporary, but a lot of the time it's permanent. At the mo-*

ment, his concern for Zade's memories was not an issue. These were Kaiden's memories they were discussing now.

"Yes, I've been warned." Kaiden studied Elric. "How could you tell?"

"Let's just say I have a kind of sight."

"Have you *seen* the queen since we've arrived?"

Elric let his hands fall to his sides. "Should I have?"

"No. I just feel a change in her." Kaiden rested his forearms on his thighs.

"Isn't that to be expected? She has just become queen, and the pressure of rebuilding Balam could be weighing heavily on her shoulders," Elric said.

"No, not that kind of change. Before, she was peace. Today, I feel only chaos." Kaiden stared at him for a long moment. He loosed a breath and buried his face in his hands. "I must sound insane."

"Not at all, Captain. It sounds as though your heart is your guide."

Kaiden peered at the sergeant. "It's like a spark in my soul. I know when she's in the room, and I've known her in sleep. I'm telling you, Sergeant, something has changed."

"Well, have you been in the same room together yet?" Elric asked.

Kaiden supposed he hadn't exactly been in the room while she was talking to Andreas. "No. Not yet."

"Okay, what needs to be done?" Elric clasped his hands.

Kaiden stared out into the distance. "We need to get her alone, but Andreas seems adamant about that not happening."

"Do you want me to . . ." Elric cleared his throat and made a slicing motion across his neck.

Kaiden raised his hands. "No."

Not yet, at least.

Elric didn't appear at all surprised. "I have an idea, but it's a bit extreme."

Kaiden cocked a brow and stood. "How extreme?"

A slight grin tugged at the corners of Elric's mouth. "You'd really have to trust me." He continued to tell Kaiden the plan.

SINCE KAIDEN HADN'T SLEPT THE previous night, he went back to his chambers to take a nap. He was jolted awake by banging on the door. Dragging himself out of bed, he answered it.

Isaac stood there in his black jacket with the onyx buttons polished to a mirror's shine. His brows rose. "Are you not going to dinner, Captain?"

Kaiden ran a hand down his face. "Shit. Give me a few minutes." Closing the door, he rushed to get ready. Kaiden smirked, knowing Blaise would likely have something to say about his tardiness.

Upon his arrival to the large dining hall, the chatter ceased. Everyone at the long dark table stared at him while he walked to the only empty chair.

For the first time in weeks, Kaiden gazed upon her.

Blaise sat with the galydrian crown on her head. She wore a long-sleeve black gown with a neck corset collar, and a yellow crystal rested on her chest. Her features seemed so different with the dark eyeliner and burgundy lips. It didn't seem to be her style, but she was still as beautiful as he remembered.

She stared at him with an unreadable expression on her lovely face. Did she not recognize him?

Nearly falling into his seat staring at her, Kaiden regarded the queen. "You look well, Your Majesty."

"Thank you, Captain." She exchanged a glance with Andreas, who sat on her right. She made no mention of his tardiness.

Perhaps she's waiting for the right moment?

Everything about Blaise should've felt familiar. To him, she was completely closed off. Kaiden attempted to reach out with his untrained satori only to be denied by some unseen force. The icy void in his chest caused a chill of unease to course through him.

Throughout the entire dinner, Andreas made small talk about the improvements to and progress of Balam and about how he was making deals with the kingdoms of the lands overseas.

Blaise avoided eye contact with Kaiden all night.

Could she still be angry at me for leaving?

If she was, he didn't blame her.

Kaiden reached out to her once more, and an icy tremor crawled up his spine, suffocating his senses. He gasped, breaking the connection. He pushed up from his seat and stood. His chair screeched against the floor, toppling onto its back.

The room quieted, and everyone stared at him again.

"My apologies, Your Majesty." He picked up his chair and set it back in place.

What in gehheina is happening to me?

He started to sit down.

"If you're not feeling well, Captain, perhaps you should retire to your chamber," Blaise said.

Silence filled the dining hall. Kaiden glanced around the table, recognizing Elric, Isaac, and Simone on the other end. His eyes snapped back to the queen. "Perhaps I should. My apologies again."

She flashed him a smile. "Find me when you're well, Captain. We'll catch up."

Kaiden walked out of the dining hall. He paused in the corridor, composing himself.

We'll be catching up sooner than you think.

9
KAIDEN

AIDEN STOOD ON THE BALCONY OF HIS bedchamber sharpening his sword. He swiped the whetstone down the length of his blade, moonlight reflecting off the steel. While his hands were busy, his mind went over the plan he and Elric had put together. *A risky one.* There was a knock at his door. He put the stone back into his utility belt and sheathed his weapon. He strode over to answer it. Elric, Isaac, and Simone filed into the room.

"Did anyone see you?" Kaiden closed the heavy door.

Simone examined the chamber. "Why is your suite so much nicer than mine?"

Elric let out a short breath at her complaint and then responded, "No one saw us, Captain. Thankfully, no one heard the cast-iron candleholder Isaac knocked over."

Isaac's lips tugged up into a wry smile.

"I thought you were going to work on your stealth?" Kaiden asked, crossing his arms.

Isaac huffed and murmured, "I said I was sorry."

Elric shot Isaac a stony glare.

"It won't happen again, Sergeant," Isaac said, hiding behind Kaiden's big body.

"Can we focus?" Kaiden snapped.

Isaac and Simone each discussed their role to infiltrate the queen's bedchamber. They would be the lookout outside her chamber while Kaiden and Elric made their entrance another way.

Simone leaned against the oak dresser with her arms crossed. "I hope this illogical plan of yours works."

Me too. It was a lot easier when her room was next door to mine.

"Ready, Sergeant?" Kaiden glanced at Elric, then walked onto the balcony, the crisp night air brushing his cheeks. He tied the high-tension rope to his utility belt and pulled on his leather gloves, waiting for Elric to situate himself.

Elric followed, securing the ropes to the thick stone railing. "As ready as I can be, Captain."

The last time Kaiden had scaled a wall was in squire training. He'd rappelled down Teaos, which was half the size of the fortress. He peered over the railing at the long drop. He wasn't afraid of heights, but he didn't exactly want his brains scattered all over the courtyard grounds. Inhaling a deep breath, he closed his eyes.

Elric strode up beside him, tugging on his gloves. "Good to go."

Kaiden nodded and did a once-over of the ropes secured to the railing. He took one more glance down the length of the vine-covered fortress. Nervousness unsettled his stomach, and tension crept through his body. He swallowed the bile threatening to rise, breathing in the crisp night air.

On his exhale, he climbed over the banister. He began to rappel as soon as his feet hit the outer wall. He descended, the wind whipping through his hair, heart pumping, adrenaline coursing through his veins. He'd always had an urge to soar through the skies.

Elric trailed, keeping Kaiden's pace. They moved quietly in the shadows, passing balconies and huge paneled windows of the fortress. Kaiden's eyes darted back and forth, looking for any sign of movement, any sign of the guards. There were far too few patrols. It had only been a few weeks since Blaise's coronation and attempted assassination. The suspect was still at large, and she needed more protection than what was here.

Did Andreas intentionally send the Alchyra away?

Kaiden spotted Blaise's balcony. He took a deep breath and let it out slowly, trying to calm his racing heart. He heard footsteps coming from the balcony above him. He signaled Elric and pressed himself against the leaf-covered wall, holding back a sneeze.

"What're you doing?" a guard said.

"I thought I heard something."

"Have you been drinking on duty again? It's probably just rodents in the vines." Their voices faded.

Kaiden and Elric exchanged glances, then looked

into the black vines. Kaiden swore Elric cringed before he mouthed, "Let's move."

With quiet precision, he lowered himself onto Blaise's balcony. Elric landed next to him with the grace of a cat. Kaiden signaled him to keep watch. The doors were wide-open. He crept up to the threshold, his head on a swivel.

Once Kaiden knew it was clear to enter, he stealthily ghosted into the dimly lit chamber. He locked eyes with the queen, who stood in front of a row of windows. Her skin gave off an iridescent glow in the moonlight. He stepped closer, a chill trickling down his spine.

"Captain Kaiden, so nice of you to visit." She wore the same dress she'd had on at dinner. Kaiden noted the dark circles around her eyes and the paleness of her usually tanned skin.

Her reaction to him made no sense. His brow furrowed. "I figured you'd still be angry that I'd left."

A slight frown crept onto her face. "Why would I be angry? You have your sentinel duties, Captain."

He stepped closer, craving her familiar lavender scent. It was sweet—too sweet, like spoiled fruit. "I don't understand," he muttered.

"What don't you understand, Captain?" she asked, tilting her head.

He reached out to caress her hollow cheek. "What happened to you, Blaise?" The question had come out as a whisper.

She batted his hand away. "You do not have permission to touch me, Captain."

You are not my Sparks.

He stepped back. "Who are you?"

"I'm Queen Blaise Everleigh Vinterhale of Balam."

"Tell me what happened to you," he demanded. "Is it Andreas? Has he coerced you in any way? Tell me. I'll make him pay."

She shook her head. "Of course not. He's my most trusted advisor."

Kaiden's nostrils flared.

What has Andreas done to her?

One of the doors to the chamber opened, and Andreas and an Alchyra woman walked in.

"Pardon the intrusion, Captain. We've apprehended two of your sentinels and found them a cozy cell in the dungeon."

"You do not have permission to be here, Captain," said the woman.

Blaise smiled at Kaiden and stepped beside Andreas. Her fingers grazed the yellow crystal around her neck. The color seemed to have faded since dinner.

Kaiden didn't take his eyes off Blaise. "What did you do to her?" he asked Andreas through gritted teeth.

"I don't know what you're talking about," Andreas replied all too calmly.

Kaiden scoffed. "Right. This is not the same woman I left here in Balam."

"How would you know? You left her here in my charge. A lot can change in a short amount of time." Andreas looked to the Alchyra. "Captain Cyrene, take the captain to join his unit."

Kaiden unsheathed his sword.

Elric charged in from the balcony, weapon in hand, his free hand outstretched. His intense gaze locked onto the Alchyra. She grabbed her head and fell to her knees, screaming in pure terror.

Kaiden wasted no time in pummeling Andreas in the face with the hilt of his sword. Andreas fell back against the wall, eyes wide.

"I'm going to ask you one more time. What the *fuck* did you do to Blaise?" Kaiden pushed the sharp edge against Andreas's throat, drawing droplets of blood.

"Might I remind you we need him alive, Captain?" Elric said.

"Shut up," Kaiden growled. His jaw clenched, and he pulled back.

Andreas straightened. His eyes blackened. "You're too late. He's already coming for her."

Kaiden glared. "Who?"

"Watch out!" Elric pushed Kaiden aside as dark leatherlike wings erupted out of Andreas's back. Two horns broke through the skin of his forehead, and he bared razor-sharp teeth, talons growing from his fingertips. A claw slashed through the air, just missing Elric.

Kaiden regained his balance.

Andreas reached for Blaise's neck, ripping the crystal away. "Kill."

Kaiden remembered wearing his mother's purple crystal infused with her akrani. Maybe the crystal Blaise wore had something to do with her sudden change in demeanor.

An ominous vibration emanated from her, and black smoke swirled around the room. Her skin began deteriorating into rotting flesh, the sweet-sour stench Kaiden had detected earlier filling his nostrils. A high-pitched shriek escaped the creature's mouth. She leaped toward Kaiden, wrapping her black fingers around his neck.

Elric dropped his hand, releasing the Alchyra. He darted toward the revenant, kicking her off Kaiden. She hit the wall, bones cracking, body contorting unnaturally—inhumanly. Like an arachnid, she crawled up the stone wall.

Andreas bolted for the balcony. Kaiden gave chase, but he skidded to a stop when Andreas leaped over the railing, taking off into the night sky.

Damn, I wish I could fly.

"What the fuck's going on?" the Alchyra screamed.

Kaiden turned back into the room. Elric flung one of his daggers, hitting the revenant in the sternum. She screamed at him and scuttled onto the ceiling. The bones in her neck popped and cracked. Her dead eyes met each of theirs as her head came full circle, a grin on her face.

"Get down here, bitch." Elric reached out in the direction of the revenant. He appeared to grab a handful of nothing. The revenant made a guttural growl, and its body was pulled away from the ceiling. With one swift motion, Elric seemed to slam what he was holding into the ground. The revenant was violently thrown to the floor, where an unknown force pinned her.

Elric's hands started to shake, sweat coated his brow, and black smoke emanated from the corners of his eyes.

Kaiden stepped forward and placed a hand on Elric's shoulder. "I got it from here." Without another word, he unsheathed his sword and spun, decapitating the revenant in one quick motion.

An end to the fake queen.

Kaiden looked to Captain Cyrene. "You must inform General Zade of everything that has happened here tonight. The queen is being held somewhere against her will."

Panting, Elric leaned against the wall. "We need to go after Andreas before I lose his trail."

"Are you okay?" Kaiden asked him.

"I will be," Elric grunted. Kaiden helped him straighten.

Captain Cyrene stood in front of the door, fear in her eyes.

"Go now. Tell everyone we're going to find the true queen," Kaiden said, and they passed her, heading out the door.

Andreas was their only way to Blaise.

"Which direction is he headed?" Kaiden asked Elric, striding down the dim corridor.

"I sense he's headed north, but I won't know for sure until we're outside." Elric was regaining his balance.

"Let's get to the stables before everyone wakes," Kaiden said.

They grabbed their horses and supplies, including warm clothes, and wasted no time heading in the direction of the trail only Elric could see.

A flash took over Kaiden's vision, and he saw Blaise chained to pillars, kneeling in an icy puddle of blood. It faded as quickly as it had come, and the cold despair coiling in the pit of Kaiden's stomach matched the void he felt in his heart. Dark clouds hovered over them, but nothing would keep him from Blaise.

10
KAIDEN

KAIDEN PULLED THE HOOD OVER HIS HEAD and buckled the top clasp of his heavy black fur-lined cloak. The thick gray fur seemed inadequate for the mountains that loomed ahead. He leaned forward in his saddle and patted Cedric's neck, praising the steed for being so resilient in the increasingly colder weather. Andreas's trail had led them west, then east, taking them in a full circle. At one point, they were nearly led off a cliff, and it took them half a day to get back on his trail.

They gradually ascended toward the frozen white-peaked Terrenmis Mountains. Kaiden was starting to hate traveling through these chilly climates. Once the sun made its descent over the horizon, the temperature would plummet. Elric rode behind him through two feet of snow and icy winds, yet he seemed unbothered by the change in weather.

Four days after leaving Balam, they rode into the ruins just as the sun set. Their supplies had run out on the third day. Luckily, the snow could be melted to fill their canteens.

Kaiden took in the surroundings as he led Cedric out of the elements. Part of the grand structure protruded from the slope of the mountain. Only four slate pillars were visible through the tons of snow and ice covering the ruins. A fallen column lay in front of the wide archway where a door had once hung.

Chiseled above the entrance was a symbol Kaiden had never seen before. Then again, he'd never paid attention when it came to learning about the history of the gods. The symbol was chipped in several places, but from what Kaiden could make out, it was half of a circle.

Maybe a full one?

Elric settled his horse next to Cedric in a small side room, then made his way to Kaiden. "Whose temple is this?"

It was irritating that Elric didn't seem cold at all. Kaiden cursed the architects for building this place of worship so far up the damned mountain.

Kaiden shrugged, hugging himself. "I don't know." Despite the altitude, the heaviness in his chest lessened with each inhale.

"Shall we?" Elric drawled, unsheathing his sword.

Kaiden retrieved a torch from the side room and followed suit, leading the way into the ruins. Once they were surrounded by darkness, Elric pulled a flint rock from his utility belt and struck it into the torch head. It sparked to life, and they continued down the drafty corridor.

Kaiden was blindsided and knocked to the ground. In the falling firelight of the torch, he made out the silhouette of a beast he recognized. The undead creature bore scimitar blades for arms and a chest of steel-plated armor.

"Son of a—" Kaiden blocked its bladed arm. The revenant struck again. Kaiden parried, but the creature lunged. He sidestepped, avoiding the strike.

With his sword at the ready, Elric struck the revenant's rib cage, and sparks erupted upon contact. "Find Andreas. He's just up ahead," he said to Kaiden.

"Are you sure?" Kaiden swung down only to be blocked by the creature's arm. In his periphery, he saw Elric's eyes darken, obsidian smoke emanating from them. Black veins protruded and crawled up his neck. Elric bared his teeth, the pain apparent on his face. His lips pulled back from a pair of sharp fangs.

Something akin to terror rose in Kaiden's chest.

What type of akrani is this?

"Go," Elric growled.

In a billow of smoke, Elric lured the monster away from Kaiden. Without further hesitation, he picked up the torch and sprinted down the corridor.

Sword in hand, he came to a chamber. It appeared to be a place where worshipers offered their sacrifices. Human remains caught his gaze, lying along with the pile of animal bones. Kaiden scanned the open room. Small mountains of snow had formed where there were holes in the ceiling. Broken urns were gathered on the stone altar in the center of the room. The altar was encircled with black candles—some broken, others missing—but none had been lit in ages.

Whose temple was this? There was nothing familiar about the symbols etched on every surface. Many of the rooms he'd passed appeared as though whole walls had been knocked down by some tremendous force. *Could this have been a battleground of the gods?*

On the other side of the altar was a vestry, and one of its walls was partially blown away. He could see debris strewn on the moonlit floor behind it. Snow fell from a large circular opening in the ceiling. A chill coursed through him. That once-empty feeling in his chest surged with serene warmth when he saw snowflakes drifting to the floor.

This is the place.

Tranquility tugged at his heart, pulling him across the room, leading him through the beams of azure moonlight and into the darkness. His snow-covered boots echoed. With each step, the oppressive void gripping his soul eased.

He crossed the threshold, and his gaze snapped to the crouched figure in the middle of the room, doused in crimson and moonlight. He stopped in his tracks, staring, hoping this was all just a bad dream. His racing heart knew her—wanted her, called her name.

"Blaise," he whispered, begging his legs to move, but he remained cemented in place. She was chained between two pillars and was as still as a statue, kneeling in a frozen puddle of blood.

She's not dead. She can't be.

The vigorous desire to hold her in his arms and feel her heart pulse forced him forward. Strands of her tangled onyx hair hung around her downcast face. Snowflakes collected like a crown on her head—the queen of Balam, chained like a common criminal.

Kaiden reached out and almost touched her, but Andreas emerged from the shadows, lunging with his sword. Kaiden blocked his attack with the downward sweep of his blade. Andreas unfurled his leathery wings, drew them back, and flailed forward, thrusting a powerful gust of icy wind. Kaiden tumbled backward, landing on one knee.

Andreas's next flurry of strikes forced Kaiden to the right. He stifled a groan while pain tore through him. Andreas's blade had slashed his arm through the gap in his armor. He climbed to his feet, ignoring the sting.

Andreas swung his blade once more. Kaiden blocked, their swords crossing in the middle. They locked onto each other, and in Andreas's dark eyes, Kaiden's reflection was upside down.

"What the fuck are you?" he gritted out, trickles of liquid seeping from his wounded arm. He needed to end this.

Andreas's chalky lips curved into a smile. "You're a smart man, Captain. Figure it out." He pushed his blade forward, steel sliding against steel. He kicked Kaiden square in the chest.

Kaiden's back collided with the wall, and all the air left his lungs. Placing his hand over his stomach, he inhaled deeply.

He's fucking fast.

"I'll give you a hint: I serve one of the gods." Andreas crept toward Kaiden, wings hovering above his head. He dragged his sword across the stone floor, leaving sparks in its wake, and a horrid screech echoed through the chamber. Kaiden observed each lazy step, trying to find a flaw in his stride.

"Why are you doing this?" He was buying time or elongating his death. Either way, he wasn't going to give up, and he sure as gehheina wasn't going to walk away. *Not again.*

"Redemption." Andreas's hand moved with a flash of the silver blade, swinging down horizontally.

Kaiden pushed through the burning in his arm, propelling his sword upward with all the strength he could muster. Their weapons clanged, and Andreas fumbled back.

Kaiden didn't want to leave any opportunity for Andreas to strike back. He gripped the handle of his sword and slashed up at an angle. Andreas swiped down at the last possible second, barely blocking the blow.

His movements are slowing.

Kaiden couldn't afford one miscalculated move. Despite the ache in his legs, he drew strength from within and attacked Andreas with a combination of strikes.

A crazed expression crept onto Andreas's face. He flung one wing at Kaiden, knocking him off-balance. With a flail of his wings, Andreas barreled into Kaiden, slamming him against the wall. Before Kaiden could react, Andreas pummeled him in the face so hard he dropped his sword. Kaiden's head jerked back and hit the stone wall. His vision blurred while Andreas held his body against the surface with his wings.

Andreas slammed his fists into Kaiden's face again and again, sending his head lurching side to side with each jab. Ignoring the throbbing pain, Kaiden struggled to get out of Andreas's hold, but he was too gods damned strong.

A warmth tingled up Kaiden's spine, settling in his chest. It burst outward, making its way to every part of his body. Muscles vibrating, he conjured the strength to swing both feet in the air, kicking Andreas in the gut. Kaiden landed on his feet as Andreas released him and stepped back, holding his stomach with wide eyes.

"How did you move so quickly?" he asked.

Kaiden retrieved his sword with a smirk. "You're a smart man, Andreas. Figure it out." He spat crimson to the speckled snow-covered floor and wiped his bloody mouth with the back of his gloved hand. Not an inch of him was spared from the agony tearing through his fatigued muscles.

This ends now.

Sentinel training had taught Kaiden to push through the pain and exhaustion, to fight until there was nothing left.

With labored breaths, he darted forward, eating up the space between him and Andreas. Kaiden slashed back and forth, Andreas ducking and dodging every swing.

It seemed Andreas could barely keep up. He panted, "She will be angry if this doesn't go as planned."

Kaiden held the tip of his sword to Andreas's chest. "Who will be angry?"

"Guess you'll just have to wait and see." Andreas thrust himself into the air and circled Kaiden. The high ceilings of the temple allowed for his wide wingspan. He dove and struck Kaiden with one of his sharp talons, knocking him to the ground.

Kaiden winced through the thrumming pain and climbed to his feet, sword still in hand. Andreas flew above him somewhere in the darkness. Kaiden could only make out his silhouette through the beams of moonlight cascading through the cracks and holes in the ceiling.

Kaiden's gaze went to Blaise still kneeling between the two pillars, unmoving. He needed this fight to end.

Where's Elric when I need him?

A gust of wind swept past Kaiden from behind. A booted foot struck him to the floor. He landed on his hands and knees.

This guy is almost as relentless as I am.

"Oh, Captain," Andreas taunted.

Kaiden tilted his head up. He focused on Blaise and the man—or creature—standing behind her. Andreas grabbed a handful of her hair and jerked her head back, baring her neck. Then he reached around and placed a dagger to her pale throat.

"She's lost quite a bit of blood already. Shall we see if she can bleed more?"

"Don't," Kaiden growled, reaching for her. He got to one knee only to falter before finally standing. "What do you want?"

Andreas chuckled. "I thought it was obvious. I need you and your unit to go back to Elatora and tell the king that everything in Balam is fine. I'll even sign that little peace treaty of yours."

Kaiden scoffed. "That's not going to happen."

"Then her blood is on your hands." Andreas pushed the blade into her neck, breaking skin. Droplets of red seeped from the cut.

"Wait." The void—the emptiness—started to crawl its way back into Kaiden's soul, stealing the warmth he'd just found. His breathing was shaky, hands trembling while he sorted out his options.

"Ticktock, Captain. I don't have all night," Andreas drawled.

Kaiden's eyes narrowed, but he grinned when he saw Andreas's bloodied lip and black eye. His garments were tattered, scrapes and cuts all over his hands.

Kaiden inhaled and searched inside himself for his mother's power. It had to be there.

The warmth from earlier ignited in his chest. He willed it to flourish and felt it ripple through him. Focusing the heat of his power to his hands, he aimed them at Andreas. Disregarding the consequences of using it without proper training, Kaiden unleashed it on him, pushing it through his palms.

The loud pulse of his akrani sent a tremor through the floor, avoiding Blaise and slamming Andreas into the wall. It fractured upon impact.

Andreas collapsed to his hands and knees, head hung in defeat. "You may have won this battle, but you haven't won the war."

Weapon in hand, Kaiden took long strides forward. "You talk too much." Kaiden raised his sword high and sliced down, cutting through skin and muscle and bone. Crimson sprayed onto his face as Andreas's head rolled across the floor, leaving a trail of blood behind it.

Kaiden dropped his weapon and crashed to his knees. Turning, he fell to the floor on his back and gave into the icy fatigue that seemed to saturate his bones. His vision blurred. He blinked once, twice, three times. Finally regaining focus, he reached for Blaise.

A spasm erupted in his mind, like a sharp blade picking at his brain. He suddenly couldn't remember where he was. He grunted in pain, fighting against it, holding his head in his hands.

Why am I here?

Through the throbbing, he managed to glimpse the woman kneeling in chains a few feet from him. A torrent of warmth tugged at his chest, and the pulse in his head dissipated. He pushed himself to sit, a groan escaping him. He glanced at the woman once more, her name coming to the forefront of his mind.

Her smile. Her laugh. Her beautiful defiance. Blaise.

Footsteps resounded in the shadows, nearing Kaiden. Elric stepped into the moonlight. From his boots to his dark hair, he was covered in a light layer of snow. It was a contrast from the fresh cuts and dried blood on his face, though he didn't appear nearly as beat-up as Kaiden. Elric helped him to his feet.

"I apologize for my extended absence. I had to . . . get ahold of myself." He took a fleeting look at Andreas's headless body. Once he gazed upon the queen, he strode to her, falling to his knees.

Kaiden wasted no time in undoing her chains, and she fell into Elric's arms.

"She has a pulse. It's weak, but it's there." Elric examined her shoulder next. "It's dislocated."

Through the aching in his legs, Kaiden knelt in front of Elric. Even though her calm flowed through him, he couldn't bear the sight of her: lips dry and peeling, dark circles around her eyes, dried blood on her tattered dress, the bolt still embedded in her stomach. Would she have survived this if she weren't a half god?

Kaiden didn't take his eyes off Blaise. "We need to minimize how much we move her during travel." He took his cloak off and wrapped her in it with Elric's help.

Elric followed suit, then gently laid her on the ground.

He and Kaiden started their search for planks around the temple ruins. They found enough to construct a sled and carefully strapped Blaise to it.

Kaiden pulled while Elric pushed her down the dark corridor and into the biting cold. They used rope to tie the sled to Cedric and started the long journey down the mountain.

After traveling through the night to the break of dawn, they rode into Meliwe Forest and stopped, watering and resting their horses beneath the shady trees. The men bandaged themselves up and took turns sleeping for an hour while one of them stood guard.

When Kaiden woke from his nap, he checked Blaise's pulse. It seemed to be strengthening, or maybe it was a false sense of hope.

"We should get to the fortress before nightfall." Elric was already sitting on his own steed, ready to move.

The warmth in Kaiden's chest flickered, threatening to go out. He stared at Blaise and placed his hand on her chest, feeling it rise and fall. "Tell me she'll be okay."

Elric's voice softened. "She *can* be okay, but we need to go."

He was right. Kaiden stood and climbed onto Cedric, following Elric down the shady path. They rode into the Balam foothills a few hours later. Through the white clouds was a view of the fortress.

Finally.

Kaiden sped up the pace to a trot, mindful of the terrain—mindful of Blaise. The crisp wind blew through his dark hair. People murmured and gasped while they rode through the small marketplace. They reached the fortress gate, and a handful of servants and stable hands rushed toward them.

Captain Cyrene darted out a few seconds later. "Gods, you found her."

"We need to get her inside." Kaiden detached the sled from Cedric, and the stable hand led the horse away.

Like clockwork, Isaac and Simone sprinted out of the fortress. *Captain Cyrene must've released them.* The four of them carried Blaise into the nearest bedchamber on the first floor. Kaiden and Elric unstrapped Blaise from the sled and lifted her onto the huge bed.

Moments later, two servants walked in with hot water and clean cloths. Simone unsheathed a small dagger from her utility belt and cut off the top half of Blaise's dress, leaving the strip of cloth across her breasts. She examined the bolt in her stomach.

Simone moved to her shoulder, grabbing her arm. She gave one quick motion, and a muffled pop rang in Kaiden's ears.

"She's going to feel that when she wakes up." Simone touched the skin around Blaise's wound. She looked at Kaiden. "I'm going to try to extract the bolt with my gitros."

Kaiden nodded his approval.

She's going to be okay.

That familiar warmth had dissipated at an alarming rate. He swallowed the lump in his throat, ignoring the pain coursing through his body. It was no match for the agony pulsing in his chest. He glanced back at the solemn faces of the servants, then at Elric and Isaac.

Simone placed her hand over Blaise's wound, hovering an inch above the bolt, a look of concentration on her face. "That's strange." She frowned as sparks emanated from Blaise's unconscious body.

"What's wrong?" Kaiden stepped closer.

Simone stopped, shaking her hand. "I'm not sure yet. Let me try again." A small surge of lightning erupted, holding Simone in place.

Kaiden touched Simone's hand, and the current lessened. Warm tingles flowed through him. The image of Blaise's beautiful smiling face invaded his mind. Beneath their hands, the bolt oozed from her stomach, and the wound began to heal. Once the injury was nothing more than scar tissue, Kaiden pulled away.

Simone gazed at him with wide eyes. "Captain, how . . . ?"

Kaiden shook his head, glancing at his palms. "I don't know." But the warmth was back, and that was all he cared about. "I'll stay with her." He looked at Elric pointedly.

Elric seemed to understand the unspoken command. "Get out. Everyone." He was the last one to leave, closing the heavy door behind him.

Gods, Kaiden felt like he'd gone to gehheina and back. He made his way into the washroom. Wincing, he unbuckled the straps on the sides of his chest plate and slid it off, flinging it to the floor. Once he'd undressed down to his trousers, he splashed water on his face and torso from the faucet. He used the rest of his energy to clean the gash in his arm and wrap it in fresh bandages.

Kaiden managed to walk back to Blaise despite the sharp pains prickling his body. He lay next to her, glancing at her stomach—at the barely visible scar. His gaze went to the rise and fall of her chest and the strong pulse in her neck.

Just to be sure, he rested his palm on her midsection, closed his eyes, and felt the cadence of life coursing through her body. His eyes welled with pure elation. His muscles relaxed, and long-awaited sleep consumed him.

11
BLAISE

Blaise's body was enveloped in a familiar warmth. She cherished it. Sank into it. Her eyes flickered open, awareness flooding her senses. Someone was holding her down. She threw her arm back, hitting something solid, then rolled. She landed on her hands and knees, the cold seeping into her limbs.

Where am I?

After taking in the surroundings of the bedchamber, she glanced down at herself—at her scarred wrists where her shackles had left marks.

"Fuck, Blaise."

Her gaze focused on Kaiden, sitting on the bed, cupping his nose in his hands.

"You're not real," she whispered, crawling backward into the corner.

"Blaise, it's me. I'm here." He crept toward her with his hands up.

"No, no, no." She shook her head. "My Kaiden left me. You're not him—not real." She squeezed her eyes shut. "He left me. I'm dead. That's the only explanation . . ." Her words were cut off by a wave of sobs. She flinched at the featherlike fingertips grazing her head. Her eyes shot open, and she stood, smacking his hand away.

"You're not dead, Blaise." His voice cracked. "I *am* here with you."

She kept fighting him until he grabbed her arm and drew her into his embrace. The pure elation of his energy was all-consuming. It was invigorating and caused gooseflesh to rise on her arms. She shifted, and a mangled breath escaped her, a vivid twinge of pain coursing through her. "Kaiden?" she rasped.

He pulled away, gazing upon her face. "Yes, Sparks. It's me." He leaned in and placed a soft kiss on her forehead.

He came back?

The vigorous pulse of her heart was too much for her to handle. She closed her eyes, and a single tear trickled down her cheek.

He reached up and wiped the tear falling down her face with the pad of his thumb. "You're safe."

She couldn't remember how or when she'd been saved, knowing death would be her only freedom.

His dark eyes bored into her the way she remembered. Her heart skipped a beat. He wrapped her in a blanket and picked her up in a gentle embrace, leaving kisses on her face. She sank into him as he carried her back to the bed. He laid her on the mattress. She winced, her body incredibly tender.

"I'm sorry." He loosened his hold to climb in next to her and coaxed her close. He buried his face in the side of her neck, inhaling deeply. "I thought I lost you."

His lips caressed the curve of her soft flesh, and her breath caught. Her body had always been annoyingly responsive to his touch. She bit down on her bottom lip.

"I've missed you," she whispered.

He rolled her closer and stared into her eyes. "What?"

Shit. She hadn't meant to say that out loud. "I didn't say anything."

He leaned in, kissing her on the cheek, working his way along her jawline. "Yes, you did. I heard it. You missed me." His lips curved up in that familiar smirk. His gaze met hers, then he kissed her, tongue slipping into her mouth. They moved in perfect synchronicity.

Gods, his citrus-sweet taste on her tongue was the aphrodisiac she longed for. His fingers reached beneath the white strip of cloth and brushed over one of her breasts. A moan escaped her throat. Her hand drifted to the bulge in his trousers, and she stroked it with her palm, his muscles tensing in response. His touch remained too gentle. She longed for his rough caress. She wanted to be wrapped around every inch of him.

He released a desire-filled groan.

She should've been angry at him for leaving, but at that particular moment, she didn't care. All she wanted was his hands exploring her body. His lips on hers. His hard length inside her.

He winced, tearing himself away. "We need to stop." His familiar hazel eyes were dilated with lust. He couldn't catch his breath. "You have severe injuries that need to heal. We both need rest."

Her excitement wavered at the loss of his lips, but he was right. She was in no condition to be engaging in the primal activities she had in mind—no matter how pleasurable they might be. She loosed a breath and flinched at the thrum of pain in her stomach. The wound was healing. She suspected it still needed more time.

Concern crossed Kaiden's handsome bruised face. "Are you okay?"

She nodded and wrapped the blanket around herself, resting her hand over the fresh scar on her stomach. "I feel . . . different. What did you do?"

He grinned and cocked a brow. "Why do you assume *I* did something?"

She crossed her arms. "Tell me you didn't."

Kaiden threw his legs over the side of the bed and straightened, the hard lines of his back on full display. Gods, he was still as sexy as she remembered. A few fresh bruises discolored his tanned skin, but they just added to his beauty.

"Honestly, I'm not sure," he finally muttered, turning around.

He didn't seem eager to talk about it, but she would definitely speak to him later.

"What happened?" she asked, clasping her hands in her lap.

"What's the last thing you remember?"

She loosed a breath. "The chamber, there was some-one . . ."

His lips formed a straight line. "Yes, that was your advisor, Andreas."

She averted her gaze. "Why would he do that to me?"

Kaiden moved to sit beside her. "It was him. He alchemized a copy of you with a revenant."

Dread trickled down her spine. "How long has it been since the coronation?"

His face fell. "It's been about a month."

"Goddess of chaos," she blurted, attempting to get out of bed. "We need to raise the alarm and assemble the Alchyra."

He stopped her, placing his hand on her shoulder. "We've already dealt with it."

"What did you do?"

"My team terminated the problem." He stood and stretched out his arms, trousers slipping lower on his hips.

She shot him a sidelong look. "You mean *you* terminated the problem?"

"Same difference."

Blaise sighed. "Are you sure it was him?"

Kaiden opened the curtains, and beams of golden sunlight streamed into the room. "I had a vision. It wasn't clear at first, but that's how I knew it was him."

Her brow furrowed. "Satori? Does it have anything to do with your ellorian bloodline?"

"I believe so. Though I've yet to attain any definitive answers about any of it." He turned and started scratching his back along the rough stone wall. "Dammit, this annoying itch again."

The corner of her mouth rose. "Gods, don't tell me you got fleas."

His eyes narrowed on her. "You've been awake all but ten minutes and you're already giving me a hard time?"

A ghost of the glacial tinge from her shadowy prison crawled up her spine. She was grateful for their banter. She raised her good shoulder. "You make it all too easy."

He grumbled. "I'm going to prepare a bath for you."

Blaise didn't miss the hint of amusement on Kaiden's face. He strode into the washroom, leaving the door slightly open behind him. Her lips curved up.

Moments later, Kaiden strolled out. "It's ready. Do you want me to carry you, or do you want to try walking?"

She heaved her legs over the edge of the mattress and attempted to stand. The cold floor stung against her bare feet. Her knees buckled, and Kaiden raced forward, catching her.

Frustrated with how weak her body had become, she let out a sharp breath. "Thanks."

"Perhaps we should try that again later." He carried her into the washroom and sat her on a black stone bench.

"Wait." She stopped him from taking off her undergarments.

He raised an eyebrow. "Really? I've seen it all before."

She huffed. "So?" She wanted to hide the gauntness of her starved and scarred body.

She tried to cover the bones protruding from under her skin, but he noticed, his eyes softening on her. "If it makes you feel better, I won't look."

Not wanting to bathe in her soiled undergarments, she conceded. He kept his promise and looked away. He proceeded to take off his trousers, exposing his nakedness to her as though it were normal.

Goddess of chaos. She didn't look away. Her nipples

hardened at the sight of his beautiful muscled body. He caught her staring, and that notorious smirk crept onto his features.

"Like what you see?" He was careful in scooping her into his arms. She knew he was in pain by how slowly he moved and the way his muscles tensed.

He cradled her against his chest. A spark ignited in her core, her pulse beating in tandem with his. The connection between them was still there—still strong.

Kaiden stepped into the large sunken bath built for spacious comfort. Once they were fully submerged, she stood, the water barely covering her breasts.

The temperature was perfect and almost instantly relaxed her aching muscles.

"I'm not sure this is a good idea," she said, keeping her gaze on the ornate galydrian vase sitting on a table in the corner.

He grabbed one of the large sponges from the tray, which had various fragrant soaps. "I'm not going to do anything questionable, if that's what you're worried about." He soaped his chest and arms, wincing occasionally. He rinsed off, drops trickling down his chiseled shoulders and taut abs.

She didn't know whether to be relieved or disappointed by that last statement. "You can't just come back into my life and expect us to pick up where we left off, Kaiden. It doesn't work like that." She studied his unreadable expression.

He squeezed out the sponge and lathered more soap into it. "Come here."

She stared, arms crossed, unmoving. He wasn't going to have his way—not if she had anything to do with it.

"Look, I thought leaving was the right thing to do at the time. The dutiful thing to do," he said.

With a sidelong glance, she asked, "Why *did* you come back? Did King Vaughn give you orders?"

He pursed his lips.

His silence answered her question, and she inhaled deeply. "The only reason you're here is because of him."

"I would've come without his approval," Kaiden said. He backed her into a corner of the bath. "Trust me, when I left, I regretted every moment of every day. I blame myself for what happened to you."

Her eyes drifted from his hard pecs to his collarbone. She stopped at his face. Was the water getting hotter? She swallowed. Hard. "Why?"

"I would've protected you." He leaned close, his face an inch from hers.

"It's not your duty to protect me," she whispered.

There was a knock on the washroom door.

Kaiden stepped away from Blaise, steam permeating off his tanned skin. "Who is it?" he bellowed, sounding annoyed.

"A message arrived from King Theod. He and his entourage will be arriving within three days." Isaac's voice was muffled through the heavy wooden door.

Why in gehheina was King Theod on his way to Balam? Blaise's brows came together, and she let out a breath.

"Thank you, Isaac," Kaiden said. "Gather the others and meet us in the throne room in thirty minutes. Tell Captain Cyrene."

"Consider it done, sir," Isaac replied.

When Blaise was sure Isaac had left, she asked, "What in gehheina is going on? Why is King Theod on his way? Where's Zade?"

Kaiden huffed. "Will you let me scrub your back?"

"Not until you tell me what's going on."

Kaiden proceeded to tell her that her double had sent her strongest Alchyra away and arranged a marriage between her and King Theod.

She conceded, turning. "I'm to marry King Theod?" She raked her hand down her face. "This can't be happening. What am I supposed to do?"

"Perhaps we can hold a nice dinner in his honor before we send him on his way," Kaiden suggested, grazing the sponge over the skin of her back, careful not to put too much pressure on her bruises.

She spun around, facing him. "How in gehheina am I supposed to do that? I don't know shit about Balam or the customs or fucking being queen. And with all of this, we're putting on a dinner party for my intended?" Her chest tightened, dizziness setting in. "What if King Theod doesn't take no for an answer?"

What if he takes Balam by force?

There was no way to defend against an attack like that. Her breathing quickened at the thought.

"Hey." Kaiden pressed his forehead to hers. "It's going to be okay."

She blew out a breath, struggling to ground herself.

"That's it, just breathe, Sparks," he said with a smirk.

"Don't. Call me. That." She inhaled. Exhaled. The storm inside her was subsiding, heart returning to its normal rhythm.

Even though her episode was passing, he continued to hold her. His grip on her arms was tight but didn't hurt. Her eyes drifted shut. He was quiet while he brushed his fingers along her back in a languid motion, the water lapping against her skin.

She refused to get lost in him again and backed away, opening her eyes. "We should get ready."

"Very well, milady."

He helped her out of the tub and assisted in drying her off. Thankfully, her legs kept her upright, though she still needed Kaiden to lean on. She was anxious to be at full strength again. He dressed first, then helped her pull on black trousers and a high-collared queen's robe.

He slipped one of her boots on.

"I'm sorry," she said.

"For what?" He looked at her, a curious gleam in his eyes.

"For being such a burden."

He slipped her other boot on, then knelt between her legs, placing his hands on her thighs. "You're not a burden, Blaise. I promise."

How could he say that? Everything that had happened thus far was because of her. Because she simply *existed*.

She averted her gaze and leaned back, gaining some distance from his intoxicating sandalwood scent. With a nod, she pursed her lips.

He straightened and offered his hand. "Shall we?"

"Thank you, Kaiden," she murmured, taking it.

He grinned, pulling her to her feet. And with a wink, he said, "You're welcome. Now, we have a dinner to plan."

12

BLAISE

The lone blond Alchyra stood out amongst Kaiden's small team of black-clad sentinels, her hair sleeked back in a neat bun. She carried her sheathed sword on the back of her shining silvery armor. The deep burgundy etchings matched those of the four small karambit daggers on each hip. The group had gathered to await Blaise's entrance into the throne room.

Even though she was able to walk properly now, Kaiden still accompanied her to the galydrian throne. She hesitated, her arm intertwined with his. He placed an encouraging hand over hers and continued forward. She allowed him to help her settle into the seat of her immanent rule.

The Alchyra approached Blaise with a reverent bow. "Your Majesty, you look much improved."

With a nod, Blaise replied, "Better by the second." She didn't know this woman's name or recognize the rank insignia on her shoulder plate.

"I'm Captain Cyrene. General Zade left me in charge when he and the troops were sent to Meliwe Forest. My loyalty is with you, my queen." She stepped back into the row of sentinels.

Through the enormous windows lining one side of the room, the sun hid behind white clouds. Water droplets trickled down the glass, blurring the view of Balam. The iron chandeliers hanging from the high ceilings provided dim lighting throughout the space. Blaise glanced at each person standing in a uniform line at the bottom of the steps.

Gods, I'm the fucking queen of a kingdom.

She stared at them, inhaling and slowly exhaling. Her index finger tapped on the armrest of the oversize throne. She had no idea how to handle this meeting.

Kaiden made his way to stand next to her, his uplifting hazel gaze meeting hers. He winked at her and faced the four warriors, giving each member of his unit a proper introduction. "If it pleases Her Majesty, we can begin discussing the upcoming visit of King Theod."

The inkling of anxiety bubbled in Blaise's stomach. "I assume everyone here is aware of the impending marriage."

They acknowledged with a "Yes, Your Majesty."

The formality of the meeting was far more than she'd anticipated. She breathed in too-thin air. The collar of her robe tightened around her throat. She fidgeted in her seat, then bolted upright and headed toward the door. "I need some ale."

Kaiden chased after her. "Blaise, where are you going?"

Blaise burst into the nearest bedchamber and started unbuttoning her robe, letting it fall to the floor. She reached into the closest armoire, grabbed a loose black tunic, and slipped it over her head. "The tavern." She walked back out into the corridor, keeping her pace, the rest falling into step with her. "Where is it?"

Cyrene strode next to her. "It's near the fortress gate, Your Majesty."

"Perfect." Blaise led the way down the corridor and out the double doors. Crisp air filled her lungs, and she crossed the gravel-covered yard to the gate, ready to walk through it.

"Forgive me, Your Majesty, but it isn't customary for the queen to go out without a proper detail. It usually takes a few days to coordinate and organize an outing," Cyrene said.

Blaise slowed, glancing at the captain. "Well then, just for today, I am not the queen. I am simply Blaise," she said with a wink.

Cyrene took a scrutinizing look at the ground, then met Blaise's gaze in agreement. "As you wish. I'd be much more at ease if we could disguise you better." She ran into the closest guardhouse and retrieved a short hooded cloak.

Blaise hoped most of the people wouldn't know what the queen looked like in regular clothes and no makeup. It didn't matter either way. Kaiden was here, and she needed to settle her nerves.

They approached the outdoor tavern. Tables and chairs were set up beneath a colorful canopy. The bar was nothing more than a small wooden shack with one bar-keep—a lovely blond-haired woman in a low-cut dress that displayed her generous cleavage. Even Blaise couldn't help but steal a glance.

"Why don't you ready a table for us all? Isaac and I will get the drinks," Kaiden insisted.

Blaise narrowed her eyes. "I'm more than capable of ordering my own drink, *Captain*." Without another word, she strode up to the bar, leaning her forearms on the smooth surface.

The woman approached, wiping out a pint glass with a rag. "What can I get for you?" She paused to stare at Kaiden for a heartbeat. "It's you again."

Blaise cocked her head, looking between the two. "Again?"

He'd better hope this acquaintance wasn't recent, or she would have to cut off his balls.

"We'll take six pints of your finest ale." Kaiden un-hooked his coin pouch from his utility belt. He seemed unbothered by Blaise's death glare.

The beautiful barkeep poured their order and winked at Kaiden. "This round is on the house."

The other four retrieved their pints and walked ahead to the table Isaac had cleared near the road. Blaise grabbed her ale and was about to follow, but Kaiden pulled her aside, away from the other patrons.

"It's not what you think." He set his pint on the bar.

Blaise sipped her ale, her eyes never leaving his face. It wasn't fair to expect him to have been faithful in her absence. They'd never established anything official as far as their relationship went.

"I gave her a polite nod when we rode through the marketplace. That's it."

She swallowed, then inhaled. "You don't have to explain yourself, Captain."

"Yes, I do. Because whether or not you want to believe it, you are my heart." He winced. "I meant you *have* my heart."

A corner of her mouth quirked up.

"You know what I mean."

Vivacious warmth filled her chest and spread through her body, blanketing her in bliss. She still didn't want to make things easy for him. With a smile, she teased, "Okay, ladies' man."

He stopped her from walking away, wrapping his arm around her waist. He closed the space between them and pressed his lips to hers. They separated, but the heat of his fervent kiss lingered.

"If I have to spend the rest of my life proving myself to you, I will." Grinning, he turned and strode to the table.

Blaise followed Kaiden and sat next to him. She noticed the looks of amusement on everyone's faces.

Shit, they probably saw that.

"Well, at least now I have some inkling of what this meeting will entail," Cyrene said, sipping her ale.

Blaise guzzled half her pint and slammed it onto the table. Holding back a hiccup, she said, "Captain Cyrene, do you have any idea why King Theod would want to unite Haven and Balam?"

Cyrene pursed her lips, her brow furrowed. "I just

remember Andreas saying King Theod would help rebuild Balam to be even greater than what it was before."

Before what?

Haven was more vast than Elatora and Balam combined. *Why would King Theod contribute to this kingdom's greatness?*

"What benefit would there be in uniting our kingdoms?"

"I'm sorry. I wasn't made aware of the politics of the situation," Cyrene replied.

"I see . . ." Blaise looked at her half-empty pint glass. "What can you tell me about Balam's royal dinner customs? We're going to have to make this look authentic."

"Normally, plans like these are underway in the kitchens and with the servants. The royal chef will begin preparations a day before. You'll need to go over last-minute details with all heads of household." Cyrene leaned back in her seat, crossing her arms. "You'll need to approve the music and entertainment for the evening with both Balam and Haven in mind."

Blaise's face grew cold. "Does that mean I'm going to have to dance?"

Cyrene nodded. "Oh yes, Balamites are known for their dances."

Blaise chugged the rest of her ale. She slid it to Kaiden, asking for a refill. He caught the mug and nodded graciously, then walked away from the table.

Of all the things she'd have to manage in the next few days, Blaise wanted to avoid the dancing at all costs. How in gehheina was she supposed to do all these tasks in such a short amount of time? She breathed in through her nose, shutting her eyes for a heartbeat, then released it. The sound of a mug thumping the table snapped her back. The full pint frothed over the edge, and she took a hearty gulp.

Isaac broke into the conversation. "I assume you want a way out of this arranged marriage?"

Blaise tapped the cool surface of her mug. "I'm not sure if that's a possibility since we don't know the specifics of the arrangement."

Simone leaned closer. "What if we make you undesirable to him?"

Kaiden's lips curved up; he was obviously pleased with Simone's suggestion. "That won't be hard."

Blaise shot him a severe expression and slapped his forearm. "Don't be rude, ass." Though she couldn't keep the grin off her face. She turned her attention back to Simone, raising a brow. "How?"

Blaise spent a day and most of the next preparing with help from Cyrene, Kaiden, and his unit.

You must find Chaos Island.

The whole time, Jynx's request remained in the back of Blaise's mind. She needed to get through this dinner and deal with King Theod, and then she could worry about following the orders of a hallucination. She didn't even know where the island was located, but maybe Isaac would.

An intense pulse stopped Blaise in the middle of the long corridor. The buildup of akrani within her overheated her insides. She hadn't felt relief since the morning she'd awoken in his arms.

Could Kaiden be that balance Jynx was talking about?

Needing fresh air, Blaise stepped out onto one of the balconies overlooking the kingdom, admiring the lay of the land. The scent of rich soil filled her nose. Young crops grew in the distance. Further inland, homes were being constructed of cobblestone and wood.

She breathed deeply, letting her mind wander to her grandmother, Helena, and brother, Daniel. Grams had raised and protected Blaise for over twenty years of her life, keeping the secret of her lineage. Blaise had learned the truth in Haven. If it hadn't been for Philippa and the memory crystal, she might've never known. At first, it had been upsetting, but now, she just missed her family. Blood related or not, Grams and Daniel were the only family she'd ever known.

"You look nice today." Kaiden stood next to her, his arms folded over his armored chest.

Blaise peered at him, straightening her dark jacket. The train hovered over the stone floor and draped around her long legs. She wore fitted black trousers and boots. Her hair was styled into a single thick row of braids with the remainder of strands pulled back into a ponytail. She still wasn't fully recovered, but it helped to at least look like it.

She smiled. "Thanks. I figured I should at least dress the part of a queen."

A corner of his mouth rose, and he stepped closer, turning his gaze to the view.

The pulsing heat of her akrani lessened. From the corner of her eye, she saw a look of sadness come over him, and she wondered if it was because of Mathias. A flash of pain engulfed her as she remembered Mathias's stoic face and the bolt piercing her body. Her hand drifted over the concealed scar.

Kaiden had told her earlier in the day that Nira had aided in Mathias's escape. Surely Nira had better sense than to aid a criminal—someone who'd tried to kill the queen she'd served. Blaise didn't want to believe that either of their friends could've been compliant in such a plan.

She decided to take a chance and asked, "Any word on Mathias?"

Kaiden stole a glance at her. "No. Andreas supposedly sent Piers and Ollie to track him and Nira. But as of yet, there's been no word."

She nodded and decided to leave it at that.

The balmy breeze caressed her cheeks, and she closed her eyes, enjoying the warm afternoon rays. She placed her hands on the cold stone balustrade. There was life in the kingdom again, and that brought her unexpected joy.

Kaiden covered her hand with his and said, "You know . . . if worse comes to worse, you can always seek refuge in Elatora."

"I can't leave my people. Besides, I don't think King Vaughn would choose to side with me over King Theod." Blaise shot him an incredulous look.

He shrugged. "Why would King Vaughn help you ascend this throne only to betray you later because you don't want to marry his cousin? I honestly don't think he would do that to us."

"You're probably right." She turned and made her way into the fortress.

He followed. "Of course I'm right."

Why would Theod want to marry her? Was he looking to gain power over her kingdom, or did he truly want to be the alliance Balam needed? If he was rejected, would it start a war?

They walked side by side, and she stared at Kaiden's profile. "What if..."

His attention went to her. "What if?"

"I agree to the marriage?" She bit her lip, dreading his response.

He stopped in the middle of the empty corridor, nostrils flared. "You're not serious."

She faced him with her arms crossed, expression resolute. "You know damn well his army is much larger. Balam wouldn't stand a chance if he were to attack."

"So, what? You're just going to give in to his demands? What about our plan?" Kaiden's hazel gaze locked on her.

Blaise turned into the sanctum, pulling Kaiden along with her. This was the room where she had nearly been assassinated. She made her way to the center and stared into the pool's crimson-tinged obsidian water. It seemed to pulse in tandem with her heart.

"I don't know what to do, Kaiden. I wasn't exactly prepared for any of this."

He stood next to her. "What about us?"

She ignored the tug in her chest and the small voice that told her Kaiden belonged to her. Her brow furrowed. "What about us? There was no longer an 'us' once you left—"

"But I'm here now. I came back. Doesn't that count for anything?" By the intonation in his voice, he sounded more hurt than angered. "Besides, you weren't exactly present either."

She scoffed. "Yes, because I was chained to fucking pillars, dying."

He remained silent, his features softening.

"You always speak of duty." She spread her arms in reference to everything around her. "Now this is mine. As queen, I will have to make my own sacrifices." She couldn't bring herself to look at him. She detested the thought of marrying King Theod, but it was probably what her mother would've done. With her back to him, she waited.

"What're you still doing here, Kaiden?"

"What are you saying?"

"You should've been gone by now."

He stepped in front of her and placed his index finger beneath her chin, tilting her gaze to his. "Is that what you want? You want me to leave again?"

She studied the glint of agony in his eyes. That was so far from what she wanted, but instead she chose to say, "Don't you have to report back to your king?"

"I need you to get past your fucking pride and accept that I'm not going anywhere."

He'd left her once. Blaise was convinced he would do it again. To save herself the heartache, she was prepared to argue her point, but the words caught in her throat.

He closed the small distance between them, and his lips captured hers, not giving her a chance to react. A warm tingling trickled down her spine. It burst through her entire body.

He pulled away, one eyebrow cocked.

"You feel it too," she murmured.

The water in the pool quaked. Blaise wondered if her power had anything to do with it. She vaguely remembered Zade saying there were certain conduits that could amplify akrani.

"Yes . . ." Kaiden's eyes glazed over, and he fell to the ground. A shriek of pain escaped him, and he clawed at his armor and tunic, yanking them off his body. His armor clattered to the gray stone floor. His screams continued, his nails digging into the flesh on his back.

Blaise's eyes widened, she placed her hand on his back. "Kaiden, what's happening?"

His back muscles constricted, bones cracking and popping beneath her hand. She jerked away, straightening, unsure of how to help him.

Am I doing this to him? She stepped back, her hands trembling at the thought of losing him. She stood there, helpless, eyes brimming with tears.

Blaise started to reach for him, but Kaiden's body contorted, bringing him up on all fours. She dropped to her hands and knees, meeting his pain-filled eyes. "What can I do?"

Whatever was happening to him seemed to ease for the moment. He straightened onto his knees, his eyes watering. "I don't think there's anything—" He gripped her arms tightly, pulling her flush against his bare chest.

She could hardly breathe. Looking over his shoulder, she made out the muscles in his back undulating beneath his tanned skin. He buried his face into the curve of her neck. His muffled screams vibrated through her chest, sending chills down her spine. She managed to pull her arms free, hoping to soothe this suffering.

Where her fingers rested on his torn flesh, she felt the first edge of a quill. She moved her hands and stared in awe. Two giant snow-white wings, stained crimson, ripped through his skin.

"Goddess of chaos," Blaise whispered. What in geh-heina was happening, and why was it happening to Kaiden?

His body relaxed, and he panted against her, his body damp with perspiration.

Taking shallow breaths, Kaiden lifted his head, and the terror in his eyes mirrored her own.

13

BLAISE

BLAISE SEARCHED THE SANCTUM.

What should I do?

Her gaze went to a large tapestry depicting the sign of Amasu. She rushed over and yanked it off the wall, then dragged it to where Kaiden knelt. She managed to pull it over his shoulders, and Kaiden hissed in pain from the weight. The huge material barely concealed his wings. She made her way over to the door and peered out, ensuring the hallway was clear.

"Come." She bent low enough for him to swing an arm around her shoulders. They hunched beneath the weight of his wings, and they slunk forward into the empty corridor. Her knees buckled, the tapestry almost falling, but she caught it, stumbling. He caught her coattails and helped her straighten. "Thanks," she whispered.

He grunted in response.

Voices echoed from the hallway ahead, and Blaise halted. Kaiden groaned, still hanging on to her for support.

She scanned the area, knowing she didn't have many options. One of the rooms on this level had a secret passageway that led to multiple places in the fortress. "I know another way."

Kaiden grunted while she pulled him into the room. She apologized, unable to be as gentle as she wanted.

"Where are you taking me?" he whispered.

With an eye roll, she said, "You *used* to trust me."

She closed the door behind them, then led him across the room. In the corner of the room sat a large oak armoire. She opened one of the doors and pushed at the back to reveal a passageway. Gesturing to his wings, she asked, "Can you tuck those in? It's a bit of a tight squeeze."

"Does it look like I can do that?" Kaiden gritted out, closing his eyes, a pained expression on his face.

On his first attempt, one wing expanded and the other folded in. On the second attempt, one wing made a sweeping motion, knocking Blaise flat onto the bed. She was tempted to just stay there.

"Do you need help?" she asked, climbing off and straightening her robe.

"Just give me a second," he snapped. A rapid series of short rasping noises came from his wings while he struggled to fold them in tight.

She placed her hands on her hips. "Ready?"

He nodded.

"Think small." She pushed Kaiden through the narrow doorway, ensuring his wings didn't catch, and then closed the door behind them. She pulled a torch from the wall, snapping her fingers. She tried to summon katai from her well of akrani, but she got no spark. There was only a buzz of power in her fingertips. She groaned, feeling for Kaiden's utility belt.

"What're you doing?"

She retrieved a flint rock and held it up. "I'm getting the flint."

"Why didn't you just ask?"

The corner of her mouth rose. "Don't act like you didn't enjoy that." She created a spark and lit the torch, then sidled past him to lead the way. They traversed the passageway, their boots echoing on the stone floor.

"How did you find this?" Kaiden asked, keeping a slow, steady pace behind her.

She replied, "I discovered it a few days before my coronation. It leads to different rooms. There's another one leading to the main floor."

Blaise's bedchamber was not far from the guest room. It didn't take long for her to find the hidden latch that opened the secret door disguised as a large mirror. Once they made it into the room, Kaiden shrugged the tapestry off with a groan. He fell to his knees, leaning against her bed.

Despite the aches and pains of her own body, she did her best to help him sit on her large velvet-covered mattress. Stepping between his legs, she leaned over to inspect the damage his wings had caused. His hand slipped around her waist. She stared at the torn and bloody skin; new tendons and muscles had formed.

His wings sprawled out on the bed behind him. She wanted to touch them.

Are they as soft as they look?

With gentle fingertips, she stroked the white feathers.

His wings bristled and expanded, fully erect. "Whoa… They're sensitive."

"I'm sorry." She bit her lip. "Wait here." She walked toward the washroom.

"Where are you going?" he asked.

She glanced over her shoulder, voice firm. "Just wait."

Blaise filled a small basin full of warm water and retrieved a clean cloth from a shelf above the bench in the washroom. She made her way back out. Kaiden was in the same spot she'd left him, his wings relaxed.

In the silence of the chamber, Blaise placed the basin on the wooden surface of the bedside table and soaked the cloth in warm water. After wringing it out, she stood in front of him once more. His hazel eyes drifted up her body, stopping at her face.

Blaise's mouth curved up, and she stepped between his legs, leaning over. His wings nearly covered the entirety of the mattress. She stared at them, dabbing the blood off his shoulder blades and spine.

Kaiden hissed. "Easy."

"Sorry." She pulled away, tossing the cloth into the basin.

He rested his hand on her hip, those hazel eyes locked on her, filled with desire. Snaking his arms around her waist, he drew her to him and rested his head over her heart. "Thank you."

Blaise's brow rose, her fingers brushing through his dark hair. She wanted to know what he was thinking. "Why did this happen?"

"I don't know," was his muffled reply.

She slipped out of his embrace and stepped over to the basin and squeezed the cloth out. She continued to wipe the blood from his back. "Did your mother have wings?"

"I never saw them." Kaiden flinched.

"What do we do now?" She moved behind him to clean his lower back.

"Simone has gitros. Perhaps we should call on her. I think she can be trusted with this."

Blaise didn't know Simone, but if Kaiden trusted her, maybe she could too. Blaise sent a servant to call on Simone, and a short time later, there was a knock on the bedchamber door. Blaise let Simone into the room.

Simone's eyes immediately went to Kaiden. "Goddess of chaos," she murmured. "Where in gehheina did those come from?"

"We're not entirely sure," Blaise said.

Simone stepped closer to Kaiden.

Kaiden grimaced, moving so Simone could reach his back. "My back feels like it's on fire," he said. "Is there anything your gitros can do for this?"

Simone's eyes widened at his mangled shoulder blades, but she didn't falter. An almost pleased look crept onto her face. "Brace yourself, Captain. This is going to hurt."

He wrapped his arms around Blaise, holding on tight.

Simone rubbed her palms together a few times, then began to work her fingers against his back.

Kaiden groaned, flinching beneath her touch. Blaise heard his teeth grinding from the pain of Simone's akrani.

Heat surged through his body and radiated into her. To distract herself, Blaise bit her bottom lip, tasting a hint of copper on her tongue.

"Be still," Simone said, sounding annoyed.

"I'm trying," Kaiden said between labored breaths.

Blaise had always been amazed by those who possessed the gift of healing. She glanced at the progress Simone's gitros had made. The muscles and tendons had woven together, and fresh skin materialized before her eyes.

If I have katai and satori, do I also possess gitros? Colvyr be blessed.

"There. Finished." Simone moved away from his back.

"Thank you," Kaiden whispered.

Simone had completely healed him. She grinned proudly at Blaise. "Don't mention it."

"I think you enjoyed that way too much," Kaiden muttered, still grimacing.

He was probably still sore. Simone had seemed to enjoy having her hands on him while she healed him.

First the barmaid, now Simone. Is there anyone else?

"I didn't know you were an ellorian, Captain," Simone said.

"It's a recent development." Kaiden pushed his wings behind him so they were out of his way.

Simone remained unmoved, staring at the half-naked man.

Blaise's stomach clenched. The thought of this woman with Kaiden left a bitter taste in her mouth. "Thank you for what you've done here, Corporal." Her tone was dismissive.

"Of course. I'll take my leave now, Your Majesty." Simone started for the door. She peered over her shoulder at Blaise. "Captain Cyrene is looking for you."

Blaise nodded. "I'll take care of it, Corporal."

Once Simone left, Blaise faced Kaiden, who was fiddling with and poking at his wings with a curious expression. A smile spread across her face at his amusement, and her heart softened.

She stood in front of him, arms crossed. "What am I going to do with you?"

His hazel eyes met hers, something akin to sadness glistening in them. "Please. Don't try to send me away, Blaise." He grabbed her hands and drew her near.

That spark inside her blazed, warming her core. "It's not like you'd even listen if I tried." A corner of her mouth rose while his fingers worked the buttons of her coat.

His mouth curved. "True." He pushed the coat off her shoulders, letting it drop to the floor, revealing the white camisole covering her. He pulled her close once more. "I just want to feel you for a moment."

Blaise's heart quickened in the warmth of his arms. She should've resisted his advances, but she didn't have the willpower to pull away from him. She combed her fingertips through his dark hair, and he moaned against her.

"You feel so good." His voice was muffled.

"Do I?"

"It is so good to hold you like this." He placed a tender kiss between her breasts and wrapped her even tighter in his embrace. "I won't ever leave you again, Blaise."

She stood there running her fingers through his hair for a few minutes more.

"Will you lay with me?" Kaiden asked.

"Yes." She drew back, and her body shuddered at the loss of his warmth. It was strange, but she ignored it, studying his gorgeous face. He bit his bottom lip. Hers turned up at the sight. He looked like he was ready to beg. She worried she would hurt him. "How should I lay?"

That roguish smirk crept onto Kaiden's face. "On your back."

Blaise climbed onto the plush bed and lay in the middle of the mattress.

He followed. He knelt on a wing, and it forced him face-first onto the bed. "Son of a bitch."

She covered her mouth, stifling a giggle.

He glared and pushed the wing aside, settling on his stomach next to her. He reached one arm around her, pulling her close, partially draping his leg over hers.

"Is this okay?" he asked, turning his head to face her.

She adjusted her arm into a more comfortable position. "Now it is."

"Good."

She stared at him.

Why, of all the people in the realm, does my heart keep choosing him?

Maybe she should've counted herself lucky that he even wanted her. She wasn't exactly the easiest woman to be with.

His eyes drifted closed, a satisfied grin gracing his features.

"We need to spend some time investigating this situation. Maybe the archives have information on the ellorians." Blaise glanced at his wings.

He opened one eye. "Okay."

His familiar warmth comforted her. It permeated her heart and radiated through her body.

"I feel empty when you're not near, Blaise. Like a piece of my soul is missing. Not being able to feel you or breathe you in has been a darkness I could hardly bear," he murmured.

He's usually so awkward with his words.

She didn't know if he was being honest or was just deliriously tired. His breathing steadied, becoming soft snores, and she smiled. She stroked a single feather, and the wing wrapped around her.

I guess they're sensitive when he sleeps too.

There were so many things that needed to be done before King Theod arrived. Blaise didn't even want to think about it. The list of tasks popped into her mind, but all she wanted was to sleep as peacefully as Kaiden was. She pushed the thoughts away only to be consumed by the voice of Jynx whispering about the portal.

Blaise closed her eyes, too tired to think, and hoped sleep would find her.

14

KAIDEN

AIDEN'S EYES FLICKERED OPEN. HE DIDN'T remember falling asleep.

How long have I been asleep for?

He stretched out his sore limbs, and his wings mirrored the action, rustling softly. His gaze drifted to Blaise grinning down at him from next to the bed, her hands on her hips. His breath hitched at the sight of her. The intricate lace detail of the burgundy V-neck gown enhanced her generous cleavage.

"Sleep well?"

He looked out the window at the setting sun. "How

long was I out?" He climbed off the mattress, careful not to kneel on a wing.

"It's time for you to get ready, Kaiden."

He straightened and stepped closer to her. "You mean to tell me I slept through all the preparations?"

She shrugged and nodded. "You *clearly* needed rest." Her eyes wandered to his bare chest, and then she turned her back to him.

Kaiden was always impressed by Blaise's ability to take charge, even when she wasn't sure of herself. He placed his hands on her shoulders and brought his lips to the base of her neck. Her body relaxed. Inhaling her familiar lavender scent, he tasted her velvety skin. He scraped his teeth across her flesh. Every instinct told him to throw her onto the bed and take her.

"This is nice, but King Theod is waiting."

His body called to hers, yet he forced himself to release her, stepping away, and starting toward the washroom.

God of peace, I need a cold bath.

"It's treason to turn your back on a queen."

His bottom lip slipped between his teeth. "You can punish me later."

"Careful with your words, Captain. I might just do it."

"I look forward to it." He winked and pushed his wings out of the way to shut the door.

He scrutinized himself in the floor-to-ceiling mirror. He rolled his sore shoulders, staring at his heavy white wings. It took so much concentration to simply move them. The muscles and tendons felt like a bowstring being drawn too tight.

Had his father and King Vaughn known this would happen to him? That he would someday sprout wings?

When did Mom get hers, and what color were they?

He was tired of all the half-truths. If only he could speak to someone who knew about his manifesting akrani. *Colvyr would know everything.*

After cleaning up, Kaiden made his way out of the washroom, a towel wrapped around his waist. Blaise sat at the end of the bed, hands clasped in her lap, patiently waiting for him.

"I don't have anything to wear."

Her face brightened. "I already considered that and had something made for you." She walked over to the armoire and withdrew a formal black uniform.

"I kept your wings in mind. The tailor made accommodations." She gestured to the white wings attached to his shoulder blades.

A grin spread across his face. "Thanks, I'd hate to have to cut it up." He didn't know when they'd truly be alone like this again. "I haven't had a chance to say this yet. But I'm sorry. I should've never left you." He pulled on the trousers, then donned the tunic with her assistance.

She blew out a breath. "None of this was your fault. Who knows what would've happened if you'd stayed. It could've been you chained to those pillars."

"And I would've willingly taken your place." He slipped on the coat and buttoned the polished onyx buttons.

"It happened. We can't change it now, Kaiden." She fixed his collar and smoothed the shoulders, brushing off any lint in the process. "I think this is the first time I've seen you wearing formal attire."

He smirked. "What do you think?"

"I think you'll have many admirers tonight." She rested her palms on his chest.

He grabbed her wrists, holding her close. "I just want one." He moved one hand to her waist, the other to her nape, and lured her in for a slow, deep kiss. His heart raced, and he relished her warmth. He wanted to do so much more but knew they were on a tight schedule. He ran his tongue over her bottom lip, then coaxed himself away from her.

"Do you forgive me?" he asked softly.

A coy smile tugged at the corners of her mouth. "What do you think?"

"I think you enjoy torturing me."

"Maybe just a little." She leaned in and kissed his bottom lip.

He fought the urge to pick her up and lay her on the bed. His heart pulsed in his neck and throbbed in other places.

She backed away, crossing her arms. Her chestnut gaze met his. Taking one last sultry glance at him, she made her way out.

Such a fucking tease. Kaiden adjusted himself in his trousers, tailing her.

Kaiden took long strides down the wide corridor toward the dining hall, following the aroma of entrées and desserts. A familiar sweet scent filled Kaiden's nostrils. *Custard tarts?* Unable to contain his excitement, his wings bristled.

Blaise snickered but kept pace. She shot him a sidelong look. "What was that?"

These cursed things. He tried to act as though nothing had happened. "What?"

"You smelled the tarts, didn't you?" She had a knowing expression on her face.

He smiled. "You added them to the menu."

"I might've." She shrugged as if it was their little secret.

He was falling in love with her all over again. A brief silence ensued.

"How are you going to address this marriage arrangement with King Theod?"

She loosed a breath. "I haven't completely decided. But once I know his motives, I'll hopefully know my next move."

There was nothing Kaiden could say. Blaise was the queen. This was her kingdom. Her people had to come first. He couldn't tell her not to marry King Theod. *It may be her duty.* Despite knowing that, a burning sensation erupted in Kaiden's chest, and his jaw clenched at the thought of King Theod being allowed to have Blaise in all the ways that should've been his alone.

Isaac fell into step with them, gawking at Kaiden. "Where in gehheina did those come from?" He gestured to Kaiden's wings, eyes wide.

Kaiden gathered some semblance of patience and replied, "They're a recent development."

"I didn't know you were ellorian." Isaac lightly brushed Kaiden's left wing.

Kaiden jerked, his wing swishing away from Isaac's touch. "Don't do that. And I'm only half. I don't have the time or patience to explain this absurd situation."

Isaac held his hands up and backed away, falling behind. Kaiden caught a glint of amusement on Blaise's beautiful face. He narrowed his hazel eyes at her. She winked in response.

The servants opened the doors and announced Blaise

and her entourage. The chatter in the hall faded. Everyone rose from their seats.

There are more nobles in Balam than I thought.

All eyes were on him and Blaise. Kaiden hoped it was Blaise's beauty that stunned the people into silence and not the heavy wings on his back.

Blaise adjusted her flowy dress and took her seat at the head of the table. Kaiden sat on her right with Elric, Isaac, and Simone. Captain Cyrene stood slightly behind Blaise's left shoulder.

The doors flew open once again, and King Theod was announced. He entered the room, and ominous strings of akrani snaked through Kaiden's body, taking over his vision.

He glanced down at his hands, barely visible in the dim lighting of the sanctum. *The sanctum?* Scanning the room, his eyes fell on Blaise holding a black crystal. The next moments occurred in flashes. Roaring white flames careened toward Blaise, hitting her, slamming her against the wall. Her body lay limp on the dark stone floor, eyes dull. *Lifeless.*

Kaiden's vision snapped back to the present. He was back in the dining hall seated next to Blaise. He placed his hand over hers to ensure she was real. She shot him a questioning look, and he snatched his hand back.

What the fuck was that? He sat there staring at the table. Why was his satori manifesting now? Had he just glimpsed the future? How was he going to change it?

"Captain Kaiden, I see my cousin may have similar interests in Balam." King Theod sat on Blaise's left, directly across from Kaiden. The king gave Kaiden's wings a once-over, face neutral.

"And what interests are those, Your Majesty?" Kaiden all but bit out.

Blaise subtly shook her head.

King Theod stared at him. "I don't believe that's any of your business, *Captain*."

A line of servants entered the hall with trays of food. They spread the entrées and platters down the center of the table. The next group of servants followed with stacks of galydrian plates and goblets.

"It appears I've underestimated your capability to plan a decent dinner, Queen Blaise," Theod drawled. He cut a hefty piece of meat and put it on his plate. "You will make a fine wife indeed."

Without thinking, Kaiden put his hand on the handle of his sword.

Elric hit Kaiden's arm, making it seem like an accident. He leaned in and whispered, "We're clearly outnumbered. Don't be stupid."

Kaiden glared at him and glanced around the hall. There were more Haven soldiers than Alchyra. *Dammit, he's right.* He conceded, releasing his weapon.

Theod didn't seem to notice or care. However, his captain of the guard did. Wilhelm stood behind the king, clad in white armor with gold accents, eyeing Kaiden, his hand resting on the hilt of his sword.

"How kind of you to say." There was a hint of sarcasm in Blaise's tone.

Kaiden couldn't help but smirk at her response.

Blaise swallowed a sip of wine from her goblet. "What do you think about Balam so far, King Theod?" Blaise asked.

The king gave a nod of approval. "It's impressive how much things have improved in such a short time frame."

He scrutinized the faces sitting at the table. "Where is Sir Andreas? I was hoping to speak with the man responsible for our pending union, Queen Blaise."

She inhaled deeply. "I'm afraid he's indisposed at the moment. I will be handling all of my own affairs from now on."

A corner of King Theod's mouth rose, and Kaiden wanted to punch the smirk off his royal face. Kaiden hated what was happening between the two, but he also knew Blaise needed to establish some sort of compromise with the king of Haven. Kaiden didn't want to be responsible for starting a civil war in her kingdom.

The king placed his fork down and clasped his hands on the table. "Perhaps we can speak privately about the details of our marriage arrangement."

"Of course," Blaise said.

Kaiden's wings flinched at the thought of King Theod and Blaise alone. *Dammit, I really need to get these under control.* He wanted to object, but Blaise could handle herself. And if she needed help, he trusted her to call on him.

After dinner, the musicians set up in the hall. Dancing commenced, and Blaise and Theod adjourned to the study down the corridor from the dining hall. Kaiden, Elric, and Wilhelm followed.

Theod stopped them at the door. "You can wait out here. We won't be long." He specifically shot Kaiden a coy wink.

Kaiden tried his damnedest not to let the king get beneath his skin. Kaiden clenched his hands into fists. His wings twitched, and something inside him snapped. *I can't allow this.* He took a step toward the study doors, but Elric placed a heavy hand on his shoulder and guided him away from the door.

They turned the corner out of Captain Wilhelm's sight, and Kaiden struggled against his hold.

Elric's eyes flashed that ominous obsidian, dark smoke escaping from the corners. "Stand down."

Inhaling a deep breath, Kaiden tried to get ahold of himself. Regardless of his feelings, he was going to have to accept the necessary evil. "Fine." His wings twitched.

Elric's eyes changed back to stormy gray. He stepped away and crossed his arms, watching Kaiden pace the width of the corridor.

Kaiden's mind flashed to that vision of Blaise, lifeless on the sanctum floor. He was tempted to start praying to Colvyr to get the answers he was searching for. His chest grew tight, and a pounding ensued in his ears. He clenched his fists, nails digging into his palms. Tension coiled in his muscles. Without another thought, he slammed his fist through the nearest wooden door.

Elric stepped forward, a blank expression on his face, and assessed the damage. "Feel better?"

"No," Kaiden said through gritted teeth. His knuckles throbbed. At least it distracted him from thinking about what was going on in that study.

"Talk to me," Elric said.

They walked down the hallway back toward the study, Kaiden's wings hovering over the stone floor.

I'm afraid of losing her. Kaiden's heart had told him she was the only one for him from the day they met. But he'd fought it like a fool. He was done fighting. "I don't want to burden you."

Elric drawled, "Too late."

Asshole. Kaiden didn't know whether to be annoyed or grateful for Elric's persistence. Maybe talking about his frustrations would help. Mathias was usually the one Kaiden confided in. "It's confusing."

"What is?"

Kaiden tossed his hands in the air. "Everything."

"Well . . ." Elric slowed his pace so they stayed out of Captain Wilhelm's earshot. "Blaise is a deime. Does she have the ability to help you sort this out?"

Kaiden let out a breath. "I was hoping not to get her involved."

"I think it's a little too late for that," Elric said.

They neared the doors of the study. Captain Wilhelm stood next to them, leaning back against the wall, arms crossed.

Captain Wilhelm cleared his throat. "So . . ."

Kaiden and Elric turned toward him.

A corner of Wilhelm's mouth rose. "When did you get wings, Captain?"

Kaiden rolled his eyes and didn't bother to answer, taking to heart what Elric had said. Blaise was already involved in this, so there was no point in trying to protect her—especially if Kaiden wanted to share a future with her.

15

MATHIAS

I T HAD BEEN A FEW DAYS SINCE MATHIAS AND Nira had been to the Scarlet Crown. Returning to his usual late-night shift opposite Nira had kept them blissfully apart, so they hadn't had the chance to speak about what they'd discovered. Sitting on his small bed in the cottage, he rubbed the sleep from his eyes. The parchments they'd found were vital evidence that could clear their names.

He wanted to go back to being Mathias Gage, sergeant in the Sentinel Order and not just a friend, but a brother to Kaiden. The man had had his loyalty since they were boys. They'd fought in many battles, both on and off the field.

They'd shared many losses. For the first time in his life, he had been unable to follow through on his loyalty. *I promise to keep a close eye on her.*

He straightened at the rapping on the front door. *Nira wouldn't knock.* He peered out the side window, careful not to be seen.

The setting sun silhouetted four men standing on the broken-down wood porch. They were all armed with swords and wore black velvet jackets with matching trousers and knee-high boots. Alarms rang through his head. *They're definitely not Haven soldiers.*

Mathias bellowed, "I'll be right there." He stashed the map and letters in a hidden pocket on the inside of his jacket, made himself look presentable, and, with a deep breath, answered the door.

"Casimir Octo?" the man with a deep scar across one eye asked.

Mathias leaned against the doorpost with his arms crossed, tamping down the nervousness crawling beneath his skin. "Yes?"

"Tarren Mandelbaum requests your presence immediately," said the man.

"What's this regarding?" Mathias's gaze swept over the other two who stood on the steps. Their hands moved to the handles of their weapons. He was sure he didn't have a choice at that point. It would probably be less painful if he went with them peacefully. *What about Nira?* "Let me just slip my boots on."

"Hurry up."

Mathias closed the door and pulled his boots on. He quickly jotted *The Scarlet Crown* on a piece of paper.

Crumpling it up and throwing it on Nira's bed, he walked out the door.

THE CARRIAGE JERKED AND ROCKED. Mathias sat slouched in silence between two burly men, their shoulders occasionally bumping. It was all he could do to find some comfort on the narrow bench seat.

Did Tarren discover the letters and the map are missing? Mathias was sure he'd been cautious about every move he'd made, but he needed to be prepared for the worst. Would Nira even try to help him? *She wouldn't leave without me.*

The carriage lurched to a stop, and Mathias almost fell off the seat. Tarren's men squeezed through the small door first. Mathias climbed out, joining the four men on the side of the road. His gaze drifted up the building. The lifeless ambiance of the Scarlet Crown was not where he wanted to be. The empty streets proved that no one wanted to be there during the early evening.

One of the men shoved Mathias forward. "Move."

"Easy." He glared at the man but obliged.

The men escorted Mathias through the empty first floor and up the stairs. The steps creaked with each footfall. They made their way down the long hallway, the four following him, swords at the ready to take him down if he breathed wrong. The men stopped at the end of the hall, crowding the office door. One of them knocked.

A deep voice called, "Enter."

The man with a dark mole on his chin walked in with Mathias, pushing him to stand in front of Tarren, who sat behind the dark wooden desk, reading a parchment, his legs propped up on the surface. The office was clean compared to how he and Nira had left it a few nights ago.

"Casimir Octo, sir," said the henchman.

Tarren plopped his booted feet on the wooden floor, straightening in the seat. He rolled up the sleeves of his white tunic. "Took you long enough, Byron."

The gruff man's eyes narrowed, and he retreated to stand next to the door, hands behind his back.

How in gehheina am I going to get through this interrogation without giving anything away?

Tarren stared at him. "Casimir."

"How do you know my name?" Mathias calmly clasped his hands.

"I am one of the most trusted men in this kingdom. I know everything I want to know." Tarren grinned. "I also know that you bought me a drink a few nights ago, and I wanted to thank you in person."

Mathias lifted a brow. "Is that why you sent four armed men to my home?" He crossed his arms.

Tarren stood, his gray eyes full of suspicion. He sidled over to one of the two windows in the room, gazing out at the empty dirt road. "One of my attendants saw you and a woman walk into my office." He met Mathias's blue eyes.

It took everything in Mathias not to react. *Fuck. I should've hidden the documents at the cottage.* "They must've made a mistake. I was on the main floor the whole night."

"You don't want to know what I do to liars, Mr. Octo." Tarren stared at his nail beds for a few seconds. "It seems a few of my important items have gone missing." He stepped over to Mathias, his lips pulled into a straight line. "I'm most positive *you* have them."

Shit. I need to get the fuck out of here. Mathias glanced at the open window next to the wooden desk, planning his escape. There was a knock. It hindered him from taking the final steps toward freedom.

Tarren bellowed, "Enter."

The wooden door swung open, and there stood Nira in the threshold. They had to have taken her straight from the tavern. Another one of Tarren's men shoved her into the office. She landed on her knees next to Mathias.

"We found her, Boss," said the man who'd just pushed Nira. "And the house is clear."

"Thank you, Silas." Tarren walked around the desk and stood in front of her. He helped her stand. "So that means one of you has my parchments." His eyes darkened on Nira as he said, "Care to introduce me to your wife, Cas? You don't mind if I call you Cas, do you?"

Mathias's pulse rushed through his ears with each rapid heartbeat. His palms became clammy, and sweat beaded on his nape. Mathias inhaled and gritted out through his teeth, "No, I don't mind. This is Veda Octo, my wife."

"Beautiful." Tarren gave Nira a charming smile. "I apologize if my men were a bit too rough with you, Lady Veda."

They better not harm a single hair on her head.

Tarren nodded to the man standing next to the door. "Search him, Byron."

Byron slammed Mathias against the wall and started running his hands along his shoulders.

Mathias grunted on impact. "You could take me out for dinner first."

Byron kicked his legs apart next and searched along his inner thighs.

"Whoa there, watch the goods." Mathias flinched.

"I'm gonna pound your face in if you don't shut the fuck up," Byron said, squeezing the outer pockets of Mathias's coat. The parchments crinkled, and Byron ripped the jacket off him. He reached into the hidden pocket and pulled out the papers and passed them to Tarren with a self-satisfied grin.

Tarren looked through the documents. "What should I do with you, Casimir?"

Shit, I need to act quick. How am I going to get us out of this? Mathias's eyes roamed the room in search of escape options, but with Nira there, he didn't know if he could protect them both. His thoughts settled on her. He admired her strength and courage in this situation. They had been caught and were most likely about to spend the rest of their lives in prison, but there was not one cowering bone in her body.

Byron threw the jacket onto the floor, then wrested Mathias away from the wall and thrust him to his knees in front of Tarren.

"First of all . . ." Tarren studied him for a moment. "Who are you working for?"

Mathias panted and responded regrettably, "I am not in service to anyone but myself."

"So, then, why would you take *these* parchments from my desk?" Tarren shook the papers in front of his face. He slammed them onto the desk and came around to sit on the front corner. "Are you having trouble remembering?" Tarren picked up a small black dagger from the desk. "Maybe this will help to jog your memory." He reached out and grabbed Nira's hair. He spun her around and placed the blade against her throat.

Nira's eyes widened, and a strangled gasp escaped her.

Mathias tried to lunge forward, but Byron's strong hand gripped his shoulder, holding him back. "I'm not fucking working for anyone," he bit out.

Tarren brushed his fingertips down Nira's bare arm. "So soft. Does she taste as good as she smells, Cas?" The tip of his tongue swiped at the corner of his mouth.

Violent heat swirled in Mathias's gut. *I'm going to fucking kill this asshole.* His jaw clenched, hands balling into fists. "Take your fucking hands off her."

"Then tell me what you were going to do with my parchments." Tarren slid his hand around to Nira's stomach, inching upward and stopping beneath her supple breast.

The heat bubbling inside Mathias turned molten. He swung his right fist into Byron's crotch. Byron howled and stumbled to his knees. Nira bit down on the arm at her throat. Tarren shrieked, and the dagger fell to the floor. With boiling rage, Mathias sprang to his feet and headed for Tarren's throat.

Silas sideswiped him, slamming Mathias into the wall next to the window. He threw a left hook. Mathias blocked with his forearm while simultaneously slamming his other fist into Silas's gut.

After a few more seconds of scuffling, Silas had Mathias on his knees in front of Tarren, and Byron had Nira next to him. There was no way Mathias could take these three men down with only his bare hands.

Nira shot Mathias a narrow-eyed expression as though telling him, "You're an idiot."

He licked his bloodied lip, tasting copper on his tongue. Mathias mouthed, "I'm sorry."

Tarren picked the dagger up off the floor and stood behind Nira once more.

A light knock sounded at the door. With an irritated sigh, Tarren hollered, "Enter!"

A woman in leathers with a scarred white eye sidled up to Tarren and stood on tiptoes to whisper in her boss's ear. Irritation washed over his face, and he flung the dagger at the wall. She turned on her heel and walked out, closing the door behind her.

"Perhaps you can be of use to me." Tarren shoved Nira toward Byron. "One of my fighters got into some trouble with the law. I could cancel tonight's event, but since you clearly know how to brawl, you can fill in."

Mathias remained quiet, staring at Tarren, struggling against Silas's iron grip.

Tarren stepped in front of the window and stared out at the empty street. "You'll be fighting my champion tonight, and fortunately for me, you'll be losing."

"Define 'lose.' " Was this going to be the only way out of this situation?

"Well, you may die, but if you survive, I'll let you both leave my city," Tarren drawled.

Mathias glanced at Nira, and there was a glint of worry on her lovely face. She shook her head as though telling him not to take the deal.

"We'll see to it that you're fully prepared," Tarren said with a devious smirk. Tarren gave a hand signal to Byron. "Escort Lady Veda to a cell with a view."

Mathias jerked forward, but Silas held him in place on his knees. "Just let her go. She has nothing to do with this."

Tarren twirled a strand of Nira's dark hair between his fingertips. "I need insurance. Just in case you don't follow through with our agreement."

"Will you at least give us a moment alone?" Mathias pleaded, knowing he had no control over anything.

She peered at him with questioning cobalt eyes.

"No." Tarren signaled the men toward the door.

Mathias resisted the urge to reach for Nira's hand as Byron grabbed her arm and dragged her out of the office. "Don't fucking hurt her."

Tarren grinned. "Don't you worry, Cas. We'll take good care of your wife."

Mathias didn't even want to know what he meant. He didn't have time to react. A burlap sack was yanked over him. He felt pain in his head, and then everything faded to black.

MATHIAS PLACED HIS PALM OVER his forehead, eyes fluttering open. *Where in gehheina am I?* Glancing around the room, he realized he was in a small cell. Once he made it into a sitting position, he thought that might've been a bad idea. His head began to ache more. Gods, he was going to kill whoever had knocked him unconscious.

"Fuck," he whispered. *I won't forgive myself if anything happens to her.*

The sound of crowds cheering resonated from beyond the thick door. Moonlight poured in from the tiny iron-barred window high above. Had he been unconscious for most of the day?

Muffled voices sounded through the door, and keys

jingled. A few seconds later, the door creaked open, and Tarren and Byron strode in.

"Ah, good. You're awake," Tarren said.

Mathias groaned. "Barely."

"Get up. Our champion awaits." Tarren had a pleasant smile on his face.

Mathias wanted to pound it off him. "Great."

"Just so you know, your challenger has three kills under his belt." Byron grabbed Mathias by the throat and yanked him to his feet. Mathias grasped the large man's forearm but couldn't break his grip. "This is for earlier, you fuckin' twat."

Byron buried a small dagger into his side, and pain seared in Mathias's flesh. Mathias gritted his teeth and groaned under Byron's grasp. The dagger slid free, and Byron threw Mathias out of the cell door.

Mathias grunted and grabbed at the fresh wound in his side, crimson staining his hand. All he had to do was endure all of this and survive long enough to free Nira. He climbed to his feet, using the wall for support. "Let's get this over with," he muttered, then followed Tarren through the narrow hallway.

Cheers echoed, becoming louder as he neared the end of the narrow corridor. Mathias stopped at the threshold, the energy of the crowd drowning him in uncertainty. Holding the wound in his side, he took a deep breath and stepped through the doorway. The scent of sweat and blood permeated the air. The rabid onlookers banged on the bars of the iron fighting cage.

Mathias approached the center ring, his breathing becoming more and more shallow. *That's not a man.* His chest tightened at the sight of his opponent standing across the ring. *That's a fucking mountain troll hybrid.*

He stood a whole foot taller than Mathias and had a dark braided beard that hung to the middle of his chest. His tanned skin was stained red, and his muscles were on full display with only a loin cloth covering him.

Mathias hadn't realized he'd stopped to stare until Byron pushed him forward. He entered the cage with a wince. His hands trembled, but he would show no fear.

Tarren placed a heavy hand on Mathias's shoulder. "I gave you my word. You both will go free if you lose. If you need a little reminder . . ." He pointed to a balcony over-looking the arena.

Mathias turned his gaze to Nira, who stood between Silas and another burly guard. Her bodice was ripped open and hanging off her shoulder, her skirt was torn nearly to the waist, and bruises were appearing on her legs and face.

She tried to fight back.

Mathias faced Tarren. "What the fuck did you do to her?"

"What was needed to keep the little whore under control. She's a fighter, but that makes breaking her all the sweeter. You better make it look real if you want her back."

Mathias started to throw a right hook, but Byron elbowed him in his wounded side. Grunting, Mathias doubled over.

Tarren grinned. "Good luck, Cas. You'll need it." He made his way to the middle of the ring and announced, "Our next match will be between our undefeated champion, Saul"—the cage shook from the roar of the crowd—"and the opponent, Casimir Octo." The room rumbled with boos and laughter. Tarren raised his arms into the air. "Place your bets!"

Mathias hated the thought of losing a fight, but if he was going to save them both, that was what he needed to do. He rolled his shoulders back and inhaled deeply, needing to focus. *One fight to freedom.*

"May the best man win." Tarren exited the ring.

A grin crept onto Saul's rugged scarred features. He closed the distance between him and Mathias like a bad dream.

He's faster than I expected. Inhaling a sharp breath, Mathias attempted to dodge Saul's left hook, but it landed. He blocked it with his shoulder, the force knocking him against the bars. Several arms reached through the bars, grabbing at Mathias. They held him in place while Saul landed a hit to his stomach. The air left Mathias's lungs, he doubled over, and his vision went blurry for a few seconds. *Fuck, he's strong.* The crowd released him, jeering in assumed victory.

Mathias ignored the pain in his side and ducked and rolled out from under a flurry of attacks. He needed to pick up his pace and stop getting hit.

The cheers of the crowd were muffled. He evaded Saul's outstretched arms and darted around him. Mathias leaped onto the giant man's back, driving his elbow into the curve of his neck. Saul reached back and grabbed Mathias's leg. Saul yanked him off, flinging him across the ring. Mathias slid into the iron bars with a grunt. Fingers started reaching for him, but Mathias scrambled to get away.

Mathias climbed to his feet, and Kaiden's voice yelled at him. *Every opponent has a weakness. Find it.* He sprinted forward and threw a roundhouse kick to Saul's knee. The only thing that happened was Saul's uppercut landed directly on Mathias's wounded side.

Fuck, I'm going to pass out soon. Where is it? With a deep breath, Mathias charged Saul and threw his whole shoulder into Saul's ribs. Bones crunched on impact, and Saul winced, faltering back.

Found it. Mathias smiled to himself. He could taste freedom. He clenched his fists and turned to the balcony, facing Nira. Tarren had a blade pressed into her throat, drips of blood trickling down. Mathias's smile faltered. *This is not a fight I have a choice of winning.*

Saul stomped toward Mathias. "You're dead, Octo!"

They both lunged at each other. But Saul's longer reach collided with Mathias's jaw. Mathias spun, landing on his hands and knees. He staggered to his feet and threw a flurry of blows to Saul's ribs. The giant man swung a heavy arm at Mathias. He dodged it, striking at his kidney again and again. Mathias needed to keep fighting, but exhaustion was setting in.

Saul caught one of Mathias's arms and swung, landing a left hook. Mathias's teeth rattled. Saul released him and hurled blow after blow. Mathias swayed and grunted with each iron fist Saul threw. Mathias flashed Saul a blood-stained grin. The giant pulled his fist back and threw one final blow to the middle of Mathias's forehead. Darkness consumed his vision.

16

MATHIAS

PAIN SHOT THROUGH MATHIAS'S BODY, JOLT-ing him into consciousness. Raising his arms in defense, he blinked a few times. His eyes focused on the person sitting next to him. Her dark blue eyes were full of concern.

"Nira?" he rasped, scanning the cottage.

Their clothes were in tatters all over the dirt floor. The cabinets had been torn off their hinges. Vegetables and dry goods were strewn across the kitchen. Knives were stuck in the walls and counters. Dishes and pots had been shattered against the walls. Not one area had been left untouched.

Tarren. Mathias's hands balled into fists. He pushed himself to sit, wincing. "What happened? How did we get here?" He glanced down at his bare chest—the wound in his side was merely a scar.

Nira soaked the bloodstained cloth in the small basin. She squeezed the excess and dabbed his brow. "Byron and two others brought us back. Tarren told me we have until the end of tomorrow to get out of Haven."

"Fuck him." He stared at the small cut on Nira's cheek. "Are you okay?"

She rinsed the rag out again, crimson seeping from the material. "I'm fine. The wound in your side took the most out of me." Her features softened and relaxed. She dabbed at the cut above his cheekbone, cleaning it off. She rubbed her thumb firmly over the small gash, healing it.

He cringed, though the pain was fleeting. He couldn't keep his attention off her while she continued her ministrations. "I just saved your life. Think you could ease up a bit?"

She rolled her eyes. "Give me your hand."

He did as she commanded.

Nira wiped the dried blood off his knuckles. She did the same to the other hand and tossed the cloth back into the water. Her cerulean gaze locked on him. She blew out and said under her breath, "Thank you for not leaving me, Mathias."

He blinked a few times, staring at her. "Are you sure you're Nira?" was all he managed to get out.

She backhanded him in the gut. "Don't be an ass."

He groaned, leaning forward. "Do you not know the meaning of 'ease up,' woman?"

Her eyes narrowed. "No." She grinned at him, and his heart warmed. It was the first genuine smile she'd given him since they'd started living together. "Where do you want to go now?" she asked.

He somehow found the strength to look away. "Back to Balam to clear our names."

Nira sat back on the couch. "How?" She peered at him.

He stared down at her. "I had proof until we were caught by that asshole."

Her eyebrows came together. "Proof?"

"What do you mean? You were with me at the Scarlet Crown."

She straightened, crossing her arms. "No, I wasn't. I went home early that night."

Mathias sat up with a cocked eyebrow. "What do you mean you went home early?"

Nira huffed. "I left about twenty minutes after we arrived. You seemed content talking to one of those barmaids."

That explained how she'd gotten home so fast. "Then who was in the office with me?" *Who was I kissing?*

She tore a loose string from the hem of her dress. "What in gehheina are you talking about?"

"She looked exactly like you."

"Are you serious? You can't tell me apart from some other woman?" She punched his shoulder.

He flinched. "Ow. I'm telling you, it was *you*, right down to your clothes." He remembered catching a whiff of charcoal from her that night. Leaning in, he sniffed her sleeve. The scent of jasmine filled his nostrils. *Gods . . .*

She shrugged away. "Did you just smell me?"

He leaned back, eyes closed, relishing her scent. "That night you smelled like charcoal."

"What?"

"You just smelled different." He opened his eyes and met her gaze.

Nira's mouth popped open at the same time Mathias made the connection. If there was a look-alike of Mathias in Balam, there could be one of Nira here.

Her brows scrunched together. "Why would anyone create copies of us?"

"Whoever it was could have been trying to help. They did give us some useful information concerning Blaise." He continued to tell her about what fake Nira had said about the Onyx Crystal and how Blaise needed to find it before King Theod did.

"How do we know we can trust anything that prestae said?"

Mathias finished telling Nira everything the doppelgänger had told him. "The map was torn out of a tome from the Balam archives—coordinates to the galydrian mines. We don't have many choices here, but the way I see it, Balam is the lesser of two evils."

Nira shook her head. "Blaise wouldn't agree to marry King Theod. She still has feelings for Kaiden. After he left, she wasn't the same. If what they told you is true, I think it's all a ploy."

He tilted his head to the ceiling and stared at the wooden beams. "I don't think she would either. Kaiden is an idiot; I'm sure he realized that once he arrived home," Mathias mused, brushing his fingers through his dark dyed hair. He didn't know what doppelgänger Nira's intentions were, but if it meant redeeming himself with Blaise and Kaiden, he had to take that chance. "We'll head to the market tomorrow and buy what we need for the journey."

"Fine. We should get some sleep. It's been a long few days." She stood and started toward her bed across the room.

He caught a glimpse of the slit on her neck from Tarren's blade. *I could've lost her.* The thought caused discomfort in his chest that he hadn't experienced since he was a child. Had Tarren cut deeper, she would no longer be there to tell him to clean off his muddy boots before walking into the cottage. He wouldn't hear her incessant humming while they cooked dinner together anymore.

Mathias jumped to his feet, pulling her back against his chest and enveloping her in his arms. He winced, still sore from the fight, but didn't loosen his hold on her, truly grateful to the gods that Tarren was a man of his word.

"Um, Mathias?" Nira glanced over her shoulder at him. "Are you okay?"

Enjoying the warmth of her body and her jasmine scent, he grinned. "Fine. Just thankful." He couldn't tell in the dim lighting, but for a split second he thought she was staring at his lips.

"We have a lot to do tomorrow." She didn't falter. "We should go to bed."

He grazed her nose with his. She inhaled sharply.

"As you wish." He released her from his hold.

Her eyes fluttered, and she caught her bottom lip between her teeth.

He went back to his spot on the couch. For the rest of the night, he couldn't shake the feeling of missing her even though she was only a few feet away.

17
BLAISE

LAISE PEERED OUT THE WINDOW OF THE study, admiring the mountain range that protected her homeland. The dark sky was dusted with stars, and the waxing moon shone high above the Balam fortress. The glass reflected King Theod standing in front of her oak desk, eyeing her. She scratched her arm, the material suddenly becoming itchy. Facing the king, she folded her hands together.

King Theod clasped his hands behind his back and inhaled deeply. "Let's discuss the terms of our betrothal, shall we, Blaise? May I call you by your first name?"

She pursed her lips. "I suppose that's fine."

His blue eyes glistened in the dim lighting. "Good. You may call me Theo, if you like."

Blaise stared at him, taking in his white dinner jacket with gold accents. His black trousers were fitted and matched his shin-high boots. "Tell me, Theo. What does Haven have to gain from the union of our two kingdoms?"

"I understand your apprehension. What does a rich ruler want with a kingdom that is in ruins?" He kept his distance, but his gaze didn't falter.

She crossed her arms and waited for him to continue.

"I've been where you are—the young ruler thrown into a pit of monsters." He smiled, rubbing the light stubble on his chin. "I want to help you, Blaise."

She walked around the desk, confronting him. "And you define 'help' as an arranged marriage? How generous."

He stepped closer. "You have so much more to offer than you think."

She resisted the urge to cringe away. *Does he simply want more territory? An heir won't do anything for my kingdom besides give him more power over me. And anyone can give him that. So, what does Balam have to offer?*

"I want to help you unlock your potential as queen." Theo glided his index finger down the front of her neck. His sudden advance startled her into taking a few steps back.

"And you think you're the man to do that?" she asked.

"Unless you have someone else in mind?" He canted his head. "That sentinel captain perhaps? There's nothing he can give you that I can't."

"This is an important decision, Theo. I'm going to need time to think this over." She wasn't going to give him a definite answer until she knew his true intentions for this marriage contract.

He stared at her, and a corner of his mouth rose. "Is there anything I can do to convince you to make the right decision now?" He leaned closer.

She shook her head. "Time. I just need time." She steadied her breath.

He closed the distance between them again, his cold blue gaze boring into her. "Time. Two days should be plenty of time."

"Two days," she echoed, their faces mere inches from each other.

He continued to stare into her chestnut eyes, silent.

It took everything in her not to falter. "I promise to make the wait worth it." Her body shivered as though rejecting the words. Hopefully he hadn't noticed.

He leaned in and placed a chaste kiss on her lips. She kept her expression neutral despite wanting to push this man away with all the strength she could muster.

"Then you'll give me your answer." It wasn't a question.

"Yes."

He stepped back and continued to talk about Balam's slow progression for a few more minutes, then ended the meeting. Blaise let out a breath. Any longer in there with his heavy presence was liable to cause her chest to implode. She inhaled deeply and followed him toward the door.

They strolled into the corridor, where Kaiden, Elric, and Captain Wilhelm waited. Theo's eyes softened on her, and he brushed a strand of her dark hair behind her ear. It took every ounce of self-control not to draw back from his clammy fingers.

Blaise glanced at Kaiden and his white-knuckle grip on his sword. She shot him a warning look. King Theod pressed his cold, dry lips to the corner of her mouth for a long moment. She pulled back, fighting the urge to wipe away the kiss. Kaiden's rage was apparent on his face. Thankfully, Elric stood in front of Kaiden, blocking him from advancing.

"Thank you for the lovely dinner, Blaise. I'll see you soon." King Theod and Captain Wilhelm started down the corridor toward the main fortress doors.

Blaise avoided Kaiden's piercing stare. She blushed and bit her bottom lip. More embarrassed than anything, she turned on her heel and headed in the opposite direction, cheeks scorching. She wasn't attracted to the king despite his good looks. Kaiden's molten gaze pierced her back.

"What happened?" Kaiden fell into step beside her, brow furrowed.

Her hands trembled, but she was proud of herself for getting through the king's visit. "I have two days to figure out what he wants from me—from Balam." She inhaled deeply, filling her lungs, not wanting to lose control. *What would happen to my people if I failed and lost my kingdom?*

"Hey, hey, look at me." Kaiden's voice was low. Demanding.

She came to a slow stop facing him, meeting those comforting hazel eyes. A wave of calm flowed through her. He didn't say anything else. He didn't have to. The silence was enough to soothe her.

"I have a feeling if I don't accept his proposal, he'll take Balam by force," she said, averting her focus to the dark stone floor.

Kaiden studied her for a moment. "What you were really doing was negotiating more time?"

She nodded. "There aren't enough Alchyra present to take on Haven's army. And there really isn't anything keeping Theo from ordering an attack. Just his word."

Kaiden looked impressed, but then he hesitated for a heartbeat. "He told you to call him Theo?"

Her lips turned up into a wry smile. "Yes. Would you focus? We need to come up with a plan."

Two guards patrolling the hallway gave them a passing salute. A look of contemplation consumed Kaiden's handsome features. "I can send Isaac to search for General Zade and the rest of the Alchyra in Meliwe Forest," he said as though that were the most obvious solution.

"You know damn well there's not enough time or Alchyra, and half of them aren't even well trained. The battalion he brought is far greater than ours, and he still has more in Haven."

"What if we seek reinforcements from King Vaughn?" Kaiden asked.

The king had sent Kaiden to establish a peace treaty. Did that mean he would aid Balam in a civil dispute? More importantly, would the sentinels arrive in time to prevent an attack?

Glancing out one of the tall corridor windows, Blaise stared at the clouds that covered the moon, beams of light outlining their shapes. *Will there always be something or someone trying to drown me in darkness?*

She glanced at him. "Do you still have that peace treaty for me to sign?"

He shot her a sidelong look. "Yes."

"You could add a passage that states the ruler of Elatora must provide any type of military assistance during a national or civil dispute." She'd never paid much attention to the politics of Crenitha, but she knew Kaiden had that power as King Vaughn's emissary.

"Shit," he muttered. "You're right. Consider it done, Your Majesty. We could send a messenger bird. It'll get there in a quarter of the time."

Would King Vaughn approve of the new terms? He had to have a certain level of trust in the captain. Hope rose in her chest at the thought that this issue with King Theod could be resolved soon.

Blaise and Kaiden continued down the dimly lit hallway to her bedchamber. Warmth emanated from the hearth, and the heavy velvet curtains of the windows and balcony doors were still open.

She stepped over to the window and gazed at the town below.

Streetlamps lit the single road leading to the marketplace and a few half-finished homes. There were some townsfolk who had decided to build farther out, toward the foothills. These were *her* people now—her responsibility.

Blaise turned and caught Kaiden rummaging through his satchel on the dresser near the fireplace. "Goddess of chaos, I could really use your guidance," she murmured. A heaviness weighed on her shoulders just thinking about every task that needed her attention.

He stared at her, and his brow rose. "What?"

Blaise decided to tell him about the visit from Jynx. She couldn't keep it bottled up any longer. "The goddess of chaos appeared to me."

"Appeared? When did this happen?" His jaw clamped shut.

"When I was imprisoned in the mountain. I thought I was hallucinating. But it seemed like she was trying to help me."

His wings twitched. "What makes you think she's trying to help you?"

"Jynx told me the high god is on the verge of escaping his bonds. He's going to kill the one who has his power, and then he'll destroy Alymeth," Blaise said.

"What if it's a trap?" He went back to his bag and pulled out a neatly folded parchment, then opened the paper and retrieved a quill and ink.

"She wants me to find Chaos Island."

Kaiden finished up with the paragraph he was writing—the new clause, Blaise assumed. "Here. Sign the treaty."

She walked over and took the quill from him. It was the first official document she would sign as queen of Balam. "Let's hope this works," she said beneath her breath.

"It will." His lips curved up, offering her assurance in the decision they'd made.

After letting the ink dry, he folded the parchment and put it back into his bag. His brow furrowed. "Wait. The one who has his power? What does that mean?"

She shook her head. "I don't know. I'm sure I can find out more once I go to her."

He stared at her, disbelief apparent on his handsome features. "I don't think this is a good idea. You don't even know if she was real."

"I know, but I need answers, and so far she's the only one who has given them to me." She took a step closer to him. "Please. Trust my judgment for once."

"I trust you, Blaise. She's the one I don't trust."

"Just think of Jynx as the lesser evil." Blaise placed her hand on Kaiden's shoulder.

His gaze drifted up to meet hers. The golden rings around his irises seemed to glow in the firelight of the hearth, and she lost herself in them. Her pulse increased under the scrutiny of his darkening gaze.

He stepped closer. "How can you be sure?"

"I can't be. Nowadays, I'm only sure about one thing." She needed him, her body needed him, her soul needed him. She wrapped her arms around his neck, bringing her lips within inches of his.

He pulled her body against his, embracing her. "And I'm sure we're in agreement."

She felt the whisper of his lips trail her jawline. "We're both still recovering."

"I'll be gentle."

His hands slid up the sides of her body to her wrists. He pinned her arms against the wall, pushing his body flush against her. Anticipating shoulder pain, she was pleasantly surprised to find none. With a slight smirk on her face, she stared at him, so close, breaths mingling.

His warm tongue slid over her pulse. Slow. Teasing. He sucked on the base of her neck, biting down. She let out a brief rousing cry.

"That sound," he growled and pressed his lips against hers, devouring her.

Her body was on fire from the inside out. She moaned into his mouth, playing his tongue with her own. He trembled. She ground her hips against his arousal. It throbbed against her through his trousers.

"I'll never get tired of you." He brushed his lips over that sensitive spot behind her ear.

She whimpered in his embrace, hooking one leg around his waist, careful not to kick his wing. She rubbed against the length of him. *Gods . . .* She was beginning to feel like pudding in his arms, and all she wanted was for him to eat her up—savor her.

"I want you."

"So have me," she panted against his lips.

He released her hands and ripped open the bodice of her dress. She cared nothing for the damage he'd done to her clothes. He peeled down the camisole covering her. He cupped her breast, massaging the supple fullness, pinching her hardened nipple between his index finger and thumb.

She arched against his touch, biting her lip.

"Take off your clothes and sit on the bed," he demanded, releasing her from his hold to step back.

In the light of the fire, Blaise slipped off her dress and sauntered toward the end of the bed. "You're not my superior anymore. What makes you think you can order me around, *Captain*?" She gave him a mischief-filled look, her lower half still clad in her white undergarment.

He rose a brow, crossing his arms. "Take them off, *Blaise.*"

His tone sent tingles to her core. She conceded, slowly sliding the thin material down her legs.

A low groan escaped his chest. It seemed he was at a loss for words.

She sat on the bed and leaned back on her hands with her legs crossed. "What now?"

He stripped off his tunic and released the buttons of his trousers, allowing his hard throbbing length freedom from its confines. "Touch yourself." His voice was low and gravelly.

She spread her legs, displaying her glistening warmth. He took himself in hand and stroked. She stuck her index and middle fingers into her mouth, then dragged them to her core, gliding them up and down her slit. She pursed her lips and inhaled a sharp breath as she pushed into wetness. Her walls pulsed with need, tightening around her fingertips. Her breathing became shallow.

Kaiden stood in front of the fireplace a few feet from her, stroking himself. "Is my queen ready for me?"

Her core clenched at his words, and she couldn't hide her smile. He looked magnificent with the firelight glimmering through the feathers of his white wings.

Blaise slid her fingers out and licked them, tasting herself. A gentle moan escaped her. "Beyond ready." She slunk off the bed and stood, gesturing for him to sit down. He obeyed. She wasted no time climbing on. She guided his hard cock into herself. "Fuck," she whispered.

"Gods, you feel better than I remember." He wrapped his arms around her midsection, biceps tensing.

Beams of moonlight streamed through the balcony doors onto their writhing bodies, their movements in sync, Kaiden thrusting up, *deep.*

Blaise took every inch, grinding her hips against him.

Kaiden's fingers glided over the scar on her rib cage. Blaise was grateful Nira had been able to heal the wound. But some of the surface damage was irreparable. She watched his wandering hand, and her movements slowed. The discoloration of her skin was a reminder of the pain

Rowena had inflicted. Did Kaiden think they were grotesque? She was sure he'd been with flawlessly attractive women.

He locked eyes with her. As though sensing her thoughts, he said, "No one compares to you, Blaise. You're my beautiful fierce queen." He grabbed her nape, pulling her in to capture her lips with his.

A torrent of warmth flooded and heightened her senses. The sheer rhapsody of their writhing bodies triggered her well of akrani to open to him. Her eyes drifted closed.

"Gods, do you feel that?" he asked, breathless.

"Yes, don't stop." Her hips quickened as she chased oblivion. She was so close.

He didn't stop, grinding into her a few more times until his abs tensed, and he spilled into her with a groan of ecstasy. Her release came with a loud cry and his name on her lips. He panted into her bosom, then trailed kisses along her collarbone. She caught her breath, leaning her forehead against his shoulder. In the silence of the moment, Kaiden traced circles on the delicate skin of Blaise's back.

Kaiden helped Blaise beneath the covers, then settled himself beside her. She positioned herself in his arms, completely sated. Despite the questionable status of their relationship, she wanted to know more about the man who had become so willing to risk his life for her.

"What would you be if you hadn't become a sentinel?" She turned over to lie halfway on his chest.

His wings spread out on the bed around them. He brushed his fingertips up and down her bare arm. "I'm not sure."

"Come now, surely you have other interests." She looked at his face in the pale moonlight.

He pursed his lips, an amused yet thoughtful expression forming on his handsome face. "In my younger years, I liked to draw."

Her eyes widened, and a grin spread across her face. "So, you'd be an artist?"

He cocked a brow. "What? I know it's quite a contrast from wielding a sword."

"I didn't say anything."

"I know what you're thinking," he said.

"I'm sure you do." She chortled. "Have you ever thought about maybe starting again?"

He shrugged. "It's crossed my mind a few times."

Blaise was surprised at his admission. It definitely wasn't something she'd expected from him. He had an appreciation for art. How could she have missed that before?

"What about you?" he asked.

She gazed into his hazel eyes but didn't allow herself to get lost in them. "I think I would've liked to be a horse tender."

"Really?" His head rose, and he glanced at her.

"Is that so difficult to believe? I find it to be quite therapeutic." She started to move off his chest, but he held her in place.

"Maybe when all this is over, we can get you a herd of horses." He grinned.

Her eyes narrowed. "You're making fun of me."

"No. I'm serious." His smile faded. "You just never cease to surprise me." He curled her into his arms and held her warm naked body flush against his.

She rested her face near the crook of his neck. "That's a good thing, right?"

His chest vibrated with a chuckle. "I think so."

Blaise listened to the sound of his heart and the slow, steady rhythm of his breathing. If she could've stopped time, she would've stayed here in this moment with Kaiden for the rest of her life.

"Blaise, I—"

She rotated onto her stomach, meeting his gaze. "I'm listening." She supported herself on her forearms, careful not to hurt his wings.

He brushed a strand of hair from her face, tucking it behind her left ear. "I don't know what I'm doing anymore."

Her eyebrows came together, and she tilted her head. "What do you mean?"

"Before I met you, I knew my purpose in life. I was going to follow in my father's footsteps and become commander of the Sentinel Order. Now . . ." He huffed. "Meeting you and discovering everything about my mother and myself, I just don't know."

Blaise pursed her lips and kept her stare on him. "It's a lot to process," she agreed. "Wait a second. Are you blaming me?" she teased, giving him a playful poke in the ribs.

Kaiden rolled his eyes. "Of course not. If it weren't for you, I'd still be living a lie."

Blaise's mouth curved up. "You're welcome. I think?"

"Maybe after we get this whole situation with King Theod settled, we can help each other with our god problems," Kaiden said, tracing circles on her arm with his index finger.

"How?" She ignored the gooseflesh that rose.

"If you really are talking to Jynx, maybe you can find out from her how I can contact Colvyr," he said, continuing his absent-minded tracings across her cool skin.

"It'll probably be dangerous."

He let out a short laugh. "What isn't these days?"

"I'm not always going to be there to protect you." She smiled.

The corner of his mouth rose. "If I recall, I was the one who saved you. *Again.*"

She rolled her eyes and attempted to scoot away from him, but he grabbed her. Pulling her back into his warmth, he said, "I'll keep saving you, Blaise. If that's my new purpose in life."

She turned to face him, still wrapped in his strong arms. "I don't want you to carry that burden, Kaiden. Don't you believe in my capabilities?"

He gave her a brief squeeze. "I do. But I also believe you don't like asking for help even when you need it."

Dammit. He's right about that. She let out a slow breath onto his chest and watched as tiny hairs stood straight up on his tan skin. "Fine. I'll try to do better."

His lips turned into a soft smile. He kissed her forehead with fervor. "Good. I'll do the same. We should probably get some rest now."

She yawned. "You're probably right."

They lay there in silence. Kaiden's wing covered her while she counted the beats of his heart. His gentle breath whispered through her hair, lulling her to sleep.

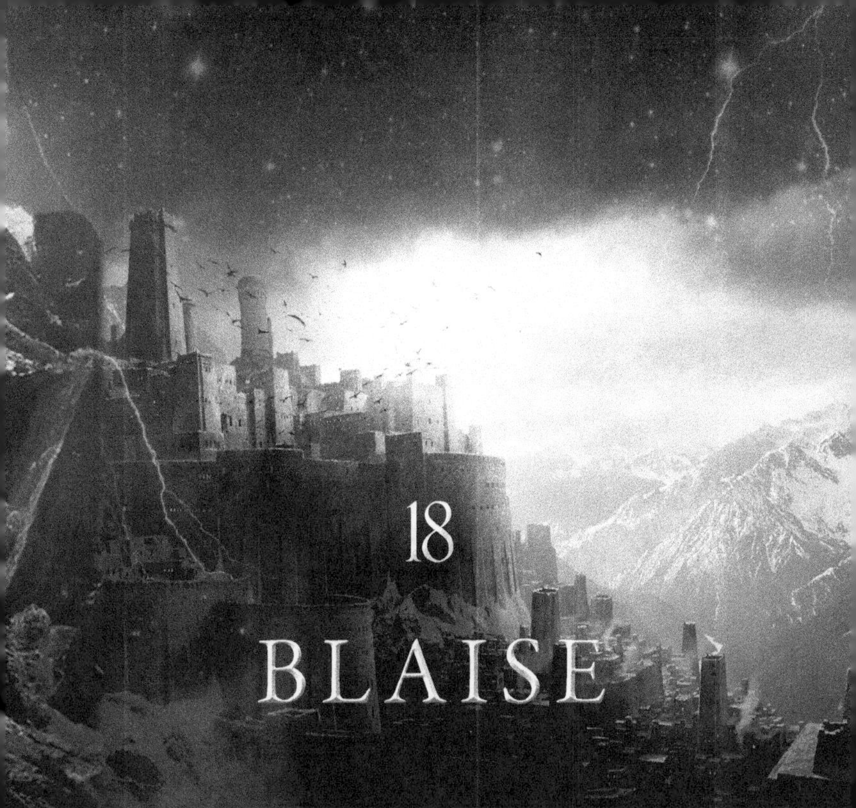

18

BLAISE

THE ANSWERS ARE IN THE FLAMES.

A gentle voice jolted Blaise awake, and for a split second, she couldn't remember where she was. She glanced at Kaiden asleep next to her, and one of his heavy wings warmed her naked body. She slipped out from beneath it, careful not to wake him, then traipsed over to her armoire.

After she dressed in black trousers, boots, and a loose white tunic, she peeked through the velvety curtains out the tall window. The first glimpses of golden sunlight emerged on the horizon.

"Good morning," Kaiden rasped.

Blaise spun around, nearly tripping over herself. "Good morning. Sleep well?"

"Like a baby." Kaiden sat up and stretched out his arms, wings following suit. Gods, they were truly impressive. Blaise couldn't help but stare in awe.

"I was planning on going to the archives. Spend the morning researching," she said.

Kaiden stood and slipped on his trousers. "Sounds exciting. We should get Isaac to help."

"Good idea. I'm sure he'll be ecstatic." She ripped holes in the back of his tunic, then helped him fit his wings through. He tucked the excess into his pants and buttoned them.

"Thanks." He strapped on his utility belt and sword next, then grabbed her hips and pulled her close. Leaning in, he grazed the top of her ear with his lips as he murmured, "What if we just spend the morning in bed?"

"Mmm . . . tempting." She placed a quick kiss on his neck. "But we have responsibilities now, remember?"

"How could I forget?" He enveloped her in his arms and breathed into the curve of her neck.

She sank into his warmth and familiar sandalwood scent, treasuring each second in his embrace.

"Okay." He looked at her, tucking a strand of brown hair behind her ear. "Let's go save your kingdom."

Kaiden and Blaise padded down the dim corridor. Beams of the rising sun shone through the floor-to-ceiling windows. A click echoed. It sounded close. Kaiden drew Blaise into the shadows against the wall.

About twenty feet away from them, Simone stepped out, briefly scanned the hallway, and ran in the opposite direction.

"I shouldn't have asked her to be in the unit," Kaiden whispered.

"Who?"

"Simone." His jaw clenched. "That's not her room. It's Isaac's. And Isaac is courting my sister."

Blaise placed her hand on Kaiden's tensed bicep. "What? That's unlike Isaac." She stared at Simone's silhouette disappearing down the long hallway. "Let's go." She strode up to Isaac's door, Kaiden trailing behind. "Maybe Simone seduced him."

"Maybe," he muttered. "I suppose I shouldn't blame him. A woman's charm can be irresistible."

She could hear his smile and stopped short. "Are you implying I seduced you?"

"I'm implying that you're irresistible," he replied.

Her cheeks warmed, and she stole a glance at him in the dim light, his wings leaving his face in the shadows. "Flattery won't work on me. You should know that by now."

He grabbed her and gave her a brief kiss on the lips. "It's not flattery. It's the truth."

She gave him a gentle pat on his chest. "Focus, Captain."

He released her and rolled his shoulders back. The movement caused his wings to rustle. "You're right. Sorry." That roguish smirk stayed on his face. He raised a closed fist to the door and knocked.

Isaac answered a few seconds later, eyes widened. "Bla—I mean, Your Majesty. Captain." He wore a black tunic and matching trousers, and his dark hair was tousled.

"You have five minutes to get ready," Kaiden said, arms crossed and a firm expression on his face.

Isaac nodded. "Where are we going?"

"The archives," Blaise replied, and his eyes instantly brightened.

"I'll be ready in three minutes." Isaac gave a slight bow and closed the door.

Blaise and Kaiden walked across the corridor to stand near one of the windows lining the long hallway. Her gaze locked on the snowcapped peaks of the Terrenmis Mountains in the distance. Fluffy white clouds were scattered across the blue sky.

Isaac kept to his word and was armored up in less than the time he'd stated. "Shall we?" He ambitiously led the way. Blaise and Kaiden glanced at each other, following the young sergeant.

They came to the door that led to the archives. Its lock appeared to have been tampered with, like someone had broken in. Blaise's brow furrowed.

"Someone was desperate to get in." Kaiden pushed against the heavy worn wood. It creaked open.

The room was dark until torches lining the walls sparked to life, lighting the entire area.

"Well, that's convenient," Kaiden muttered, closing the door after Blaise and Isaac walked inside.

"Must be akrani." Blaise scanned the archives. The walls were covered with wooden shelves lined with tomes of all sizes. In the middle of the octagonal room was a single six-person table.

Kaiden nodded. "Of course it is."

Isaac's gaze roamed the space, a pleased glint in his eyes. Clearing his throat, he asked, "What're we looking for precisely?"

Blaise let out a breath, trying not to be overwhelmed by the amount of information they had to sift through. "We need to look into the history of Balam and figure out why King Theod is so intent on marrying me." She pointed to the shelf next to the door.

They spent the day going through the dusty shelves, reading through tome after tome in search of anything useful. Later, Elric delivered a big platter of bread and cheese to munch on. Then he strode out, returning to whatever it was he'd been doing.

The leather covers were brittle, and the pages were yellowed with age. The air was thick with the musty smell of old parchment.

Thoughts of Mathias came rushing through Blaise's mind. She looked at Kaiden and said, "You know, I don't think it was him."

Kaiden was flipping through a leather-bound tome, dust coming off the pages. He coughed, waving the specks away. "I can't read your mind. What're you talking about?"

She knew that was meant to be a joke. "Mathias. I don't think he tried to kill me."

He stared at her, an unreadable expression on his face. "You don't?"

Isaac stood nearby, probably eavesdropping.

She shook her head, placing that tome back in its place and grabbing the one next to it. "Back in Meliwe Forest, when we were ambushed by the Balam refugees, Mathias was wounded by an arrow."

Kaiden sniffed. "Idiot."

She gave him a severe look. "He was shot trying to defend me."

"Oh."

Blaise's eyes wandered the pages of the tome. "After Nira healed him, he told me he'd made you a promise to protect me and couldn't imagine telling you that he'd failed."

Kaiden let out a shaky breath and remained quiet.

Blaise knew the topic of Mathias was a touchy one. A detail in the book drew her attention. "Interesting," she muttered, walking to the center of the room and placing the oversize tome on the dark oak table.

Isaac joined her. "What is it?"

"Old maps. It says *The United Kingdom of Crenitha*."

Isaac peered over her shoulder. "This is over a thousand years old, from when all the kingdoms were one. When Queen Naava ruled. That'll never happen again."

"Look." She pointed to the top of the page, which had been torn away. "The entire eastern side is missing."

"That *is* interesting. What lands are on that side of the map?" Kaiden asked.

Isaac replied, "Half of Balam, the Terrenmis Mountains, the Onyx Mountains, part of Elatora, Wyndover Woodlands, Blackrock Harbor, and part of the Daagan Forest."

Blaise bit her lip, her chestnut eyes narrowing in thought.

Kaiden pulled another book off the shelf. "Is this whole book about the three levels of gehheina and the creatures in it?" He flipped through the pages while striding over to the table, then placed the book in front of them.

Isaac glanced over at it. "Seems to be."

"Does that mean someone actually made it through

to know all this?" Something seemed to catch his eye. He stopped to try to read it. "What language is this?"

"It's the old language," Isaac answered.

"Do you know what it says?" Kaiden asked.

"I know some words." Isaac grinned and pointed to the page. "These creatures are called algeaa. They dwell in the second level of gehheina and feed off the fears of realm dwellers." He flipped the page, trying to read a bit more. "The algeaa are why nightmares exist."

A shiver crept down Blaise's spine. She hoped never to encounter any of these creatures. She turned to a page of creatures that dwelled in the Onyx Mountains.

Kaiden stopped her from closing the tome. "Wait. What is that?"

Blaise stared at the jagged-toothed creature, studying its black bat-like wings and the burgundy scales covering its body.

Isaac read it out loud for them. "The vissera was created by the goddess of chaos and is a guardian. It protects a hidden portal to nehveina."

"That's the thing that attacked us on our way here," Kaiden said.

A spark of akrani ignited, startling Blaise. She clutched her chest but was able to remain steady.

"It's bigger in person," Kaiden muttered.

"I bet . . ." She wanted to keep staring at this fascinating creature. Taking one last glance, she slammed it shut, dust flying into the air. She waved them away, strolling over to a shelf near the fireplace.

The answers are in the flames, a feminine voice echoed in her mind.

Who is that? Jynx? She stared at the cold empty hearth, feeling drawn to it.

"Blaise?" Kaiden seemed to notice her confusion.

"I'm fine." Her eyes were still locked on the fireplace. Making her way over, she examined the stones around the mantel. She didn't quite know what she was looking for. Her fingertips brushed across the cold uneven surface. One of the stones rattled. She withdrew the dagger hidden in her boot and used it to pry the stone free, revealing an opening.

Kaiden grabbed her wrist to stop her from sticking her hand into the dark space. "Careful."

"You do it, then." She placed her hands on her hips.

Without hesitation, he reached inside. The hole enveloped most of his forearm. A few seconds later, he pulled out a small leather-bound book. He handed it to her.

She examined the dark bindings and intricate designs etched into it and ran her fingers over the green oval crystal embedded in the center.

"Who do you think hid that there?" Kaiden asked.

A commotion echoed in the corridor. Four large Haven soldiers burst through the archive doors.

Gods dammit, that untrustworthy excuse for a king . . . She tucked the book into the waistband of her pants. The closest object to Blaise was a fire iron. She grabbed it and whacked one of the soldiers in the head, knocking him off-balance. The other two engaged in combat with Kaiden, who wielded a five-foot candle holder.

Blaise felt Isaac at her back, and swords clanged against one another. She shielded herself with a tome from the table. She tried to summon her katai but failed. Her akrani was festering inside her like a sickness she didn't know how to cure.

Her instincts weren't as sharp as they'd once been. She managed to parry and block each blow the soldier threw her way, but she struggled to predict his movements. The other soldier recovered from the strike she had delivered earlier. He charged, knocking her against a shelf. She grunted, pain shooting up her spine on impact. Adrenaline rushed through her veins, numbing the pain for an instant. She recovered long enough to front kick the soldier away while the other one approached.

Fuck. I don't know if I'm strong enough to take them both on. She didn't falter, didn't allow them to see her doubts. She moved toward them, swiping at the midsection of one. With all her might, she spun and kicked the other, sending him crashing forward onto the wooden table. It shattered into pieces.

"Blaise, duck!" Isaac bellowed from somewhere behind her. She did. He threw a dagger over her head but missed the soldier he was aiming for. The blade hit the wall and clanged to the floor. "Gods dammit!"

Kaiden's wing came slicing through the air, hitting the other Haven guard in the face. And with one sweeping motion, Blaise knocked the soldier's feet from under him.

"We need to get out of here." Kaiden grabbed her hand and pulled her from the floor. Isaac fell in behind them, and they cut between shelves to make it out of the archives. They funneled into the corridor in time to hide from a group of soldiers entering the room. Once the doors closed, they sprinted down the hallway and rounded the corner straight into Simone.

"There you are. The entire fortress has been compromised. Quick, this way." Simone led them up a staircase to the floor the sanctum was on.

Isaac was the first to follow her.

"Shouldn't we be going the other way?" Kaiden asked.

Blaise tried to loosen his hold on her hand, but he wouldn't let go.

Simone led them down the empty corridor and into the sanctum, where King Theod, Captain Wilhelm, and a dozen Haven soldiers stood waiting.

The king shot Blaise a devious look. Simone walked up to him. He placed his hand on her shoulder. "Well done, my dear."

Simone stepped to King Theod's side and grinned at Blaise and Kaiden. "This is for my sister."

Kaiden's eyes narrowed. "Your sister?"

"Yes, you might remember her. Audrey Black." Simone glared at Kaiden with pure hatred. "You let those monsters take her. It's because of *you* she's dead."

"Do you think I didn't try to save her? That I would just let her go like that?" Kaiden growled, fists clenched, wings tensing. "You don't think I blame myself for the deaths in my unit—for her death?"

Blaise didn't know Simone all that well, but she'd never expected this.

"Surrender now and I won't order my men to kill off what's left of your precious Alchyra," drawled the king.

"What happened to my two days?" Blaise bit out. Gods, she wished she could use her lightning on him.

"I'm an impatient man. I can't say I'm sorry about that."

Blaise gritted her teeth. "Oh, you're sorry all right."

"Careful, Queen." The king stepped closer. "You don't want to see me angry."

"What do you want with my kingdom?" Blaise demanded, fighting the urge to step away from him.

A grin crept onto King Theod's face. "Oh, darling. There's a lot you need to learn about being a ruler."

Elric burst through the doors of the sanctum, tendrils of dark smoke surrounding him and trailing in his wake. He crossed the threshold, entering in a blur of blades. Daggers flew in every direction, and soldiers fell at his feet. "Get the queen out of here!" he bellowed, swinging his sword and slicing through the arm of another soldier.

Simone pleaded with the king, "Your Majesty, this is not a fight you can win. We must go now!"

Kaiden grabbed Blaise's hand, pulling her in the opposite direction. Darting toward the exit, they were stopped by more soldiers. Kaiden guided her away, detouring to the balcony, where the moon shone high.

Kaiden lifted her onto the stone railing, and her heart pounded violently in her chest at the height of the drop. Bolts from the soldiers' crossbows whizzed past them.

Gusts of wind tested her balance, and Blaise screamed, "What're you doing?"

"Just trust me." Kaiden yanked her into his arms, a bolt nearly missing her. He squeezed her before diving over the edge, and they plummeted through the crisp night air.

19

MATHIAS

Fuck." Mathias reached for his hood, covering his head. Keeping Tarren and the two Alchyra trackers in his peripheral, Mathias prayed to the gods they wouldn't recognize him. It was Ollie and Piers. *They must've told Tarren we're wanted.*

He needed to get going to meet Nira. She and crowds didn't mix well for long.

The trackers were about twenty feet from Mathias. His pulse pounded in his neck as they passed him. He held his breath, holding on to hope.

"Okay, Peregrine is ready for you, Sir Casimir." The dealer handed the reins to Mathias.

Gods dammit, he said that a little too loud. Mathias didn't bother bidding the man goodbye. He took the horse's reins and pelted down the street without looking back. He could feel eyes on his back while he rounded the corner. Thankfully, the streets were crowded.

Nira stood on the side of the street with a satchel on her shoulder. The hood of her cloak covered her head, but Mathias could recognize her figure from any direction. A smile crept onto his face.

"You there with the horse, stop!"

Mathias ignored the call and ran, grabbing Nira's hand as he passed her. She stumbled, dropping her satchel, trying to catch up with his long-legged strides. There would be no way to mount Peregrine in this crowd. The end of the street was still quite a distance from them.

It had been a long time since Mathias had tried to mount a moving horse, so he hoped he wouldn't land on his face. "Get on first," he shouted back at Nira.

"What?" Her eyes widened, terror apparent in them.

He dragged her forward faster. "Put your foot in the stirrup." She did, and he swept her up onto the saddle.

"Shit, my ankle." Frantically, she grabbed Peregrine's mane. She managed to steady herself on the horse and gripped the reins.

Once he had enough space, Mathias leaped, simultaneously throwing his leg over Peregrine's back, landing behind Nira. He gripped the saddle horn and kicked the horse into a gallop.

Mathias noticed Tarren and the others had mounted horses but were still several blocks away. He couldn't afford to stop. It wouldn't take long for them to catch up.

Mathias glanced back—Tarren and the two best

Alchyra trackers in Balam, Piers and Ollie, were closing the distance between them.

He tightened his arms around her. "We're going to lose them in Grelan. Hold on."

"I thought we were going to Balam," she shouted, keeping her eyes on the path ahead.

Mathias and Nira made it through the gates, but Tarren and the trackers were gaining on them.

"That's what they'll be expecting us to do," he replied. "I thought we were past this already."

She groaned. "Fine."

They sped through Grelan Forest, leaping over fallen branches, going off the main path. The trees were tall and thick, their branches intertwining overhead, forming a dense canopy. The only light came from the occasional ray that filtered through the rustling leaves, creating dancing patterns on the forest floor. Trees blurred past them, and the sound of their pursuers grew fainter. Weaving through the trees, dodging low-hanging branches, Mathias and Nira gained more distance and finally lost them.

Sweat trickled down Mathias's temples. He was grateful for the shade and the crisp breeze coming in from the coast.

"Well, that was eventful," Nira muttered.

Mathias inhaled, then exhaled. He didn't have the energy to respond to her remark. They remained silent, traveling toward Balam.

Mathias and Nira made their way through the Azureden pass, and the temperature plummeted. As long as they escaped the mountains before sunset, they would avoid the kynarah that dwelled there. He was in no way equipped to fight off those bloodthirsty flying creatures.

When they made it to the Meliwe Forest, Nira's body started to relax against his. He didn't blame her. He was exhausted as well. They had been riding for hours, and the sun was beginning to set. A chill crept down his spine. Only the clip-clop of Peregrine's hooves could be heard. He didn't know if it was the cold or the ominous quiet of the forest.

He tightened his grip around her waist. "Let me take the reins for a bit," he said, gently coaxing the leather from her hands.

She tensed at first, then let go and relaxed her head against his chest. "Thanks." She yawned.

Mathias brought his mouth close to her ear. "I have you. Just sleep."

Nira's breathing became even and slow. She was definitely asleep. A grin spread across his face, and he shook his head in amusement. He'd always envied how quickly she found slumber.

Mathias kept the horse at a slow, steady pace, riding deeper into the forest. With Nira asleep in his arms, he didn't want to disturb her by riding too fast. His mind drifted over past events. He remembered what the other Nira had said about the parchments and the Onyx Crystal.

The sun set over the horizon, and the waxing moon took its place in the star-speckled sky, lighting a path for Mathias. His eyes grew heavier with each passing minute. They needed to stop and rest.

He leaned in close to Nira. "Wake up," he whispered, inhaling her jasmine scent.

She murmured something inaudible and stretched out her arms. "Where are we?" she rasped.

"We're a few hours into Meliwe. If I had to guess, we're about a quarter of the way to Balam," he said, dismounting.

Nira jumped off the saddle, yelped, and began falling.

Luckily, Mathias caught her.

"Shit, I must've twisted my ankle."

He sighed and shrugged his jacket off, draping it around her shoulders. "Here, let me look at it." He helped her sit beneath a large cypress tree.

He tugged on her boot, and she hissed, "Ouch, that hurts."

"Sorry." He finally managed to get it off her foot and examined her ankle. It was swollen to the size of a grapefruit. "Can you move your toes?"

She nodded.

"It's definitely sprained."

She loosed a breath. "Thank you, Captain Obvious."

He tore a strip of cloth from her underskirt and wrapped her ankle.

Mathias tended to the horse, then dragged a log over to Nira for her to prop up her foot. He sat next to her on the damp ground, settling against the cypress trunk. Mathias crossed his arms and stretched out his legs. He leaned his head against the bark, eyes drifting closed.

She rested her head in his lap.

He looked down, meeting her tired cobalt gaze. "Did you need something?"

"Is it okay if I sleep next to you tonight?" She was still shivering.

With a deep inhale, he propped her up. Standing, he moved the log in front of them so she could rest her foot.

Her lips curved up as he plopped down next to her.

"I'll warm you with my body." He hadn't meant for it to come out so suggestive.

She stared at him, beams of moonlight illuminating the unreadable expression on her face. "Only because I'm desperate for heat."

He cocked a brow. "Really?"

"Hurry up before I change my mind." She rolled onto her side, keeping her foot on the log.

Mathias settled behind her and was pleasantly surprised when she shared the jacket with him. He wrapped his arm around her midsection, and warmth immediately radiated between their bodies. He didn't care they were in the middle of a forest amidst the darkness. With only the moonlight shining from the black sky, Nira in his arms was all that mattered. In minutes, Mathias fell asleep, enjoying the Nira he rarely got to be with.

MATHIAS'S EYES FLICKERED OPEN WHEN he felt cold steel against his neck. He peered into the eyes of the blade's wielder. Piers stood over him, his silver armor glinting in the sun barely ascending over the horizon. The scent of dew lingered in the air.

"Shit," Mathias murmured in his sleep-induced haze. He reached over in search of Nira. She still lay next to him, wide-awake.

"We almost fell for your little trick," said the dark-haired man. "Get up. Slowly. Both of you."

Mathias obeyed, helping Nira to stand on her one good foot. He wrapped his arm around her waist, giving her extra support.

Another familiar soldier trod up, sword in hand. "General Zade is in for a pleasant surprise," said Ollie, the young green-eyed Alchyra.

"Ollie, you know me. I would *never* have involved myself in that assassination attempt on our queen." Nira's brow furrowed.

"It's Sergeant Ollie to you," he said, pointing the tip of his sword at her. "Let's get these traitors back to camp." He yanked her away from Mathias. She stumbled and screamed in pain. Ollie ignored her, tying her hands behind her back.

Mathias struggled against Piers. "She's injured, you idiot," he growled. "And we're not traitors." He didn't get a response while Piers restrained his arms behind him.

Ollie pushed her forward. "I used to look up to you."

"This is all a misunderstanding." Nira winced, limping down the path.

"You can explain yourselves to General Zade." Piers shoved Mathias ahead.

ON HORSEBACK, THEY TRAVERSED THE forest for half a day before finally arriving at the Alchyra camp. The guards at the entrance nodded at Piers and Ollie, allowing them to pass. They made their way to the large tent in the center of the basecamp. The two Alchyra guarding the entry stepped aside, pulling the flaps open for them to enter.

Once inside, Piers and Ollie pushed Mathias and Nira to their knees in front of a large wooden table.

Zade stood across from them, studying a map of Crenitha. The insignia on his silver armor indicated the rank of general he'd risen to. With his dark crimson cape shrouding his shoulders and a firm expression contorting his pale features, he scrutinized Mathias and Nira.

Piers and Ollie took a few steps back.

Zade crossed his arms over his armored chest. "Well, well, well, if it isn't Sergeant Mathias and his little accomplice."

"As I live and breathe." Mathias straightened on his knees.

"For now," Nira added under her breath.

Mathias shot her a glare. He turned to Zade. "I did not try to kill Blaise. You have to believe me, Zade."

"It's General Zade to you, and I don't *have* to believe a word you say. Anyway, nothing can be done until we get you back to Balam. Until then, you two are prisoners." Zade looked at Piers and Ollie. "Tie them up in the cage, and watch them closely."

Piers yanked him to his feet.

"Wait, I have proof," Mathias said. "Just let me explain."

"Save it for your trial," Zade replied.

Trial? We're actually going to be put on trial? He didn't know what he could do to convince Zade to listen.

At least this would guarantee an audience with Blaise. He hoped he would be able to regain her trust once she heard his evidence. Even though Blaise had started out as a huge pain in Mathias's ass, he had grown to appreciate her strength and attitude. And she definitely knew how to handle Kaiden. Mathias had never seen his best friend so incredibly flustered by someone.

Eyes bored into Mathias and Nira. With bound hands, they were dragged through the camp. Mathias found it difficult to swallow the bitter shame coating his mouth. Whispers could be heard amongst all the Alchyra they passed. He steadied his breathing and found comfort that he had proof of their innocence. *If they would only give us a chance.*

BLAISE

Her own screams rattled her brain as she sliced through the sky in Kaiden's arms. Blaise's heart thrashed. She couldn't bear the sight of the ground nearing. "Anytime now," she shrieked, squeezing her eyes shut. "We're going to die!"

"No, we're not." He panted. At the last possible second, Kaiden's wings spread out, catching an evening gust. With power and grace, he flew higher into the pale light of the moon.

Blaise's eyes drifted down to the fortress. The soldiers standing on the balcony shot their crossbows, but they were well out of range. Elric and Isaac still fought. She hoped to the goddess of chaos that they'd make it out alive somehow.

Her eyes followed the road to the rolling foothills of Balam. From this height, her kingdom seemed so diminutive.

"Do you have to go so high?" she squealed into his ear.

He looked at her with that roguish grin of his.

She scowled back and wrapped herself around him more tightly. The book began to slip from the back of her waistband. "Kaiden, the book."

His brow rose. "What book?"

"It's in my pants. Grab it. Don't let it fall!"

He reached around her waist and carefully coaxed it out from her trousers. "Why do you still have this?" He chuckled, flying past the hills. They were miles from the fortress at this point.

Her cheeks warmed. "It called to me."

He drew back, gazing into her eyes. "There's been a lot of that lately. Not sure how I feel about it."

She noticed drips of blood on the side of Kaiden's neck. "Gods, you're wounded."

"I don't feel anything. Where?"

She searched his throat for any injuries, but when she pulled away, crimson dripped from a cut on her own hand. "Oh, it's me."

"Are you okay?" he asked, concerned.

"It's just a flesh wound. Can you give me the book?"

He nodded, handing it over her shoulder. The movement caused them to tilt slightly to one side, making Blaise squeal.

"Here, take it," he complained.

She peered into the green crystal embedded in the

leather cover. She freed one hand to grab the book. A faint glow seemed to pulse in rhythm with her own heartbeat. Her well of akrani overflowed with warmth, sparking to life. She pressed the book into her chest and felt the stone slip out of place. Tingles shot up her arm.

Blood.

She looked at her palm—the glowing crystal had attached itself to the cut. Her vision started to blur.

"K-Kaiden?" She stuttered, and everything shifted into darkness.

BLAISE'S VISION CLEARED. HER HAND still tingled, but the green stone was no longer there. She peered up from her hand. She stood in the sanctum of the Balam fortress. An unfamiliar warmth made it seem like a completely different place. The colors were vivid. The golden daylight shone in from every angle. She'd never realized the fortress could be so full of life.

A handsome man with dark hair and chiseled features stood near the pool. His somber light gray eyes peered into the depth of the water. A heavily pregnant Queen Maxima walked up to him and kissed him on the lips, running her fingers through the silver streak on the side of his head.

Wait a minute. Is this my father? Her brow wrinkled as she watched the scene unfold before her.

"I don't want to leave you. I'm willing to stay with you, but it's your choice," the man said, embracing Maxima.

"I know, love, but it's the only thing I can truly have of you." Tears trickled down her cheeks. "Our child will never know their father."

The man gestured to Maxima's swollen belly. "That baby is a curse to the gods."

Maxima frowned. "You don't really believe that though."

"I love you, Maxi. But you have chosen it over me," said the man, cupping her cheek. "I would've chosen you. Every time. I broke my own law for you."

Those words crushed Blaise to the point of tears. *How could he? My own father.*

"I'm sorry," Maxima sobbed. "I love you. There has to be something we can do."

He stared into her eyes. "As long as that child lives, I cannot exist in this realm."

The pool rippled and quaked, and the goddess of chaos sprang from its depths. She landed on her feet between Maxima and the man. Water glistened on her skin, and her silver armor dried instantly. She didn't even acknowledge the queen of Balam. "Everything is in order, Father."

Blaise's eyes widened. Jynx's father was the high god, Amasu. *She is my sister.*

"We could've ruled forever, Maxima. But now I have to pay for your choice. Remember this day. It'll impact everything that happens from now on." Amasu gave the queen one last kiss on the forehead and stepped away. "You'll never be able to take this back."

Maxima reached for him, but he'd already jumped into the water, Jynx following shortly after.

The queen fell to her knees and sobbed.

Blaise blinked back tears, swallowing a lump in her throat. She wanted to hold her mother, to comfort and console her shattered heart. These memory crystals she had encountered brought her nothing but visions of pain and hardship. She didn't know if she could handle another.

Maxima's sobs lessened as she opened one of her clenched hands, revealing a familiar green crystal. She caressed her belly with her other hand. "When the time is right, my darling child, you'll find my memories." She sniffed. "The gods are more complicated than you know. They're not perfect. They have emotions like everyone else. Laws forbid them to interfere with the lives of realm dwellers. We will never be safe, my love. When you find this crystal, it will unlock the path to the power your father fears most. The book contains everything you need. The answers are in the flames. Be brave. Be strong. Never forget I love you."

Tears streamed down her cheeks. "I love you too, Mom," Blaise whispered, a wave of darkness consuming her.

BLAISE'S HEAD THROBBED. A FAMILIAR male voice echoed in her ears as she came to. *Who in gehheina is that?* Her eyes flicked open and focused on Zade's handsome features. His short auburn hair had grown out since the last time she'd seen him.

"Am I still dreaming?" she rasped, taking in her surroundings. She lay on a small cot and was covered with a wool blanket. A table with an iron basin and cloths hanging off the edge was in the corner.

Zade grinned and helped her sit up. "It's good to see you again, Blaise."

"Where's Kaiden?" The blood rushed from her head to her heart. She placed two fingers to her temples and closed her eyes, trying to regain her bearings.

"I'm here." Kaiden came in from outside the tent and knelt next to her cot, wings and all.

Relief escaped upon her breath.

"I'm assuming that was a memory crystal." Kaiden gestured to her hand. "Nothing knocks you on your ass like one of those."

She opened her palm, now dried with blood, and the clear stone dropped onto the wool blanket.

"What did you see?" Zade made his way over to the basin and squeezed out the cloth. Sitting next to her, he placed his hand on hers. He tried to access her mind, but she held firm against his akrani.

Blaise met his emerald eyes with a steadfast gaze.

"Interesting." Zade cocked his head. "Something has changed since the last time I saw you."

Kaiden reached for the cloth from across the cot, taking it from Zade. "It wasn't her you saw last," he answered, cleaning the dried blood from her hand.

Annoyed, Zade turned his attention to Kaiden. "Explain."

With help from Blaise, Kaiden told Zade everything that had happened since she'd last seen him during her coronation. Kaiden filled in the gaps about the fake revenant queen and the meta crystal and how his wings had seemingly come out of nowhere.

The last thing they told Zade about was King Theod's attack on Balam—how he had lied and attempted to take Blaise by force.

"Interesting," Zade muttered again.

"You keep saying that," Kaiden huffed.

"You're ellorian—"

"Half."

"Very interesting." Zade placed a finger to his chin.

"Stop telling us how interesting it is, and tell us what you know," Kaiden snapped, running his hand through his windswept hair.

Zade straightened. "Well, I've read ellorians don't grow their wings until they've met their aniivasei."

"Their what?" Blaise and Kaiden said in unison.

Zade inhaled deeply. "Aniivasei is when akrani is perfectly balanced. It's like harmony."

Blaise's brow furrowed. "But why now? Why not when we first met?"

Zade shrugged. "Akrani does work mysteriously. There are many things that can affect it. One or both of you may not have *fully* come into your power yet. Perhaps one of you activated an amplifier? Has there been a change between you?"

Kaiden raked his hands down his face. "This is making my head spin."

Blaise shared the sentiment.

Aniivasei. Is that all that's been drawing us together this whole time? Was it the only thing attracting him to her? *Is this the only reason he stayed?* She wanted them to be able to choose from their heart, not because of this akrani bond.

Zade cleared his throat. "By the way, we caught Mathias and Nira."

Kaiden stood. "Where is he?"

"They're in a cage at the edge of camp." Zade pointed to the north.

"Take me to him." Kaiden's wings shuddered.

Blaise didn't want to think about how that reunion would go. Kaiden's anger radiated off him as he walked out. *Would he hurt Mathias?* She needed to follow him before he did something he might regret.

Zade helped her stand. "He doesn't even know where he's going. Come along, let's catch up to him." He reached around her waist and helped her.

She grinned, following him through the camp.

21

KAIDEN

AIDEN STOMPED THROUGH THE BUSTLING Alchyra camp, the noon sun high above. The infantry tents were set in a uniform line encircling the larger ones. In a clearing ahead, Alchyra sparred. All around him, soldiers carried out their daily duties, but there was no sign of captives. Kaiden's steps slowed. It dawned on him that he had no idea where he was going.

He came to a complete stop, looking north, but he could only see tents. He spun to question Zade and spotted the cause of the general's slow pace. *Idiot, you just left her behind.* He raked his hand down his face.

Zade maintained Blaise's hobbling gait, her arm around his neck.

At a clipped pace, Kaiden returned to her side and glanced at Zade. "I've got her."

"Very well." Zade stepped out from under her arm.

Kaiden reached for Blaise and swept her gently off her feet, cradling her against his chest.

"I can walk." Her brows rose.

Zade took the lead, and Kaiden trailed behind. He smirked at her. "I know."

She interlaced her fingers around his neck. "Why do you have to be so—"

"Handsome?"

"No."

"Amazing in bed?"

"No." Her cheeks reddened. "Obnoxious."

"Oh, come on, Sparks." He leaned in close, his lips grazing the shell of her ear. "Admit it. You're thankful for the ride." He winked.

Her eyes narrowed. "And you should be thankful I still allow you to touch me."

He shook his head, that roguish grin still on his face. "Oh yes, I'm grateful for *all* I'm allowed to do."

She rolled her eyes and sighed in defeat.

Kaiden stared, admiring Blaise's beauty. They neared the edge of the camp, and the words she'd quoted from Mathias sprang to mind. *He told me he'd made you a promise to protect me and couldn't imagine telling you that he'd failed.*

The tips of Kaiden's wings skimmed the dirt. They came to a large jail wagon with thick iron bars parked between two tents. Inside, Mathias and Nira sat back-to-back, their hands and feet chained.

Kaiden set Blaise down, steadying her. He strode up to the bars. Mathias sat cross-legged on the wooden planks. His clothes were tattered and stained with blood. He was muddy from his grungy black boots to his darkened hair. His thick, scruffy beard made him look older than his years. When their eyes met, Kaiden could see how much the exhaustion had dulled the brightness of his blue eyes.

Mathias had the audacity to squint at the sight of Kaiden and say, "What in gehheina happened to you?" Even tied and bound, Mathias couldn't help but be the smart-ass Kaiden had always known.

"I could ask the same of you." Kaiden crossed his arms. "You look like shit, by the way."

Nira's tired gaze met Kaiden's. "We didn't do it, Captain."

"Then how do you explain the scar on Blaise's stomach?" Kaiden asked.

Zade scoffed, stepping next to Kaiden. "Personally, I think they're hiding something."

Amusement glistened in Mathias's eyes. "Are we all just going to ignore the fucking wings?"

Kaiden pointed his index finger at him. "Don't try to change the subject."

"It's not what you think," Mathias said.

Kaiden's nostrils flared. "Then what is it?"

Mathias tilted his stare to the solid wooden ceiling and loosed a breath. "You're not going to believe me."

Nira interjected, "The night of the assassination, I saw a prestae leaving the sanctum after Mathias had already been taken to the dungeons. That's how I knew it wasn't *Mathias* who'd tried to kill the queen." She snorted. "I wouldn't have gotten myself mixed up in this mess if I'd known otherwise. But the man didn't deserve to die for something he didn't do."

"Aww, you do have a heart," Mathias quipped.

She elbowed him. "I'm trying to save your life *again*, stupid."

Mathias's mouth clamped shut.

Blaise finally spoke up and asked Zade, "Can you use satori on him?"

"Well . . . yes, but it will be painful. For the both of us. His head will feel like scrambled eggs for a while." Zade looked at Mathias with empathy.

Kaiden let out a breath. "Did you do it, Mat? Did you try to kill Blaise?"

Mathias's brow ruffled, and his eyes glistened. "How could you ask me that? You really don't know the answer to that?"

Kaiden wanted the allegation against Mathias to be false. He sighed, brushing his fingers through his hair. *I don't want to torture my best friend, but I can't stand by him without the truth.*

Blaise strode up on the other side of Kaiden and placed a comforting hand on his shoulder, giving it a gentle squeeze.

Nira jabbed Mathias once more and snapped, "Tell them the rest."

Mathias rested his head back against Nira's and said, "We found evidence at the Scarlet Crown in Haven that can help clear our names and save Balam from King Theod."

Zade let out a short incredulous laugh. "Right."

Kaiden demanded, "Show us what you've found."

"I don't actually have it on my person," Mathias muttered.

Kaiden groaned. "Then how do you expect to prove your innocence?"

"I was hoping you would trust me at my word," Mathias replied.

Kaiden was aware of the necessary course of action. He turned to Blaise and said, "Do what needs to be done."

Blaise's gaze drifted to Zade. "Will you please confirm their innocence with your satori?"

With a sigh, Zade unlocked the door of the cage and took a step toward Mathias, studying him. "I suppose this was inevitable." He placed his thumbs on the Mathias's temples, then rested his fingers on the top of Mathias's head. They stared into each other's eyes. "Are you ready?" Zade asked.

Mathias nodded once. "Yes."

Their eyes glazed over, going entirely white, and Mathias groaned. Beads of sweat accumulated on Zade's forehead and arms. Kaiden could feel the pulse of powerful akrani in the air.

Blaise held her head, shuffling backward. Kaiden ambled toward her, wrapping his arm around her waist, keeping her balanced.

"You okay?" Concern swept through him.

She nodded, breathless. "I'm fine. Thank you."

Mathias screamed, trying to shake out of Zade's hold.

Nira spun around and attempted to prop Mathias up with her chained hands. She held his arm and began whispering into his ear.

Kaiden stepped up to the bars of the jail. He reached through and grabbed Mathias's hand and squeezed tightly. "I'm here, Mat. I've got you, brother." His skin buzzed with energy that caused the hair on his arms to stand on end.

Zade's eyes turned back to their normal green color several minutes later. "He is innocent. And it seems there are more truths to be revealed, Your Majesty," he said, breathing heavily. He stepped down from the wagon, reaching for the keys on his belt, and handed them to Kaiden.

Kaiden hopped up into the cage and released Mathias and Nira from their bonds. "I can't believe you planned on convincing us with nothing but your word. I thought you were smarter than that, Mat."

Mathias groaned. "But it worked, didn't it?" he said to Kaiden with a half grin.

Zade helped Nira down from the wagon, and she turned to wait for Mathias.

Kaiden lifted him to his feet. Mathias staggered forward with his guidance.

Nira helped him down, and he slung his arm over her shoulder.

He swayed into her. "You're a g-good wife," he slurred.

"And you're an ass," Nira retorted. She looked to Blaise and asked, "Is there any place we can put him down?"

Kaiden's fists clenched. "Why didn't you send *me* a message?"

Mathias glanced at him. "I couldn't risk being caught." He leaned forward, grabbing his head.

Kaiden and Nira stopped him from falling. Wincing and limping, she continued on. The three started toward the center of camp.

"I was fucking worried about you," Kaiden said.

"And you think I wasn't worried about you?" Mathias backhanded Kaiden in the chest.

Kaiden's wings ruffled from the forced breath. "It's been too long, Mat."

"Tell me about it," Mathias murmured.

Zade led them back to the tent Blaise had woken up in. Kaiden and Nira laid Mathias on the cot and covered him with the wool blanket.

"You need a bath. You smell like a horse's ass," Kaiden remarked.

"You're a horse's ass," Mathias groused.

Kaiden laughed, shaking his head. *Same ol' Mathias.*

Mathias's eyes drifted closed, and he let out an audible sigh.

"Get some rest." Kaiden patted his hand and stood.

"So . . . everything's good with you two?" Nira asked.

Kaiden placed his hand on her shoulder reassuringly and said, "Yes, we'll be fine."

NIRA LIMPED INTO THE TENT with a warm plate of food for Mathias. Kaiden, Blaise, and Zade filed in, their own platters in hand. They all sat at the table that had been placed in the center of the tent.

"Wake up, sleepyhead." Nira gently shook Mathias awake.

Mathias pushed himself into a seated position. He took in everybody in the space, eyes glossy.

"How're you feeling?" Kaiden asked with a mouthful of food.

"Like my head was put into a vise." Mathias massaged his temples while Nira placed the tray of food in front of him. He took a few bites of bread and sipped water from the cup.

"Now, what was Zade talking about before?" Kaiden prompted, leaning back in the chair.

Mathias glanced at Nira, then met Kaiden's hazel eyes. "Gods, where do I begin?"

"How about the beginning?" Nira ate a few spoonfuls from her own plate.

"Well, we know a prestae was made for Blaise," Kaiden said. "So there very well could have been a prestae made of Mathias as well."

Zade swallowed his food and said, "Then the only purpose for there to be a prestae of Mathias would be to set him up."

Nira agreed, "Yes, that's why I involved myself."

Mathias said, "The two parchments I found at the Scarlet Crown seemed to explain part of the plan. One was a letter from King Theod."

"Is it true you were planning to marry him?" Zade asked.

Blaise's nose scrunched. "I would never. That's what my prestae was there for."

Mathias finished the bread. He swallowed the last bite and said, "The letter said something about the Onyx Crystal. Do you think that's what they're using to make all these prestae?"

Kaiden said, "You're the one who saw the letter."

"Yes, but I couldn't read it because it was in the old language." Mathias took a gulp from his cup. "Nira read it."

Everyone's gaze locked onto Nira. She peered up from her plate, eyes wide. "Not me. They must've made a prestae of me too. He says I was with him when I was home in bed." She shrugged and continued eating.

All eyes returned to Mathias.

"I deciphered a portion of the letter Mathias saw," Zade chimed in. "It confirmed their plans to overthrow Blaise and take Balam by any means necessary. But taking Balam isn't all he's after."

Blaise let out a breath. "What else could he possibly want?"

"King Theod is searching for something called the Onyx Crystal," Mathias said to Blaise, then looked to Zade. "That must've been in the part you couldn't read. Nira said it's something you need to find before he does."

Zade said, "The second parchment was a map that looked to have been torn from a tome."

Kaiden rested his forearms on the table. "What lands were included on the map?"

"I'm not sure because it was written in the old script as well," Mathias replied.

Zade tapped his index finger on the wooden surface of the table. "It appeared to be a map of the United Kingdom of Crenitha prior to the rise of Rowena."

"Do any of you know what the Onyx Crystal is?" Blaise asked, pushing her empty plate away.

Mathias replied, "I was told it's valuable."

Kaiden brushed his fingers over the stubble on his jaw. "This is a lot to take in at dinnertime."

"It's been a long couple days," Blaise said. "We should take time to rest. Tomorrow we begin planning how to take back Balam."

"My men will bring a bigger cot to accommodate Nira," Zade added. "I'll have them bring a change of clothes also." He excused himself and left the tent.

Blaise let out a giggle, her attention on Nira. "Let's give these two a moment alone."

With a nod, Nira followed Blaise out of the tent, their empty plates in hand.

Kaiden stepped to Mathias's bedside. He twisted at the waist to look at Mathias, shifting his wing to see over his shoulder. "They're pretty crazy, huh?"

Mathias reached forward, brushing his fingers along the feathers. "Oh my gods. They're so soft."

Kaiden shivered, gooseflesh forming on his back and arms. "Don't do that." He turned, hitting Mathias's hand with the other wing.

A few moments later, one of the Alchyra sergeants brought Mathias some clean clothes, placing the fresh tunic and trousers over the back of a chair. Mathias thanked him, and the Alchyra walked out of the tent.

"We have a lot to catch up on, my friend," Kaiden said. "I'll see you in the morning."

22

BLAISE

LAISE FOLLOWED ZADE TO A TENT IN THE middle of camp. Nira trailed behind, limping. The two guards standing at the entrance opened the flaps for them to enter. Blaise stepped inside, and warmth engulfed her. A wood stove sat across from the plush mattress. She brushed her fingers along the comforter's velvety threads. A dark wooden table sat in the corner with a basin and clean washcloths.

Zade and Nira waited while Blaise examined the space. "How has training been going?" she asked him.

He took a step forward. "They learn fast. Some of them

have akrani. To be honest, I'm surprised Meliwe hasn't been destroyed."

Blaise's lips curved up. "Thank you again for taking on such a heavy task. For being my general."

"I will always be allegiant to you, my queen." He bowed his head.

When Zade straightened, their gazes met. They studied each other for a moment. Blaise tilted her head.

Why is he looking at me like that? She pushed the thought away and stepped back.

Zade averted his emerald eyes to Nira. "I can get you some ointments for that ankle and a change of clothes." He turned back to Blaise. "We can talk more later, my queen." He held the flap of the tent open for Nira to exit, then strode out, closing it behind him.

Blaise released a heavy breath and plopped down onto the bed.

Jynx's voice echoed in her mind. *Where are you, Little Flame?*

Slipping off her boots, Blaise answered, *I got a little sidetracked.*

Stop wasting time. I have the answers you desire, Jynx said.

How in gehheina am I supposed to do that when my kingdom is being invaded? Blaise needed to get her priorities straight. The possibility of a high god escaping from gehheina was certainly up there. However, she was the queen of Balam. *There's no one else who will protect my people.*

I have thousands of years of knowledge to pass on to you, sister. It only requires you to come to Chaos Island. Jynx's voice faded.

Blaise took off her clothes and utilized the basin in the corner, cleaning herself with a wet cloth. She grabbed the oversize tunic that lay on the bed and threw it on, letting it slip off one shoulder. The flimsy material barely covered her thighs. *It'll have to do.*

Kaiden swept through the flaps moments later, tying them shut behind him. His wings almost touched the top of the tall tent. He faced her, his hazel eyes drifting up her body. His bottom lip slipped between his teeth.

Blaise wasn't wearing anything under the tunic. She crossed her arms over her chest. "Thought you'd be catching up with Mathias still."

He stared at her lips. "I figured he needs more rest."

Heat rippled through her core with each step he took toward her. "Shouldn't we rest too?"

His gaze darkened on her, and the corner of his mouth crept up. "If that's your wish."

She took a few slow steps to the table in the corner and leaned her backside against it.

He stared at her like this small distance between them killed him. Part of her wanted to accept the akrani bond between them, but she didn't want him to choose her *because* of it. She wanted to know he would choose her regardless.

Kaiden was now a few inches from her, his hazel eyes roaming over every part of her. "How are you doing with everything you've learned today?"

No matter how hard she fought it, her whole being called to him—begged for his lips, his touch. She focused on his question, ignoring the blatant magnetism between them. "I'm taking everything in stride." Her gaze averted to the ground, but he stooped down and caught it.

"Hey, talk to me." His voice was a mere whisper.

The list of everything she needed to do rushed through her mind: Jynx's request; the mystery of her mother's book; and most importantly, the invasion of Balam. A breath caught in her throat, and her breathing became shallower after each intake of air. She shook her head. "What do you want me to say?"

"Don't do that."

"Do what?" She tapped her index finger on the table, grounding herself.

"Don't shut me out. I know we're both dealing with a lot." He placed his hands on her hips and held her close.

She braced her hands on his firm pecs. "I feel like I'm being pulled in so many directions."

He gave her a look of understanding. "I know. But you're not alone. We'll get through this."

She stared into his eyes, determined to mask every emotion that threatened to bubble to the surface.

He wrapped his arms around her, his euphoric warmth breaking through the defenses she struggled to keep in place.

"Just because we have some bond, I don't want you to feel obligated to stay with me." She slipped out of his embrace, stepped around him, and stood next to the bed. She felt completely vulnerable under his scrutiny.

The flecks of gold around his irises sparked with intensity, and a muscle in his jaw ticked. "I've never once felt obligated to be with you. Sure, we've had a few instances where we didn't have a choice."

Blaise's mind flashed back to the time in Lerwick when she'd teased him with toast. They'd slept in the same room—in the same bed. Her lips turned up.

He snaked his arms around her waist and pulled her against him once more. "This . . . wanting you is *my* choice." He buried his face in the side of her neck, inhaling deeply.

Ripples of pleasure shot down her spine to the heat between her legs.

"I haven't been able to stop thinking about you since the day I left you in Balam," he murmured into her ear. "The very thought of you haunted me. Your scent. The way you taste. How you feel beneath my fingertips."

She bit back a moan. "Did you practice that in front of a mirror?"

His lips curved up against her neck. "No. It's pretty good though, huh?" He grazed the shell of her ear and made his way down to her racing pulse, teeth scraping her soft skin.

She giggled.

His hand roamed to the small of her back. The other one skimmed the outside of her oversize tunic and gripped her ass cheek, eliciting a small squeal from her.

He drew back, eyes wide. "Are you not wearing any undergarments?"

She stared at him in silent confirmation.

"Fuck," he whispered, then lifted her onto the mattress. He crouched in front of her and spread her legs. His warm tongue sent chills of ecstasy through her entire body. No man had ever done this to her before, but she wasn't complaining. *Not at all.*

"Gods." Her head lulled back, and her eyes rolled as he continued to lick and suck and push into her with his tongue.

"I love how your body responds to me," he growled, pushing one finger into her warmth.

Blaise whimpered. She clamped her hand over her mouth. He inserted another finger and began to lick her again. He maintained a vigorous rhythm, fingering her and swiping his tongue in circles on her swollen bud.

If he kept going like that, she was going to—

"K-Kaiden, I'm c-close . . ." Her back arched as her cunt squeezed and pulsed around his fingers.

"I love the way you taste." He trailed kisses along one of her inner thighs and straightened. "My only regret is I didn't get to take my time with you the first time."

"You're already making up for it." She pushed herself up onto her forearms.

He threw off his shirt. His gaze never left hers. He undid the buttons of his trousers and released his hard arousal. Standing naked between her legs, he lined up his girth at her entrance, easing the tip of his cock into her. "Gods. Dammit." He gripped her waist.

She stifled a breath.

He sank his whole length into her with a grunt. "I'm not sure how long I'll last, love," he whispered against her lips.

She gyrated her hips against him. "You underestimate yourself."

He pulled out only to thrust all the way in again and again until she could no longer be quiet. His mouth covered hers, silencing her, but he never slowed his pace. He drove into her, filling her so deeply and completely that stars blurred her vision. She forgot all the reasons why she should resist this.

Her head fell back, and a wave of pleasure consumed her, her walls pulsating around his cock. He tasted her parted lips, and with a few more quick thrusts, his muscles tensed. He throbbed inside her, releasing himself with a sated groan. Staying in her warmth, he pushed all the way into her one more time.

She lay on the mattress in silence, panting while the corner of her mouth rose.

Kaiden drew himself out of her, glanced between them, and grinned. "I think I made a mess." He dressed quickly, then grabbed the basin and a clean cloth. He squeezed out the excess water and made his way to her.

Kaiden wiped the damp towel over her skin. "I'm yours, Blaise. I hope you know that."

His words caused her chest to constrict. He'd already risked so much just rescuing her from the Terrenmis Mountains.

"You could die, you know," she blurted.

He stared at her for a few seconds. "Is that supposed to deter me?" He tossed the cloth into the basin.

Her brow wrinkled. "Yes, but I know it won't because you're a stubborn ass."

Kaiden sat next to her. "You're right about that."

If keeping her loved ones at arm's length meant they stayed safe, she would endure the aching loneliness weighing in her heart. She'd not realized that being queen would isolate her from the people she wanted to be close to. "There's a lot going on right now…"

He placed his hand over hers and intertwined their fingers. A smirk tugged at the corners of his mouth. "Okay."

She tilted her head. "You're not going to fight me on this?"

"No. I don't want to pressure you into a decision you're not ready to make." His eyes locked on hers for what seemed like the millionth time that night. "Come on, let's get some sleep."

"Your Majesty? May I come in?" Nira's voice came from outside the tent the next day.

Kaiden had left early that morning to find Mathias.

"Yes, come in," Blaise announced, standing from the bed.

Nira strode in, her limp barely noticeable now. She had a change of clothes and a towel hanging from her arm. "I'm not disturbing you, am I?"

"No. I was just resting."

"This won't take long. I just wanted a quick word."

Blaise nodded. "Okay." She needed to get to Jynx before she suffered her wrath. Kaiden should be gone until the afternoon. *I just need to wait for the right moment. I'll go to the cartographer's tent to find a map with Chaos Island on it.*

"Am I going to be punished?" Nira asked as though she couldn't contain herself anymore.

Blaise furrowed her brow. "Punished? For what?"

Nira laid her change of clothes on the bed. "I wasn't there at your coronation. I should've been. But I found Mathias, and the next thing I knew, we were being chased. Everything happened so fast."

Blaise stepped closer. "None of that was your burden. I don't want you to feel responsible for anything that happened. And no, you won't be punished. You were simply in the wrong place at the wrong time."

Nira's usually stoic face expressed relief. She loosed a breath and curtsied. "Thank you, Your Majesty."

"Will you take back your place as my handmaiden?"

Nira seemed to hesitate for a second. "Actually, I would very much like to be part of the Alchyra."

Blaise's brow rose. "Are you sure? A soldier's life isn't an easy one."

Nira shifted her weight to one leg and held her arm. "I'm sure. If I had proper training, I'd be of better use to you."

Blaise turned away and paced a few steps. "Very well. I'll speak with Zade about training you immediately. Truthfully, we'll need all the help we can get if we're going to claim Balam back."

"It's a miracle you escaped." Nira tilted her head.

"Kaiden and I wouldn't have if it weren't for—" Blaise cleared her throat, becoming lightheaded just thinking about how close they'd come to death. "His wings."

"And how, precisely, did he get those?" Nira asked.

"Zade said it's because I'm his aniivasei," Blaise replied.

Nira's blue eyes widened. "Wow. Are congratulations in order?"

Blaise took her hair out of the messy bun, glancing at Nira. "Yes? No? We haven't had the chance to talk about it. My trust is fragile these days."

"Allow me, Your Majesty." Nira picked up the comb from next to the basin on the table, then gestured to the mattress. Once Blaise sat, Nira moved behind her and brushed through her thick dark hair. "Well, I certainly haven't done anything to earn your trust."

Blaise cocked a brow. "Are you saying I shouldn't trust you?"

"No, I was merely stating the obvious." Nira was gentle in untangling the mess that was Blaise's hair. "But I want to be someone you feel you can trust."

Blaise believed she could trust Nira despite what had happened with Mathias. Nira had been trying to do the right thing, and it wasn't her fault they'd been falsely accused.

Blaise went on a rant about what had happened in the sanctum the day of the coronation and everything after, except the part about her sister. Nira sat there in silence, working the last of the tangles out.

"Well?" Blaise finally asked.

"I'm processing," Nira murmured. If she was surprised, she didn't show it.

Blaise started to wonder if she'd made the right decision in telling her about all the past events.

That thought was quickly snuffed when Nira said, "If this is a secret, it's safe with me."

Blaise faced her with a kind smile. "Thank you." She wrapped Nira in her arms.

"You really shouldn't be hugging me in this state. I haven't bathed yet," Nira mused, coaxing herself free.

Blaise chuckled. "Go on. We'll talk more later."

Nira picked up the clothes and towel, then walked out.

Zade stopped by the tent to give Blaise the book she'd found in the archives of Balam. "You should keep this close," he said.

Blaise took it from him and hugged it to her chest. "I've been trying. Thank you." Zade turned to leave, but she stopped him. "Wait. Something has been happening between me and Kaiden. It's like he's been relieving me of my excess akrani somehow."

"Relieving you?"

She nodded. "Does it have to do with our bond?"

Zade raised a brow. "From what I know, only a certain bloodline of ellorians have that capability. It sounds like he's an enophii. He can take akrani from you without killing you."

"How many ellorian bloodlines are there?" she asked, a curious look on her face.

"I only know of three. The satrevo serve Colvyr directly, mandistiri are the warriors of nehveina, and the iipiretis ensure justice is served throughout the realm." Zade took a breath. "I believe it's the mandistiri bloodline that has the gift of enophii."

Blaise frowned. "I thought you said they were the warriors?"

"They are. We should speak about it more with Kaiden present. I need to get the troops in order now." Zade bowed and said no more about it, leaving the tent.

She wanted to know more about Kaiden and his ellorian bloodline and what he could do. Every question she asked just led to more questions. She let out a heavy breath and threw the book onto the large bed.

Blaise stood in the middle of the round tent for a moment longer, gazing at the black leather-bound book lying on the plush mattress. There had been so many things occupying her mind that she hadn't had time to read its contents.

She strode toward the bed and sank into the softness of the burgundy covers. Her hand trembled over the book at the thought of what truths it could contain. Part of her wanted it to remain secret, but the other part was desperate to unlock the information. She picked it up and stared. Taking one final breath, she peeled it open to the first page.

It's blank . . .

She flipped through more pages.

The whole fucking thing is blank!

Blaise slammed the book shut and tossed it to the floor.

23
MATHIAS

ATHIAS CHERISHED THE WARMTH OF the midmorning sun on his walk to the stream a short distance away from camp. He stood on the bank, the scent of fresh mountain water filling his nostrils. He slipped off his tunic and trousers, washing them. He laid them out to dry on a nearby boulder.

He walked into the icy stream and gasped, the shock stopping him from going any deeper. While scrubbing the dye out of his hair, he looked down at the small scar on his chest. An arrow had nearly pierced his heart once, in this very forest. He found it amusing Nira had been the one to heal it.

"Are you almost done?" The irritation in Nira's voice stung.

He faced her. Despite the dirt on her dress and her frizzy hair, she was still beautiful; she was *always* beautiful. Blood rushed straight to his cock. He sank his lower half into the water, hoping she hadn't noticed. "No. I'm not done." He scowled.

"How much longer?" Her eyes were averted from his nude form. She placed a hand on her hip, holding her change of clothes and towel in the other.

"Here's an idea. Why don't you go farther down and wash there?" He turned his back to her, wishing his cursed hard-on away. *Traitor.*

She sighed. "The water's too rough."

He smirked. "That sounds like a personal problem."

She groaned. "Why do you have to be such an asshole?"

"I was afraid you hadn't noticed."

There was nothing but silence for a long moment. Mathias looked over his shoulder at Nira.

Her eyes were squinted, staring into the trees. "What is that?"

"What?" He faced her and started walking toward the bank. Thick black mist drifted between the trees, enveloping the forest in darkness.

Mathias wasted no time in dragging himself through the current to Nira, water sloshing everywhere. He forced her to the ground, shielding her body with his. He supported himself on his forearms, gazing intently into her cobalt eyes. The cloud flowed over them, dissipating into nothingness.

"You okay?" His focus drifted to her dusty-pink lips.

"Fine." Her eyes widened, and it took him a few seconds to figure out why. His half-hard cock was pressed firmly against her inner thigh.

The corner of his mouth rose.

"Ugh, get off." She shoved at his chest.

He climbed to his feet and slipped on his trousers, adjusting himself in the process. "I would love to. Care to give me a hand?"

She rolled her eyes, smoothing out her skirt. "You're a pig."

Mathias scanned the thicket, spotting two figures lying on the damp mossy ground. He rushed over and examined each of their faces, immediately recognizing one of the men.

"Gods, it's Isaac." Mathias checked their pulses. "They're alive."

Nira knelt on her heels next to Isaac's unconscious body. She rubbed her palms together, something she'd always done before using her gitros. Mathias admired how she never hesitated to help.

She hovered her palms over Isaac's chest, and dark strands of akrani drifted from them. "Get help. I'll stay with them."

Mathias hesitated. He didn't know how safe it was for her, didn't know if anyone was following Isaac and the strange man.

Nira glared at him. "What're you waiting for? Go."

With a huff, Mathias tossed his tunic on and sprinted toward camp. He passed the guards at the entrance and spotted Zade striding out of the war tent.

"General Zade!" Mathias ran up to him and proceeded

to tell him about the two unconscious men near the stream. After calling a small squad of Alchyra, Zade followed Mathias through the trees. The soldiers trailed behind with stretchers.

On their way out, Kaiden fell into stride. Mathias summarized what had happened and who he and Nira had found.

Mathias's legs ached from pushing wayward branches out of his path and leaping over fallen tree trunks. When they arrived, Isaac was barely regaining consciousness. Nira lay in the dirt, passed out. Mathias clenched his fists, chest tightening the longer he stared at Nira's unmoving body. *Did she use all her akrani on them?* He ran to her side. She had risked her life by pushing the limits of her abilities. He could only hope she recovered from this.

The Alchyra hauled Isaac and the tall dark-haired man into camp. Mathias recognized his bloodstained sentinel's armor but had never met him. Something about the man Kaiden called Elric left an uneasy feeling in Mathias's gut.

Mathias cradled Nira's limp body against his chest, her warmth seeping into him. He fought against the soreness in his muscles, carrying her through the forest.

"Do you want me to take over, Mathias?" Kaiden was a short distance behind, helping Zade and two other men lug Elric along.

Mathias narrowed his eyes on his best friend. "I have her, thanks." He adjusted her in his arms, and despite the ache in his legs, he kept a steady pace.

They rushed through the cluster of tents toward the doma gitros not far from the entrance. Mathias carried

Nira inside and requested a bed for her. A healer led him to a clean empty cot. With great care, Mathias laid her down.

The healer examined Nira. "What happened?"

"I'm not entirely sure, but she was using her gitros." Mathias stood next to her cot. "I think she might've over-exerted herself."

"Unfortunately, there's not much I can do for her." The akrani gitros started to walk away.

Mathias grabbed his arm, stopping him. "What do you mean there isn't much you can do?"

"An akrani gitros cannot heal their own kind—not without suffering dire repercussions. If I try to heal her, we could both die from repulsion," the man said.

Mathias nodded. He had learned of repulsion while he was a squire. When two akrani could not come together in harmony, the energies are negated. They become volatile and destructive, especially to its wielder.

"I'm sorry." The man bowed and took his leave.

Mathias sat at Nira's bedside. He checked the pulse in her neck. *Still strong. Good.* He brushed the strands of hair from her beautiful face.

He scanned his surroundings. Two rows of cots lined the large tent. Isaac had been assigned to the cot directly across from Nira's.

Kaiden strode up to her bed and cleared his throat. "Is she okay?"

Mathias glanced at him. "She will be."

"The healers said Isaac and Elric will live," Zade said, approaching them. His silver armor clinked with each step. "And if it weren't for Nira, Isaac would've probably died."

Mathias's gaze went to her once more. "It was reckless. And I plan to tell her that when she wakes."

Kaiden crossed his arms, and the corner of his mouth cocked up, but he remained quiet. Mathias glared at him, knowing he was holding back some snide remark.

"Isaac's awake." Zade said, then strode across the tent to the young sentinel's side.

Mathias was good at reading Kaiden's expressions and body language. It was both a blessing and a curse. "Just say what you're thinking." His voice dripped with annoyance.

Kaiden placed a heavy hand on his shoulder. "Maybe later. She's waking up." He walked over to check on Isaac.

Nira's eyes fluttered open and met Mathias's irritated face. "What happened?" she rasped, pushing herself onto her forearms.

"You almost killed yourself." He stood, balling his hands into fists.

She rolled her eyes and straightened into a sitting position with a huff. "You're being overdramatic."

"No, I'm not. You almost died, Nira. You do have limits, you know," he scolded.

She kicked her legs over the edge of the bed. "Of course I do." She ran her hand through her long dark hair, flipping it to one side.

"So, what? You just ignore them?" He helped her stand.

She struggled at first, placing a hand on his chest, steadying herself. "I don't like failing."

"Even if it kills you?" His voice rose, and his hold on her tightened.

Her brow furrowed, those royal-blue eyes still dull as she gazed at him. "Why does it matter? You hate me, remember?"

"I don't hate you, Nira." He couldn't believe he had admitted it.

An unreadable expression crept onto her face. "I can't do this with you right now." She pulled away and made her slow way over to Isaac.

Despite all Mathias's experience with women, he couldn't figure Nira out. Whenever he tried to get close to her, she'd find a way to push him away. *Why though? Maybe she just enjoys torturing me.* He let it go for the moment and joined the rest of them on the other side of the tent.

"It wasn't Isaac's fault," Nira said to the group. "It was his."

Kaiden frowned. "Elric?"

Nira rolled her shoulders back. "I'm not sure what kind of akrani he has, but I can sense the darkness he wields. The terror." Her hands trembled.

Mathias frowned. "But it's the gods who gave us akrani. And there is no god of darkness or terror."

Nira glanced at him. "That's true, but I've never encountered that kind of akrani." Her cobalt eyes drifted to Elric, who was still unconscious on the cot.

"Elric seems to have a pretty good hold of it. We wouldn't have escaped without it," Isaac added.

"Can you heal him, Nira?" Zade asked.

Nira loosed a breath. "If I can get past his akrani, I can."

"You should rest before you try again," Mathias interjected, shooting her a severe look. He didn't expect her to concede, but she did, although hesitantly. A small victory for him, though he feared he would pay for it later.

Mathias pushed the thought away and sat on Isaac's bedside. "How're you feeling?"

"Fine. Thank the gods I remembered the tunnel passages in the dungeon." The corner of his mouth rose.

A few more minutes of small talk passed. Mathias noticed Nira swaying. He rushed to her side. Just as her knees buckled, he wrapped one arm around her waist.

"You okay?" He helped her straighten.

She nodded, placing her palm to her forehead.

"Let's step outside for a moment," he suggested.

Mathias led her out of the tent and over to a water barrel just a few feet away. He sat her on a wooden bench. When he knew she was steady, he retrieved a ladle of water and gave it to her.

The soft breeze rustled through the trees and whipped at the tents surrounding them. Despite the obstinate irritation Nira caused him, he found himself wanting to be near her more and more.

"Thank you," she said, her voice bland.

"You're welcome."

Mathias sat beside her, wanting to know so much more about her.

How was she feeling? About him?

Something seemed to have shifted in their relationship since they'd left Haven, but he couldn't figure out what.

"I'm staying here to train with the Alchyra." Nira gazed ahead at the soldiers sparring in the green clearing.

Mathias was speechless. No sarcastic remark. Nothing. What in gehheina was going on with him? He met her eyes. "When did this come about?"

Her brow furrowed slightly. "I asked the queen to let me join her army so I can be of better use to her."

"You can heal people. How much more useful can you be?" he asked. Audrey immediately came to mind. "You shouldn't have volunteered yourself so willingly. Do you have a death wish or something?"

"No. Do you have something against me protecting myself?"

If resolve could cut, hers had slashed at his heart.

"I need to be able to fight," she continued. "Why else would I want to train?"

"You can learn how to fight without joining the ranks."

She scoffed. "It's nice to know you don't believe in my competence."

He scooted closer to her on the bench, straddling it. "That's not what I meant."

She stole a glance at him, then averted her eyes once more. "We don't have to do this anymore."

His eyebrows came together. "Do what?"

She shook her head. "Pretend. Continue acting like we're together."

The thought of being separated from her disturbed him because he had stopped pretending before they'd left Haven.

Nira interrupted his thoughts. "Are you afraid I'll kick your ass in a duel?"

"No. Although that *would* be terrifying." He feigned a shiver, and a corner of her mouth rose. "By the gods, is that a smile?"

Her lips pursed. "I don't know what you're talking about."

He grinned, his fingers brushing a strand of hair from her face. "You're beautiful when you smile."

Her brow rose. "So, I'm ugly when I don't?"

He huffed. "Why can't you just take a gods damn compliment?"

"Is that what you call a compliment?"

He leaned in, his blue eyes meeting hers. "Why do you always make things so difficult for me?"

"You would lose interest otherwise." Her face paled as though she realized what she'd just said.

He tilted his head to the side, his smile widening. "What did you just say?"

She cleared her throat and stood. "I should get back in there." She started walking away.

He grabbed her wrist, bringing her to a halt. "Not so fast, sweetness." He rose from the bench and adjusted his hold on her. Towering over her, he stepped closer until they were mere inches apart. "Please. Don't enlist."

She met his gaze. "Look, you're not my husband anymore. You can go on with your life and be with whomever you please now."

He let go of her arm. Searching her eyes, he was desperate to find some kind of feelings for him. "Who says I want to go back to that life?"

She didn't falter. "Please. A few weeks in a pretend marriage and you're suddenly a changed man? I saw the way you looked at those women at the Scarlet Crown."

His face came within a hair's breadth of hers. "That's interesting, because you haven't paid any attention to the way I've been looking at you."

She licked her lips.

The temptation to lean in and kiss her was palpable. *How would she react?* He lingered there. Her chest heaved, gaze drifting to his mouth. He didn't know whose pulse was thrumming faster.

"What we had wasn't real." Her eyes became glossy. She turned away from him, hugging herself.

Something inside him shattered from those words. No other woman had ever made him feel that way before. And he couldn't figure out what was so gods damned special about Nira. He'd been attracted to many women, but none had challenged him like she did.

Well, it's real now. He ran a hand through his blond hair and turned to walk away. Where was he going to go?

Anywhere away from these wretched feelings.

24

KAIDEN

KAIDEN STEPPED OUT OF THE INFIRMARY tent, stretching his arms overhead. Carrying Elric's heavy body through Meliwe had been no easy task. The leaves of the cypress swayed back and forth amongst the crisp ocean breeze. He gazed around the area in search of Mathias.

Kaiden spotted Nira sitting on a wooden bench nearby. He strolled up to her. She stared far off into the distance. "How're you feeling, Lady Nira?" he asked.

She peered up at him. "Better. Thank you, Captain."

Kaiden looked around once more. "Where'd Mathias go?"

She told him he'd headed toward the ocean cliffs with a sword in hand. Kaiden thanked her and darted in the same direction, his borrowed blade clinking on his hip. Mathias was probably practicing his sword techniques, which usually meant something was bothering him.

Mathias stood near the cliff's edge, swinging his sword with precision, nothing but pure concentration on his face. Waves crashed into the rocky cliffside, and the salty air hit Kaiden's face.

Mathias paused, glancing at Kaiden, then continued in silence.

Kaiden kept his distance, arms crossed. "What's wrong?"

Mathias lunged at his imaginary opponent. "What makes you think something's wrong?"

"Well, for one, you're training. You hate training." Kaiden couldn't help but smirk. "Second, you look pissed."

"I just needed to clear my head," Mathias muttered, coming to a stop and staring out into the blue-green sea.

Kaiden unsheathed his sword. "How long has it been since we've sparred?"

Mathias shrugged and turned to him. "A few months."

Kaiden stood a few feet in front of his best friend. "And I won that match, if I recall."

"Only because you cheated, as always." Mathias pointed his sword at him.

The corner of Kaiden's mouth rose. "You have no room to talk." He made the first move with a downward strike.

Mathias blocked. Their blades crossed with a clang. He shoved Kaiden away and sidestepped.

Kaiden struck him horizontally. Mathias parried. With a huff, Kaiden kicked Mathias in the stomach with his boot. Mathias grunted and rolled backward on one shoulder, landing on his feet. Kaiden lunged, and Mathias met him blade to blade. With a twist of his sword, Mathias knocked the weapon from his hand. Kaiden turned hard and flared one wing out, hitting Mathias full force in the chest and knocking him to his ass.

"That was a cheap shot." Mathias coughed, sprawled out on the green grass.

Kaiden picked up his sword and sheathed it. He rested his hands on his hips, standing over Mathias. "Are you ready to talk yet?"

Mathias heaved. "Just finish me off already."

"Gods, you're so dramatic." Kaiden offered his hand, and Mathias took it. Kaiden yanked him to his feet.

Mathias stood, staring at the rolling ocean below. Sweat coated his brow, and his chest rose and fell. With one deep inhale, he chucked his sword toward the tempestuous ocean.

Kaiden's eyebrows rose. The weapon soared through the sky and hit the cerulean water, waves swallowing it in an instant. "Well, that was unnecessary."

"This is the last time I let that woman get under my fucking skin," Mathias blurted. He blew out a breath, wiping the sweat from his forehead with his sleeve.

Kaiden had an idea who he was talking about. "Nira?"

"She's infuriating."

"Okay. Explain."

"I can't." Mathias kicked a rock off the cliff.

Kaiden grinned. "You can't or won't?"

Mathias tilted his head toward the sky. "She's not my type."

"I didn't know you had a type. Thought you just went around sticking it in anything," Kaiden teased.

Mathias rolled his eyes. "Fuck you."

"This isn't about me."

Mathias heaved a heavy sigh. "I don't know what I'm supposed to do. I kind of told her how I felt."

"What do you mean, *kind of*?" Kaiden asked, eyeing Mathias warily.

Mathias shrugged. "Well, I basically told her I hadn't been looking at anyone else but her."

Kaiden cocked a brow. "You *basically* told her? Mat, you either told her or you didn't."

"I don't fucking know what I said anymore. She's insufferable," Mathias exclaimed.

Damn. Kaiden had never seen his best friend like this before. He was completely smitten, and the poor guy didn't have a clue how to handle it—not that Kaiden knew any better. "For someone who has a plethora of experience with women, you're kind of an idiot."

Mathias deadpanned, "Thanks. That's no help at all."

"Women are a beautiful mystery." Kaiden stretched out his arms and wings, nearly hitting Mathias on the back of the head.

Mathias ducked at the last second. "Hey, watch it." He stared at Kaiden's rustling wings. "Never in a million years would I have thought my best friend would end up with something like those."

Kaiden glanced back at them. "Yeah, well . . . I'm just as amazed as you are."

"How about we test them out?" Mathias had a mischievous grin on his face.

"What? Here?" Kaiden laughed. "What do you want me to do, dive off this cliff?"

"Unless you can take off from here?"

Kaiden tried to flap, but for some reason they wouldn't sync up with each other. He let out a frustrated breath and considered Mathias's suggestion. "This is a stupid idea," he said, running a hand down his face.

"It's not the worst one I've had."

"This is true," Kaiden muttered. He inched forward and peeked over at the waves crashing into the rocky cliff-side. It was definitely good motivation to get them working together. *Why am I even considering this?*

"You want me to give you a little push?" Mathias rushed Kaiden and pushed him toward the edge.

Kaiden slid on the gravel. At the last second, Kaiden turned and caught the playful gleam in Mathias's eyes. He reached out, grabbing Mathias's arm before he dropped over the side of the cliff. "If I'm going, you're coming with me."

"Asshole!" Mathias screamed.

Kaiden's wings seemed to react faster than last time. They spread and tilted, catching the wild sea breeze and lifting them into the golden sunset. Willing his wings to obey, Kaiden flew even higher above a patch of white clouds.

"I hate you," Mathias bellowed through the wind. His arms were wrapped around Kaiden's torso, clutching for dear life. If he were anybody else, this would've been awkward.

"It worked," Kaiden mused.

"We've established that. Can we go back down? I think I'm going to be sick."

The corner of Kaiden's mouth rose, and he tucked his wings, taking a nosedive toward land. Mathias screamed curse words Kaiden hadn't even known existed. He extended his wings, catching the air to glide above the cliff. He dropped Mathias a short distance from the ground.

Kaiden's feet touched down, and he slid to a stop, the gravel crunching beneath his boots. *That went better than I expected.*

Mathias ran to the cliffside and doubled over, puking into the ocean. He straightened and dusted off his trousers and tunic, then stomped up to Kaiden and slugged him in the shoulder.

Kaiden just laughed, not fazed by Mathias's reaction. "At least I know how they work now."

"I never want to experience that again," Mathias murmured. "But thanks for getting that woman off my mind."

A fogbank rolled over the sea. "We should head back before that gets here," Kaiden suggested.

Mathias groaned. "Fine."

They trod back toward basecamp at a steady pace.

Kaiden's mind wandered. *I've been away for too long. I hope Blaise doesn't need me.* Flashes of her death played out in his mind. A sharp pain thrummed through his heart. He had to prevent that future. *At any cost.*

"What's going on in that head of yours?" Mathias kept his pace.

Kaiden shook his head. "You're going to think I'm crazy."

Mathias stopped and crossed his arms. "Nothing's crazier than those wings."

Kaiden faced him, inhaling a deep breath. "I had a vision."

"A vision."

"Yes. It was all a blur, but there was this crystal and white flames and Blaise's body . . ." Kaiden swallowed the lump rising in his throat. "Lying on the sanctum floor. I think she was dead."

Mathias's brow furrowed. "So, are you trying to tell me you have satori?"

"The hell with the satori. I'm telling you Blaise is going to die. I can only assume it's a potential future, and I don't know how to alter it—if it can be changed," Kaiden said.

"Do you think Zade might be able to give you some sort of explanation?" Mathias asked, continuing toward camp.

Kaiden followed. "Possibly. He knows a lot about everything. There's just so much I don't know. My mother, our history, my father's secrets, and what the hell I'm supposed to do with all of it."

Mathias placed his hand on Kaiden's shoulder. "That's a heavy burden, but you're not alone in this."

"Thanks, Mat. You're not as bad as they say you are." Kaiden clapped a hand on his back while they strolled through Meliwe.

They neared the outskirts of camp, the sounds of battle echoing throughout the woods. Metal clanged against metal. Men and women screamed out in agony. Caught by surprise, Kaiden started running toward the fighting, Mathias on his heels. *Why in gehheina are the Alchyra fighting one another?*

It wasn't a field exercise. Bodies and blood were strewn across the forest floor.

Mathias wasted no time grabbing a sword from the nearest weapons rack.

"I need to find Blaise," Kaiden shouted, rushing through the melee.

"I'll go for Nira," Mathias bellowed.

Two Alchyra charged Kaiden. Their faces remained stoic and eerie, completely blank as obsidian eyes stared at him. One Alchyra swung high, the other swinging low. Kaiden managed to dodge one strike and parry the other. Four more armed men surrounded him. Two rushed in.

Kaiden shot both wings out and spun, sweeping the men off their feet. *These are handier than I thought. What in gehheina is wrong with everyone?* Alchyra fought Alchyra throughout the site. *Is this some kind of akrani?*

Kaiden sprinted through camp, slicing and swinging at oncoming soldiers with only one goal in mind: *Blaise.*

"Captain." Zade caught up to him, bloody sword in hand.

"Why are they fighting one another?" Kaiden shouted, coming to a stop.

They stood back-to-back, fighting the onslaught. Zade ducked while Kaiden lunged over his head, plunging his sword into a soldier's neck. Straightening, Zade tripped another and stabbed him through a weak point in his armor.

"I don't know. I think they're possessed," Zade managed to say, dodging a strike. With one final blow, Kaiden killed the last blank-faced Alchyra.

They stood near the firepit in the center of camp. Kaiden scanned the area, taking in the bodies. This definitely wasn't going to help their numbers. He hoped none of the possessed soldiers had escaped.

Zade stopped an Alchyra passing by and said, "You there, take a small squad through the forest and secure the perimeter."

Without any questions, the young woman obeyed.

Zade cleaned off his weapon and sheathed it. He just stood there, staring at his fallen comrades.

Mathias strode up with Nira trailing behind. "What in gehheina was that about?"

Isaac and Elric walked up from the opposite direction.

"Everyone okay?" Zade examined each one of them.

"For the most part," Elric said.

When did he wake up?

"You should be resting still," Kaiden told Elric, though he was glad he'd regained consciousness.

Elric held his side. "I'll be fine, Captain. Like a spring cock." He smirked and ran a hand through his dark hair.

Kaiden asked, "Does anyone know why this happened?"

Elric stepped forward. "The algeaa did this."

Kaiden recalled reading about the creatures of gehheina in the Balam archive. "I didn't know they had the ability to take control of someone's body."

"Unfortunately, I've seen it firsthand," Elric replied.

A sense of emptiness overwhelmed Kaiden. The familiar excruciating void returned with a vengeance. "Has anyone seen Blaise?"

"She was in her tent," Nira said.

Zade shook his head. "No, she wasn't there. I checked."

Kaiden's heart sank. "We need to find her."

Zade gathered units of Alchyra and ordered them to search the camp for the queen.

Some time later, the lead Alchyra returned from searching the small base. "Negative findings on Queen Blaise, General. And all the dead have been accounted for."

"How many casualties?" Zade asked.

"We've lost nearly half our battalion," replied the soldier.

Nira asked, "If she's not with the dead or in the camp, then where is she?"

Kaiden glanced at Elric. "Would these algeaa kidnap her?"

"No. Their purpose is to inflict pain and torment the souls of the dead in gehheina. They can only leave the second level through an open portal," Elric said, a worried look in his blue-gray eyes.

"Okay, tell me more," Kaiden demanded, standing near the unused firepit.

"The problem is once the algeaa escape, they're free to terrorize the living." Elric folded his arms. "There's a portal open somewhere, and if we don't close it soon, the worst of gehheina could escape."

Kaiden let out a breath. "What does that mean for Blaise?"

"I don't know what it means for her, but she is the queen, and I don't think she would want her kingdom to suffer." Elric met each of the eyes in the group.

Isaac cleared his throat and raised his hand. "I might have some useful information."

Kaiden's attention snapped to Isaac, and he stalked toward him. "Why didn't you say something sooner?"

"I didn't want to interrupt," Isaac muttered, stepping back.

"Well? Out with it," Kaiden ordered.

Isaac glanced at Mathias and Nira, and then his frantic gaze focused on Kaiden. "Before the fight broke out, I saw her leaving the cartographer's tent."

"And you're just now telling me this? It would've been useful ten minutes ago." Kaiden groaned.

"I'm sorry," Isaac whined.

Kaiden shot him a severe look, raking his hand through his hair. *Chaos Island.* He grumbled, "I have an idea of where she went." *What in gehheina is she thinking?*

Kaiden couldn't understand why Blaise hadn't come to him before leaving. Warmth rose in his chest, and his nostrils flared. He ran his palms down his face and muttered, "This woman is going to be the death of me."

Mathias stared at Nira. "I share your sentiment."

She shot him a narrow-eyed glare, then turned to Kaiden. "Where do you think she's going?"

"I think she's going to Chaos Island," Kaiden replied.

"Chaos Island?" Zade asked. "Why would the queen need to go there?"

Kaiden looked Zade straight in the eyes. "Jynx."

Isaac's brow furrowed. "What does the goddess of chaos have to do with the queen of Balam?"

"Jynx has been communicating with Blaise," Kaiden murmured.

"What do you mean?" Zade asked, taking a step toward him.

"Blaise told me Jynx came to her while she was imprisoned in the Terrenmis Mountains," Kaiden said. "The goddess told her Amasu is trying to escape. My thought is Blaise thinks she can prevent that from happening."

Elric stared at Kaiden for a few seconds. "If Amasu is trying to escape and the algeaa are already here, that means he's not far from his end goal."

"I need to go after her. It could be a trap." The more Kaiden talked, the more distant she became.

Mathias nodded. "I'll go with you."

"I don't think you'd enjoy the flight." Kaiden winked at him. "Besides, I need you to stay here and help the general relocate the remaining Alchyra. We can't take any chances staying near Balam." He turned to Zade. "Head toward the Azureden Mountains. Set up camp there until I return. There's a peace treaty between our kingdoms. King Vaughn should protect your people."

Kaiden exchanged glances with all of them before landing on Zade again. "I've been meaning to speak with you." They walked toward the outskirts of camp before he continued, "I had a vision back in Balam."

"So, your akrani has surfaced. That's good," Zade said.

Kaiden stopped, head tilted toward the darkened sky. "I beg to differ."

"Tell me about this vision," Zade said, leaning against a tree trunk.

Kaiden told him every detail of the vision, including the mysterious black crystal. "Is that the future I have to look forward to?"

"It could be. The future isn't set in stone like the past," Zade said.

"So, you're saying I could change it?" Kaiden massaged his nape. His head ached just thinking about the complexities of his satori. The situation would've been so much simpler if he didn't have it.

Zade grinned. "Would it *really* be simpler?"

Dammit. Kaiden had let his mental barrier down. He glared at Zade. "Don't do that."

"Anyway, I'm saying the future has many paths. They connect and cross, but our choices are what determine our outcome." Zade studied Kaiden for a moment. "If you want to alter the future, you're going to have to make life-altering choices," he said, an amused look on his face. "You should get going. She couldn't have gone far."

Kaiden asked one more question. "The crystal from my vision. Do you think it's the same one King Theod is searching for?"

"I don't have all the answers, Captain." Zade pushed off the trunk and headed back to camp. "Bring *my* queen back in one piece."

25

BLAISE

LAISE SPRINTED THROUGH THE FOREST, leaping over fallen trees, her lungs aching. She pushed through the burn in her legs and avoided low-hanging branches. Heart pulsing in her ears, she pushed through shrubs. The waves of the ocean crashed against the cliffside. The mist cooled her cheeks.

She peered out at the moonlit sea, tightening her grip on the strap of the satchel she wore. *What in gehheina am I doing?*

Gods, those three weeks of being imprisoned had taken a toll on her stamina. These tumultuous waters were going to eat her alive.

Moonlight silhouetted Chaos Island a few miles off the coast. Blaise stood on the cliff's edge, her chest tight with dread.

She inhaled, trying to access her well of akrani to contact Jynx. Steadying her breathing, she focused, thinking of Jynx. Her mind tried to find the invisible path to the goddess, but nothing worked.

"Jynx!" she screamed in the direction of the island. "I'm here. Now what?"

No response.

Blaise groaned, dropping to her knees. "A lot of fucking help you are . . ." Maybe if she stared hard enough, the goddess would appear.

A large shadow flew overhead. She jerked her gaze up, but the sky was dark. Standing, she rushed toward a clump of bushes to hide. She held her breath, listening to every sound, hoping whatever the creature was would pass.

Her heart thrummed in her throat, and she clenched and unclenched her fists. She attempted to reach into her well of akrani once more, but all she got was tingles throughout her body.

"Blaise. What the fuck are you doing?" Kaiden's voice resounded through the wind and surf.

She yelped and leaped out of the bushes, ready to run. Standing a few feet behind her, Kaiden's form towered over her. She felt a wave of relief upon seeing him. Her eyes narrowed. "What're you doing here?"

He paced closer, a vein pulsing in his neck. "What am *I* doing here? I thought we agreed to do this together."

She looked away, turning to the salty sea once more. "I'm sorry, but I need to do this on my own."

"You're so fucking stubborn. You know that?"

With a wrinkled brow, she faced him. "I am not. I'm trying to protect the people I love. My kingdom. I thought you'd be more understanding."

He gripped her arms, holding her in place and staring into her eyes. "This isn't a choice you can make for me. I *want* to be here by your side. I *want* us to fight for each other—with each other."

Kaiden didn't understand the risks involved. She couldn't believe she was admitting this.

"I can't stand the thought of losing you," she said, and her voice trembled.

He just stood there, staring. "I feel the same."

Suddenly aware of what she'd said, she averted her gaze. She wanted him safe. He probably thought she was acting childish about this whole situation. She couldn't have any more lives lost on her account. *Not if I can help it.*

Kaiden reached beneath her chin with his index finger and brought her focus back to his handsome face. "You should know by now that I'm not easy to kill. I mean, I did survive your lightning."

That roguish smirk on his face caused Blaise's lips to curve up. "It was only a little bolt. Most of it hit the troll, remember?"

He let out a light chuckle. His lips formed a straight line. He leaned forward and rested his forehead against hers. "You have to stop running from me, Blaise."

"I'm sorry," was all she could say.

"I would never stop looking for you. I would scour the fucking realms to find you." His words jolted her heart, permeating her soul and ingraining his commitment into her spirit.

Truth. She could feel every syllable was spoken from his heart. Akrani may have bound them together, but only true love would solidify it. And the sooner she accepted that, the better off they would be.

Kaiden cupped her face and pressed his lips to hers gently. "Are you ready to take to the sky with me?" he whispered against her mouth.

She couldn't help but melt into his embrace, cherishing the warmth that was Kaiden Atherton, her aniivasei. "On one condition."

"Anything."

"This is my duty. I need to know you'll follow my lead." She crossed her arms and stepped away from him.

His hazel eyes narrowed on her. With a sigh, he replied, "Fine. You have my word."

Heart pounding against her rib cage, she let him pull her against his body. She didn't dare peer over the edge of the cliff. Instead, her gaze went to the waxing moon.

Kaiden wrapped his arms around her. "Do you trust me?"

Blaise leaped, straddling his waist and interlocking her legs around him. "With all that I am."

He placed a reverent kiss in her hair before falling off toward the rocky cliffside.

All the air left her lungs, and the crisp sea breeze swept across her face. She couldn't scream—couldn't speak. She squeezed her eyes shut, and the roar of crashing waves filled her ears. *Did his wings catch the wind yet?*

For just an instant, she felt a sudden sinking in her stomach and an odd lightness in her head. She was no longer falling, but hanging from Kaiden, legs still encircling his waist.

"Blaise." Kaiden had held her tightly against him the entire time. "Open your eyes."

She raised one eyelid, then the other. She gasped, the cold air stinging her cheeks. Stars shone so brightly in the darkened sky they seemed to be within arm's reach. In the miles of ocean, shades of blue green glistened in the waxing moonlight. "Gods, it's beautiful."

Kaiden pulled back and gazed into her eyes. "My thoughts exactly."

They approached a small cluster of islands. The largest landmass had a stone temple built on the highest cliff top.

Drifting closer to the island, Kaiden steadied them. His wings fully extended, tilting to catch the air. He landed and skidded to a stop on the gravel without dropping Blaise.

"Impressive." She kissed his cheek.

His lips curved up into the biggest grin she'd ever seen. "Thank you."

The wild waves of the ocean contrasted with the serenity of the jungle surrounding the structure ahead. The architecture was angular and symmetrical with pitched red tile along the rooftops and sweeping corners. Each corner supported a stone head of the vissera. The clean lines gave Blaise a sense that Jynx's chaos could take on a more militant and calculated approach.

Dark clouds rolled in front of the moon, blocking the light. The scent of ozone filled Blaise's nose, and the sky rumbled. Lightning unfurled, cracking against the ground once, twice, three times.

Through a wisp of smoke, Jynx sauntered up to them.

Blaise placed herself between Kaiden and her sister, taking in the goddess's appearance. Her tight red curls flowed past her shoulders, and she wore no armor this time. A silky black gown draped over her tall curvy frame. The flowing fabric shimmered with blue flames that rose from the long train and up her body with each step.

Jynx strode up to them, her burgundy lips pulled tight. "Took you long enough, Little Flame." Her gaze went from Blaise to Kaiden. "Who do we have here?"

"My apologies, milady. This is Captain Kaiden Atherton." Blaise hoped the goddess would allow him to live.

Kaiden stepped beside Blaise, a resolute look on his face. "I'm her aniivasei."

Jynx placed a finger to her chin, curiosity filling her glowing red eyes. "He can stay. Come along." She turned on her heel and headed inside the massive structure.

Even though Blaise knew Jynx was her sister, she still questioned her motives. As a god, was Jynx capable of any selfless act? "I thought your temple was in Grelan Forest?"

Jynx glanced over her shoulder at Blaise. "It is. This was my first temple, but the pilgrimage was much too difficult for my followers. My brother, Colvyr, annoyed me into taking the one built in Grelan. That was before you stopped believing in us."

Blaise and Kaiden followed Jynx through the temple. Intricate designs were etched into the dark walls and polished obsidian floors, a story of how the goddess of chaos had come to be. Amidst the archaic aura of history, an unsettling eeriness hung in the air.

"So, what has Father been telling you?" Jynx asked, turning to face them.

Blaise stepped in front of the goddess, who was about six inches taller. "How do *you* know about that?"

"The chaos whispered his secret. And it was your blood that weakened the veil of the portal." Jynx crossed her arms.

Blaise tilted her head, eyebrows scrunching.

Jynx rolled her eyes. "The pool in the sanctum of the Balam fortress is a portal."

Blaise stood there, incapable of forming sentences.

Jynx took a step closer. "Blaise, once he regains his strength, he will come to claim his power. You will die, along with all you love."

Blaise swallowed and glanced at Kaiden, whose brow was furrowed.

"What am *I* supposed to do?" Blaise asked the goddess.

"You'll have one chance to close the portal," Jynx said, placing her hands on her hips.

"What if I don't get to the portal in time?" Blaise couldn't understand why Jynx had any faith in her.

"Then you'll have to kill him," Jynx said nonchalantly.

Blaise scoffed. "I can't kill a high god. Why can't you do any of these tasks?"

Jynx sighed. "My physical form cannot leave these islands. Plus, a god can't kill another god. It is an edict cemented by akrani and created by Amasu himself. But you are not a god; therefore, you *can* kill him. Now you see the primary reasons we are not to fraternize with realm dwellers." She gestured to one wall, at the depiction of Amasu weaving akrani and creating the laws of the gods. She turned away from them and continued down the corridor of the temple.

Blaise and Kaiden trailed behind.

"Aren't there any others like me who might be more qualified?" Blaise asked.

Jynx scoffed. "I certainly hope not."

"So . . . you don't know?" Kaiden asked.

Jynx glanced back at him with that annoyed look on her face. "I do not keep track of my siblings' playthings."

They turned the corner and entered a large circular room with tall, wide windows. The moonlight reflected off the dark floors, giving dim light to the space. Through the windows, the waves of the ocean crashed against the cliff below.

"This is where I will train you most of the time," Jynx said. She led them out of the room and through another corridor and into a chamber with two single beds. "This is where you two will sleep. *Separately.*"

Kaiden glanced at Blaise, a corner of his mouth rising. She blushed and shot him a piercing glare.

"There is a washroom just across the hall." Jynx pointed. She made a circular motion in the air with her hand, and a wild gust whipped around the room. Clothes flew in through the doorway, hitting Blaise and Kaiden in the chest and face. "Rest up. Training starts tomorrow."

Blaise retrieved the clothes that had fallen. "Wait. How long are you going to keep us here?"

"For as long as it takes," Jynx stated before walking through the thick wooden door, leaving Kaiden and Blaise to their own devices.

Kaiden examined the clothes Jynx had thrown at him: black trousers and a matching tunic. "These might be a bit tight on me."

Blaise knew she would have to help him customize the tunic to fit his wings.

She started toward the door, clothes hanging on one arm.

"Wait." Kaiden let out a breath. "What am I supposed to do while you're training?"

Blaise shrugged. "Maybe if you annoy her enough, she'll send you home."

He narrowed his hazel eyes. "Are you calling me annoying?"

Her gaze wandered the length of his body, fingertips tingling with the desire to touch him. She stepped closer until there was about a foot between them. "What're you going to do about it, *Captain*?"

He leaned in, his lips grazing the shell of her ear. "Unspeakable things, *Your Majesty*." He dropped the clothes to the floor and wrapped his arms around her waist, leaving gentle kisses along the curve of her neck.

Gods, his lips on her caused her mind to go blank. She hummed, and he bit down on her collarbone. She inhaled a sharp breath and felt his lips curve up against her skin.

This wasn't fair. He was using their attraction to each other to his advantage. *Stupid bond.*

He captured her lips with his, tongue entering her mouth. He held her tighter against him, and she molded herself to him.

She wanted to be his more than anything, but losing him would break her. He would be safer if she kept him at a distance. She broke the kiss, chest heaving. "We should probably stop."

He nodded, releasing her to slide down his body. "You can bathe first."

Escaping her urges, she didn't give herself the chance to change her mind about taking him then and there. She rushed out of the bedchamber and locked herself in the washroom.

Blaise had been at this all morning with no rest. The sun shone high noon, and sweat trickled down her temples. She hauled a sack full of sand across the beach, her chest heaving with each step. She tossed the bag onto the rest of the pile.

Jynx stood on the cliff's edge, monitoring Blaise, arms crossed. Strands of red curls drifted across the goddess's gleaming face. Her gaze locked on Blaise, giving no signal for rest.

She enjoys torturing me. Blaise could be doing worse exercises, like crawling through a foot of mud. She stared past the waves crashing onto the shore at the miles of ocean.

"I didn't tell you to stop," Jynx bellowed.

Blaise bit back a groan and continued hauling sandbags across the beach. Gods, her legs ached, and her lungs burned. She pushed through the fatigue, Kaiden coming to the forefront of her thoughts. His strong build was way more accustomed to this sort of training, though Blaise had always been athletic and taller than the average woman.

This is the strongest I've felt in a while. Blaise added the last bag to the pile, and then a bolt of lightning struck the beach a short distance from her. She spun on her heel, facing the settling smoke.

Jynx traipsed up to her through the settling smoke.

"Whoa . . . Will I be able to do that too?" Blaise rested her hands on her hips.

"Maybe one day, Little Flame."

Blaise huffed, stretching out her sore arms. "What's next?"

That smile stayed plastered on the goddess's face. "How's your defense?"

Blaise started to respond, but Jynx snapped her fingers. A small orange flame sparked into her palm and began to grow.

Blaise stumbled back. "What in gehheina are you doing?"

"You better start running. If you reach the temple before I get to you, you're safe." The goddess's eyes flickered in tandem with the flame she held. It took the shape of a chaotic sphere.

Blaise's chest tightened with panic. "Are you insane? I can't use my akrani right now."

"You're wasting time," Jynx said in a singsong voice.

"Fuck." Blaise took off toward the steep grade of the cliffside. She didn't even want to imagine what Jynx was going to do with that raging orb of fire. She was beginning to regret ever coming to this island.

Blaise climbed and climbed. The ball of fire collided into the rock mere feet from her. She slipped but managed to stabilize herself. Glancing down at the goddess and clinging to the rock, she screamed, "Are you trying to kill me?"

Jynx had already sparked another flame. "Enough talk. More action."

With aching limbs, Blaise pulled herself up to the top of the cliff. She rolled and landed on her feet. Her lungs burned, and she struggled to catch her breath. There wasn't time. She needed to get a move on. *I'm going to die here.*

Blaise burst into a sprint, crashing through the tropical foliage. Her foot caught on a vine, and she stumbled. Peering behind her, she discovered Jynx had used lightning to transport herself to the top of the cliff. The flame was still growing in her hand.

"Cheater." Blaise didn't stop. The red roof of the temple was within view. Pushing her way through the tree line, she spotted the stone steps a few paces away.

I'm going to make it.

Jynx's fireball hit the ground, barely missing Blaise's heels. Heat engulfed her from behind. The impact knocked Blaise onto her hands and knees, and she tumbled forward on her shoulder. A crippling wave of pain rippled through her entire body. She coughed and curled into the fetal position. All she could do was endure and hope it would pass.

Jynx approached, clicking her tongue in disappointment. "It seems you have a lot of work ahead of you."

"You cheated." Blaise peered up at her with bleary eyes.

"And you think Amasu will play fair? He'll kill you to take what he wants." Jynx grabbed Blaise's collar and yanked her to her feet. "I will not waste my time playing with you."

"You're right," Blaise muttered.

Jynx released her and massaged the space between her eyes. "Let's move on."

Blaise closed her eyes, and a tinge of dread trickled down her spine. Then again, that could've just been sweat.

26

KAIDEN

KAIDEN SPENT THE DAY EXPLORING CHAOS Island while Blaise was off training with Jynx. He returned at sunset. Blaise was fast asleep on one of the beds. Her long dark hair draped over the sides of her pillow, and she snored softly.

Kaiden settled onto the bed across from Blaise. Thoughts swirled through his mind. He tossed and turned for an hour, maybe more, before giving up on sleep. He walked down a few steps and found himself in the large kitchen. It had no windows, reminding him of a cave. The walls were dirt, the counters were carved from stone, and there was an open fireplace in the middle of the room.

Jynx sat at a wooden table in the corner, enjoying a pint of foamy gold liquid. "Care for a glass?" she asked without looking at him. A glass of that same color liquid appeared in his right hand. She gestured across the table. "Take a seat."

He joined her in staring at the fire roaring in the fireplace. Taking a sip from the glass, he savored the sweet, bitter ale. He swallowed, and the bubbles tickled his throat and settled in his stomach. "This is good. What is it?"

"Honey peach ale. My special recipe." Jynx still didn't look at him.

It had been a while since he'd enjoyed a nice ale. "Why aren't the other gods helping you stop Amasu?" he asked.

"Teival and Karasi are hiding away in Theitaa, the god haven. Colvyr is in nehveina greeting those who pass on from the realms," she said.

"So, they don't care?"

"Teival and Karasi want things to go back to the way they were, to the times when they controlled the will of the realm dwellers," Jynx explained before taking a big gulp from her pint.

"And you don't want that?" Kaiden questioned.

"It would weaken chaos and disrupt my akrani, ellorian."

"Half ellorian." He chugged the rest of the ale and hiccupped.

She sighed. "That's insignificant."

Kaiden pushed his empty mug away. "Are ellorians' visions significant?"

Jynx held her hand up. "I'm not the one you need to speak to about this."

He let out a breath. "Well, can you direct me to the *one*?"

She shot him a sidelong look. "I'll see what I can do."

"Great." He stood. "Thanks for the ale."

She waved him away.

He reached the doorway.

"Your mother was a brave, resilient warrior. You're a lot like her." Jynx stared distantly at the dancing flames in the hearth.

Kaiden came to a halt and didn't know how to respond. A short pause later, he bowed and walked back to the bedchamber. His mind swam with thoughts. The waves crashing against the cliff vibrated the temple walls. What else did Jynx know about his mom?

The vision of Blaise's death flashed in his mind. He pushed it away, determined to keep it from becoming a reality. *Will Blaise be able to unlock her katai in time?*

KAIDEN SLEPT IN UNTIL NOON the next day. Blaise's bed was empty. He assumed she'd gone for training. After getting ready, he strode outside for some fresh air. There were two green mountains adjacent to each other, and far off in the distance was the coast of Crenitha. It appeared miniscule from where he stood. A sudden wave of tranquility washed over him.

"Not even the gods get to sleep this late," a voice said behind him.

Kaiden turned. A man with short dark hair wearing long black robes stood before him. The god's translucent white eyes glimmered with amusement. Kaiden could only assume this was the god of peace himself, Colvyr.

"You're correct. I am him. My sister told me you're in need of some . . . assistance."

Kaiden stepped closer and waved a hand in front of Colvyr but received no reaction from him. "Can you see me?"

"In this form, no. I'm not completely solid," Colvyr said.

Kaiden cocked an eyebrow and folded his arms. "Why can't you?"

"We can only take a solid form in our own temples. My sister is allowing me to siphon some of her akrani so I can make this visit. You can pay homage to her later. I will only be able to visit sporadically." Colyvr clasped his hands. "Shall we begin?"

Kaiden nodded. "Yes."

"Let's start by climbing that mountain." Colvyr took the lead.

"I could just fly us up there," Kaiden offered.

Colvyr didn't stop. "Can you control your wings without jumping off a cliff?"

"Well . . . no."

"Controlling your wings takes a certain amount of satori," Colvyr said. "It requires you to have control of your mind. Ellorians perform better when their mind and body are one. You are not there . . . yet."

Without further argument, Kaiden followed. He couldn't believe this was happening. The god of peace had entered the realms to train him. *Maybe they aren't so bad after all.*

Kaiden peered at the mountain. It was going to be quite a climb to the top. "So . . . did you know my mother?"

Colvyr's pace slowed. For a blind god, he really knew where he was going. "What was her name?"

"Beatrice." Kaiden trailed behind.

Colvyr's shoulders slumped, and he remained silent for a few paces. He turned to face Kaiden. "How could I forget Bea?"

So, he did know her. Kaiden's eyebrows rose. "Bea?"

The god nodded. "She loved you and your father dearly."

"That's what I keep hearing," Kaiden mumbled.

Colvyr tilted his head. "Let me guess. You want to know what it means to be ellorian. Or in your case, a half blood."

"Are there others like me?" Kaiden lingered a few paces behind the god.

With a quick breath, Colvyr replied, "No. When I created the ellorians, I thought I ensured they couldn't reproduce." He continued onward.

Kaiden trod on his heels. "Where did that go wrong?"

He shrugged. "We can create things, but we have no control over how the akrani manifests. It's not like a painting where at some point it's done. Akrani evolves in mysterious ways."

It was difficult for Kaiden to wrap his head around all of it. He'd always thought the gods had complete and total control over the source. "So, it was akrani that brought forth my sister and me?"

"Essentially," Colvyr said through the breeze.

Kaiden let Colvyr's words sink in while they continued the rest of the climb. The god taught him about satori and how he could wield it. With enough conditioning, he would be able to see the memories of Crenitha. He would even be able to control another's will if he so desired.

"Controlling another's will is a violation of their inner peace. Rowena chose to abuse the power. As a result, it shattered her," Colvyr said.

"Yeah, no kidding."

It took them a few hours to finally get to the top of the mountain. Kaiden took in the view, inhaling the salty sea air. Nothing but blue for miles. He could get used to this feeling of tranquility.

"Take a seat." Colvyr gestured to the soft grass.

Kaiden listened, sitting cross-legged.

"Now close your eyes."

"Now what?" Kaiden asked.

Colvyr shushed him. "Listen," he whispered.

Okay, this god had some divine rocks loose in his head. Kaiden cocked a brow. "To what?"

"Everything."

Kaiden opened one eye to find Colvyr sitting next to him in the same sitting position with one hand resting on each thigh. He inhaled deeply and exhaled slowly.

With all the effort he could muster, Kaiden closed his eyes once more and focused on his surroundings.

Waves crashed against the rocks and cliffside. The mist cooled his skin, and the breeze caressed his wings' feathers. Seagulls squawked high above them. He even homed in on the blades of grass whipping in the wind.

The waves roared.

The birds screeched.

The sound of the grass was like blades slicing through the air.

It was too much at one time. He couldn't quiet his mind. His breathing became shallow. His pulse thrummed in his ears, growing louder until he could hear nothing else.

Kaiden's eyes shot open, and he gasped, desperate for air. He climbed to his feet, hands interlaced on top of his head. He sucked in gulping breaths and paced, trying to steady himself.

"It seems you have a lot of work ahead of you," Colvyr drawled, unmoved from his spot on the grass. "It's amusing you think highly of your ability to focus when you can't even sit quietly for five minutes."

Kaiden rolled his eyes, but he couldn't argue with the god. Colvyr was right, after all. "It's not the kind of focus I'm used to."

"Let me guess, you'd much rather focus on your anii-vasei." Colvyr stood and clasped his hands behind him. "What if I told you that what you will be learning could save her from the fate you had in your vision?"

"You know about my vision?"

"How could I not? It lingers in your mind like an annoying itch," Colvyr said. "Now sit down. Try again."

COLVYR CAME AND WENT WITH the passing days, training and teaching Kaiden the fundamentals of satori. He not only conditioned Kaiden's mind, but his body as well. Colvyr believed a strong mind required a strong body.

Kaiden decided to trust Colvyr and his process. He spent time balancing on his hands on top of the windy mountain—controlling his thoughts. The first time he'd done it, he fell after only a few seconds, his wings catching a gust. Kaiden couldn't figure out how doing handstands would save Blaise.

At the week's end, he'd beaten his time by a minute.

Kaiden sat alone on the mountain, quieting his mind. It had been the longest he'd maintained his control. He experienced a familiar sensation. Warm akrani flowed through him. *Another vision . . .*

In a flash of light, he was in the pool of the Balam fortress. He held that same black crystal he'd seen in the vision before. Bright light devoured him. His life source was being stripped away. This time, he was the one dying.

27

BLAISE

LAISE WOKE UP BEFORE KAIDEN. HER HEAD pounded, but that wouldn't stop her. She was ready to make her katai work. She dressed and made her way to the training room down the hall. When she entered, the large space was empty. She scanned the area and gazed out one of the windows. It was overcast outside, and the sun was hidden behind dark storm clouds.

Where in gehheina is Jynx?

Blaise padded to the center of the room. A dark figure swooped down and threw swift jabs. Blaise tried her best to block and dodge. Jynx was too fast.

Blaise took a direct kick to the chest, and it knocked the air from her lungs. She lay on the stone floor, gasping for air. "What the fuck are you doing?"

"What I'm here for. You're wasting my fucking time." Jynx brought her leg up, then down into Blaise's stomach, forcing her to curl into a ball. "You want control but for you, it is unattainable." She picked Blaise up by the front of her uniform. Jynx threw her like a doll against one of the stone pillars. "Let go."

Has she lost her fucking mind? Blaise climbed to her feet in time to block another combination of quick jabs. Jynx side kicked Blaise, knocking her a short distance away. Blaise stumbled. She regained her balance and lunged, attacking with a hammer fist to the goddess's chest. Rearing forward, she kicked Jynx in the stomach. The goddess doubled over momentarily, then stretched a hand toward Blaise. The goddess unleashed a torrent of white lightning from her fingertips.

Blaise ducked and tumbled out of the way, rolling to her feet. "Are you insane? Are you trying to kill me?" she screamed.

Jynx's eyes flashed crimson. "Yes," she shouted back, shooting more electricity from her hand.

Blaise dove and flipped around the room. *Why is this bitch trying to kill me?* She needed to figure it out.

"Katai requires you to let go of control and embrace the unknown." Jynx stopped, catching her breath. She winced and shook her sparking hands. "You have to let it go." She rushed up to Blaise in the blink of an eye, throwing a right hook. Pain shot through Blaise's jaw. Jynx threw a left. Another left. "You have to let go of your need for control." Another right.

Thankfully, the agony of the goddess's hard blows was dulled by the adrenaline coursing through Blaise.

What is she talking about?

"I don't have enough control." If she couldn't control her katai, how was she supposed to use it to protect everything she loved?

Jynx threw a right hook into Blaise's swollen cheek. "If you want answers, you have to let go."

Tears welled in Blaise's eyes, stinging the small cuts on her face. "How am I supposed to do that? I can't think straight with you trying to kill me!"

Jynx ran up to her and grabbed her throat, squeezing. "Fighting Amasu will be infinitely worse. He won't hesitate to kill you and destroy everything you love."

Blaise fought against the lightheadedness from Jynx's grasp. The goddess's words echoed over and over in her mind.

Bright light flashed in the periphery of her vision. With every flash, she sensed her katai ready to erupt. The pressure within her boiled hot, starting in her stomach, working its way through her body. *Gods, not that familiar darkness again.*

Jynx's red eyes softened. "Just let go, Little Flame."

As much as her mind fought against it, Blaise surrendered her worries, surrendered her control, and surrendered herself, letting it flow into the universe.

Jynx dropped her and stepped back.

Blue sparks ignited on Blaise's fingertips. They grew. The chaos within her raged, yet without fear or control, she could work with it instead of against it.

She aimed at the goddess, and the lightning unfurled. Electricity enveloped Jynx, shooting her across the entire length of the training room. Wisps of azure lingered on Blaise's hand, dissipating. Jynx wasn't moving.

Blaise sprinted over. "Jynx. Jynx, I'm sorry." She placed her ear to the goddess's chest. *She's breathing. Thank the gods.*

"Why're you sorry? You finally did it," Jynx said, eyes still closed. She winced, pushing herself to sit up. Dust covered her black clothes and boots, and her tight curls were in disarray. She pushed them from her face and grinned.

"I'm glad you find this amusing, but I thought you were dead." Blaise helped the goddess to her feet.

Jynx giggled. "I'm a goddess. I've taken worse hits than that."

Blaise loosed a breath. She was right. How could she have hurt the goddess of chaos?

Jynx placed a hand on her shoulder. "You have the akrani of a god. You underestimate yourself far too much."

Blaise glanced out the window at the overcast sky. "I'm still having trouble understanding what all of this means."

"It means you can wield not only katai, but satori, alchime, and gitros. Though if you're not careful, it can kill you. You're still mortal and not equipped to handle that much power," Jynx said. "That is where your aniivasei comes in. He has enophii, and it'll help you regulate. You will balance each other."

That wasn't what Blaise wanted to hear. She didn't want to rely on anyone to control her akrani.

Jynx took off the training jacket, revealing the sleeveless white shirt she wore beneath it. "Now that you've released your katai, we'll have to focus on the more detailed aspects of your abilities."

EVERY NIGHT FOR A WEEK Blaise passed out exhausted from the intense training she underwent with Jynx. They started before sunrise and continued well beyond sunset. It left her no time to spend with Kaiden, but she was glad he'd been able to train with Colvyr.

Blaise woke early Sunday, readied herself in the black uniform Jynx had provided, and strode into the training room. The goddess was nowhere to be found. Blaise stood in front of one of the large windows, watching the morning sky fill with oranges, pinks, and purples. The sun continued its rise over the horizon, cascading warm light into the room.

She'll find me when she wants me. With a sigh, Blaise walked out, making her way back to the bedchamber.

Kaiden stood next to his bed, buttoning his tunic. He cocked a brow, wings fluttering at the sight of her. "What're you doing here?"

It was amusing that his wings gave away his emotions. She grinned. "This is my room too, you know."

He deadpanned, "You know what I mean."

"I couldn't find Jynx, so I came back." She traipsed over to her bed and sat, leaning back on her hands.

He continued to work the buttons of his tunic. The sleeves stretched over his well-defined arms. He caught her gaze on him, and her cheeks warmed.

He smirked, stepping closer to her until their bodies were inches from each other.

The heat rose in her core. She peered at him with curiosity. *What's he going to do?* It wasn't the usual look he'd get when he wanted her. This was something entirely different.

He knelt between her legs, slid his arms around her waist, and placed his ear to her heart. "I missed you." His deep voice rumbled against her chest.

Despite her rapid pulse, her muscles relaxed, and she melted into his embrace. Was it wrong for her to feel the same?

"I missed you too." She hadn't meant to say it out loud. *Dammit.* She reminded herself that keeping her distance wasn't for her alone. Though, with him in her arms, she was beginning to forget the reason why.

Kaiden remained unmoved. He seemed content with listening to her breathe. "I want you, Blaise."

She tilted her head, not fully comprehending what he meant.

"Not just your body." He gazed into her eyes. "I want to fall asleep with you in my arms every night and wake up next to you every morning. I want to spend every moment of every day knowing you're mine and I'm yours."

Blaise blinked back the emotions that threatened to spill down her cheeks. She fought against the urge to tighten her arms around his broad shoulders. "We may not have that luxury, Kaiden."

"I want a future with you—whatever that may look like."

"What if it's not the future you want?" she asked.

He squeezed her closer. "As long as you're there, it's what I want."

She drew back and thought about what Jynx had told her in the training room.

Let go.

"We seem to be at an impasse. Maybe we should let fate decide this one?" She smirked. There was only one way she could think to settle this. "Shall we duel?" She reached for her sword.

"Duel?" His eyes glinted.

She nodded. "You're not scared to take on a little ol' half god, are you?"

Kaiden's eyes narrowed, and he retrieved his sword from where it hung on his bedpost. "Just so we're clear, if I win, you'll give yourself to me *completely*?"

Blaise readied her weapon and took her fighting stance. She inhaled a deep breath. "Yes. But if I win, you'll stop trying to force ridiculous notions of our future."

He grimaced, the hurt apparent in his hazel eyes. He conceded with a nod.

Their room was small. Blaise would have to utilize her close combat skills, but she was confident she could beat him this time.

They kept their weapons sheathed for safety. Pushing away all thoughts, Blaise swung her sword, its weight becoming an extension of her body. She moved in. Kaiden smirked, staggering back against the bed. He set his feet and rushed her.

She sidestepped, avoiding his massive body, but quickly met the stone wall. He whirled around, striking at her. She parried, then swung once, twice, three times. He blocked and dodged each of her blows. The impact of their sheaths rang out.

Blaise lunged, but Kaiden knocked her sword aside with a downward sweep. She centered herself once more and sliced in fluid motions. Kaiden sank into a slight crouch, a move he'd used to win the first time they dueled. He surged ahead, ready to collide with her, shoulder to shoulder.

This time, Blaise was prepared. She shifted her foot back, moving her hips sideways. He slipped past her. She swung her arm around with all her might, hitting him just below the neck, knocking him on his ass.

Blaise spun around, placed a foot on his stomach, and pointed her sword at his heaving chest. "Holy shit . . ." She hadn't expected to win.

Kaiden stared, an unreadable look in his eyes. "It seems you've won."

She turned her back to him, a million thoughts rushing through her mind. *I never wanted to win.*

"It was a good match. Your training has paid off," he said, pushing to his feet, his wings rustling.

She closed her eyes before turning to face him once more. How had she won? She snapped, "Were you even trying?"

"I won't raise the issue further." He started to walk away.

"Wait." She hadn't thought about it. Maybe she was wrong about what she wanted.

He didn't face her. "Please don't make this more difficult than it has to be, Blaise." His voice trembled with an emotion she couldn't stand hearing from him: *pain.*

She knew what she had to say—what she *needed* to say. "I surrender."

He turned, meeting her with a heated gaze. "What did you just say?"

Her sword clattered to the floor. She swallowed. "I surrender."

His long strides ate up the distance between them. He stood inches from her, glancing at her lips before focusing on her eyes. "Say it again." His voice was low, filled with desire.

She looked away.

He stepped closer and hooked a finger under her chin, tilting her gaze back to his. "Don't do that."

"Do what?"

"Don't offer me the universe and then try to take it away." His eyes darkened.

"That's not what I'm trying to do. You deserve so much more, Kaiden."

"I want you, Blaise. Nothing more. Nothing less."

The corner of her mouth rose, and she leaned in. "You have me. You've always had me."

His wings quivered as he attacked her lips with his, pushing her back against the bed.

She squealed and writhed beneath his warm hard body. *Is this sacrilege?* His lips on her pulse and hardening length grinding against her center distracted her from any other thoughts. She needed him in every way he would give himself to her.

Blaise broke the kiss. "I want you inside me." She shimmied off her trousers and lay there bare for him.

Kaiden released his hard length and readied himself at her glistening folds. "Are you sure?" He stared into her chestnut eyes.

"Yes."

He slid into her, grabbing her waist, then pulled out and pushed in again. "I'm yours now, Blaise. Body." His nails dug into her skin. "Mind." He thrust into her and gritted out, "Soul. And you're mine."

She wanted to scream from the mixture of heartache and pleasure, but instead she bit down on her hand, silencing herself. He moved her hand away, replacing it with his lips. He kissed his way to the curve of her neck, then one of her breasts, maintaining the consistent push and pull of his cock into her warmth.

He wrapped one arm around her waist, elevating her hips. He buried himself deeper than he'd ever been. Her back arched, breasts bouncing as he drove into her again. Again. Again.

"Kaiden." His name left her lips like a desperate plea. She wanted her release—needed it.

Their bodies melded together, strands of akrani flowing through them, around them. A moan escaped her as she came, legs trembling. He thrust into her for the last time, spilling himself into her.

A flash of light obscured her vision. She was in the throne room of the Balam fortress. Kaiden's body materialized into view. He lay on the stone floor, lifeless.

Another flash brought her back to the present and the worried look on Kaiden's face. He'd already pulled out of her, but his pants still hung around his thighs. He hovered over her, his lips forming a straight line. "What did you see?"

She stared at him, tears streaming down her face. "I saw you . . . dead." That last word was only a breath. His mental barrier had slipped. Was that a vision he'd already seen?

He tugged his trousers up, averting his gaze. "You weren't supposed to see that."

"I thought you said no more lies?" She threw her legs over the edge of the mattress.

"I didn't lie to you about that," he said.

She began dressing as well. "Withholding important information is the same thing. Just like when you didn't tell me about that little side mission in Haven."

He tossed his hands up. "I apologized for that. I was on orders."

"Well, that just makes everything better, doesn't it?"

He crossed his arms, wings bristling. "This is different. I didn't think it was important."

Her eyes narrowed. "Your death isn't important?"

"You want to know the truth?" The volume of his voice rose. "I saw you die too. And to be honest, I'd rather it be me than you."

She straightened, confronting him. "Once we get back to Elatora and I get the necessary reinforcements from King Vaughn's army, you're staying there."

He scoffed and took a step toward her. "You're insane if you think I'm going to let you do this on your own."

"It's not your problem, gods dammit." She didn't falter.

"It *is* my problem. Whether you like it or not, we're connected," he retorted.

Blaise leaned her weight onto one leg. "Here we go with the bond bullshit again. I'm going to find a way to sever it." She ripped her eyes away from his. She knew it was a lie the moment those words left her mouth. She'd let her anger take over.

Kaiden's face contorted with anger. Hurt gleamed in his hazel eyes. "I'm *never* leaving you again, Blaise. It's more than just a bond." He made a straight line for the door and walked out of the bedchamber.

28

BLAISE

LAISE BATHED, BUT SHE WASN'T QUITE ready to deal with Kaiden. She wandered the island until her stomach started to grumble. *I should head back before sunset.*

Blaise strode back to the temple a short time later. She made her way to the kitchen and found Jynx sitting with a solemn expression and a pint in her hand.

The goddess gave Blaise a sidelong look. "I'm surprised you're not with your aniivasei, Little Flame."

Blaise approached her, passing the built-in fireplace in the middle of the kitchen. "Where have you been?"

"You finally released your akrani. That might need to

marinate for a while." Jynx waved her hand, and a frothing pint of ale appeared on the table along with a full pitcher. "Shall we?"

Blaise took the seat next to her sister, grabbed the pint, and gulped until she had to stop for air.

Jynx smirked. "You want to talk about it?"

Blaise stared at her mug, tapping her fingers on the cold glass. "So much has changed in such a short time. I'm having trouble coping."

Jynx tilted her head. "Tell me about it."

"It feels like yesterday I was guarding Teaos. I went from being a lowly sergeant in the Sentinel Order to a queen, and a half god at that. I have an aniivasei I spent the day avoiding, and now I'm drinking honey peach ale with a goddess." Blaise took another swig.

"Sounds *chaotic*," Jynx mused.

A grin tugged at the corners of Blaise's mouth. "I just . . ." She released a breath. "I needed to take my mind off things for a moment."

Two pitchers of ale later, Blaise and Jynx ended up in front of the warm hearth a few feet from the table. Blaise lay with her head in Jynx's lap on a large fur rug. She couldn't ignore the swirling. *At least I'm numb.* Her eyes grew heavy while the fire crackled and popped.

Jynx brushed her fingers through Blaise's long hair.

"Can you tell me more about Amasu?" Blaise slurred.

"You don't want to know more." Jynx guzzled the remainder of the ale straight from the pitcher.

Do gods get drunk? Jynx didn't seem fazed by the amount of alcohol she'd consumed.

Blaise's eyes moved with the flicker of each flame. "Um, yes, I do."

Jynx stared down at her, brow slightly creased.

Blaise awaited her response, nearly falling asleep.

"He was not a good father. He was strict, cold, unyielding. Until he met your mother." Jynx leaned back on her hands. "That's when he changed."

Blaise rolled over and ungracefully pushed herself up to sit next to the goddess. "In what way?"

"I think it was love. It might've been a superficial love, but I guess some kind of love is better than none at all." Jynx's gaze drifted from the doorway to the fire. "Unfortunately, for him, the laws of a high god are hard to break. His love of power was so great he thought he'd never desire anything more."

Blaise cocked a brow. "What does that mean?"

Jynx shot Blaise a fleeting look. "It means you're in for the fight of your life."

Kaiden walked through the arched doorway, his wings sweeping in behind him. "What in gehheina is going on here?" His eyes roamed the nearby wooden table with its empty pitchers and pints. Another empty pitcher sat between them and the hearth.

"What does it look like, ellorian?" Jynx grinned. "Maybe you should escort her to bed. You're probably very familiar with that task."

Blaise snickered.

Kaiden rolled his eyes, then stepped next to Blaise, bent low, and tossed her over his shoulder. "You're not going to be laughing in the morning."

"Good night, sister," Jynx said in a singsong voice.

Everything was upside down while Kaiden carried her down the long hallway to their bedchamber. She somehow managed to get a handful of his feathers in her mouth. She spit them out. Kaiden kicked the door in and smacked her ass before he tossed her onto the bed. He tucked her in and said, "You're such a pain in the ass." He placed a light kiss on her forehead and walked over to his bed.

BLAISE FOUND TRAINING TO BE a little less intense in the days that followed. She learned all she could from the goddess, including her style of hand-to-hand combat techniques. Blaise learned how to wield the yellow flame, which was the least damaging of them all. Once the goddess approved of how well Blaise could control it, she moved on to red, then blue. Jynx warned Blaise about using the white flame. It was the deadliest for the opponent as well as the wielder.

At the end of a long day of training, Blaise strolled away from the temple into a field of long grass swaying in the ocean breeze. She inhaled slowly, trying to gather her thoughts, and grounded herself in this moment.

With her mother's book in hand, she continued up the slight grade. She made it to the middle of the field, tall blades rustling against her black trousers. She examined the leather-bound book in her hand, warmth stirring in her stomach. *How in gehheina am I supposed to read this thing?*

The golden sun started its descent toward the horizon. Blaise continued to stare at the book.

The answers are in the flames. I can wield my flames now. Would that work? She strode over to a flat rock and placed the book down on it. *What if I burn the only thing I have left of my mother?*

Blaise conjured yellow flames on her fingertips. She doused the book in them, closing her eyes. Fear coated her insides at the damage she'd done to the only thing connecting her to her mother.

The smoke cleared, and the book was still there, unharmed by her flame. She tapped the leather cover, making sure it was cool enough to pick up. Flipping through the pages, she groaned. *Still blank. Maybe that flame isn't strong enough.*

Red fire flickered from her fingers. She repeated the process. Once again, the book was unharmed, and the pages remained blank.

She slammed it back down onto the rock. "I'm not going to kill myself trying to read you. It better work this time." She summoned her blue flame and threw it at the book. The impact caused the cover to fly open. The fire became an incandescent blue. Ink appeared on the pages while the azure flames faded. She couldn't wait to read her mother's words.

> My darling girl. I knew you'd figure this out. If you're reading this, your father is on the verge of escaping his prison, and you're running out of time. I've done everything in my power to ensure your survival. You must find the Onyx Crystal. It will be at its strongest during the darkest moment of the solar eclipse. Helena will help you find it. Keep this book close—it holds the keys to your future. There will be more to learn once you retrieve the crystal.
>
> Always remember, I love you.

Blaise slapped the book shut and sprinted toward the temple. She found Jynx drinking tea in the kitchen. She explained everything, excluding the location of the crystal. In the midst of the conversation, excruciating pain shot through her head. Her visions blurred, and she doubled over, grabbing her head. From the depths of her mind, Amasu's voice manifested, louder than ever before.

I'll be seeing you soon, my little abomination. You have no right to defile my power. You have no understanding of the consequences of your irreverence.

The pressure was too much. She pushed back, drawing strength from her akrani. With pure will, she tried to force him out of her mind. *Stop! Why're you doing this? Why do you hate me?*

The day your mother chose for you to live was the day I stopped being a high god. With your first breath, you destroyed everything I desired. Because of you, the realms have lost their faith in us. But once I relieve them of their will, their faith will return.

Tears rolled down her cheeks. *You can't do that. They won't survive.*

It has happened once before. The survivors shall be cleansed.

Blaise gritted her teeth. *I'll never let that happen.* She gave one last shove of satori, and her vision cleared. She was back in the kitchen again, Jynx holding her up.

"Let me guess. Our dear father?" Jynx asked while Blaise straightened.

Kaiden burst through the door. "What happened?" He rushed up to Blaise and embraced her. "I couldn't sense your akrani. It felt like you vanished. I was terrified."

Blaise gazed into his hazel eyes, that glint of fear still in them. "I'm fine." The corners of her mouth tipped up, and then she pursed her lips.

"I'm afraid we've run out of time, Little Flame," Jynx said. "You must return to the mainland. Take what I've taught you and use it wisely."

"What will you do?" Blaise asked her.

"I'll be in nehveina with Colvyr. We will be watching." Jynx studied her for a long moment, then let out a breath. "Believe me, if I could be there to help you, I would."

Blaise nodded. "I understand. Thank you. For everything."

Jynx pulled her in for a brief hug. Releasing Blaise, she turned away and disappeared into a cloud of chaos.

Blaise had become accustomed to her sister's dramatic exits. She faced Kaiden. "Look, I'm sorry about what I said about the bond. I didn't mean it." What she'd seen in that vision wasn't the future she was going to accept.

He shook his head. "It's okay. I should've learned my lesson the first time I kept something from you."

A faint grin crossed her lips. "So . . . have you gotten a handle on those things yet?" She gestured to Kaiden's wings, then placed her hands on her hips.

He shot her a severe expression. "What do you think I've been doing the whole time we've been here?"

She raised her shoulder. "I don't know. What else is there to do on this island? I've been too busy training."

"I like when you're like this." He kissed her on the lips and started toward the exit.

Blaise didn't let him get very far. She swung, her hand landing hard on his ass cheek. "How's that for a pain in the ass?" With a smile, she turned and headed to the bedchamber.

29

BLAISE

BLAISE STRODE UP TO THE TOP OF THE CLIFF, the satchel strapped to her back and a solemn expression on her face. Kaiden stood next to another man. "You must be Colvyr," she said.

"Hello, sister," the god said.

"Thank you for keeping Kaiden out of trouble while I trained with Jynx." Blaise shot Kaiden a teasing expression.

Kaiden narrowed his eyes at her.

Colvyr chuckled. "To be honest, we did quite a bit of our own training. I have a few words for Kaiden before you leave." Silence ensued for a heartbeat.

"Whatever you have to say, you can say in front of

Blaise." Kaiden interlaced his hand with hers, drawing her next to him.

Colvyr nodded. "Beatrice loved your father so much that she sacrificed true love in the name of duty."

Kaiden's brow wrinkled. "What does that mean?"

"It's time for you to talk to your father," Colvyr replied.

Blaise muttered, "It seems we're all having that problem."

"Well, be on your way, and let tranquility guide you in mind and body." His form faded before their eyes.

Kaiden turned to Blaise and held out his hand. "You ready to go back?"

She took it and pursed her lips. With a slow blink, she said, "No, but we don't have a choice."

He pulled her close, wrapping his arms around her midsection. "Hold on tight." Extending his wings, he launched into the sky.

Blaise shrieked in his arms and wrapped her legs around his waist. They soared through the clouds while she clutched him for dear life. "Do you have to be so turbulent?"

He glanced down at her. "Would you rather I jump off the cliff again?"

"No. But you could try to be more graceful," she gritted out.

He smirked. "Yes, *Your Majesty*."

She said nothing else, squeezing him more tightly, pressing the side of her face against his warm neck.

Approaching Crenitha, they descended, flying lower and lower. The land seemed to draw near far too fast, but Kaiden adjusted his wings and slowed.

The closer they flew, the more Blaise had to use her mental barriers. A pulse in her head distracted from her fear of heights. She assumed it was Amasu.

Blaise didn't even feel the landing. She unwound her legs from his waist, her booted feet crunching onto the gravel.

He didn't release her from his hold. "Was that graceful enough for you?"

She peered at him from beneath her long lashes, eyes glimmering with mischief. "It was. Thank you, *Captain*."

"What's on your mind?" he asked, furrowing his brow.

She scanned the cliffside and whispered, "Shit, it's all very real now." She shook her head. "We should get a move on so we can get to camp before sundown."

"We're going to have to go on foot the rest of the way. The forest is too thick to fly through, and we'd be clear targets in the sky." Kaiden started walking toward the tree line.

They remained concealed in the thicket, staying out of any clearings they came across, remaining alert of their surroundings. Blaise agreed, knowing King Theod could have scouts searching Meliwe.

Blaise and Kaiden continued their trudge through the forest. Half a day passed until they came upon the camp. The Alchyra had set up between the coast and the Azureden Mountains. They approached the entrance. Two guards gave a greeting and escorted them to the general.

Zade called for a meeting in the war tent. Mathias, Nira, Elric, and Isaac filed inside. In the middle of the space was a wooden table with a map of Crenitha on top. They all stood around it in the candlelight. Banter from passing

Alchyra could be heard through the thin material of the tent. It took a few hours for Blaise and Kaiden to divulge the new information to the group.

"I know who can figure out when the next solar eclipse will occur," Isaac remarked.

Kaiden stated firmly, "As do I, Isaac."

Isaac stepped back from the table.

Blaise left Kaiden's side and walked next to Zade, staring at the kingdom of Balam on the map. "Amasu won't be at full power. And if we can close the portal before he breaks free, we can avoid the confrontation with him."

"Do you know who has this crystal?" Elric crossed his arms.

Blaise glanced at him, guarded about Grams, knowing this vital piece of information. "I do. I'll take care of that matter personally."

Elric huffed and gave a short nod.

"We'll need to speak to King Vaughn about the adjustments I made to the peace treaty between Elatora and Balam." Kaiden looked to Zade.

Zade grimaced. "That should be an interesting conversation."

Once the meeting was over, Blaise headed out of the tent. She needed to breathe. Everything they'd spoken about in there had left her with a bitter metallic taste in her mouth. A short walk around the camp would help lessen the tightness in her chest.

"Blaise." Nira caught up with her, falling into step as they passed a few Alchyra. "Everything okay?"

Blaise nodded, giving her an assuring smile. "Fine, I just needed some air."

"This is all a bit wild, isn't it?"

Their pace slowed, and they ended up sitting on a bench that overlooked the makeshift training grounds where a unit of Alchyra sparred.

Blaise missed the sentinel life. All she'd had to worry about was training and guarding the wall. "Yeah, that's one way to put it," she muttered.

"Are you sure you won't need me to accompany you to Elatora?" Nira asked, angling her body toward Blaise.

"I'm not going to need a handmaiden on this trip. I can dress myself." Blaise added, "It would do you well to continue your training here. You won't fight Amasu himself, but there will be war if King Theod chooses to remain in Balam."

Nira stared at her clasped hands in her lap. "I won't let you down, Your Majesty."

"Nira, you deserve to have the life you choose." Blaise stood, walked a few feet, and then faced her. "So . . . what's going on between you and Mathias? I sensed a bit of . . . tension in the tent."

Nira fiddled her thumbs. "What makes you think something's going on?"

Blaise shot her a severe glare. "It feels like there's electricity in the air when you two are near each other." She laughed.

Nira giggled. "Don't be ridiculous. He can barely stand me. And besides, Mathias has a reputation to uphold. I'm not the type that could support that kind of reputation."

Blaise's brow creased. She sat next to Nira. "What makes you think you're not his type?"

Nira shrugged and stared out into the field. "I've been told my whole life I'm no one of importance. Being an akrani gitros doesn't make me special."

Blaise's eyes softened, and she placed her hand over Nira's. "Is that why you want to be an Alchyra? To make a name for yourself?"

"That's part of the reason." Nira's gaze met Blaise's.

Blaise loosed a breath, squeezing Nira's hand. "But it's incredibly special to save a life, and you've saved many, including mine. You *have* to know how important you are in this realm."

"Maybe someday." Nira's lips curved into a faint grin. "Thank you for saying so."

Blaise shook her head. "I should be the one thanking you."

Nira blushed. "Enough about me. What about you and the captain?"

Blaise pulled her hand away. A gentle breeze filled with the scent of cypress caressed her cheeks. She didn't know how to answer. She and Kaiden hadn't come to terms yet. She wasn't sure where she stood in their relationship. Of course, they were aniivasei, but she wasn't willing to let him risk his life for her.

"I can see it's a touchy subject," said Nira, a studious look in her cobalt eyes.

Blaise sighed. "It's complicated."

Nira nodded and seemed to fully comprehend that answer. "When is it not?" she mused, and then her mouth formed a straight line. "I pray to the gods we all come out of this safely."

"I don't think the gods will be able to help with that this time," Blaise murmured with an eye roll.

"How do you feel about going back to Elatora?" Nira straddled the bench, facing Blaise. "Are you nervous? Excited?"

"I'm not sure." Blaise hadn't had the chance to think about what it would be like to be back in Elatora again. "I'm looking forward to seeing Grams and my brother again." Now that she'd thought about it, she couldn't wait to hold them in her embrace.

"I'm sure they'll be over the moon at the sight of you," Nira said.

Blaise focused on Nira and the kindness in her eyes, the smile on her face. She was truly lucky to have someone like Nira in her life, especially during these difficult times. "I want to apologize to you."

"Whatever for?" One of Nira's brows rose.

"For ever doubting your allegiance to me."

Nira pursed her lips. "I understand why you would have doubts. Andreas took advantage of your inexperience as queen. He orchestrated everything to kill you and take your kingdom. It would've been impossible for you to discover the truth by yourself."

"I'm sorry you had to go through that." Blaise glanced down at her hands.

"I don't know what Andreas would've done if I hadn't found Mathias," Nira said.

Blaise's lips curved up. "He really needs someone like you to care for him."

Nira stood from the bench. "Despite his arrogance and careless attitude, I can't deny that I've grown a fondness for the big ass."

Blaise laughed. "I should probably begin preparations." She stood and started walking away.

"You won't tell him, will you?" Nira caught up to her.

Blaise narrowed her eyes. "You really think I would after everything you've done for me?"

Nira held up her hand, palm facing Blaise. "No, it's not that. I don't normally share these things with others."

Blaise halted. "Any words between us are *only* between us. Agreed?"

Nira nodded, her smile reaching her eyes. "Agreed." A dutiful expression came over her face. "Now let's get you packed. You have a long journey ahead of you."

KAIDEN

DARK CLOUDS FILLED THE SKY, BLOCKING the sun's warm rays. The air was thick with the smell of rain—earthy and clean with a hint of ozone. The birdsong ceased, and a chill rippled down Kaiden's spine.

Kaiden wanted to leave the Alchyra camp before the downpour. He gathered provisions and loaded Cedric's saddlebags, then waited at the edge of camp for the rest of his traveling companions.

With his horse in tow, Mathias joined Kaiden. Some-thing about Mathias seemed different. He didn't appear as carefree as he usually was before a mission. *Does he still trust me after everyone falsely accused him?*

Kaiden caught Mathias staring at Nira, who was sparring in the clearing. He wondered how *close* they'd gotten in the three weeks spent hiding in Haven.

"She's a talented woman," Kaiden said.

Mathias's gaze snapped to Kaiden, and his nostrils flared. "More like stubborn and frustrating." He mounted his horse.

Kaiden followed suit. "You could use a bit more of that in your life."

Blaise joined the conversation on her own horse. "What're we talking about?"

"Mathias has a thing for Nira." Kaiden grinned.

"Anyone can see that," Blaise teased with an eye roll.

Mathias let out a forced breath and deadpanned, "You two are hilarious."

Nira walked into earshot, her training sword still in hand. "Enjoying the show?"

Mathias tilted his head toward the overcast sky, irritation apparent on his face.

Kaiden smirked. "Mathias was just admiring your technique."

Mathias's blue eyes widened, and he stared at his best friend with disdain.

Nira glared. "Really? That's a rare occurrence, especially when it comes to me."

"And why do you think that is?" Mathias glared at her, gripping his horse's reins.

Her challenging gaze met his. "You don't want my opinion."

"Stop saying that," Mathias retorted, dismounting his horse and getting in her face. "Yes, I do."

Nira stepped back. "You're an ass, that's my opinion," she said, pointing her sword at him.

He smirked, swiping her blade away. "And you need to work on your insults. They're getting old."

"Do you two need a moment?" Blaise asked with a cocked brow.

Nira stared at Mathias for a few seconds, then said, "No. We're done here." She turned to Blaise, and they started their own conversation.

Mathias made a hand gesture and shot Kaiden a look that said, *You see what I'm dealing with?*

Kaiden shook his head, letting out a quiet chuckle.

Zade rode up on horseback. "Everything is in order. I told Piers to continue the training regimen until I return."

Elric steered his horse next to Kaiden, his face aloof, as usual. Kaiden's satori was beginning to manifest more potent intuition. Elric's visible scars told Kaiden the man had gone through some rough times in his life. It was Elric's dark energy that felt dangerous. Maybe one day, if they survived this, Kaiden would take the time to know the obscure Elric better.

"Travel safe," Nira said, then strolled back to the training field.

"Shall we?" Zade asked Blaise.

Elric lingered and waited for them to ride ahead of him. "I'll take the rear."

Isaac took the lead while Kaiden and Zade rode on either side of Blaise.

"Could you two give me a little space?" she asked, waving her hand at each of them.

Kaiden shot her a tight-lipped glare. He nodded at Zade to back off. They opened some space between them, though not so much that Kaiden couldn't get to her if they were attacked. He watched her from behind and couldn't help but feel the distance. However, it was the intense weight of her emotional detachment that was tearing him apart.

The sun was getting low behind the clouds. They planned to take the Azureden pass. Nearing the mountains, they would need to pick up pace if they were going to get through the pass before sundown. Once the sun set, kynarah and trolls would come out to quench their bloodlust.

The wind shifted. A chill trickled down Kaiden's spine. He shivered. Stopping Cedric, he scanned his surroundings. Cypress trees lined the dirt path, their dark green leaves rustling in the dreary breeze. Something was wrong, like a piece in the grand scheme of things was out of place. The hair on the back of his neck stood on end. His gaze swept the forest once more. There was no evidence of a threat approaching.

Elric caught up to him. "I sense it too. We all need to be extra watchful."

"Agreed. I'll ride ahead and inform Isaac." Kaiden trotted up to Isaac, who rode ahead of Blaise. "We need to talk."

"O-okay." Isaac appeared caught off guard.

"Keep your eyes peeled. There's an odd energy near," Kaiden said.

"Yes, Captain."

Kaiden gave him a sidelong glare. "I'm going to get to the point. Are you a spy for King Theod?"

Isaac appeared taken aback. "What? I would never. N-no. I'm not, I assure you, Captain."

"What else am I supposed to think when you were fucking that traitor Simone?" Kaiden growled, gritting his teeth.

Isaac tripped over his words. "I-I wasn't thinking." He took a deep breath and rested his eyes on his hands gripping the reins.

Without a thought, Kaiden reached over and grabbed Isaac by the neck of his armor. "Of all the things to not be thinking of, why did it have to be my sister?"

"Kaiden!" Blaise bellowed from behind them.

"Elizabeth was all you should've been thinking of." He managed to gain control of himself and let Isaac go.

Blaise rode up, scowling at Kaiden. "Do you think your sister would appreciate you meddling in her personal affairs?"

Dammit, she has a point. Kaiden let out a breath. "No, I'm sure she wouldn't," he muttered, then turned back to Isaac. "Clearly, you'll need to tell my sister what you've done, then never speak to her again."

A look of sadness and regret overcame Isaac's boyish features. "I will, Captain." He sped up, taking back his place in the formation.

Blaise grabbed Kaiden's arm and squeezed gently. "I understand that Elizabeth is your sister and you want to protect her, but I don't think Isaac was alone in his fraternization." She said nothing more and rode ahead, catching up with Isaac.

An all-consuming darkness weighed heavily in the air.

Sinister chills crawled up Kaiden's spine. The grim vibration in his chest matched the murky atmosphere. Light seemed to be disappearing, along with all the trees of the forest. He leaped off Cedric, searching the space for his unit. They were nowhere to be found. *What in gehheina is happening?*

"Blaise? Mathias? Isaac?" He held his hands out, reaching into the darkness. "Elric?"

Kaiden's vision flooded with the massacre of his comrades—his friends. He squeezed his eyes shut for a moment and reopened them. Nothing changed. *No. This can't be real.* It took him a few seconds to focus because his world was covered in red. When he did, his heart sank into his stomach. Blood stained the ground. Bodies were spread out, their limbs contorted in unnatural ways. He willed his legs to move and staggered to each of them.

Elric lay on his back with one leg bent beneath him, his intestines splayed across the ground. A few feet from him was Isaac, his face barely recognizable. Kaiden's insides turned to ice at the sight of Blaise's limp body. He sprinted over and slid to his knees next to her. She lay in a puddle of her own blood, a weeping gash in her neck. He opened his senses and checked their bond. It was alarmingly weak.

"Hold on, Blaise. You're going to be okay." Kaiden held her blood-soaked hand.

Tears trickled down her pale cheeks. She met his gaze. Kaiden could feel her warmth emanating through the anii-vasei, but the sparks of life in her chestnut eyes were fading. *This can't be happening.*

Cackles echoed all around Kaiden. He looked up into the glowing eyes of a dark figure, its sword dripping with blood.

The creature said in a deep ominous voice, "Your friends are dead. We will find all that you desire and destroy it."

Kaiden unsheathed his sword and ran toward the figure. He launched forward with his wings, striking down at his opponent. The dark figure moved sideways, crouched, and swept at Kaiden's legs. Heart hammering in his chest, Kaiden leaped, avoiding the creature's attack.

The hooded figure seemed to be made of ash and ember. *How in gehheina am I supposed to defeat this creature of smoke and shadow?* He tapped into his speed and retaliated with a swing only to be blocked.

The figure's eyes glowed an orangey red. It struck upward. Kaiden jumped back, avoiding the blow. He held the handle of his sword with two hands, waited for the creature to get closer, and then lunged.

Kaiden's sword penetrated the creature's chest. His vision swirled and warped. He heard Mathias call his name from the shadows. Meliwe Forest materialized, and his surroundings shifted. The creature transformed. It spoke his name.

"Kaiden."

"Mathias?" Kaiden choked out. Eyes wide, he carefully withdrew his sword from his best friend's shoulder. Mathias collapsed into his arms. "I'm sorry, I didn't know." His eyes welled up with tears. "What can I do?" He had to do something.

Mathias coughed up blood. "It's not your fault."

Kaiden scanned the area. Elric didn't seem affected by whatever had possessed them, but he was in the middle of fighting with Blaise.

"Elric!" Kaiden called.

"They're under the influence of the algeaa." He knocked Blaise to the ground and held his hand over her eyes. His eyes turned black. "Get out of her, you son of a bitch."

A shadow seeped out of her eyes, coiling around his wrist and hand. He held the shadow, and with a swift yank, he extracted the dark spirit from her body. He hurled it into the beams of sunlight breaking through the clouds. The dark entity dissipated into cinders.

Blaise sat up, catching her breath. "What happened?"

Zade and Isaac were still fighting, making their way farther from the rest of the group.

"Can you do the same to those two?" Kaiden asked, still holding the injured Mathias. Blood soaked through to his hands and onto his tunic. This wasn't good. He was bleeding slowly, but Kaiden needed it to stop. "Fuck." He didn't want to think of losing Mathias. "Keep your eyes open, Mat." Kaiden shook his body.

Blaise stumbled over and knelt in front of Kaiden. "Gods," she whispered.

"Can you do something?" Kaiden begged her, tears escaping his eyes.

She frowned. "I don't know how."

"Try anything. Please?"

Kaiden held tight to Mathias, his mind flashing back to all the trouble they'd gotten into, the pointless fights over women, his inappropriate jokes. *I can't lose him. My best friend, my brother.*

Kaiden couldn't imagine a life without Mathias. The way they could communicate with each other without having to say anything at all. His stupid, off-the-wall ideas. Regardless of how insufferable he might've been, it was Mathias's presence Kaiden would miss most of all. Kaiden's heart clambered up in his throat as he stared at his best friend. "Don't you leave me."

Elric, Zade, and Isaac walked up. Kaiden glanced at each of their solemn faces, then back to Mathias. His eyes drifted shut. His grip on Kaiden's arm weakened. "Hold on, Mathias."

Blaise looked to Zade. "We have to get him to Nira. Can you connect with her using satori?"

"I can try, but I might need your assistance." He walked away with Blaise on his heels.

A few moments later, they returned to say Nira was riding to meet them halfway.

"I'll take him. If I fly just above the treetops, we should remain unnoticed," Kaiden said. "The rest of you can keep watch from the ground."

They wasted no time in strapping Mathias onto Kaiden. With a burst of power, he used his legs and wings to launch them through the canopy, and then they were speeding over the thick forest back toward the Alchyra camp.

"We're gonna get you healed, just hang on," Kaiden said, his best friend hanging limply from his body. Mathias was weakening; Kaiden could sense it.

The sun drifted closer to the horizon. Nira came into view, the chill of night setting in. Kaiden landed and quickly cut away the bindings holding Mathias to him. He laid Mathias's unconscious body on the forest floor. Nira leaped off her horse and stumbled a few times, reaching the two.

Nira went to work on Mathias. "His pulse is weak. I don't know if I'll be able to save him."

"Please," Kaiden choked out. "Try."

The rest of the unit caught up moments later. He felt a hand on his shoulder and knew it was Blaise. The memory of Blaise on the verge of death invaded his mind. Nira had nearly exhausted herself with the effort, and Blaise hadn't even been completely healed.

Kaiden felt so hopeless. So pathetic. He hated being unable to help Mathias.

"Tell me how I can help," Blaise said, kneeling next to Nira.

"I'm going to need a shit ton of akrani to heal the worst of the damage," Nira said. "Is there any way you can transfer some of your energy to me?"

Blaise looked to Kaiden. "Do you think we can use your enophii power to transfer akrani?"

Kaiden didn't know what to do, but he would try. He nodded, taking Blaise's hand. He placed his hand on Nira's shoulder, completing the connection. Nira placed her hands over Mathias's chest.

Misty healing tendrils of smoke emanated from her palms, enveloping Mathias's body.

This is what I'm meant for. Kaiden sensed the two women's energy. He ensured the flow of akrani between them was clear and unfiltered. The surge of power sent waves of intense pulsations through his muscles. He clung to hope while the akrani continued to flow from Blaise's hand and into Nira, but he sensed their energy waning.

Nira's smoke dissipated, and the wound was mostly gone. Both women crumpled together, working to catch their breath, holding each other for support.

Mathias still lay there unconscious. He wasn't breathing.

"Come on," Kaiden murmured over and over. "Breathe, gods dammit!"

Mathias's eyes shot open and landed on Kaiden. "So bossy," he rasped, lips curving up.

"Fucking idiot." Kaiden helped Mathias sit and hugged him. "I thought I lost you."

Mathias wrapped his arms around Kaiden. "Nope. Afraid you're stuck with me."

Kaiden helped him get to his feet, and then he assisted the two ladies off the ground.

Nira's and Mathias's eyes met. Kaiden knew that look. He'd shared it with Blaise countless times.

"Well, I guess I should be getting back," Nira said. She turned, making her way back to her horse.

Mathias grabbed her wrist and pulled her close. He embraced her and buried his face in the crook of her neck. "You need to quit saving me, woman."

Nira grinned. "Never."

Mathias and Nira stared into each other's eyes for a long moment until Kaiden cleared his throat. "We should get back on the road if we're going to make it through the Azureden pass before dark," he said.

Nira was the first to pull away. "Safe travels." She climbed onto her horse and rode away.

31

BLAISE

THEY FORMED UP AGAIN AND HEADED toward the Azureden Mountains. This time Kaiden stayed closer to Blaise in the silence of the forest.

Kaiden tilted his gaze to her. "It'll be nice to see Grams and Daniel again."

Blaise raised a brow and stared at him. "Again?"

Kaiden replied, "Uh . . . yes. I visited them every now and then after I returned from Balam."

She canted her head. "Why?"

He swallowed. "Just to check on them, and I'd deliver her elixirs from the apothecary."

Her face softened, eyes becoming glossy. "You brought the medicine to her?"

"Yes. Daniel was completing his final trials to graduate to sentinel, so he didn't have time to pick them up for her."

She took a breath and turned away. "Thank you for doing that." She didn't know what else to say about what his kindness meant.

The group made it through the Azureden Mountains without incident. They gave the horses and themselves a few hours of rest and planned to push on to Lerwick, where they would be able to get a full night's rest. Not many outside of Balam knew what the new queen looked like. If they checked in to the Lerwick Inn under aliases, they should be safe for a night.

Kaiden insisted on sharing a room with Blaise. She conceded. They all seemed too tired to argue about sleeping arrangements. Mathias and Elric shared a room while Zade and Isaac shared another. Blaise was relieved their room had single beds.

She was exhausted after the long day of travel, but she hadn't wanted to stop until they made it to Lerwick. They had little time to waste. With every passing hour, her father's attacks on her mental barriers grew more intense.

She sank into the bed and didn't even bother to remove her boots. Kaiden pushed his bed next to hers and followed suit. He tucked his wings as though that would make him fit in the tiny bed. The springs creaked, and his body covered the entire mattress.

At the moment, she couldn't care less where he moved his bed. Her eyes drifted shut.

"Thank you." Kaiden's whisper caused Blaise to jerk awake.

"W-what?" she half grumbled, eyes still closed.

His hand slid over the sheets to hers, interlacing their fingers. "Everything you did saved Mathias. I didn't know how much it would mean to me . . ." He inhaled as if to compose himself. "You have my undying gratitude."

Her lips curved up. "It was a team effort. He means a lot to me too, but don't tell *him* that."

"I won't. His head is big enough as it is," Kaiden mused.

A moment of silence lapsed, and then Kaiden said, "We were so young when his parents died. He came over almost every day. He didn't like being in his huge house all alone."

Blaise opened one eye and glanced at Kaiden. "How did they die?"

"His father was put on a task force. It was supposed to be an 'easy' mission. The unit was assigned to transport resources to Lerwick, but they were attacked by steel revenants on the way. Mathias's father didn't make it, and his mother died of a broken heart just a few months later," Kaiden said.

Blaise's chest constricted. She couldn't tell by Mathias's playful, carefree nature that he'd gone through so much heartache. Hearing his story helped her see him in a different light. "How tragic."

Kaiden squeezed her hand.

Blaise now knew how Kaiden valued the camaraderie within his small circle. They both cherished friendship as much as family. And both would sacrifice anything to keep them all safe.

After an amazing night of sleep, Blaise and the rest of the unit wasted no time in saddling their horses and getting back on the road. Elatora was about a half day's ride. They rode through Grelan Forest, the familiar scent of pine filling Blaise's nostrils. The Teaos wall came into view a few hours later. She peered up the length to the wall-walk. There weren't nearly as many sentinels as she remembered.

Once the unit checked in with the guards at the gate, they followed the dirt path, passing fields of wheat and corn. The lay of the kingdom was quite ingenious with its circular barriers in case of an enemy attack. They would first need to get through Teos and cross the miles of farmland before finally getting to the city. The business zones encircled the residences and sentinel estates, which surrounded Cloveshire Castle.

Blaise squinted her eyes as the four towers of the castle came into view. Her chest tightened at the possibility King Vaughn might contest Kaiden's revision of the peace treaty.

"Do you think the king will have time for me today?" Blaise asked Kaiden. They rode up the incline to Cloveshire Castle.

"I'm not sure." He shot her a smile. "We're going to try though."

Her heart sped up, and she bit back a grin. He winked at her, and the corner of her mouth rose. *Damn, my face.*

The streets were crowded with people. Many stopped to stare at Kaiden and his wings while the unit made their way through the marketplace. He appeared unbothered for the most part.

King Vaughn's servants were very accommodating toward the group upon their arrival. Kaiden was able to schedule a meeting in the war room with the king that evening, and then they were escorted to the guest wing to freshen up and rest.

Blaise changed and cleaned up in her room, then strode out into the wide corridor of the castle. Elric and Isaac fell into close step behind her. Commander Stephen had summoned Kaiden and Mathias to speak with them at the Atherton estate.

Adding to Blaise's frustrations, Kaiden had left Elric and Isaac to watch over her. It seemed pointless to argue with him now. She stopped and shot them each a tight-lipped expression. "You know, this is a little overkill. I *am* an ex-sentinel."

Elric kept his blank gaze straight ahead. "Apologies, Your Majesty."

She let out a breath. They were just following orders. She couldn't fault them for that. "It's fine."

"Blaise?" A familiar voice fell upon her ears.

Her heart thrummed, and she spun toward the voice. Daniel threw his arms around her. With wide eyes, she moved swiftly, enveloping him in her arms, inhaling his musky scent and taking in his warmth.

"Daniel," she whispered.

Elric and Isaac lingered behind them.

Blaise kissed her brother's cheek and pulled away to get a better view of him. His hair was longer, and he had a bit of stubble on his chin. She smiled. "Look at you. You look like Dad. Gods, I've missed you."

"Thank the gods you're alive." His voice shook with emotion. He wrapped her in his embrace, tighter this time.

If only he knew. She held him close, tears trickling down her cheeks. He sank his face into her shoulder.

"Barely," she whispered, her own voice wavering.

"My unit kept telling me there was no way you'd make it, but I didn't have a doubt in my mind," Daniel murmured. He stepped back, swiping the wetness from his cheeks. "You did it, and now you're the queen of Balam." With mischief curving his lips, he gave her a proper bow.

"Stop it." She pushed his shoulder.

He stumbled and laughed. "How much time do we have to talk?"

"A few hours, but I do need to go see Grams at some point," she replied.

Daniel greeted Elric and Isaac.

Blaise said, "I need to do some research on the upcoming solar eclipse."

"That's perfect. There's space in the archives for us to chat." Daniel led them to the gigantic library. Tall stacks filled with tomes surrounded them. The scent of oak and leather hung in the air. Blaise and Daniel took a seat in front of a huge bay window.

"Yeah, perfect," Isaac muttered under his breath, and then he and Elric wandered in different directions.

Daniel sat on the small couch at an angle, facing Blaise. "I didn't know they assigned Elric 'Mad Dog' Maddock to guard you."

"I didn't know he had a nickname."

"I heard he was locked in a dungeon for years because he couldn't control his akrani." Daniel was the biggest gossip, and she'd learned long ago to take everything he said with a grain of salt.

She gave a short laugh. "I'm sure you're exaggerating."

He shrugged. "Believe what you want. But have you seen the smoke come out of his eyes yet?"

"Well, yes, but that doesn't mean he's out of control." Her eyes roved over the shelves. "You wouldn't happen to know where the astronomy section is, would you?"

He cocked an eyebrow. "No, I don't. But I know the archivist."

Loud voices echoed through the cavernous room, distracting Blaise from their conversation. *What in gehheina?* She stood and started searching between the shelves, Daniel trailing behind her. She turned down a row to find Isaac and a petite woman with dark blond hair in a heated argument.

"How could you? I thought you loved me. We had plans!" the young woman screamed, tears in her eyes.

"Liz, I'm so sorry, it just happened," Isaac said just as loudly.

"Fuck you, Isaac. That can't *just* happen," she yelled.

Blaise squinted at the woman and recognized her amber eyes. That had to be Kaiden's sister, Elizabeth. Gods, she was beautiful with her high cheekbones and full lips. She wore a simple blue dress with quarter sleeves that hugged her curvy frame.

"I promise you it won't ever happen again," Isaac said, trying to grab her hand, but she yanked away.

"You're gods damned right about that. It won't happen to *me* again," Elizabeth snapped.

Blaise could swear the small woman was getting louder with each word. She tried to interrupt them only to be ignored. *Are all the Athertons stubborn?* It was clear they were both consumed with their emotions.

Elric turned the corner without hesitation and tugged Isaac away from Elizabeth.

Isaac spun around, confronting him in a rage. "This has nothing to do with you, *Mad Dog*."

"Enough," Elric said. His voice was calm but radiated power.

Isaac stepped closer to him. "You have no authority over my personal life."

"And I'm no longer a part of your personal life." Elizabeth started to walk away.

"Wait." Isaac reached for her arm once more.

Blaise stepped forward to intervene, but Elric threw his left fist into Isaac's jaw, knocking him to the gray stone floor.

All Blaise could do was stare at the scene unfolding before her with no idea how to handle it. This was such a strange situation.

Elizabeth stepped over Isaac and up to Elric. She stuck her index finger into his armored chest. "I don't know who you think you are, but I don't need you to fight my battles."

Blaise couldn't keep the grin off her face. Gods, this woman was snarky. She had to be, especially having Kaiden as a brother.

Daniel stood next to Blaise, obviously entertained with this whole situation.

Great, the whole city is going to know about this by the end of the night.

Isaac recovered, climbed to his feet, and rubbed his jaw. Daniel had enough sense to lead him out of the archives.

Elric stared at Elizabeth with no emotion on his face. "I was trying to keep the peace."

"Punching people in the face is not peaceful." Elizabeth's voice resonated throughout the archives.

Elric crossed his arms over his broad chest. "It stopped the argument, didn't it?"

Blaise tilted her head. This was the most she'd ever heard him say.

Elizabeth groaned. "Were you raised by wolves?"

"From what I know, he deserved it," Elric replied nonchalantly.

Blaise cleared her throat to disguise her laugh.

Elizabeth turned to her. "And who are you?"

"I'm Blaise." She wasn't quite comfortable introducing herself with her title.

Elizabeth's eyes widened, and she curtsied low. "Forgive me, Your Majesty. I had no idea you were visiting Elatora. My brother never mentioned he'd be bringing you back with him."

"No. It's all right, Lady Elizabeth—"

"Please, call me Liz."

A smile crossed Blaise's mouth. "Very well, Liz. You may call me Blaise."

Liz pursed her lips. "As you wish, Blaise. Is there anything I can do for you?"

"Actually, I need information about the next solar eclipse," Blaise said.

Liz folded her arms and pressed a finger to her chin. "What precisely do you need to know about it?"

"I need to know the timing of the darkest moment during the solar eclipse," Blaise replied.

"Let me look at my astrolabe." Liz reached into her skirt pocket and withdrew a circular metal plate with dials. She sniffled and sauntered to the nearest table, laying the device on the surface. She started to spin the discs.

Elric leaned in, reaching out to touch the golden contraption. Liz slapped his hand away and glanced up at him with squinted eyes. "Don't touch it."

Elric stepped away, his eyes narrowed slightly. Blaise assumed he was growing impatient with Elizabeth.

Blaise tried to read the chart, but it was like reading a different language. Liz seemed to comprehend the information with no difficulty.

After several minutes, Elric heaved a sigh. "Are you sure you know what—"

Liz's gaze snapped to him, and she placed a finger to her lips, shushing him. Her attention fell back onto the astrolabe. She changed out the plates.

Blaise pursed her lips, hiding her smile. Elric actually had a look of incredulity on his usually blank features.

Liz muttered something Blaise couldn't hear. "What?" she asked.

"The sun celebration is in four days, so the darkest moment is at the peak," Liz said, setting something on the astrolabe. She peered up at Blaise. "It'll be at precisely 3:33 in the afternoon."

Balam was a three-day journey from Elatora, and that was only if Blaise made it through the Onyx pass with no delays. *That doesn't leave much time to find the crystal and close the portal.* Blaise tapped the wooden surface with her index finger while she stared at Liz in silence.

"Blaise?"

Her mind snapped back to Liz's curious face. "Thank you." She turned her attention to the tall sentinel standing a few feet away. He towered over them both. "Now, Sergeant Elric, if you will, please escort Lady Elizabeth back to the Atherton estate."

Blaise regarded him. *That's a lot of man.* She wondered

how the armorer had ever managed to fit him. She read the slight glint of disagreement in Elric's blue-gray eyes. He followed Liz out of the archives.

Blaise blew out a breath, thankful that whole ordeal was over. Daniel returned from taking Isaac to cool off. She thanked Daniel and asked him to escort her home. He conceded with that familiar smile she'd missed.

BLAISE AND DANIEL RODE THROUGH the black iron gate of the Carrington estate. The house she'd grown up in didn't feel like the home it had once been. Nothing about it had changed, even in the time she'd been gone. *This isn't my sanctuary anymore.*

Normally, Daniel would talk Blaise's ear off, but the ride had been abnormally silent. *Maybe he's matured during my absence.*

She dismounted in front of the house, and Daniel took the reins of her horse. "Go inside, I'll take care of the horses," he said.

"Okay. Thank you." Blaise turned and approached the dark wooden door. The day she left Elatora was a vivid memory. She pushed open the door, and the hinges creaked.

A familiar gentle voice resonated from the kitchen. "Daniel, is that you? Were you able to pick up eggs from the market?" Grams walked into the foyer, coming face-to-face with Blaise for the first time in what seemed like a lifetime. The bowl slipped from her hands and shattered on the stone floor.

Blaise stood there, staring at the woman who'd raised

her, the woman who'd believed in her even before she had come into her power, the woman who'd lied to her about her life. Despite everything, she sprinted toward the white-haired woman and fell into her loving embrace. Tears poured down her cheeks. She hugged Grams as tight as she could without breaking her.

"Oh, my Pooka. I knew you could do this. I knew you would come back to us."

Blaise pulled away. Tears pooled in Grams's eyes as well. She helped clean the broken pieces off the floor.

"Come, sit, tell me everything." The old woman led Blaise into the kitchen, where a fresh cup of hot tea sat on the wooden table. Grams sat down and blew into her mug.

Blaise took a seat across from her and summarized all the events that had unfolded in the months she'd been gone: discovering her true lineage, putting an end to Rowena's reign, taking her place as queen of Balam, and last but not least, the attack. By the time she was finished, Grams's tea was gone.

A brief silence deafened the space between them.

Grams finally said, "I'm sorry I had to keep the truth from you for so long. It was for your own protection."

"I know," Blaise muttered. "But you hid everything. How much do you really know about my lineage?"

"I don't know much, only what your mother was comfortable sharing. I didn't know the truth about your father." Grams stood and made her slow way to the sink. She placed her empty mug in the basin, then faced Blaise.

"I found my mother's journal during my short time in Balam. You should have something for me. It's the Onyx Crystal," Blaise said.

Grams shook her head. "I don't have that, Pooka."

Blaise's brow furrowed. "What do you mean you don't have it? I need to have it to close the portal."

"I understand, but when we sought refuge here, Jocelyn and I thought it would be best to keep you separated from it due to the potential amplification of your akrani." Grams sat back down at the table and folded her hands on the surface.

"Okay. So, where can I find it?"

"We gave it to a guardian for safekeeping—someone who would protect it with their life."

Blaise's body tensed, a million questions bombarding her mind. "Who is this guardian?"

"It was Beatrice Atherton."

Heat rose in Blaise's chest, and her nostrils flared. *Does Kaiden know?* It wouldn't be the first time he'd withheld something important from her. "Of all people, why did you choose her?"

Grams replied, "We didn't. She approached us."

"Why would *she* do that?" Blaise asked, raking a hand down her face.

"She told us we were in possession of a powerful and potentially destructive relic," Grams said. "She warned us that, in our hands, the risk to the realms was too great."

Aware of the time, Blaise thought it best to cut the conversation short. She hugged her grandmother. "Thank you for everything, Grams." She tried to pull away, but the old woman only held her tighter.

"We may not be blood, but we will always be family." Grams looked at Blaise and cupped her cheek. "You will always be my Pooka."

Blaise's eyes started watering again, and her chest tightened. She swallowed, not wanting to break down, and said, "I know, Grams. I love you."

"And I you. Now, you better get a move on." Grams walked Blaise to the door.

Daniel waited in the courtyard with the horses, ready to escort Blaise to their next destination.

"Take care of your sister, Daniel," Grams said.

The two mounted to leave the estate, and Blaise took one last glance back at the white-haired old woman. Exhaustion from her travels and the day's events was setting in. She ignored it, determined to retrieve the crystal from the Athertons.

32

KAIDEN

KAIDEN RODE THROUGH THE MARKETPLACE next to Mathias, his eyes roaming the wooden stalls of produce and products the merchants were selling. Whispers caught his ears; he assumed they were about the huge wings protruding from his back. Perhaps he should've flown instead.

"Seems like you're giving the realm dwellers something new to talk about," Mathias said, flashing a charming smile to a woman at a fruit stand. She just about dropped her melons.

Kaiden rolled the tension from his shoulders, his wings rustling with the motion. "It seems so."

"How do you think the commander will react?" Mathias gestured to Kaiden's wings.

"Honestly, I don't know," Kaiden replied.

Cedric didn't appear to like all the attention. He huffed at one of the passersby.

"Don't be rude." Kaiden patted the horse's neck.

Mathias steered closer. "You could at least smile at people."

Kaiden's lips formed a straight line.

"Or not." Mathias held his hand up, palm facing Kaiden. "Now I know where your horse gets his attitude."

Kaiden's eyes narrowed. "You know I'm not a big people person. You're lucky I like you."

They neared the end of the street. Only another mile or so until they arrived at the Atherton estate.

"Blaise is a queen; therefore, you, my friend, would be king by marriage. And that kind of requires you to be a people person," Mathias said.

They passed the last few shops in the marketplace.

Kaiden released a breath. "I'll deal with that if it happens."

Mathias's smirk remained on his face. "Okay. Just seems a bit counterproductive."

"What're you talking about?"

Mathias shrugged. "Why deal with it later? You could start practicing now. Here's your chance. Just offer him a friendly smile."

A young man who appeared to be in his twenties was making his way toward them. He wore a leather apron over his tunic and trousers. His boots had black marks on them as well. Kaiden assumed he was a blacksmith.

Before the man could pass, Mathias nudged Kaiden's arm with his own.

"Hello there, how're you this fine afternoon?" Kaiden said.

The man didn't stop. He peered at Kaiden and winked. "I'm doing well now that you're here."

Kaiden canted his head. He didn't stop Cedric from continuing forward. "Well . . . have a good day, then."

The blacksmith waved. "You too, handsome."

Once they were out of earshot, Kaiden's gaze snapped to Mathias, and he gritted out, "Why do I listen to you?"

Mathias laughed. "What's wrong? I thought that went well."

They finally came upon the Atherton estate, with its linear structure, stone pillars, and huge windows. They passed under shady oak trees, riding up to the courtyard. He and Elizabeth used to walk down a thin gravel pathway lined with shrubs that led to a stream behind the house. Kaiden used to call this home.

Kaiden and Mathias settled their horses in the stable and walked into the house through the foyer. Commander Stephen stood in front of the hearth in his study, staring into the fire, his hands clasped behind his back.

Kaiden's heart swelled at the sight of his aging father despite his flaws and misgivings. Stephen's shoulders seemed more weighed down by the trials of his years as commander. His father wasn't the spry man he'd once been. There looked to be more gray in his hair than Kaiden remembered.

Commander Stephen turned his attention to Kaiden and Mathias entering the room. The wrinkles and dark circles around his russet eyes had become more prominent. "Well, it seems you've returned with two surprises."

Kaiden and Mathias stopped within a few feet of the commander.

"Mathias in one piece and"—the corner of his father's mouth lifted—"wings."

With a frown, Kaiden said, "You don't seem surprised about either." He ruffled his white wings.

Stephen looked at Mathias. "Why don't we start with you? What in gehheina have you gotten yourself into, boy?"

Mathias gave a slight wince at the question. "That's a bit complicated."

"What isn't when it comes to you? I could swear the end of the realms was upon us," Stephen half joked.

Kaiden and Mathias exchanged fleeting looks. They continued to tell the commander he may not be wrong. Stephen's face appeared to pale despite the warmth of the fire. He took a seat next to the hearth.

"Elaborate," Stephen said with a sweeping hand gesture.

They laid out what had happened in Balam when everyone thought Mathias had tried to assassinate Blaise, that Andreas had been behind everything and had kept Blaise prisoner at some ruins in the Terrenmis Mountains and had used alchime and a meta crystal to create a prestae of Blaise and possibly others. They informed the commander of Theod's invasion of Balam and finished the debrief with Amasu's potential return.

At the end of their long-winded explanation, Commander Stephen remained silent for a few moments before muttering, "That . . . *is* quite the turn of events. The king will not be pleased with his cousin's actions." He looked up. "Sergeant, I would like to speak to my son for a moment."

It took Mathias a second to process the request. "Oh, yes, sir. I have plans at the Bootless Sentinel anyway."

Kaiden frowned. "You're not going to the meeting in the war room tonight?"

"Am I required to?" Mathias paused halfway to the door.

"No. I don't believe you are," the commander said.

"Well then, you know where to find me." Mathias snapped his fingers.

"We'll talk about your adventures later, my boy," Stephen said.

Mathias's shoulders slumped. "Yes, sir." He strode out with a bit less pep in his step.

Kaiden let out a slow breath. If Mathias wasn't *required* to be at an official event, he usually never went.

"I suppose you're looking for answers," the commander said.

"I can't avoid the issue anymore, obviously. I need to know about my mother," Kaiden said, his voice resolute.

Stephen huffed. "What do you want to know first?"

"Did she have wings?"

"Yes, she did. An ellorian is able to grow wings after their twentieth year, though only after they meet their anii-vasei." Stephen stared into the flames of the hearth.

Kaiden ran his fingers through his hair. "And you didn't think that was important for me to know?"

"Well, you'd spent time with so many women, I wondered if maybe you hadn't been born with your Mother's abilities." Stephen rested his elbow on the armrest. "Never in my wildest dreams did I think your match would be Blaise Carrington of all people."

Kaiden cocked a brow. "You don't think we're a good match?"

"That's not what I said, son. I was only stating a fact." Stephen's gaze went to the only window in the study. "I want you to have something." He stood and strode over to his desk, then pulled out a wooden box. Flipping the lid open, he retrieved a ring of jet-black metal. "It's made of galydrian. I gave it to your mother on our wedding day." He handed it to Kaiden. "It seems it's time for you to have it."

"Are you sure?" Kaiden observed the ring's texture and how it glistened in the light.

Stephen nodded. "I'm sure. She wanted you to have this one. There was one specially made for your sister as well, though she may not be in need of it," he murmured.

"I don't understand," Kaiden said.

Stephen waved a hand. "It doesn't matter now. What's important is that you know."

"Thank you, Dad." Kaiden tucked it away in his pocket.

"I'm honored to know who you'll give it to once the time is right. Consort to the queen is no easy feat." Stephen grinned.

Kaiden's cheeks warmed. He gave a short nod. "I have one more question about Mom. I don't remember ever see-ing her wings. Why is that?"

"She knew how to use her akrani to control them."

"I'm assuming I should have that ability as well," Kaiden said, crossing his arms.

Stephen shrugged. "I'm not sure, son. That's something you'll have to discover for yourself. I've never had any akrani to speak of, but when I was with your mother, it was as if I could feel hers flowing through me. As if we shared it. As if we were one person."

"So, what about Elizabeth?" Kaiden asked.

"It's difficult to say." Stephen had a worried look about him.

"You lost me again," Kaiden stated.

Stephen met Kaiden's gaze and took a deep breath. "I think it's time for you to have a man-to-man with King Vaughn."

"King Vaughn?" Kaiden and the unit already had a meeting arranged with him. "I guess I could speak with him at the meeting tonight. What exactly am I asking him about?"

Stephen looked away. "Your mother."

Kaiden heard the front door open and slam shut. He strode into the foyer and witnessed Elizabeth stomping up the staircase, tears in her eyes. Elric stood at the bottom step, that unreadable expression on his face.

"What did you do?" Kaiden's brow wrinkled.

"I might've reinjured Isaac," Elric replied in his monotone voice.

Serves him right. Kaiden held back a grin. "Explain."

A knock sounded on the heavy wooden door.

"Thank the gods." Elric sighed and opened it to Blaise and Daniel standing in the doorway. She did not look pleased.

The commander joined them in the foyer.

"Blaise, I thought you were going to visit Grams," Kaiden said by way of greeting.

She stepped through the threshold, Daniel trailing behind. "I did," she bit out.

Why did she seem royally pissed at him? Kaiden couldn't think of anything he'd done wrong. "Is everything okay? How'd you get here so fast?"

She ignored his question. "Where is it?"

Daniel shut the door behind him.

Kaiden's brows came together. "Where's what?"

"The crystal."

Was she officially losing her mind? "What makes you think I know where it is?" he asked.

Commander Stephen stepped forward. "Because I know where it is."

Kaiden's eyes widened. "How?"

"Your mother left it in my care before she went on her last mission to Balam," Stephen said, glancing down at his clasped hands. His gaze drifted to Blaise. "Kaiden knew nothing about this, Your Majesty."

Blaise let out a breath as though she was relieved. "Please, no formalities. Just tell me what you know."

How could his dad have kept something like this for so long?

Kaiden inhaled, calming the anger in his stomach from rising. "Where is it?"

Stephen's gaze met Kaiden's. "Beneath Cloveshire. After your mother died, it was the last safe place in the realm. It's part of the reason *you* need to speak to King Vaughn, Kaiden."

"I appreciate everything being done to help me and my people, but this is my responsibility, not the captain's," Blaise said firmly.

Stephen bowed. "I apologize, Your Majesty. I meant

no disrespect. It's just the reason the crystal is in the king's possession has to do with our families' connections."

Blaise's expression softened. "Oh, I was unaware. It's a good thing we're meeting with the king tonight, then."

Kaiden nodded, looking at Blaise. "Head back to the castle. I need to check on my sister."

Elric, Daniel, and Blaise bid the commander goodbye and headed out the front door. As Kaiden walked upstairs, Stephen asked, "Are you angry with me?"

"I'm sure you had your reasons, like everything else," Kaiden said. He left it at that. If he discussed the matter further with Stephen, they would probably end up arguing.

Kaiden walked through the hallway to the last room on the right and knocked on his sister's door. "Liz? Everything okay?" he called through the door.

"I'm fine."

He folded his arms. "Really? You didn't sound fine when you barged into the house like a hound of gehheina."

Silence.

He sighed. "You were so upset, you didn't even notice my wings."

The door flew open. His petite sister stood in front of him, gawking at his white feathers, her big amber eyes wide with disbelief. "Um . . . What in gehheina?"

He stepped into her bedchamber, taking in the space. "Not until you tell me what happened with Isaac." Stacks of books sat in every corner and rose from her oak desk like towers in front of the huge bay window. Papers were scattered about the surface, and a few had fallen to the floor. A small pile of books took the place of a bedside table next to her messy bed.

Kaiden remembered Liz helping him study for written tests, and if he was being honest, she was the only reason he'd passed them.

"I'm pretty sure you know of Isaac's treachery." She sniffled, sadness brimming in her eyes.

He brushed his fingers through his hair. "I'm so sorry that happened."

She shrugged. "Looks like I'm destined to be alone." She padded over to her desk. "It's just going to be me and the archives."

"Don't say that, Liz. The right one will come along when you least expect it," he said.

She shot him a faint smile.

"Are you going back to Cloveshire? You don't need to be here alone."

"I'll leave with Dad. He hasn't been in the best spirits, so we can walk together, and I can go to the archives while you're both in the meeting," she said, picking up a leather-bound book and skimming through the pages.

"I see." Kaiden wanted to talk more about their father, but time was running short. He needed to return to Blaise. "We'll talk about it more later. I'll see you tonight." He kissed the top of her head and walked out of the room.

WHEN KAIDEN ARRIVED AT CLOVESHIRE, he was immediately approached by a fellow female captain with bright green eyes. "The king would like to speak with you before the official meeting begins," she said, and Kaiden couldn't tell if she was staring at him or his wings.

Kaiden followed her to the throne room, where the king sat waiting, his fingers tapping on the armrest.

King Vaughn stared at Kaiden's heavy wings. The king's façade rarely fell, but Kaiden could swear an unreadable cascade of emotions rushed over the man's face.

"It seems there have been many changes," the king said, straightening in his seat. "Tell me when this happened."

Kaiden summarized the situation between him and Blaise and how his wings had sprouted out of nowhere. "I didn't know what was happening to me. I'd never learned much about my mother's lineage. And thank the gods for them; they were the only way I could save Blaise when King Theod invaded."

The king took a deep breath and released it, taking off his crown and running a hand through his wavy chestnut hair. "There's no need to worry about the treaty. My cousin is an imbecile." He said it like a curse. "We'll speak about this more with the queen tonight." The king stood, walked down the steps to Kaiden, and examined his modified tunic. Kaiden couldn't exactly fit his armor over his wings anymore.

"Remember when I said the ellorians used to fight alongside the sentinels?" the king asked.

"Yes, Your Majesty."

"Follow me." King Vaughn led Kaiden into the war room of the castle. He walked up to a stone wall filled with many ancient weapons, most likely wielded by legendary kings and sentinels. He pulled on a weapon attached to the wall, and it slid open. "Not many people know about this room. Not even my commanders."

King Vaughn sparked a torch, lighting the narrow hallway. The door closing behind them, he led Kaiden down the damp corridor, and at the end was a solid wooden door. The king unsnapped a key from his belt, then unlocked and pushed the door open, revealing an exceptional arsenal. Swords, axes, and maces decorated the wall farthest from them. Bows and shields covered another. Full suits of armor lined the last wall of the room.

"This is incredible. There are weapons in here I've never seen before, Your Majesty." Kaiden examined a broadsword hanging on the far wall.

The corners of the king's mouth quirked up. "These are a few of my favorite pieces. This is my personal armament." He walked over to a built-in cabinet and opened the double doors. Inside was the finest leather armor Kaiden had ever seen. King Vaughn retrieved a black leather aegis with galydrian fasteners. The pieces were pliable, and it looked like it would protect his back and the base of his wings. "This is the armor the ellorians wore when they served Elatora. This should protect and accommodate your wings comfortably."

"These are your favored items. Are you sure, Your Majesty?" Kaiden remained unmoved from his spot in front of the broadsword.

"They are, but I have plenty, and it seems you're in more need of it than I am. I look forward to seeing an ellorian in our skies once again." The king walked up and held the armor out to Kaiden. "It's covered with a special resin that came from your mother's people. It makes the material as strong as steel, but light and flexible."

"I'm only half ellorian."

"Take the armor, Captain," King Vaughn ordered.

Without further hesitation, Kaiden took it from him. "Thank you, Your Majesty."

The king nodded. "I will send my tailor to fit you for some tunics as well."

"That's not necessary—"

"I will not accept no as an answer, Captain." The king strode out of the hidden room, Kaiden trailing behind.

"As you wish, Your Majesty." Kaiden was always appreciative of everything the king provided him. He had always been so accommodating to Kaiden, even at a young age.

The king lifted his torch to a sconce on the wall. "Now, I trust you can keep this a secret?"

Kaiden replied, "Of course, Your Majesty."

He shoved the torch into the sconce, and the wall opened up. The flame was extinguished upon their exit. The wall returned to its place.

"Your Majesty, I was told by my father I should speak to you about my mother." Kaiden held the armor in one arm. "I know she was part of the Sentinel Order, but I don't know why my father has sent me to *you* to find out more about her."

"When your mother was in the Sentinel Order, she fell in love with a man before meeting Commander Stephen. But because of their positions in the realm, they knew they could never truly be together." King Vaughn sighed. "In time, they had to choose duty and honor over love. Even though they'd made that difficult decision, they were unaware of the power of their bond."

That word.

"Bond?" Kaiden's eyes widened. He sat on the closest bench, his attention unwavering.

"When your mother married Stephen, it showed solidarity between the ellorians and the realm dwellers of

Crenitha. They were once again guardians. However, the result of the bond grew inside her—"

Kaiden loosed a breath. "What does any of this have to do with me? This had to have happened long before I was born."

King Vaughn shook his head, melancholy in his dark eyes. "This has everything to do with you."

Kaiden leaned over and buried his face in his hands. His eyes welled with tears, heart hammering wildly in his chest. *This can't be true.* Stephen was the only father he'd ever known.

The king's boots came into Kaiden's view through his trembling fingers. The weight of every word the king had said made his chest ache. His fear of the truth kept him from meeting King Vaughn's gaze. Swallowing the lump in his throat, Kaiden asked, "If Commander Stephen is *not* my father, then who is?"

The king placed a heavy hand on Kaiden's shoulder. His voice shook with emotion. "I am."

33

BLAISE

BLAISE STOOD IN FRONT OF THE MIRROR, making sure she looked presentable for a meeting with the king. The door creaked open. Light from the hallway streamed into the room, and Kaiden walked inside. His arms were full of what looked like leather armor rolled into a ball. His pale face startled her. "Kaiden, what's wrong? You look sick."

He met her gaze. His eyelashes had remnants of moisture.

She strode up to him. "What happened? Why're you upset?"

Kaiden staggered to the bed, tossing the ball of armor onto it. He turned and pulled her into his tight embrace, burying his face into the side of her neck.

Blaise frowned. Wetness soaked into her bodice. Pulling away, she stared into his tear-filled eyes. "You're scaring me. Tell me what happened."

"I know the truth," he choked out. Drawing her to the bed, he sat on the edge. He leaned forward, resting his forehead against her stomach. The strongest man she knew broke down in her embrace.

She brushed her fingers through his dark hair and held him through his pain. She gently massaged his shaking shoulders and caressed the base of his wings. Confusion and sorrow lingered in the air, consuming her. She couldn't keep her own tears from flowing. She was content to stand there and comfort him for as long as he needed her.

"Commander Stephen is not my father. King Vaughn is," Kaiden blurted.

Blaise crouched to his eye level. "I know there's nothing I can say to make this better, but maybe through our bond we can share this heartache. I've been in your place and have come to terms with similar truths. Let me help you."

Kaiden's gaze met hers. "I don't know how."

She cupped his face in her hands and pressed her lips to his. She trailed kisses down his chest and started to unbutton his trousers. He showed no signs of protest. She peeled his pants from his waist, releasing his hard length. He lifted his hips to let her slide them down his thighs. Leaving his trousers at his knees, she watched his cock throb.

Blaise stood and began taking off her own pants. He watched her with heat in his eyes. Remnants of emotion still lingered in his voice. "We don't have to do this."

"Let me." She put her hands on his shoulders and straddled him. Lining herself up with his impressive erection, she settled onto him, sinking down until he filled her completely.

He wrapped his arms around her waist, thrusting up deeper. Grabbing her nape, he drew her into a claiming kiss. She fell into him, enraptured by the moment. It was as if the rest of the realm had fallen away. They were all they would ever need.

They paused their kiss, their bodies still moving as one. Kaiden whispered, "I'm yours until the end of eternity." *I love you, Blaise.*

Her eyes widened at the sound of his beautiful voice in her head. *And I'm yours, Kaiden.*

He looked at her with surprise and exultation in his hazel eyes. He captured her mouth with his once more, quickening the thrust of his hips. Holding her body tight to his, she ground her hips against him, fueling the fire between them.

Everything changed since Kaiden came into my life, and now I can't see a life without him. Her world shattered with the thought and her powerful release. Her body shook, and he tensed beneath her, burying himself deeper. The need for air broke their kiss, and they held each other tightly, both breathless. Satiated.

Kaiden traced circles on her back and said, "Thank you."

She smiled and placed a light kiss on his lips. "I will always be here for you."

Blaise and Kaiden helped each other dress quickly. He explained his new gear and the talk he'd had with King Vaughn. She helped him fit the armor over his wings and fastened it up. She stepped back and took him in. *Gods, he's beautiful.*

He cupped her cheek and stared deep into her dark eyes. His lips tilted up in that roguish grin she was all too familiar with. *And so are you.*

"You weren't supposed to hear that," she said, cheeks warm.

He gave her a quick peck on the lips, then stepped back. "I have something for you. This might be the last time we'll get to be alone."

She met his gaze.

"I wish I were the type of man who could make grand gestures, but there's just not enough time." He pulled something out of his pocket and lowered to one knee.

Blaise stepped back and covered her mouth with both hands, aware of the significance of his gesture.

Kaiden peered up at her, holding a beautiful galydrian ring between his fingers. "Being away from you made me realize how empty my life is without you."

She couldn't believe he was doing this right now. Tears welled in her eyes and threatened to spill down her cheeks.

"I know there are no guarantees in life, but I can guarantee this." He took her left hand and slipped the ring onto the third finger from her thumb. "As long as I have air in my lungs, I will love you." His voice trembled with emotion.

"You've had my heart since the moment I saw you on Teaos wall. I love you, Blaise."

Tears flowed down her cheeks. She stared at the ring for a long moment before focusing on his hazel eyes. There was no denying it anymore. "I thought I was happy on that wall, but then you came along and showed me what had always been missing from my life." She bent at the waist and placed her forehead to his. "It was you. I love you, Kaiden. With all that I am."

Kaiden straightened, bringing his lips to hers, slow and reverent. Nothing could ever come close to this. He was the only thing that made sense in her chaotic life. She wrapped her arms around his neck and sank into his kiss.

His chest rumbled in approval, and he pushed her up against the door. Grabbing the backs of her thighs, he spread her legs and pushed his hips between them. "Don't start something you can't finish," he whispered, his breath tickling the shell of her ear.

He ground his hard arousal into her. A moan escaped her. "Don't blame this on me." She trailed kisses down his neck and licked his pulse.

He let out a small grunt. "The king won't appreciate our tardiness."

She sighed. "You're right. We should stop before you end up inside me again."

"Don't tempt me, Sparks." He let her go, and she slipped down, her boots clacking loudly against the stone floor. They shared one last kiss, then made their way out of the bedchamber.

BLAISE AND KAIDEN MADE IT to the war room on time. She took her place to the right of the king, and Kaiden stood directly across from her, a slight grin on his face.

Blaise briefly scanned the guests at the long oak table. Everyone in Kaiden's unit stood behind him, minus Mathias. Zade stood with Kaiden while Commanders Peter and Stephen took their places next to Blaise.

King Vaughn thanked everyone for coming to the meeting. His gaze fell on Blaise. "Gods, I can't get over how much you look just like your mother."

Blaise tilted her head and asked, "You knew my mother?"

He nodded. "I did."

She'd just met this man and already had so many questions. "I see," was all that came out of her mouth.

King Vaughn didn't take his eyes off Blaise. "You're probably wondering how I knew her."

She clasped her hands in front of her to calm her nerves. "Well . . ." She cleared her throat. "Yes."

"I met her when I was a mere prince. She'd just been crowned queen. And what a regal and commanding queen she was." His eyes twinkled with admiration for Blaise's late mother.

Blaise pursed her lips.

The king let out a breath. "She visited often. We exchanged letters while apart."

Blaise couldn't hold back the question any longer. "Your Majesty, did you—"

"I loved your mother dearly, child. She was a loyal friend." He interlaced his hands in front of him. "So you can imagine my sorrow when I heard of Rowena's betrayal."

She studied the king's graying features, which were filled with years of wisdom and experience. "It sounds like you knew her well. I have no memory of her."

King Vaughn stared at Blaise as though she were an old friend. "Well, I remember Maxima to be quite the prankster. She used to shock me with that katai of hers. On purpose." He chuckled. "Her whole situation was quite unfortunate. A horrible chain of events."

Blaise remembered Rowena telling her she was a bastard. "Could you tell me the story of what happened to her?" She wanted to know what the people of Crenitha believed.

The king began, "There were many suitors pursuing Queen Maxima, but the one who caught her heart had no status. Your father was a farmer in Balam. She told me about him and how she hoped to marry him, but unfortunately, he was murdered before he could ask her."

Though Blaise knew the real truth, she asked, "Murdered? By whom?"

"The assumption is Rowena killed him, but I don't know for sure," King Vaughn replied.

Who came up with this story? No one could know that Maxima had been carrying the child of a high god. Blaise nodded.

He continued, "I made a promise to your mother." The king's eyes swept around the room of intent listeners. "We took many precautions throughout your childhood to ensure Rowena couldn't find you with her satori. When you became a sentinel, I had to have you assigned to the safest and most isolated part of Teaos. Then our scouts discovered Rowena was planning to attack. After the first team failed, I knew you were our last chance."

Blaise stood there, taking in all the information. Her eyebrows came together. "But there was no guarantee we'd be successful. What would you have done if we'd failed?"

"I would've lost everything to Rowena. But I would not have let it go without a fight." He placed his hand on her shoulder. "The important thing is you're here now and have taken your rightful place as queen. For that I am incredibly thankful."

"So." She shot him a brief look. "Did I even earn my position in the sentinel ranks, or was that all part of the precautions as well?"

He squeezed her shoulder, then let his hand drop back to his side. "My dear, the hounds of gehheina couldn't have stopped you from becoming a sergeant. You earned every one of your accomplishments while you were in my military."

Blaise's cheeks warmed nearly as much as her heart. She glanced at Kaiden's prideful grin from across the table. He was sending her soothing akrani, calming her nerves.

"I received a message from my cousin, King Theod, not too long ago. It seems he does not want me to interfere in your civil dispute." King Vaughn clasped his hands behind his back and began pacing at the head of the table.

Blaise froze. *Does that mean he can't help us?* But why would they be here if he didn't intend to help? She didn't think he was afraid of Theod in the least. Even though Theod had a larger army, King Vaughn's sentinels were highly trained.

"If you think I'm going to heed his warning, you're mistaken." King Vaughn winked at Blaise, and the corner of his mouth quirked up. "I didn't harbor you in my kingdom for most of your life so my idiot cousin could destroy the balance of this realm with his greed," King Vaughn said. "No. We'll teach him a lesson. I've been wanting to kick his ass anyway."

Blaise frowned. "But some of his men joined our cause a few months ago."

"Trust me, that wasn't his choice. Raijinn and Zade had been waiting for the true heir of Balam to rise. They chose to join your ranks of their own accord," said the king.

Zade nodded in agreement. "His Majesty is correct. King Theod was not aware we'd been training for your return."

Blaise had never considered that Kaiden, Zade, and Raijinn had trained most of their lives in order for her to regain the throne. This made her more disappointed in herself for failing to keep King Theod from invading Balam.

"Commanders, one of you will gather enough sentinels to drive the Haven soldiers out of Balam," the king said to the two men.

"It would be my honor to lead an army for Her Majesty," Commander Stephen said.

Kaiden looked at his father. Blaise wondered how he felt about that. It wouldn't be a safe mission, and Commander Stephen was nearing retirement.

"I'm extremely honored by your noble gesture, Commander." Blaise bowed her head to Stephen, and then she met the king's gaze. "I am forever in your debt, Your Majesty."

"The peace treaty will stand as is. Consider me your ally from here on out, Queen Blaise," King Vaughn said.

The king dismissed everyone, and they filed out of the war room. Commander Stephen met Blaise and Kaiden outside. The full moon shone through the tall hallway windows while they strolled through the castle.

"Where did you hide it?" Kaiden asked as though he'd read Blaise's mind.

The commander turned a corner, leading them through a door, then down a winding staircase and into the lower-level corridor. He glanced back at Kaiden. "When your mother died, we decided to hide the crystal deep in the castle. As her husband, I was chosen to carry out this burdensome task. We had to ensure no one would have access to it—not even the king himself."

Jynx hadn't explained what the crystal could do, and Blaise was angry she hadn't bothered to ask. "Is the crystal dangerous?"

Stephen peered over at her. "When in the wrong hands."

"What are its capabilities?" she asked.

"I'm not supposed to know anything about it, but Bea and I talked about it once. She said it could amplify akrani hundredfold, and if not used correctly, it will kill. Unlike its counterpart, it requires the strength of a god to harness its power." The commander shot Kaiden a fleeting look. "Bea felt its power once, and she never touched it again. She called it the mortis crystal."

Nausea rolled through Blaise's stomach, and her breath trembled. Would she be willing to die for her kingdom?

Kaiden grabbed her hand and gave it a reassuring squeeze. His gaze locked on her as though he could sense her concerns.

"What do you mean by counterpart? Is there more than one Onyx Crystal?" Kaiden asked.

"No. But like everything in the realm, it has an equivalent. Its counterpart has the same power and requires the same akrani, but the Azure Crystal is of the light and therefore cannot be overcome by darkness. No one knows its location." The commander glanced at his son. "Well . . . no one mortal, I should say."

They continued down several staircases, and Blaise didn't think it would end. After one more descent, they came to a long dark hallway. Stephen took a torch off the stone wall and gestured for them to follow.

"You didn't have to carry this burden on your own." Kaiden's voice softened. "I've been trying for years to understand why you were so closed off after Mom died. I had grown to resent you, Dad. I thought you didn't want me anymore."

Stephen stopped in the middle of the hallway, the orange firelight from the torch illuminating his face and the melancholy glistening in his dark eyes. "I had no idea, son." He stared at his boots. "I had to protect you." He looked up at them. "Both of you."

"Thank you, but your task is complete." Kaiden threw his arms around his father and embraced him. The commander's eyes widened, then softened, and he returned the hug from his son.

"Please. No more secrets," Kaiden said, stepping back.

Stephen swallowed. "I promise."

The light from the torch caught Blaise's ring, making it glimmer into the commander's eye. He grabbed her hand and stared at the galydrian band on her finger. Then his gaze bounced back and forth from Blaise to Kaiden.

"It appears congratulations are in order," Stephen said, a smile forming on his rugged face.

Blaise nodded. "Yes, but it's still up in the air."

A quirky smile tugged at the corners of Kaiden's lips, and she couldn't keep the foolish grin off her face.

"Well, nonetheless." Stephen pulled Blaise in for a hug. "Welcome to the family, my dear."

They arrived at a thick worn wooden door. In the middle was a star-shaped keyhole with ridged edges. Commander Stephen detached a leather string from beneath his chest plate. He tugged, snapping it from around his neck.

He eased the key in. "This has been a long time coming." He gave it a rough twist and a jerk, pushing hard to open the heavy door. He handed the key to Kaiden. "I won't be needing this anymore."

The room was enveloped in darkness. They passed through the threshold. The torch did little to illuminate anything around them. The dank space smelled of mildew and was uncomfortably warm.

Stephen touched the torch to an unlit one on the wall near the door. It sparked a chain reaction, lighting the entire room. In the middle of the space was a stone chest with no markings.

Blaise sensed akrani through the gray stone, and she was still about twenty feet away. She breathed in, tamping her power down deep inside her. She stepped toward it. Inside the chest was a wooden stick. Stephen retrieved it and inserted it into a small hole in the wall farthest from them. A stone shifted, and he struggled to pull it out. He reached in and emerged with a small wooden box, which he then handed to Blaise.

"You'll have to use akrani to open it. Be careful. Beatrice said it's extremely powerful." Stephen disclosed a black velvet bag from his utility belt. "The inside of this bag is lined with stardust; it should neutralize the crystal while in transport." Stephen wasted no time in dropping the box into the bag, pulling the ties, and sealing it shut.

She took the bag from him and tucked it into her jacket pocket, then shot him a gentle smile. "Thank you."

Stephen grinned.

They made their way back up the winding staircase to the dungeon hallways. They walked through the last level, and a trickle of akrani rippled up Blaise's spine.

"Do you smell that?" Kaiden asked.

The scent of burnt leather and rotten eggs filled her nostrils.

Three large snarling beasts filled the hall and then sprinted toward them. Black saliva dripped from their mouths as they bared razor teeth, ready to tear into their prey. The flesh beneath their cracked dark leathery skin glowed a reddish orange. Their burning red eyes focused on her.

Blaise's eyes widened. She reached for her sword, but it wasn't there. "Shit." She was going to have to use akrani.

"Hounds of gehheina!" Stephen unsheathed his sword, ready to fight.

How did they get into the castle? Sparks of lightning manifested from Blaise's fingertips. As the creatures neared, she released azure streams of lightning. They hit one hound, but the beast didn't slow.

Blaise started to sprint toward the razor-clawed creatures. Kaiden shouted at her, telling her to stop. She didn't listen. Falling to her knees, she slid between the middle hound's legs. She rolled and managed to get behind them.

Her plan to lure the beasts away from Kaiden and the commander was beginning to work. She sprinted down the hallway and passed a large hole in the wall where the hounds had most likely come from. There was one right on her heels. *Shit, where are the other two?*

Blaise sprinted up the staircase. Conjuring akrani, she used wind to try slowing the creature. Its claws dug into the stone, and it was only held back for an instant. She made it to the upper landing of the floor and continued running through the corridor.

Just as the beast leaped for her, she manifested another burst of wind, knocking the hound onto its back. Her tactics were failing her. Fire and wind hadn't worked.

The last element she had was water. Although Jynx had spent a few days training Blaise, she wasn't quite comfortable with wielding that element.

She summoned akrani once more, the cold power crawling through her veins, ending at her hands. The pressure built and built until she could no longer contain it. She pointed her palms at the hound, and a powerful flow of water crashed into it, knocking her down. The hound tumbled backward from the force but regained its footing quickly.

Her well of akrani was running low. She stood, steadying herself for this last attempt to kill the creature. Letting the power course through her once more, she pushed the water from her palms, transforming it into shards of ice. The hound shrieked, attempting to dodge them. It was unaffected. The hound leaped forward, and the force of the blow sent her flying into the wall behind her. The snarling beast closed in, and darkness fully engulfed her vision.

34

KAIDEN

THE LAST THING KAIDEN SAW WAS BLAISE sliding between the creature's legs and disappearing behind them. The hounds started to follow her. Kaiden wouldn't allow it. He tried to get the dogs' attention, but he couldn't extend his wings in the cramped hallway. He managed to propel himself forward, spiraling over the creatures, landing in front of them. Steadying himself, he stood in front of the snarling beasts, sword at the ready.

A barrage of daggers flew toward the hounds from his father. The commander ran toward one hound, jumped onto its back, and wrapped his arms around its neck. He squeezed, trying to cut off its airway.

The hound focusing on Kaiden snapped at him. He sidestepped and lunged, but the beast shook off the attack. *Fuck, their skin is impenetrable.*

Commander Stephen stabbed the hound he was on, breaking the tip of his sword. He unsheathed a dagger and plunged it through a crack in the hound's skin. It shrieked and jumped to the side.

The beast Kaiden was fighting turned. Its large jaws clamped down on the commander's right shoulder, teeth penetrating his armor. The creature whipped its head back and forth, the commander's blood spewing everywhere. His shrieks echoed through the corridor.

"Release him!" Kaiden screamed in desperation.

"The crevices are the weak points," Stephen bellowed.

Kaiden spun and tried to lunge at the already-injured hound. He pierced his blade through the cracks in its chest. Burning vibrations resonated through the steel. He could sense the akrani within the beast.

Can I absorb it?

Focusing, he drew out its life source. The creature squealed, its body shuddering. The hound jerked back, trying to retreat from the blade. It yanked Kaiden forward, but he spread out his wings to steady his stance.

The other creature tossed the commander from its jaws and charged toward Kaiden. He ripped his blade out of the dying hound's chest, and lava ran like blood to the floor. Vibrations flowed through his sword. He spun on his heels and, in one swift movement, sliced the creature's head off.

Kaiden rushed to his father, who lay in a puddle of blood. He cradled Stephen in his arms. "I'm sorry, Dad, I tried—"

The commander held up a weak hand. "It's not your fault." His breathing was shallow.

Stephen's life was fading from his eyes. His gaze went to Kaiden's. "I've always loved you, son. Have no doubt. Tell Elizabeth I love—" Upon his last breath, Stephen's hand fell to the stone floor, his body limp in Kaiden's arms.

Tears trickled down his cheek, and Kaiden pulled Stephen's body closer and mourned. "I love you too, Dad."

35

MATHIAS

Nira haunted Mathias, and he hated it. He hated the way he didn't hate her at all—not even a little. He hated that he wanted to fall into her deep blue eyes. The way her humming brought him peace while she did chores. Her smile. His desire to taste her ripe, kissable lips.

His mind had gone so far off, he hadn't even realized the girls had stopped dancing. The women at the tavern had been playing to his favor. But when one of them had tried kissing his neck, jawline, and lips, Nira was all he could see. His rejection of them had left him remembering his own. It was her cold dismissal that had brought him to this place where he didn't want to be.

His arousal hadn't been piqued in the slightest, and it annoyed the gehheina out of him. He was Mathias Gage, ladies' man and legendary tail chaser of Elatora, and yet the only one he wanted to chase didn't want him. *What the fuck is wrong with me?*

Since he wasn't going to be doing anything with these women, he chose to put his confidence in the ale. He was determined to drink Nira out of his head. He shuffled through the crowd of patrons to the bar with his empty mug. "Another pint."

The bartender obliged.

Mathias brought his mug back to his table. A familiar dark-haired woman sat with him, and even though he wasn't alone, there was a wretched yearning in his chest.

"You look distant tonight, Sergeant. Should I grab another girl and take you up to one of the rooms?" Charlotte asked. "We can go upstairs, and I can bring you a little *clarity.*"

He took a sip of ale and swallowed. "Not tonight, sweet—" He was about to call her sweetness, but the nickname only reminded him of Nira. *Gods, release me from her sorcery.*

"Are you sure? We haven't seen you for quite some time," Charlotte said.

Mathias had no idea why he was so taken with Nira. All they did was fight. The only times they did get along were when they cooked dinner together or while she was reading. He enjoyed her presence and the banter. He enjoyed the challenge she presented.

"Sergeant?" Charlotte stared at him.

Mathias chugged the rest of his ale and stood, his chair scraping against the wooden panels. "I'm afraid I must say goodbye, Lady Charlotte." He made his way out of the Bootless Sentinel.

He was glad to be out of there, even though he would probably regret it later. The nearly full moon lit his path home. He stumbled with each step, kicking up dirt in his wake. What was Nira doing? Was her training coming along? Did she ever think about him? They *had* been living together as husband and wife. Would she have moved on, or was he just the guy she had to keep saving?

He came to a crossroads and halted. He studied the marketplace buildings; everything had closed down. The evening breeze had an eerie chill. The sound of galloping hooves filled his ears and was nearing fast. He turned around and was met by an unfamiliar sentinel bearing down on him.

"What's the meaning of this?" he asked, stumbling back.

"You must return to the castle, Sergeant. There's been a breach," the lower-ranked sentinel bellowed.

Without hesitation, Mathias climbed on behind the man, and they took off toward Cloveshire.

36

KAIDEN

KAIDEN CRADLED THE COMMANDER—HIS father—in his arms. *He's dead. I couldn't save him.* He buried his face in Stephen's neck, sobbing uncontrollably. "Dad. Come back." His voice was muffled.

Minutes passed, and Kaiden's sobs lessened. He laid his father's body on the dungeon floor and climbed to his feet. The tips of his bloodstained wings dragged across the ground. He turned, tears stinging his eyes. His knees buckled, and he caught himself against the wall, his heart shattering for the man who'd raised him. The man who'd knowingly protected him and everything he cared for. The man who'd accepted him and always given him love.

He wiped the tears from his cheeks with his palm.

A few sentinels made it down to him, and their eyes widened at the scene before them. Kaiden needed to pull himself together. He inhaled a deep breath, then straightened and faced the lower-ranked guards.

"Take the commander's body to the throne room," Kaiden ordered. "Make sure you shroud him in linens."

They followed his orders and carried the commander's body out of the corridor.

A large group of people had gathered outside of the throne room, and amongst them were Kaiden's unit and Elizabeth. *Gods, Elizabeth.* Tears started to surface again. They were all each other had now. *And Blaise.* "Has anyone seen Blaise?"

Everyone shook their head.

Elizabeth ran into Kaiden's chest, throwing her arms around him. "What happened, Kai?" She examined his crimson-splattered armor. "Where's Dad?" Her voice trembled.

Kaiden swallowed the lump in his throat. He rubbed circles on her back. "It's okay. I have you now, Liz. We're going to be all right." He didn't know if he was saying it for her or himself.

Behind him, Kaiden could hear the shuffling of sentinels carrying the body to the throne room.

Liz looked past his shoulder. "Who is that, Kaiden?"

He kept his eyes straight ahead, tears brimming. "I'm sorry, Liz." His voice cracked. "I couldn't save him."

King Vaughn and Commander Peter entered to view the body. They'd spent years in service with Kaiden's father.

Sadness gleamed in their eyes, and Kaiden knew his father would be deeply missed by these men.

The king walked up to Kaiden and Elizabeth. "Commander Stephen was a great man. He will *never* be forgotten." His voice wavered on those last words.

"You have my condolences. I'll have the battalion ready to go after the burial," Commander Peter said.

"Thank you, Commander," was all Kaiden could get out.

Once King Vaughn and the commander had left the throne room, the rest of the unit gathered around the body, each wearing a solemn expression of honor and respect.

Liz buried her face in Kaiden's chest and sobbed. "Please don't make me go home. I don't want to be alone."

Kaiden eased himself out of Elizabeth's embrace. "Liz, Blaise is missing. I have to find her."

Liz peered up at him and stared. "Dad just died. You can't just leave me!"

"You don't know what's at stake here, Liz," he said.

Elric stepped up to the two. "Captain, I'll take care of her."

She started backing away from them. "No. I'm not going with him. I don't even know him."

Kaiden grabbed her arms, steadying her. "Liz, look at me."

She stared into his eyes.

"Please, you'll be safe with Sergeant Elric. I need you to go with him," Kaiden urged.

Liz huffed a breath and nodded, hugging herself. Kaiden gave his thanks to the sergeant, and then Elric escorted her out of the throne room.

"Has anyone seen Blaise?" Kaiden repeated.

"Wasn't she with you?" Mathias asked.

"We got separated when the hounds attacked. She tried to lure them away," Kaiden explained. He stared at his father's body, the bloodstained shroud that covered him.

"How could you let her out of your sight again?" Zade asked, and the muscles in his jaw ticked.

"Mathias, take a squad and search the north and west sides of the marketplace. I'll take the south and east. Zade, search the dungeon where the hounds escaped from," Kaiden ordered.

"No, Captain. I'll accompany Mathias." Zade rolled his shoulders back. He walked out, Mathias trailing behind him.

Kaiden wasted no time taking flight over the kingdom. He searched every possible path out of the city until the sun began to rise.

THE SCENT OF MORNING DEW still lingered in the crisp air. Kaiden's marched steps carried him into the armory, where his unit had gathered. His grief was nearly tangible, but he needed to find Blaise. Wood crackled and popped in the hearth, the scent of pine filling his nostrils.

Kaiden spoke first. "I found nothing. Hopefully you all had better luck."

"I'd say we got lucky," Zade remarked, shooting Mathias a shit-eating grin.

"Explain." Kaiden tilted his head, pacing in front of the wooden mantel of the fireplace.

Elric, Isaac, and Daniel stepped closer. Daniel had joined the search late last night after hearing his sister was missing.

Mathias blew out a breath before he said, "Charlotte from the Bootless Sentinel stopped us during our search. She saw Blaise being carried away by 'a huge dog.' She said it was headed toward Teaos's north gate."

"We found the hound's tracks leading out of Elatora. They looked to be going toward the Onyx Mountains," Zade finished.

Kaiden's lips quirked. "Lady Charlotte. That's an interesting informant." There was no time to waste on sarcastic quips. His lips formed a straight line, and then he nodded. "I'll fly out ahead and start following the tracks."

He turned to the three standing on his right. "Elric, Isaac, Daniel, you'll ride with Commander Peter and the battalion to Balam." He looked to his left at the other two. "Zade and Mathias, ready the Alchyra and wait in the west of Balam for the signal."

The unit of sentinels accepted their orders and slowly began dispersing. Elric lingered behind while the others walked out of the armory.

"Should you be going alone?" Elric crossed his arms, leaning back against the table nearby.

"I can cover more ground alone."

Elric pushed off the table, stepping closer. "I have my shadows."

Kaiden shook his head. "Save that for the real fight."

Elric stared at Kaiden like he wanted to say more. "Very well. Your sister's waiting for you at the burial site."

"Thank you, Sergeant. I hope she wasn't too much of a handful." Kaiden started toward the door.

"Not at all," Elric replied.

Commander Stephen's burial site was within walking distance from Cloveshire. Kaiden approached swiftly, Elizabeth's short frame coming into view. Her long dark blond hair flowed in the morning breeze, and she wore a flowy white dress.

Kaiden kept his focus straight ahead, stopping next to Liz, loose dirt crunching beneath his boots. Everything around seemed to mourn the commander; even the birdsong had ceased.

Standing over the grave with his heart thrumming in his chest, he found the courage to look down to where their father's body rested. The bloodstained shroud was still exposed.

Kaiden blinked back his tears and crouched to grab a handful of damp soil. He rose, praying for Colvyr to bless him with the strength to cross the river Akran. Then he let the dirt slip through his fingers.

With a deep breath, Kaiden turned, adjusting the white strip of cloth he'd tied on his right arm. "I have to go now, Liz."

She tilted her blank tearstained gaze to him. "I understand," was all she said.

Kaiden started to pull her in for a hug. She shrugged away, averting her eyes. An ache weighed heavy in his chest at her resistance, but he respected her need for space. "Goodbye, Elizabeth."

"Wait."

He stopped in his tracks and didn't face her.

"Tell me you'll return." Her voice trembled like she was holding back her sobs.

His throat tightened, eyelashes damp with emotion. "I

will fight tooth and nail to come home to you." He turned in time to see tears streaming down her beautiful face. "I love you, Liz."

"I love you too, Kai," she whispered, though it was barely loud enough for him to hear.

Blaise better still be alive, for everyone's sake. Kaiden sprinted and stretched his wings. Catching remnants of the morning breeze, he glided into the sky.

37

MATHIAS

THE AZUREDEN MOUNTAINS HAD BEEN relatively easy to pass, except for a single troll Mathias and Zade had managed to evade. Thankfully, the sunlight kept the kynarah in their caves. They sped through, hungry shrieks ringing in their ears.

Mathias wanted to know how Nira was doing in her training. *Is she a natural with weapons?* He rummaged through his saddlebag, brow furrowed. "Have you seen my canteen?"

Zade shot him a crooked grin. "Perhaps Lady Charlotte could tell you."

Mathias groaned. "You're never going to let that go."

Zade scanned the trees swaying in the gentle breeze. "Never."

They were finally entering Meliwe Forest.

"I'll find something about you, General. You just wait." Mathias narrowed his eyes.

"You can try," Zade drawled, stifling a yawn. He glanced at Mathias, the horses' hooves clip-clopping on the path. "Tell me, Sergeant. Do you have any talents? Anything entertaining?"

"I'm a sergeant in the Sentinel Order, what do you think?"

"I don't know. That's why I asked." The corner of Zade's mouth rose.

Mathias rolled his eyes. "I have many talents." The melody of Nira's favorite song lilted through his head. His body responded to the tune she'd sung while they'd cooked dinners together. He couldn't stop himself. "Lady Nira has the voice of a siren," he muttered.

"Nobody said anything about Lady Nira." Zade stole another sidelong look at Mathias. His lips began tilting upward. "Ah . . . You fancy her."

Mathias couldn't believe he'd let that slip—and in front of Zade of all people. He ran his palm down his face. "No." His denial hadn't come out as resolute as he'd wanted it to.

"Liar," Zade teased. "I don't blame you. She's an amazing woman. Unfortunately, she's too good for the likes of you."

"Yeah, I know," Mathias murmured, but that comment was meant to be offensive. "Hey, what makes you think I'm not good enough for her?"

"You have an outstanding track record," Zade said. "Actually, I think it stretches across all of Crenitha. I'm sure Lady Charlotte is well aware."

Mathias rolled his eyes again, ignoring the last part of Zade's remark. "Is that why you don't like me? Because I get all the women?"

Zade sighed. "I guess I can't expect a brute to understand the complexities of emotion." He sped up his horse's gait.

Curiosity overcame Mathias. *What's that supposed to mean?* He caught up with Zade. "Hey, wait, tell me what you mean."

"My mother was like you. She professed her love to my father multiple times, but she repeatedly gave herself to others. He gave her all his love, but she never truly returned it. He died a lonely man." Zade had a bitter, sad look on his face. "I'll never understand how someone can give their heart to one person, yet just give their body to anyone."

"What if I told you I have no intention of being that way with Nira?" Mathias asked. He couldn't believe the words. And why was he opening up to Zade? *Is he using some kind of satori on me?*

Zade kept his gaze on the path ahead. "You think you can give all of that up just for her?"

Could I? He remained silent the rest of the ride into the Alchyra camp, and Zade didn't prod the issue further.

LATER, MATHIAS AND ZADE ARRIVED, and they tied their horses with the others on the outskirts of camp. Passing the guards at the entrance, they made their way through

367

the rows of tents. Some soldiers sparred on the makeshift training field. That was when Mathias spotted *her*.

Nira stood in the middle of the field, gleaming in traditional Alchyra armor. She fought two men, though she was smaller than both. She wielded a shortsword in one hand and a dagger in the other. Moving with the grace of a dancer, she struck like a viper. The two men had no time to calculate her moves.

"It appears she has improved immensely in the days we've been gone," Zade said, observing Nira as well.

A few moments passed. Her opponents surrendered and walked off the field. Nira walked up to Zade and Mathias. She gave the general a proper Alchyra salute.

"You've been hard at work," Zade said by way of greeting.

She stepped over to the water barrel a few feet from them and drank from the ladle. "I didn't want to waste any time."

Even covered in sweat with strands of dark hair sticking to her face, she was more radiant than Mathias remembered. "It's nice to see you again, Lady Nira."

She walked away toward a row of tents, barely giving Mathias a second glance.

"It feels like the temperature dropped." Zade placed a heavy hand on Mathias's shoulder, a look of amusement on his face.

Mathias stomped off after her, digging his fingernails into his palms. He followed her into a small tent. "Is that how it's going to be between us?" He flung the flap of the tent closed, crossing his arms.

Nira sighed, still not meeting his gaze. "I really don't understand what you want from me, Mathias."

"I don't know, how about some decency? I know things haven't been the greatest between us, but I thought we were at least going to be friends." He stepped closer to her, knowing damn well that wasn't what he really wanted. But he was afraid to lose her completely.

She rolled her eyes. "Friends? We tolerate each other at best."

"That's just how we are now." Mathias didn't know what he was saying anymore. "I know you like bickering with me."

She shot him a sidelong glare. "You expect me to believe friendship is enough?"

He swallowed, nodded, and hated himself for the lie. "Yes."

"Fine. Friends it is."

He peered down at the sword hanging from her hip. "How about we initiate this fine friendship with a little sparring match?" The corner of his mouth rose.

Her eyes narrowed. "Are you sure you can handle that kind of humiliation?"

"As much as you can, sweetness." He winked at her and came within inches of her face. "So, what do you say?"

She leaned in, her breath warm on his face. "Let's go, *Sergeant*."

Mathias led the way back to the training field. They retrieved practice swords from a barrel and walked out to the center. A crowd of Alchyra encircled them, keeping their distance.

"First person to concede wins?" She held up her sword and staggered her stance.

"Sounds good." He anticipated she'd make the first move and was pleased when she did. He parried and spun around her. She crouched down and swept at his legs with one of hers. He leaped over it and rolled forward, landing on his feet.

She darted toward him, swinging. She made contact with his backplate once, twice, three times.

He stumbled forward. "Ouch." He looked at her with a cocked eyebrow. He *had* planned on going easy on her, but apparently, that would be a foolish move. She continued her onslaught. Leaning down and angling his body, Mathias turned and elbowed her in the side, gaining distance from her.

She grunted her frustration, but the speed of her blade was a blur. She pressed in, swing after swing. He stayed just ahead of her, deflecting each blow. Gods, she was fast and so precise with that damn weapon.

He didn't want to hurt her. He didn't want to lose either.

Nira lunged, overstepping.

Mathias grabbed her arm and pulled, spinning her away from him. That only angered her more. She glared at him, and he shot her a mischievous grin.

With a shriek, she lunged, taking two powerful steps before she threw her body forward. She pushed off the grounds using her hands and propelled herself into him. Her feet landed square on his chest. He huffed and stumbled backward, falling flat on his back. She landed straddling his chest. The blunt edge of her sword pressed against his neck.

She leaned over him, grinning, their faces inches from each other. "I win."

He smirked. "I always wondered what it would feel like with you on top."

The corners of her mouth tipped upward. "I guess this proves you can't handle it."

His brow rose. *Oh really? You think I can't handle it?* In one swift motion, Mathias pushed the sword away from his neck, grabbed her backplate, and yanked her onto her back. He climbed to his feet and stood over her, holding his blade above his head.

Mathias looked down at Nira, ready to deliver the final blow, but the serene and joyful smile on her face caught him off guard. He quirked his head, trying to figure out her expression.

At that moment, her gaze dipped to the tip of her dagger, which was ready to pierce his balls.

"I said I win."

WITH THE MOON LIGHTING THEIR path, General Zade and Sergeant Mathias rode through Meliwe with one hundred Alchyra following close behind. The balmy evening breeze brushed against Mathias's cheeks. Despite being on his way to probable death, he couldn't get Nira out of his mind. Her words contradicted her eyes.

Zade kept pace, riding next to him. "Something on your mind, Sergeant?"

"No," Mathias answered, short and clipped.

Zade had a firm look about him. "I'm just trying to make sure your head is going to be in the battle. Wouldn't want your woes to get us all killed."

Mathias could always count on Zade to be honest even though he wasn't tactful. He let out a slow exhale. "Don't worry, I'll be ready."

"What is your loyalty to Queen Blaise anyway?" Zade asked, scanning their surroundings.

"It's because of Kaiden."

One of Zade's brows rose. "Honestly?"

Mathias groaned. "You're really going to make me explain?"

"Well, I could always pry it out of you." A smile crawled up Zade's face, and he placed two fingers to his temple.

"No, no. Not necessary." Mathias released a breath. "It's simple. When we were twelve years old, Kaiden and I were put on the same team for squire training. He was so excited the first time we won against the opposing team. I never thought he noticed my efforts. As we walked off the training field, Kaiden ran up and hooked his arm around my neck. He said, 'I want you on my team from now on. Okay?' I was so honored. From that moment on, we were inseparable. Now Kaiden loves Blaise. She is part of him. Losing her would absolutely destroy him, and in turn, that would crush me as well."

Zade's emerald eyes softened. "I see. You and the captain have been very close for a long time, much like Raijinn and I were."

Mathias nodded. It hadn't occurred to him that Zade was still mourning the loss of Raijinn. It could've been difficult being around him and Kaiden. "I'm sorry," was all he could think to say.

Zade gazed at him in surprise. "Thank you, Sergeant."

Mathias found solace in the silence as they journeyed onward, a nervous anticipation lingering in the atmosphere. The only sounds were the rhythmic steps of the valiant Alchyra advancing toward war.

Hidden under the cover of night and the tall crops growing in Balam, Mathias took it upon himself to scout ahead. The small town just outside of the fortress appeared to be heavily guarded by Haven soldiers. If he had to guess, they were making sure the people couldn't escape the kingdom.

The Alchyra had hidden in the foothills and were awaiting the smoke signal.

The wheat near Mathias rustled softly. In one smooth yet silent motion, he withdrew his dagger.

Nira crawled up next to him, her movements muted. "Sorry," she whispered, her eyes on his blade.

"What in gehheina are you doing here?" Mathias asked with indignation.

"I couldn't let you get all the action," she replied with a grin.

Her bravery made her even more attractive, if that was possible. Mathias wanted to be closer to her, feel the warmth of her body against his, lose himself in the taste of her lips—and cursed himself for wanting it all. "Get back in formation," he said through gritted teeth.

She frowned. "And risk blowing our cover? I'm here now, so why not just let me stay?"

Gods dammit, she made a good point. "Fine, stay."

With a smug grin, she moved into a more comfortable position beside him, supporting herself on her forearms. She didn't seem to realize his stare on her. Without her noticing, he managed to avert his wanton gaze.

"Now what?" she asked, her focus on the moonlit town in the distance.

"We wait for the sentinel battalion." Mathias pulled a cloth from beneath his chest plate.

"What is that for?" Nira asked, her eyebrow raised.

Her curiosity was endearing. "It produces thick red smoke when lit."

"I see," she muttered, looking out at the soldiers patrolling the small town. "Did you let me win?"

He kept his focus ahead. "What?"

"The duel."

"If I say no, will you be quiet?"

She cast him a squinty-eyed glare and snorted softly. "I'm quieter than you."

Why is she here? "Why don't you just tell me what this is all about, Nira?"

She rested her chin on her forearms sheepishly. "I had time to think about things when I left you in Meliwe . . ."

His heart skipped a beat. *So, she has been thinking about me.* He met her cobalt eyes while he cocked a brow. "And?"

Nira lifted her head and leaned close to him, and her eyes went to his lips, but she remained silent. Distracted.

Mathias placed a finger beneath her chin and brought her gaze to his. "Tell me," he prodded gently.

She let her bottom lip slip from between her teeth. Mathias couldn't help but stare, wanting nothing more than to lean in and taste it.

"After everything we've been through, I'm glad we can still be friends." The corners of her mouth tugged up into a genuine smile.

His lips matched hers, and he flicked her nose play-fully. "Me too, sweetness. Me too." He tore his thoughts away from her, setting his attention back on the town.

Mathias hadn't intended to go into battle like this, feeling utterly pitiful and dejected. In the company of his chosen family, all he yearned for was someone worth fight-ing for, someone to return home to—a desire that eluded him throughout his life.

38

BLAISE

A FAMILIAR SENSE OF MISERY ENVELOPED her—cold iron chafing her wrists raw. Blaise opened her eyes, vision hazy. Her eyes finally focused, and she scanned the room. *The sanctum. I'm in Balam.* She couldn't remember anything beyond being knocked unconscious at Cloveshire. Gods, she hoped Kaiden and the commander had made it out unharmed. She was chained between two pillars on her knees. She still had scars from her time in the Terrenmis Mountains, so she tried to minimize her movements.

King Theod strolled in. Simone and a small squad of soldiers followed. "Good, you're awake," he said.

Blaise shot him a haughty glare, the warmth in her stomach rising with every passing second. "You are a sorry excuse for a king."

Theod chuckled and acted like he was going to turn away, only to slap her across the face. A pained cry escaped her lips, but she managed to keep her scowl. He grabbed her chin and jerked her gaze to his. Her cheek throbbed.

"You're in no position to speak to me like that, little bitch." He brushed his thumb over her lips, then pushed her away. Her arms twisted, and the cuffs gouged into her wrists.

The sun came into her view behind him. The eclipse was going to begin soon. She needed to free herself from these chains.

"Let me go," she ground out. The warmth in her stomach turned molten.

It's time, Little Flame.

"Or what?" Theod stepped closer.

Her sweltering chaos was so consuming that the tears brimming in her eyes dried up. The power worked its way to her wrists, heating the iron that shackled her.

Theod's eyes widened. "Fuck." He stumbled back.

The cuffs turned scarlet and melted off her skin. She peered through thick lashes at the soldiers staring in utter shock. Theod and Simone had already begun to retreat.

"Unless you wish to meet Teival," Blaise said, and her voice sounded eerie and disconnected, "you should run." She kept her well of akrani open, and orange flames hovered in the palms of her outstretched hands.

The small group of Haven soldiers were smart enough to take her suggestion and fled the sanctum, slamming the doors behind them.

Blaise made her way out to the balcony, letting her fire die. She tilted her head skyward. *Did he escape?* She searched her mind, trying to connect with Amasu. His source was untraceable. She glanced back at the dark pool. Its waters had begun bubbling and overflowing onto the stone. *The portal.*

Blaise started to reach for the Onyx Crystal, which hung from her belt. A large claw reached through the liquid and slammed onto the floor, shattering the tiles. A hound of gehheina pulled itself from the depths. Ripples of fear spiraled through her body, but she remained steadfast.

I can't seem to escape these wretched creatures. With a circular motion of her arms, she conjured a gust of wind and pushed it into the beast, knocking it against the far wall.

She didn't have time for this. The portal needed to be closed.

The hound recovered and charged toward her. She'd received the crystal, but she'd not had the opportunity to study her mother's journal.

Blaise sprinted out of the sanctum, skidding across the wide corridor, nearly crashing through the tall window. The hound barreled through the doors behind her, and a handful of Haven soldiers scattered. Some tried to fight the beast only to be torn apart. The monster bared its razor teeth, and crimson-and-black drool dripped from its mouth. *So much blood.*

She ran.

The hound was on her heels and getting closer, closer, closer, but she was getting farther and farther away from the sanctum. Warmth consumed her insides once more, charging the power within. She summoned her blue flame. With a groan, she contained the fire pulsing inside her body. *I have to get back to the sanctum before it's too late.*

Blaise reached the staircase. She spun and faced the creature, unleashing an inferno. The creature whimpered and cried inside the cyclone of azure flames. She stepped in, pushing toward the beast. Her shoulders ached from the surge of akrani. She basked in the power of havoc.

The dog's skin began to char, and the scent of burning leather filled Blaise's nostrils. Every part of her body was ablaze in her chaos. She gritted her teeth, immersed in the euphoric heat. With a final push of her outstretched palm, the monster collapsed onto its side. The cracks in its skin no longer glowed.

Enthralled by the chaotic flares, she chased after her objectives with unbridled resolve. All that mattered to her was being enraptured by this power.

Chaos is calling you. Don't let him have you. Jynx's voice pulled Blaise out of its hold.

She fought to will her gateway closed. Once her chaos was contained, she fell to her hands and knees, panting. She peered up as the hound smoldered and slowly crumbled into ash and embers.

I'm not done yet. She climbed to her feet, and a sharp jolt of pain pulsed through her, but she ignored it and limped toward the sanctum doors.

The sounds of battle echoed through the corridor. She rushed up to one of the hallway windows. Sentinels, Alchyra, and Haven soldiers were engaged in combat. Her heart lamented, eyes welling with tears, but she had no time to dwell on the blood spilling below.

Blood. My blood opened the portal.

Blaise hurried into the sanctum and shuffled toward the edge of the pool. She glanced out at the sun, which was nearly eclipsed by the shadow of the moon, and withdrew the small dagger she kept in her boot and cut a gash into her palm. She let a few drops of blood fall into the murky waters. Then, with that same hand, she reached into the velvet pouch. She used her power to release the crystal from its wooden confines.

Strands of akrani emanated in large quantities from her well. Lightning struck the balcony three times, and a downpour erupted from the dark skies. A strong gust almost knocked her off her feet. She waited. The dark waters stopped bubbling, so she placed the Onyx Crystal back in its pouch.

Completely exhausted, Blaise sank to her knees on the wet stone floor. She coughed and spat up globs of blood. *Must be a broken rib.* She stared at her pale reflection. *Is it over?*

A familiar, calming warmth coursed through her. "Blaise." Kaiden knelt next to her and placed a hand on her back.

She looked up at him, still panting. "Kaiden. I did it. I closed the portal."

He helped her stand and drew her into him. "I never doubted you." He tilted her head up to face him, placing a fervent kiss on her lips. "I thought I lost you."

"You didn't really think it would be that easy, did you, *daughter?*"

His voice. She heard him as clear as day. *This is impossible.* Her father's voice would haunt her until the end of her days.

Blaise stepped out of Kaiden's embrace and turned.

Her eyes narrowed, meeting the dark gaze of the high god, Amasu.

He crept toward her, his black robes rustling against the stone floor, his hands clasped in front of him.

"How?" She nearly choked on the word.

"How did I get here?" Amasu's grin widened. "Through the portal, of course."

"But I closed this portal." She gestured to the pool.

"It seems you've overlooked the temple ruins in the Terrenmis Mountains. I thought you were a highly trained sentinel."

Her akrani vibrated in her chest at a weakening rate. She had no strength left to fight, but that didn't mean she wouldn't try. "You're not getting this power back."

"You have your mother's courage. Something I admired and loved about her," he said.

She needed time to recharge. "I don't understand why you feel the need to return the realm dwellers to an existence they do *not* want."

He studied her. "They no longer believe in the gods, and because of that, we're weakened. I am their high god. I will make them fear us. They will worship us again."

Blaise shook her head. "That is not the way. You cannot use force and manipulation to regain devotion. It is a legacy of belief and dedication bestowed upon you out of mutual love and abundance."

"We've tried that. But I ended up with *you*." The boom of his voice shook the sanctum floors. "I will take my power back. You can give it freely, or I will rip it from your cold dead body."

Kaiden stepped in front of her, blocking the high god's path.

Amasu grinned. "How gallant of you, half blood."

Kaiden attempted to throw a left hook at him. Amasu caught his fist and twisted Kaiden's arm, then kicked him in the gut. Kaiden stumbled back but quickly recovered, unsheathing his sword. He glanced at Blaise, giving her a nod. *The crystal.* He lunged at the high god while Blaise reached for the pouch.

The high god watched Blaise, managing to sidestep Kaiden's attack. He kicked the open pouch from her grasp. It flew into the air.

Blaise blocked Amasu's incoming right hook. The crystal hit the water with a plunk. Kaiden sliced at the god's shoulder, but nothing seemed to slow him. Amasu thrust a palm into Kaiden's chest, and he tumbled across the sanctum floor.

A stream of red light escaped the high god's hand and beamed toward Blaise, connecting. Her power began to drain. She gritted her teeth. It felt like insects ripping at her flesh beneath her skin. She focused all her will on keeping the chaos within.

"Stop resisting." Amasu pulled his hand away, attempting to yank the power from her body.

"No," she bit out.

Moving in a blur, Kaiden knocked Amasu off his feet and slammed him into the wall, making an indent in the stone.

Even though exhaustion riddled Blaise's body, she found the strength to sprint toward the pool. She jumped into the waters and held her breath and dove to the bottom, searching for the crystal. Giving up on her search, Blaise surfaced, and darkness enveloped the sanctum. A wave of panic washed over her. This was her only chance to use the akrani from the crystal to defeat the high god. *The waters are an amplifier.* She hovered her hands just above the liquid. It began to boil.

Kaiden and Amasu circled each other, eyes locked in deadly focus. The air crackled with tension, and Kaiden's fists clenched. Across from him, Amasu smirked, a cruel glint in his eyes.

The first strike came fast and fierce, a lightning jab aimed at Amasu's jaw. He deftly dodged. Retaliating, Amasu swung a powerful hook, but Kaiden weaved away, a mere shadow in the onslaught. In a symphony of grunts and thuds, they traded blows, the rhythm of the fight intensifying.

Blaise's head jerked back, and she managed to summon katai, flinging red spheres of flames at the high god in rapid succession. Kaiden used the wall as a springboard, pushing off and barreling into Amasu. They both crashed into the water.

The high god burst through the liquid, his furious gaze meeting Blaise's. "Come now. You're not supposed to exist anyway. Just give me what's already mine." The high god flicked his hand out.

Beams of red pierced her once more, draining her well of akrani; she had almost nothing left to give.

A hand squeezed her shoulder. She turned her head, and Kaiden's bright hazel eyes locked onto her. *I have you, Sparks. Let go.*

With the entire fortress rumbling, she faced Amasu once more, the last of her source emerging. The crystal pulsed. Shocking tendrils of akrani sliced through her from the inside out. In the water, white flames formed on her hands and began to steadily grow.

She used her katai to freeze the water surrounding Amasu.

"You don't know what you're doing," he shrieked. "There will be consequences."

"Don't listen to him," Kaiden said. "Don't stop."

Kaiden's essence revitalized her and allowed her to hold tight to both connections. She no longer had a choice. She would have to drain every drop of akrani from her cursed father.

Tears of black blood began streaming down Amasu's cheeks. His body began to shrivel, and his skin aged and cracked. She continued drawing from his well.

She glanced over her shoulder at Kaiden, and her heart jolted. He looked like he had a terrible sunburn. His skin was beginning to peel from his flesh. She didn't want to continue. "Let go of me," she demanded.

"No."

She tried to push him away, but he wrapped his arm around her, holding her tight. "Don't. This is the only way, Blaise," he whispered into her ear.

Her heart skipped a beat, and tears sprang from her eyes. The pain in her body was nothing compared to the utter agony pulsing through her chest. With labored breaths, she said, "I can't. I love you, Kaiden."

Amasu's screams rose to a crescendo. "Daughter, don't do this."

"You were never a father to me," Blaise cried, twisting her wrists.

Kaiden pressed his lips to the side of her neck, lingering there for a moment. "I love you, Blaise, with all that I am. Thank you for helping me find my purpose. Don't hold back. You have to let go."

Through the slicing pain and her sobs, she lifted her palms, elevating her power and pushing it to its limits.

Amasu's skin crackled, his bones popped, and light seared through his pale skin. The high god gazed at the ceiling. "She will not be as lenient as I have been." His teeth ground together, disintegrating. Her white flames consumed him, engulfing the entire room. She averted her eyes when the high god burst into a million bright particles of light.

The tumultuous water became serene. Silent. Blaise turned and fell against the edge of the pool. She turned to Kaiden. "We did it." Her chest tightened at the sight of him floating face down. "No." She concentrated on the beating of their hearts. *Thump. Thump. Thump.* They were getting slower.

Memories of Kaiden flashed through her mind: the first time she'd seen him on the Teaos wall, the first time he'd smiled at her, every time he'd laughed.

Lips curving up, she laid her head against the stone and closed her eyes. "I love you," she said with her last breath. *With all that I am.*

39

MATHIAS

RENCHED IN SWEAT AND COVER IN THE blood of Haven soldiers, Mathias swung his sword, slicing a limb from one opponent. They came from all directions. Mathias brandished his dagger. Fatigue riddled his body, but he wouldn't give up. He needed to get into the gods damned fortress.

Where the fuck did Nira and Zade end up? Mathias had no time to search for them with the constant barrage of soldiers attacking him. He took a heavy blow to the shoulder. His armor protected him, the force knocking him off-balance.

The soldier swung again, but Daniel skidded in front of Mathias, blocking the blow. "Fancy seeing you, Sergeant." Daniel appeared to have the energy he was lacking, striking down one opponent after another.

Mathias grunted. "What the fuck took you all so long?"

"We ran into some beasts in the mountains," Daniel hollered, plunging his sword into the soldier's neck. Blood spewed into the air when he yanked it free.

Mathias stood back-to-back with Daniel, fighting the incoming enemies. "Great timing." He sliced at one soldier's leg, cutting deep. Through the carnage, he caught sight of King Theod and Simone together on horseback, fleeing through the fortress gates.

"Fuck, King Theod's escaping!" Mathias yelled, kicking a soldier square in the chest, blocking his sword.

"Retreat!" Haven's Captain Wilhelm yelled from a distance.

The soldiers obeyed, falling back as ordered. Some of them sprinted away on foot, and a small portion of them mounted horses and galloped away toward the Balam foothills.

Sentinels and Alchyra cried out in victory, but Mathias knew it wouldn't be the last time he would encounter the soldiers of Haven.

Daniel stalked beside Mathias, his sword at the ready.

"They'll be back," Mathias said, catching his breath. He scanned the battlefield for familiar faces while the dust settled. Bodies littered the ground, most lifeless. This was the worst part of being a sentinel. The sacrifices, lives lost. He glanced down at his crimson-soaked sword and the blood smeared on his skin and uniform. He hoped to the gods his friends had survived.

Sentinels and Alchyra began gathering the bodies and triaging the wounded. Nira hobbled up to him, bloodied, bruised, and battered, looking exhausted. Defeated. *She's alive.* He threw his arms around her and pulled her close. She shoved at him, pushing out of his embrace. Her eyes roamed the rubble of the town.

A lower-ranked sentinel called, "Sergeant, come quickly." He led them into the fortress.

The remainder of the unit had been waiting at the entrance of the sanctum with Elric, Isaac, and Zade. All had downcast expressions.

Mathias's heart sank at the sight of Blaise's dead body. *It can't be.*

Daniel pushed past him, rushing to her side. He cradled his sister and sobbed into the side of her neck. "Wake up. You can't be dead. Open your eyes, Blaise. Please," he begged.

Mathias looked away, eyes watering. His heart splintered at the sight of his friend—his brother. "Kaiden." He sprinted, crashing to his knees on the stone floor. The pain was no comparison to the utter sorrow coursing through him. He grasped Kaiden's hand like so many times before. He still carried Kaiden's words. *I'm here, Mat. I've got you, brother.*

"I'm sorry, brother," Mathias choked out. "I couldn't get to you."

How could this happen?

He should've been here fighting beside him. He placed his forehead to Kaiden's. "I should've fought harder." He watched Kaiden's chest, waiting for it to rise. Nothing happened. His tears poured down, mixing with the blood on Kaiden's armor.

He heard the voice of twelve-year-old Kaiden. *I want you on my team from now on. Okay?*

Mathias hadn't said it enough, hadn't expressed it enough. "You were the best thing that ever happened to me. You were my family. My only brother." He sat up, sobbing. "You can't leave me." He pounded his fist into Kaiden's chest. "Come back, gods dammit!"

Mathias didn't know how much time passed before he composed himself, the tears like a never-ending wave. But he finally straightened, inhaled a long, deep breath, and ordered four sentinels to take Kaiden's body into the throne room of the Balam fortress.

Nira walked up to Mathias, her features soft, tears in her eyes. "I'm so sorry."

Mathias's gaze went to his boots. He would break again if he had to look her in the eyes. Swallowing, he walked past her, determined to keep his emotions in check.

Her warm hand grasped his forearm, bringing him to a halt.

That simple gesture sent Mathias spiraling into his grief once again. He couldn't hold back. He wrapped Nira in his arms; she didn't pull away, didn't say a word.

Standing there in the middle of the sanctum, Mathias lost himself in her embrace. Her jasmine scent eased what was left of his heart. They cried together, Nira rubbing comforting circles along his back.

Across the room, Daniel knelt, cradling Blaise's body in his arms. Two Alchyra were attempting to move her, but he pushed their hands away, pulling his dagger on them. "Don't touch her! You can't take her from me!" His cries echoed through the sanctum.

How will we ever move past this?

40

BLAISE

IT'S TOO BRIGHT. BLAISE FOUND HERSELF LYING in a field of long green grass. The only sound was the wind whipping through the blades. She sat up, her dark eyes taking in the surroundings. The field stretched in all directions for as far as she could see. The cloudless sky was a pale milky white.

Where am I? She had been in the Balam fortress. She'd taken her last breath. *Is this nehveina?* She pushed to her feet and straightened slowly. She hadn't crossed the river Akran. Blaise sensed a familiar akrani.

A figure appeared in the distance. Jynx strode up, clos-ing the distance between them. Once within earshot, she greeted Blaise with a calm smile. "Hello, sister." Her white dress caressed the curves of her body, and her curly red strands wisped in the breeze.

Blaise stood a couple feet from her. "Jynx. Where am I?"

"You're in the Nethers, a realm between the living and the dead," she replied. Her tall form stepped closer.

Blaise hadn't known such a place existed. Then again, she had never died before either.

Jynx studied her. "You used your white flame."

"I didn't have a choice."

"I know." Jynx turned her back to Blaise and gazed across the acres of grass. "But you're not done yet, I'm afraid."

Blaise cocked a brow. "What do you mean?"

"You've made great sacrifices. Now it is my turn." The goddess outstretched her palms. "Place your hands in mine." Her burgundy eyes swirled.

Blaise studied her with a sidelong glance. "Wait. What're you going to do?"

"Give me your hands, sister," Jynx said, her tone hard. "There's nothing to fear."

Blaise did as she was asked. Upon contact, chaotic tendrils of akrani snaked from Jynx's body. They coiled and flowed around their bodies. Blaise gasped at the overwhelming power.

The burgundy of Jynx's stormy eyes flickered and faded to a pale gray. Her hair lost its luster, turning ashen.

"What are you doing?" Blaise tried to pull away, but Jynx continued to hold firm. "Stop, that's enough."

The goddess's grasp didn't falter. "It's okay, Little Flame."

"No, it's not. You're going to kill yourself," she cried, tears springing from her eyes.

Jynx's hands grew cold, her skin becoming translucent. "This was always my plan. I have given myself to chaos for far too long, and it ruined me. He will no longer be my master."

"What am I going to do without you? Without your guidance?" Blaise continued to struggle against her. "Please, Jynx. Don't do this."

But Jynx was too strong.

A faint smile tugged at the corners of her lips. "You'll be fine, sister. You have the will I never had." Jynx started to glow from the inside out. The goddess's breathing became shallower with each strand that escaped her. "I'm so sorry I wasn't there for you sooner. I hope my sacrifice will aid in protecting all you love." Tears rolled down her cheeks.

Blaise didn't think about it. She didn't have to. "I love you, sister."

Jynx's eyes softened. "And I you. It's been so long since someone has said those words to me." She inhaled a deep breath.

Blaise swallowed, shaking her head. She couldn't allow Jynx to do this. She'd already lost so much, she couldn't bear another. "Please, I'm begging you, don't do this." She sobbed.

"You shall be the first." Jynx reached out, her fingertips caressing Blaise's cheek. "The first of the gods to live amongst the realm dwellers." *Take care of them, my sister. My Little Flame.* "I will always be with you. You have everything I've ever been." The last burst of akrani shattered Jynx into a thousand chaotic sparks.

LIGHT ERUPTED. BLAISE'S EYES SHOT open. She gasped for air. Daniel's face was the first to come into view. He gazed down at her in disbelief. He was cradling her close to his body, his dagger pointed at a nearby Alchyra. She was alive. Back in the Balam fortress.

What in gehheina had happened to her? Daniel helped Blaise into a sitting position. "How is this possible?"

"I'm not sure I know." She climbed to her feet with Daniel's assistance.

Mathias rushed up to her and threw his arms around her, holding her tight. "Thank the gods you're alive," he whispered.

She stepped back.

Sorrow glistened in his blue eyes, red and puffy. Mathias stared at his boots.

"Take me to him." Her voice trembled.

Elric, Zade, and Isaac bowed respectfully to Blaise. Mathias and Daniel led her and the others out of the sanctum. Zade notified her of King Theod's cowardice and how the sentinels and Alchyra had forced the Haven soldiers to retreat.

An unsettling warmth ignited in Blaise's chest. *Theod will pay for this.*

Nira rushed in, embracing Blaise.

Closing her eyes, Blaise returned the hug. "I'm so glad you're okay."

Nira pulled away and gave Blaise's arms a gentle squeeze. "You're different."

Blaise canted her head. "Am I?"

Nira's eyes shifted towards the imposing doors of the closed throne room. "Do you want me to go with you?" she offered, her concern evident.

Blaise, grappling for words, could only manage a subtle shake of her head. The weight of unspoken emotions lingered in the air between them.

Acknowledging Blaise's silent wishes, Nira nodded understandingly, releasing her hold.

Mathias and Daniel lingered behind. Blaise approached the doors.

"We'll be right here if you need us," Mathias said.

Blaise tugged one door open and stepped inside, closing it behind her. She stared at the toes of her damp leather boots, bracing herself—preparing for the dreaded truth.

He can't be dead. Her heart pounded against her chest as though it wanted to escape. She didn't want to turn around. She didn't want to see him like that, but this would be the last time.

Kaiden's body lay on a white cloth in the middle of the large room, his wings neatly folded beneath him. She took one step, then another, until she was only a few inches from him.

She knelt beside him, touching his bare forearm. *So cold* . . . She lifted his hand, interlacing their fingers—his didn't respond. *Too still* . . . If she waited long enough, maybe his chest would rise and fall again. Maybe his hazel eyes would open and he'd flash her that roguish smile she'd grown to love.

Blaise laid her head on his chest. "Wake up, you idiot," she sobbed. Her eyes drifted to the ring on her left hand. The galydrian shimmered in the beams of sunlight streaming through the window. It would forever be a reminder of the man who'd irritated her into loving him. This stubborn, insufferable, amazing, selfless . . .

She tasted a mixture of her salty tears and copper. "It wasn't supposed to be this way. Please . . . Come back," she cried. "I've got you, Kaiden. You just have to come back to me."

Her plea went unheard. She lay next to him while the tears continued to flow. "I need you. I love you with all that I am."

"Such a waste," a voice said.

Startled, she sat up, wiped the tears from her eyes and turned to face the intruder. Her eyes widened at the sight of Mathias. "I thought you were waiting outside?"

"It's crazy, really, how seamlessly my plans fell into place so we could all end up here, in this moment." Mathias's clothes transformed into a long blue dress. His features and body shifted into Nira. "Your friends did well, but they're not very smart."

"What are you?" Unease roiled through Blaise as she climbed to her feet.

The imposter approached. Nira altered into Philippa, the woman who had given Blaise the first memory crystal in Haven.

Questions swirled in Blaise's mind. Eyes still wide, she stood there, protecting Kaiden's body.

Philippa's gray hair turned silvery white. The wrinkles in her skin smoothed and firmed, and her body became thick and toned within a few seconds. The baby-blue dress was snug against her curves. Her voice went from raspy to silky. "Allow me to *properly* introduce myself. I'm Lasya, goddess of the moon." Her lips curved into a devious, seductive smile.

Blaise had no memories of anything about this goddess standing in front of her. A hurricane of questions swirled in her mind. "What are we all doing here? Why have you planned for so much devastation?"

"Devastation? You are just pawns in a centuries-old game between lovers. You've yet to experience devastation like I have. But . . . there's still time." Lasya glanced at Kaiden's dead body. "What a pity. I don't think you'll be needing that anymore." Shadows crept up from the stone floor, slowly enveloping Kaiden and the goddess.

"Stop!" Blaise shrieked. "You cannot take him from me!" She fell to her knees and sobbed.

In the commotion, she heard Daniel's voice coming from the other side of the door. "Blaise, what's happening? Open the door! We can't get in!"

She tried to cover Kaiden's body with her own to shield him from the dark source. The shadows consumed him and Lasya. Blaise's hands passed through his vaporous form.

Kaiden and the goddess disappeared into nothingness.

ACKNOWLEDGMENTS

I want to thank my Badass Publishing Group, Lana, Kasey, and Brittany, for working with me through not only this series but all my crazy chaotic projects. Thank you for helping me through the times when I just wanted to give up. I owe you girls the world!

To the team over at Enchanted Ink Publishing, I've said it once and I'll say it again: Natalia, Thea, Greg, you are amazing and talented. What you've been able to do with the aesthetic of my books is beyond my expectations.

Thank you to my amazing beta readers, Veronica Hernandez, Elizabeth Lewis, Jordan Matoe, Lady Elizabeth, and Chloe Marjot. You all really helped me evolve that draft into what it is today!

I'd like to thank my husband for his continued support. You're always hyping me up and telling others about my books. Love you, honey!

To Mom, Dad, Amber, Alex, Annamarie, Angelica, and Aliyah, thank you for always pushing me to follow my dreams. I'm publishing now because you all told me I was good enough. I love you!

Glossary

AKRANI

A life source said to be gifted by the gods.

Katai: The ability to control the four elements in all their forms.
Satori: Premonitions, mastery and control over the mind.
Gitros: The ability to repair and heal.
Alchime: The ability to reanimate and create artificial life.
Shadow: Unknown.

AKRANI CRYSTALS

Infused with the source.
The color fades when all power has been drained from it.

Yellow: Meta crystals can create prestae (clones).

Purple: Mind shield.

Blue: Teleportation.

Green: Memories.

THE HIGH GODS

Amasu: Possesses all akrani. "The universe holds limitless power."

Lasya: Shadow akrani. "You don't want the moon jealous of the stars."

The Lower Gods

Karasi: The goddess of life. "To live is to know what you could've had."

Teival: The god of death. "Death isn't the end."

Jynx: The goddess of chaos. "Finding peace in chaos."

Colvyr: The god of peace. "The purest path to peace is mastery of the mind."

Servants of the Gods

Ellorians: Created by Colvyr. Peacekeepers of the realms. They receive their wings once they've met their other half, their aniivasei. The satrevo serve Colvyr directly, mandistiri are the warriors of nehveina, and the iipiretis enforce their justice on the realms.

Grysills: Created by Teival. They typically wreak havoc amongst the realms. They are created with wings and horns but can hide them when they're amongst realm dwellers.

Creatures

Kynarah: Creatures that live in the Azureden pass and feed on blood.

Siren: They swim in the depths of Thessalynne Lake. Their song hypnotizes their victims.

Mountain trolls: Giant hairy monsters that dwell inside the Azureden Mountains. They come out at night to hunt and quench their bloodlust.

COMMODITIES

Gald: Common.

Galydrian: Rare; mined from the Onyx Mountains.

THE AFTERLIFE

Nehveina: A place of serenity for souls. One must cross the river Akran to get here.

Gehheina: A place for the souls of the damned.

Theitaa: Where the gods dwell.

Nethers: Exists between the living and the dead.

THE REALM OF ALYMETH

Crenitha

Koshmena

Tarquinn

MISCELLANEOUS

Doma gitros: Medical center

ALYSSA GREEN

Alyssa is a US Navy veteran with a degree in psychology. She's a multifaceted person who enjoys a variety of activities. When she's not writing or reading, she can be found editing for clients, traveling the United States with her husband and dog, Fiona, or hiking and exploring the outdoors. She's also a lifelong learner who has been taking classes through the Editorial Freelancers Association to improve her skills as a freelance editor.

WWW.AUTHORALYSSAGREEN.COM

Instagram: @author_alyssa_green

Facebook: @authoralyssagreen

TikTok: @authoralyssagreen